Gate in the Fence of Time
A Journey to the Birth of America

David Robert Berry

Gate in the Fence of Time

A Journey to the Birth of America

ISBN-13: 978-1480232884   ISBN-10: 1480232882

BISAC Historical Fiction, Time Travel, American Revolution

© 2015 Fairhaven Lantern Media, info@fairhavenlantern.com

Order Gate in the Fence of Time at

https://www.createspace.com/4027994

Acknowledgments

Thank you to everyone who contributed to this book. Trudy Gold and Linda Winrow provided major editing. Many friends made useful comments: Elizabeth Berry, Sarah Berry, Jeremy Berman, Tracy Bowen, Peter Boag, Rev. Drew Christiansen S.J., Sue Conklin, Rosalie Fedoruk, Sharon Franquemont, Lama Sonam Gyatso, Myra Jackson, Pamela Jayson, Mary LaBarbera, Murray Liebman, Cheryl Little, Lark Lovering, Perri K. McCary, Michael Mitchell, Connie Neil, Marion Neiman, Rabiah al Nur, Bill Sanda, Betsy Stang, Don Stauffer, Mariama Thera, Sandy Wiggins, Alice Olsen Williams, Anna Woods, Matt Wright..

Thank you to the Colonial Williamsburg Foundation for making journeys to the birth of America possible for millions of travelers and for confirming that this book does not infringe upon the Foundation's intellectual property.

Photo Credits

Declaration of Independence on Cover from National Archives
http://www.archives.gov/exhibits/charters/

All other photos: David Robert Berry

Contents

Day 1-1:   On the Road to Williamsburg

To the people of the Virginia Colony in 1775, the forests and fields flanking Interstate 95 would look familiar. The smooth highway from the Potomac to the Tidewater would seem a marvel. But the cars hurtling through a misting rain early this Friday morning in May would be beyond their wildest imagining.

Peter Sinclair, a sandy-haired college senior, steered the family's Ford through a curve on the only interstate connecting what were once the thirteen original colonies.

In the back seat, his eighteen year-old sister Megan, fussed with her curly hair to feel if it had grown out enough for a new hair clip. "Isn't there an outlet mall down there? Let's hit that."

"If we hit a store at this speed, we'd crash right through it—definitely no time for shopping," Peter teased.

"No morbid thoughts! Peter, slow down." Susan Sinclair, sitting next to her daughter, nervously bit her lower lip, pushed her glasses up the bridge of her nose, and brushed her long auburn hair away from her face. She focused her blue eyes at the road ahead.

Megan rolled her eyes and sighed. "Why did we have to leave so early?"

Her mother replied, "Once again, Megan, we want a full day in Williamsburg today. Peter is home on a break and we're doing this trip together before you go off to college next year. It will be fun. You guys can do your own exploring."

John, reclined in the passenger seat, muscular arms folded on his chest. His jaw tightened under short dark brown hair flecked with gray. "Slow down, Peter.

1

Megan, quit griping. You have a paper to write—you'll get ideas in Williamsburg." He did not open his eyes but Peter and Megan were immediately quiet.

Along the median, a double row of blossoming trees flashed past, two trees per second as the car sped by. Peter moved to the left lane behind a white van that was passing an eighteen-wheeler to the right.

Up ahead, the driver of a red Hyundai had overshot his exit and used the service drive "for authorized vehicles only" to make a U-turn. His vision blocked by the treed median, he pulled out in front of the white van, which at sixty miles per hour was seconds away.

Suddenly, brake lights lit ahead and the van left black skid marks, then it hit a wet patch. Peter jammed the brake pedal; his tires skidded over the wet stretch of pavement, the Ford gaining on the van. The big truck on the right seemed to leap ahead and Peter swerved into the opening. The left front of the Sinclairs' Ford narrowly missed the van's tail light as the car went into a slow rotation on the wet road. Peter struggled to steer out of the skid without success.

Within the slowly spinning car, John entered the space of a timeless moment for the first time since his days in combat. Back then, senses alert, he scanned for the tip of a weapon protruding from behind a rock or a place to dive behind a natural shelter. Back then, as shots were fired from a hidden location, the interval between heartbeats seemed an eternity. Now, without hesitation, he called out in a commanding voice, "Hold on!" as his right hand braced against the dashboard and his left shielded his face in case of flying glass.

The sense of time decelerated. Each second seemed a long time... sliding at forty, thirty, twenty miles per hour, the occupants waited... let go...

As the van bore down on him, the driver of the Hyundai swerved into the lane where the truck had been and went into a spin—right in the path of the Sinclairs. The Hyundai spiraled at twenty, ten, five miles per hour as the Ford slid closer...

Peter stared through the windshield. The landscape became streaks of color blending into each other. It was the strangely familiar but forgotten experience of newborn babies before they begin to distinguish among objects.

Susan experienced a faint luminescence and a familiar sense of a long-ago loss. "Lord, help my family," were the only words arising from the silence within her as her arm went out to protect her daughter.

Megan watched the kaleidoscopic patterns of branches streaming past the window. As the car slowed, she exhaled. For once she was speechless, her irritation dispersed, leaving stillness.

The two cars came to rest on the asphalt shoulder facing in opposite directions— seven inches apart—no room to open doors on the passenger side of either car. In both vehicles the people breathed deeply, adrenaline subsiding.

Peter stared at the blossoming tress on the median. The colors seemed more vivid. John looked into the wide-open eyes of two Asian-American children in the back seat of the Hyundai. Susan felt a wave of gratitude that her family was unhurt. No one moved.

The white van was pulled over on the shoulder ahead. A man in painters' coveralls walked back to the two cars. "Are you OK?" The sound of his voice broke the trance-like silence.

"Yes. I think so, thank God." Susan relaxed her grip on the armrest.

Megan watched a dragonfly glide past the trees.

"That was close!" The van driver shook his head. "You folks wait until these next cars go by and then straighten out. I'll wave you out when the way is clear."

Once the cars were moved safely onto the gravel, the Sinclairs and the Asian family in the Hyundai got out. The air held the scent of grass and blossoms but no trace of blame. "Sorry," Said the driver of the red Hyundai.

"No harm done," said Peter. "I sorry I was too close to the van for a wet road. We're all lucky to be alive," Peter said.

"We're always lucky to be alive," John said quietly. He exhaled slowly.

"I was afraid we were going to crash. It feels like we just shared a miracle," whispered Susan, touching her husband's tanned arm, wishing he would pat her hand.

The contractor scratched his chin. "There's no damage and no one hurt, so this wasn't an accident. We can go on our way." Wishing each other well, everyone got back into their vehicles and, being very sure the road was clear, pulled back onto the highway.

Peter drove just below the speed limit.

"You could have left more room between you and the van..." his father said. Peter drew a breath. "...but you showed good reflexes and instincts." Peter relaxed again and turned the radio to classical music for the first time anyone could remember. After an hour without conversation, he asked, "Where do we go from here?"

Susan looked at her phone. "Exit 238 won't be long now. Follow the signs to the Colonial Williamsburg Visitor Center."

Day 1-2:   Peter and the Woman in the Garden

In the Visitor Center beams of light streamed down from windows high above as they walked past shops, flags, and historical images to the long ticket counters. John picked up passes, maps, and keys to their colonial-era quarters. In the bookstore, Susan bought a guidebook and John got colonial currency.

Outside, Susan stopped by a bronze model of Williamsburg. "I feel strange as if I'm in an altered state looking down on the town from somewhere else."

"What do you know about an altered state, Mom?" Megan asked pointedly.

Susan ignored the question and the Sinclairs climbed into a shuttle to the Historic District. The bus rolled past woods and pastures enclosed by white picket, split rail, and worm fences. "Capitol Bus Stop!" called out a recorded voice. Peter took the lead as they stepped with a crunch on a path of crushed oyster shells.

Peter felt a breeze on his face as they walked to their rooms. They stepped through the gate in a white picket fence. An iron ball hanging in the middle of a chain pulled the gate closed behind them. Inside, the rooms were quaint and comfortable with eighteenth century décor.

Suddenly Megan shrieked "Eeew! There's a wasp on the window. Can somebody kill it?"

"Calm down!" Peter grabbed a towel from the bathroom and seized the wasp in it. He opened the door and with a flick of the towel, the wasp flew away. Peter was impatient. "Let's go."

"Do we have to stay together? I want to look around by myself."

"Is being with your parents so embarrassing, Megan?" Susan asked.

"We'll start together and then you can go off to find something to write about."

"But Dad, aren't we on vacation?"

They followed Peter down the street to benches shaded by a tree. Susan opened a map. "OK, that brick building is the Capitol. Where should we begin?"

"We began on the bus then walked a few blocks. This sure has been fun so far."

"Peter!" exclaimed Megan, nudging her brother.

"Good day! Would you care to join the Powell's in their parlor for a look at family life in 1775?" A maid in a blue-and-white-striped cotton dress, white linen apron, and mobcap stood on the porch of the tiny brick building behind them.

"No waiting in line?" asked Peter.

"No, Sir. You may join these other guests and come right in."

Peter made a sweeping bow, "After you." Passing through the building, they entered a yard surrounded by buildings with brick foundations and white siding.

The maid said, "You entered through the office. These buildings behind the house are the kitchen, laundry, smokehouse, sheds, milk house, and outdoor oven. You shall have a chance to explore but first please join the family in the parlor."

As they climbed the steps to the porch, movement caught Peter's eye. A tall African woman gracefully crossed a garden, a basket on her arm, wearing a white bonnet and blouse that contrasted with her deep brown skin. The hem of her full print skirt floated as she glided by. Beyond a fence a pair of draft horses white as fresh laundry, grazed in a perfect postcard image. Peter was enthralled until a thought hit him. That beautiful woman is a slave! Why does she have such a peaceful look? I would be furious. I wouldn't stand for...

"Please join us in the parlor for children's games and a chat," the maid said.

"Oh, excuse me; I was looking at the garden."

Peter followed his family into the centuries-old house over a plank floor buffed by millions of visitors' footsteps and the feet of inhabitants long before. A prim reenactor in a long blue linen dress sat in a rocking chair by a fireplace next to two girls sitting on the floor. The hearth was empty but for the andirons.

"Welcome, everyone. Please choose a seat." Peter sat in an oak spindle-back chair next to his father. The room was sparsely decorated with prints on white walls.

"My husband undertakes construction projects and employs men from the building trades." The reenactor in the role of Annabel Powell wore sleeves to her elbows and a bonnet. To her guests she looked dressed for a formal occasion but as a middle-sorts woman in the Virginia Colony, she was in everyday attire. She chatted while embroidering a fine-chain floral border for curtains.

"Mister Powell erected the steeple of Bruton Parish Church. Have you seen it?" A few visitors indicated they had. "Mister Powell's largest undertaking was the first Public Hospital in all the colonies for poor souls so troubled of mind that their families cannot care for them. We started our life humbly but through his work Benjamin has provided well for us and improved the prospects for our daughters to marry into better-sorts families."

Yeah, thought Peter, bitterly, prosperity built on the labor of slaves!

The Powell children played a game of Bilbo Catcher—a wooden ball attached by a string to a wooden peg with a shallow cup at one end. The children held the peg and tossed the ball to land in the cup. The guests discovered how tricky it was when the Powell children coaxed them to try and the ball missed or bounced out every time.

Peter fumed. Don't the people of this house see how beautiful that woman is? This family has a slave in the backyard, people! They play happily in the living room as if slavery is normal! What a graceful walk. What a perfect face. She must descend from African royalty...

Peter's thoughts were interrupted. "Would you like to try, young man?"

"Huh?" Peter's mind replayed the question he missed. "Oh, OK." He took the peg the girl offered and tossed the ball. It made a circle the length of the string, orbiting the peg. "Hold on. Let me try again." A challenge, particularly in front of an audience, usually got his attention.

"Toss it straight up and catch it as it falls," Hannah encouraged. Peter waved the peg and the ball flew up and jerked back from the end of the string. Peter had the cup under the ball but it bounced off as far as the string allowed, causing Susan to duck and Peter to blush.

"Good reflexes," Missus Powell complimented Peter. "With practice you shall have it. These games teach children to be sharp of eye and quick of hand to prepare them for their work as adults in a craft or running a home."

"Is there talk of war around here these days?" John asked the reenactor.

"More than talk I'm afraid," Missus Powell replied. British troops occupy Boston. Colonies have committees of correspondence to work in concert when needed."

"Are any people here still loyal to the King?" asked Susan.

"Heavens, yes! Our Burgesses resist acts by Parliament that violate our rights as Englishmen, but we are all loyal to the Mother Country and our King."

I want to slip out to the garden, Peter thought. Why did I sit far from the door?

"The servants are preparing dinner in the kitchen out back. Please look around our home and then see how the cooking is done." It was a cue that this was the end of this part of the visit.

The visitors crossed the hall to a bedroom. To dally until the others left, Peter pretended to study two candlesticks that had dripped wax on the mantle. Looking out the window, he was disappointed — no one was in the garden. He followed an elderly couple onto the porch. They started down the steps, and Peter suddenly found himself one pace from the slave woman. She was tying a knot in a thread. He was speechless.

The other people moved on and Peter found his voice. "What are you sewing?"

The woman looked up at him with a look of mild surprise that he should be interested in what she was doing. "It be a doll for little Hannah, Sir, one of the Powell girls."

"I saw Hannah inside. Do you have children?"

"Yes, I got two boys. The older one is helping in the kitchen."

That surprised Peter who had guessed the woman to be about his age. He hesitated then spontaneously decided to get into a role as the reenactors did. "I live north of here. I'm on my way home from buying uh, rum in the West Indies. I came to Williamsburg ... to add tobacco to the shipment. Where I come from," he lowered his voice, "we don't mind paying a good day's wage for a good day's work."

The woman continued sewing. A couple and their young daughter wandered onto the porch. Peter leaned his left shoulder against the wall to make room for them to pass. The little girl hurried ahead of her parents to the woman and asked, "Hello, what are you sewing?"

"Good day, Miss. I'm sewin' a rag doll for Hannah."

"Is she your little girl?"

6

"Hannah is one of the Powell girls. They like to play wit' dolls I make."

The mother caught up with her daughter. "OK, Honey, we need to keep moving."

"Is she a slave, Mom?"

The mother looked embarrassed and turned to Peter, "I'm sorry. Jenny has a vivid imagination." They walked down the stairs and toward the kitchen building.

Peter watched them go. "The mother acted as if you weren't even there. Are you a slave?"

"Yes, I is one of three slaves in this house. I do laundry and help in the garden."

"Do you wash laundry by hand?" Peter did his best to make conversation.

"Yes. We also get spots out of fine cloth by rubbin' wit' bran or powdered sheep bones to absorb grease like Massa's blotter do ink. Some call that 'dry cleaning.'"

"Where do you find powdered sheep bones?"

"We save bones after boilin' them for soup stock. We bake them and grind them wit' a mortar and pestle." The woman had a scent Peter took a moment to recognize. It was plain unperfumed soap. He had not smelled that since his great grandmother died.

When no one else was in hearing range, he asked, "Do you know the group of stars that makes the shape of a drinking gourd or big dipper?

"No, what do you mean, Sir?"

"The two stars on the pouring side of the dipper are the Pointer Stars. Imagine a line from the star at the bottom front of the dipper to the one at the lip and follow that line out about five times the depth of the dipper. You will see a bright star called Polaris or the North Star."

The woman raised the doll to eye level to examine the recent stitches, straightened a pinch of material that had slipped out of alignment on the last stitch, and resumed sewing.

"That bright North Star is directly north of where you are. If you follow it each night, you will come to the far northern colonies where slaves can be free."

She stopped sewing. "How do you know this 'bout the stars?"

"My grandfather taught me. He told me he learned from his father. I've heard there are churches and good-hearted people who would help along the way."

"You talkin' 'bout the Church of England where most vestrymen own slaves?"

"I'm not sure if that's the only church. I don't really know."

She looked into Peter's face. He sensed uneasiness in her brown eyes. "Sir, the kindness of Missus Powell might stop if she angers at me runnin'. She gave me a white dress her girls wore to sew into shirts for my boys. I dried them in the sun so you can't see the spots. When my boys wear those shirts to church they feel handsome and they knows I love them. How would they feel if they saw their Mama take a whippin'? What would if I got sold away?" She looked furtively toward the kitchen. "I heard 'bout folks runnin'. Most was brought back and whipped or sold. Some we never hear from again and we don't know if they is alive or dead. When I was a girl, people ran to Spanish East or West Florida but some was caught in raids from the Carolinas. Now the Floridas is British so they ain't no place to run."

The woman sighed. "I heard life is a gift flowin' through us like a stream. We should help others wit' that gift. You tryin' to help but I need somethin' to run to, not just to run from."

Peter was about to ask where she heard those ideas when a woman in a long green dress walked through the gate and asked the slave, "Is lunch ready for the prisoners?"

"It should be done, Ma'am. They have it in the kitchen." The slave woman stood to enter the house and nodded to Peter as she turned.

Peter left the porch and walked the short path to the kitchen. He squeezed into the group gathered across from the open hearth. He realized he had not even asked her name.

Day 1-3:   John—Bearing Arms

The Sinclairs walked along the oyster-shell path leading to the Capitol. Peter stopped suddenly and behind him, Megan, looking to the side, accidently stepped on his heel.

"Hey, watch where I'm going!" she taunted.

"Good move, Megan. Always alert." Peter was unprovoked.

The family sat on benches along the low brick wall where people waited to enter the building. "It will be less than twenty minutes before you enter the Capitol," a man in a tricorn hat trimmed in fine gold braid called out from the gate.

A woman squinting in the sunlight and pursing her thin lips walked slowly past the line of seated visitors, her hair tucked under the hood of a brown broadcloth cloak too heavy for the season. Beneath the cloak, a white apron covered a faded gray dress. Someone wished her a good morning. She returned the greeting, "A good morrow unto thee. I confess I am fearful about the rise in savagery in the North. War cannot be the answer to the problems we face."

John's attention drifted to soldiers in an encampment across the grounds. He had lived in tents or in the open for a year in the jungles of Nicaragua and two years in the dry mountain valleys of Central Asia. War had assaulted his eyes and ears and crept into his nostrils. War had punctured and torn him and he had doled out the same. He rarely brought these experiences to mind. He was forbidden to talk about them. Other than the First Gulf War, he fought in secret operations in which America was not officially a combatant. A thin coil of smoke wafted in a light westerly breeze. Too easy for an enemy to spot, John knew. "I'd like to visit that camp if you don't mind holding my place."

Susan was curious about the strangely familiar woman coming down the line. "You boys go ahead. Come back when you see we're close to getting in."

"Good. Should we make reservations for lunch? John suggested.

"The Guide Book says Christiana Campbell's is open for dinner. Shields Tavern has lunch."

Megan saw an opportunity for liberation. "I'll go make reservations and meet you there!" She jumped up from the bench.

"Am I being abandoned completely?" Susan asked.

"Peter and I can visit the Capitol with you," John assured her. "Megan, reserve dinner at Christina Campbell's and lunch at twelve-thirty at Shields Tavern." Megan was instantly off.

John and Peter crossed to the encampment. A reenactor stood with one boot on a stack of firewood inserting a flint into his musket as he spoke to a group of visitors.

"How often do you have to change flints like that?" asked a boy.

"A flint is a piece of stone. It could take fifty rounds to wear down, but could shatter any time we pull the trigger. We need fast volleys in battle, so soldiers must change a flint fast."

"How many shots can you fire from that rifle?" Peter asked.

"This is not a rifle. It is a Brown Bess musket. It takes twenty seconds to prime, load, and fire one round. Not accurate beyond fifty yards, it misfires often. I'll show you how it works."

The militiaman took a paper cartridge from a leather box on his belt, and bit it in two at the mid-point where it was twisted thin. He opened the base of the barrel, poured a bit of black powder into the priming pan from the half cartridge in his hand. He poured the rest of the powder down the barrel, spat in a musket ball from the paper in his mouth, and wadded the damp paper behind it. Taking the ramrod from hoops below the barrel, he gently tamped the musket ball, and powder down. "Somebody give the order to fire."

Voices shouted, "Fire!" The musket fired a grey ball into a target on straw bales.

"That was a quarter charge of powder and a papier maché ball. A real lead ball would knock a hole in that target. The musket has a smooth barrel so the ball flies out with no spin. At fifty yards, I'd often miss" He picked up another weapon. "The flintlock's barrel is rifled inside with spiral grooves to spin the ball as it speeds out for greater distance and accuracy."

The reenactor continued, "A strange vagary of war proved fortuitous for the American Colonies. A British officer named Patrick Ferguson developed a rifle that did not need a ramrod. The soldier dropped a ball into the breech and sealed powder behind it. With a cock of the hammer, it was ready. He demonstrated it in 1776, hitting a target six times a minute at four times the range of a musket. He then fired while walking forward, hitting the target almost every time on a rainy day, in conditions when muskets often misfire. The British ordered a hundred breech-loading rifles to test in action. They gave Ferguson command of a regiment that sailed for America in 1777."

John felt they were being watched. Past Peter to his right, a gray-bearded man in a militia uniform leaned on a post. The man nodded and John returned the nod.

The reenactor continued, "At Brandywine, Pennsylvania, Ferguson saw a colonial officer riding beyond the creek beside an officer in French uniform. He ordered riflemen to shoot them, but called them back, disgusted; he said later, that the officers were helpless victims at that distance. Whom did Ferguson spare? It was General Washington and the Marquis de Lafayette. The date, September 11, could have been remembered for centuries as the anniversary of an American disaster. Later that day, the rifles held little advantage when the British attacked within range of the Americans' muskets, fired from behind stone walls. Ferguson lost his right arm and forty of his men were killed or wounded. The rifle company was disbanded and most of the rifles were somehow lost without a trace."

"Where did those breech-loading rifles go?" John asked, "Had they been used to their capacity, it would have been devastating. Losing Washington would have changed history!"

"No one knows how the rifles were lost. The Continental forces had a difficult time as it was. The British won most major battles using Brown Bess muskets."

"Thanks for the demonstration." John was curious about the disappearance of the rifles but he felt strongly drawn to talk with the man leaning on the post. They sauntered over to the man whom John recognized by his insignia to be a sergeant. He had a rugged scar that began at his cheekbone and disappeared into his trimmed gray beard. "Good day, gentlemen," he said, his eyes confident and flashing a glint of humor.

"Good day," said John.

Peter asked. "Can you tell us why the British wore red uniforms that were so easy to see?"

The sergeant drew a breath before replying. "There are myths that are not true. Redcoats need not hide. They concentrate so much firepower it doesna' matter if ye are hidden. The puff of smoke from your musket gives away your location. Lad, are ye good at arithmetic?"

Peter nodded, hoping he would get the answer right in front of his father.

"With three lines of infantry firing, each line able to reload, and fire a musket three times a minute, how much time is there betwixt volleys?"

Peter was quick. "Nine volleys a minute, so a volley every six or seven seconds."

"Right! The ranks fire in turn: ready, present, fire! The volleys sweep the field like a scythe. Now add cannon balls that cut men in half, grape shot that can kill a whole group, and cannons firing lengths of chain that shred men and the bushes that hid them. What does that add up to?"

Peter did not respond. John saw in the sergeant's bearing that he spoke from experience. He felt, without knowing why, that the sergeant saw the same in him.

"If ye made it to British lines you'd be met by this." He fixed a bayonet to the end of his musket. Redcoats win most of their battles. A militia can make a surprise attack but they best move on before the British mount a coordinated response. Wars are not glorious. They are 'gorious' if ye get my meanin'. 'Tis chaos amidst screams of the wounded, the smell of burnt powder, and parts of your friends flying about."

John did not think about "his wars." Yet this sergeant's stories resonated so strongly with his experience that he shuddered. It was strange that no one else had joined them to listen.

"The myth that you defeat Redcoats by shooting at the bright red coats from behind a tree may have arisen from the hapless campaign of General Braddock in 1755. He marched northwest into Indian country building a road as he went. Everyone for miles knew where he was. He forded a river without meeting resistance then marched into an ambush. Troops in the rear marched into retreating troops and all discipline was lost. Braddock was killed."

"Building a road as you advance is not the best way to surprise the enemy," observed John.

The sergeant studied John. "Young George Washington was there. He wrote his mother, 'I luckily escaped without a wound though I had four bullets through my coat, and two horses shot out from beneath me.' He told his brother John he was spared 'by the all-powerful dispensations of Providence'. Those who survive a battle may assume they were protected. Those killed stop assuming altogether.

"At twenty-two years of age, the year before Braddock's defeat, Washington led His Majesty's Virginia Regiment to the western frontier of Pennsylvania where he was outgunned by superior French forces. His men hastily built Fort Necessity. The French offered Washington terms of surrender. His captors treated him well in spite of his surprise attack on them just weeks before, killing ten."

Peter noticed Susan talking to the woman in the hooded cape. One group had been led into the Capitol and Susan was close to the gate. He nudged his father; it was time to go.

"You know a lot of history," John acknowledged the sergeant.

"I witnessed more than I wanted to see. Ye are familiar, have we met before?"

"I don't think so. I haven't been to Williamsburg before."

"But an old war fighter knows another by a look in the eye. I would'na be surprised if ye had a tale to tell yourself," the sergeant ventured.

"Possibly so, but my son and I must get back to the Capitol. Good to meet you."

As they walked to join Susan, Peter asked, "Was war like that for you, Dad?"

"I hope you never have to experience what that sergeant told you," was all John replied.

Day 1-4:   Susan Meets Jane Pleading for Peace

As she watched the woman in the cloak move along the line, Susan thought about war, too. She had marched for peace before the Iraq War. Why did leaders choose to send their young people to kill and to come home wounded, traumatized, or not at all, leaving families in grief and uncertainty for the rest of their lives? She could see her own features and those of her husband in both her children. She was grateful they had not been caught up in a war.

"The troubles with Britain can be settled peaceably," exhorted the woman. "Why discard abundance and safety to make war? Why send our children forth to kill other people's children? Why doth Britain send soldiers against her own people? Do our leaders pray? Their choices seemeth of neither sound mind nor spirit."

"You said that you've seen terrible things in war. Has fighting reached Williamsburg?"

"I was born in western Pennsylvania on the frontier. The French and Indian War was a mighty struggle betwixt the French and English. Both sides armed the Native peoples and set them against settlers of the other side." Her eyes narrowed. "That was long ago."

"I'm sorry," said Susan quietly. "Did you lose someone in that war?"

"My father and my brothers Nathanial and Adam were killed." She crossed her arms over her breast like a troubled child hugging itself. Susan recognized her discomfort and wondered why a reenactor would be so strongly into character.

"My name is Susan Sinclair."

"I am Jane."

"Jane, I married a man who fought in wars," said Susan, remembering. "He still does not talk about it. Were your father and brothers soldiers?"

"They were peaceful farmers, my brothers but boys. The memory pains me." She looked around nervously. "Amidst the strife men do not recall the lofty notions that sent them forth. They fear for their lives or become filled with hate against the enemy. For every man who has scars on his body, more have scars of fear, rage, or regret in their souls."

"It is hard for them to find help," said Susan quietly.

Jane flashed emotion. "They were marched off under banners to the sound of drums, filled with ideas about the sins of the enemy and their leaders' assurances that God was on their side. They hoped to help their nation but rare is the man who returns at peace. No community can be whole when many fathers, husbands, and sons are wounded in their hearts. If you have a son, keep him away from hateful hostilities." The woman's suffering seemed genuine.

"I pray for peace, Jane, but I'm not optimistic." Susan thought of her own kids.

"It looks dark I grant thee, but if our prayers and actions cannot stop the war, perchance it might end soon or both sides might take more prisoners and treat them better. If that much can happen, the victors, the defeated, and the world shall be the better for it."

"Amen," whispered Susan. As Jane left, Susan felt again the hidden sadness that war had bequeathed her, a grief she had never shared with her children, or even fully with her husband.

Day 1-5:   In the Capitol

Susan took John's arm by the curved brick walls of the Capitol. The man in the tricorn hat described the pattern as Flemish bond, courses of headers, bricks placed edgewise, alternating with stretchers, placed lengthwise. Crisscrossing bricks made the wall stronger. The ends of some headers were vitreous blue from being next to the fire in the kiln. The precision and grace of the Capitol implied authority.

The Sinclairs entered the high-ceilinged House of Burgesses where a brass chandelier hung low to illuminate note taking by the clerks. Light poured through large round windows. Rich dark-stained hardwood panels suggested that serious matters were discussed here. John led them to benches at the perimeter. A tall Burgess in colonial costume stood addressing the assembly. "Britain sends troops to quell this turbulence because Massachusetts Bay is in revolt."

"Not so! A Provincial Congress is the People's right as British subjects. The philosopher, John Locke, said when there is 'a long train of abuses, prevarications and artifices' the people would 'rouse themselves to secure the ends for which Government was at first erected.'"

"But Locke also said that after past revolutions, our government of King, Lords, and Commons was reestablished. God gave us a King to maintain order, security, and prosperity. We have no need to rise in arms to alter what is now satisfactory."

"Satisfactory? Why are the Boston Port Bill, Quebec Act, Quartering Act, Administration of Justice Act, and Massachusetts Government Act called the 'Intolerable Acts'? They violate our rights as British subjects."

A student in the gallery shouted out, "No taxation without representation!"

"Young man, you are late. Have you not heard of the repeal of the burdensome Stamp Act and Townsend Duties years ago."

Bang! The gavel startled everyone. Peyton Randolph, Speaker of the House of Burgesses, as imposing as the massive chair he sat in, called out, "Order, or the Sergeant at Arms will clear the gallery!" There was an immediate hush. "We are here to discuss proposals for the Continental Congress in Philadelphia. Leave the unjust taxes in yesteryear where they belong. Scribes are busy writing opinions and rumors of events that never happened to burden our grandsons in their history studies." Randolph looked around at several raised hands. "The Speaker recognizes the gentleman from Richmond."

"At the Albany Conference of 1754, Benjamin Franklin called for a federation of colonies as the Iroquois Six Nations had done. There are thirty British colonies in the New World, about twenty on the mainland. Mister Speaker, when you resume your post as President, I suggest we form a federation to resist injustice..."

A Burgess rose, recognized by a gesture of Randolph's chubby hand. "Only twelve colonies joined in the First Continental Congress. The Floridas and Georgia did not. Our fellow Colonials in Nova Scotia, many of them settlers from Massachusetts, petitioned His Majesty to avoid the fighting. They get rich supplying Royal Navy ships at Halifax. Even the people of Quebec, defeated by the Redcoats a dozen years ago, decline to resist and why should they? The King gave them lands west of the Appalachians and left their laws, language, and the Church of Rome. They trade muskets for furs with Indians who prey upon our settlers."

"But Virginia is the most populous colony, having half a million souls, more than twice that of New York," said another. "Georgia may join soon, so thirteen colonies will gather in Philadelphia. The rest will follow."

"I doubt it," a Burgess in a white wig to make him look older retorted. "If settlers stayed on our side of the Proclamation Line, they would not be preyed upon..."

"Gentlemen, can we please work together?" interrupted a wealthy Burgess, keen to change the subject from western settlement. "Britain ignored these colonies for a century and we made our own decisions. Her renewed attention is an affliction. We have more freedom than people do in Europe. The English do not have those 'rights of Englishmen' of which we speak. Thousands make a perilous journey here to seek freedom and property, refusing the bondage our King conspires to impose, just as Spanish and French autocratic kings bind their subjects!"

"Britain was nearly bankrupt after the war, yet Parliament cut taxes for landowners and squeezed us for more. Our German King hires soldiers from his kin on the Rhine as we dither. We must help Boston 'til Parliament comes to its senses. Friends like Pitt and Barré, support us. We toast Wilkes and the 45!"

"Those friends have failed. We have one English Lord here, Lord Thomas Sixth Earl of Fairfax, who owns millions of acres in Northern Virginia. His namesake, Thomas, Third Earl of Fairfax, led Parliament's Army when King Charles lost his head. Perhaps our Fairfax shall follow those footsteps."

"Fie! We'll have no talk of treason here!"

"Standing up for freedoms won over five centuries since the Magna Carta is not treason, Sir! It is our obligation to our ancestors and our progeny. Mister Speaker, I suggest when you resume the presidency, we offer the Virginia militia to the cause at Boston and name George Washington as General of a Continental Army. He was a fine colonel many years ago."

Susan became aware of vague scents—a musty trace of wool, old leather, lye soap, and tobacco. She leaned close to John's ear, "Did you know any of this?"

"No. What thirty colonies and why call this man President?"

Peter brooded about the hypocrisy of slave-owners speaking of freedom.

The crack of the gavel again jolted everyone. "Silence in the benches! Gentlemen, it has been an edifying discussion full of worthy ideas to take to the Continental Congress. The hour is late and my stomach rumbles. We shall reconvene at two to select delegates to the Congress and put a motion to offer the Virginia Militia to the cause. My next order of business is an ample slice of roast beef and a flagon of ale. I enjoin you to follow your own priorities in that regard. Session adjourned."

The Sinclairs followed the other visitors out and walked to Shields Tavern.

Day 1-6:   Megan at the Forge

Megan breathed in the aromas of savory soups and grilled meat as she made the reservations. She wandered on Francis Street past houses and gardens but saw no shops so she sat to look at her map. She was not good at maps, having declined to navigate on family trips. She shuddered at the memory of the incident on the highway that morning. Aha! Most of the shopping is one street behind me.

A short skinny man in a dirty shirt that had once been white and a red vest suddenly dashed past her to cross the street. He nodded and made a quick smile, put his index finger to his lips, slapped both hands on a fence post, vaulted into a garden, and disappeared behind a house. Megan stared but was startled again as two men ran to her bench, the fat one wheezing. He gasped, "Did he come by here?"

"Who?" Megan did not like these angry, sweaty men.

"A little man in a red waistcoat, thin as a reed, bolting from the high street."

"Which way did he go?" the other man asked. "He escaped his servitude. There is a prize for his capture and return to his master."

This rough man frightened Megan. "Escaped his servitude?" She pointed in the opposite direction from where the thin man had run.

"Back on Waller Street then, maybe to the squatters' huts north of town!"

"Can you catch him?" Megan asked, stalling for time.

"We shall catch him!" snarled the man and Megan felt fear stir within her. He reached behind his back to pull a long knife from its hidden sheath.

"That's a big knife," Megan said shakily, her heart pounding.

"Come on, Dagger!" panted the fat man, as he started off in the wrong direction.

The man sheathed his knife. His grin was threatening. "Maybe I shall keep the prize myself." They disappeared around the corner.

Megan hoped she did the right thing. Her heartbeat still quick, she walked to Duke of Gloucester Street and stepped into Tarpley's Store, amidst an array of china, baskets, pewter, hats, soap, and candles. Her sense of foreboding subsided.

"May I try on hats?" she asked a store clerk. She had colonial currency from her dad and, in hopes of getting to a mall, had brought other money along. She chose a white linen mobcap and an apron to look like a middle-sorts woman.

Leaving the store, she found the sidewalk blocked by students clustered around a teacher holding a yellow umbrella. Megan detoured down a lane. Metal rings leaned against a building. She sniffed a familiar smell and looked around. Near a fence was a pile of shiny black rocks. She picked one up, made a face at the black dust on her fingers, and tossed it back. Movement caught her eye as an Indian in a deerskin jacket slipped through a door. She walked over and looked in.

In the dim light, she saw a row of chimneys, each with a brick platform in front. A miniature fireplace opened to the platforms and on the nearest was a small fire

17

in a mound of the black rocks she had seen outside. There was a smoky, metallic smell in the place. A man in a leather jerkin explained the work to visitors. The Indian in deerskin spoke quietly to a smith working on an anvil.

"A smith manages the fire using bellows, water, and a poker," explained the man in the jerkin. "He sprinkles water on the coal at the perimeter to keep it from burning at once. The heat cooks out impurities leaving coke, which burns hotter than coal. Most colonies export iron because abundant forests provide the fuel needed for the iron works."

The blacksmith used a poker to move coke to the center of the fire. Holding tongs, he put a metal bar in the coals until it glowed red and then bright yellow-orange with the tip radiant and almost white. He then hammered it on the anvil.

"He's making a tyre for the wheelwright. 'Tis called a tyre because it ties together curved sections of the wood rim of a wheel." It was an iron ring like those outside.

"In this shop we make wrought iron goods and mend tools for wrights and joiners. An experienced smith here makes six score or a hundred and twenty nails an hour. In England, a skilled man makes ten score for less pay, so English nails cost less, but no nails are cheap. When people move west after depleting their land, they burn houses to the ground to reclaim nails from the ashes."

As the smith pulled a rope, a bellows behind the chimney compressed with a whoosh pushing air through a pipe in a windy rush. The fire on the forge flared and the coals glowed orange. The smith turned the hot iron with tongs and hammered the metal on the anvil to shape the tyre. He placed the metal in the coals again. Each pull of the bellows gave his face and short beard a ruddy glow. With each flare, Megan took more notice of the blacksmith.

The smith did not notice the young woman in the apron watching him. His movements were rhythmic and his eyes were on the glowing iron. He listened to the Indian. "They spotted him behind the old forge at the back, and he ran like a yearling buck through the gardens."

Megan stepped close to the two men and said, "If you're talking about the short man in the red vest, he got away." The two men looked up. "Pardon?" said the startled blacksmith as the Indian assessed Megan with a steady gaze.

"I was sitting by the next street when he ran across and jumped a fence between two houses. I told a man with the knife and a fat guy chasing him that he went the other way. They were scary. Was helping him get away a good thing to do?"

The Indian put a hand on Megan's shoulder. "That was a very good thing to do. That man with the knife is dangerous." Then he turned to the smith, "I will tell the people to help Simon if they see him," and without a goodbye he walked out.

"Why was he running away?" Megan asked.

"Can you read those?" The smith nodded at notices on the wall. Megan read a faded sheet offering a reward for a runaway slave: "Escaped the last market day in March wearing a gray osnaberg shirt. Has two missing teeth when he smiles." A newly posted notice described Simon, a runaway indentured servant: "A small boney man with thick eyebrows wearing a red waistcoat over a white linen shirt."

"That was him!" exclaimed Megan. The smith put his index finger to his lips. She moved close to the blacksmith and whispered, "What's an indentured servant?"

"In the Virginia Colony, many of us English and perhaps most Scots and Germans struggle in indentured servitude to pay the cost of our passage over, for other debts, or for crimes committed. You have heard of a bondsman in the Bible?"

"I don't think so," Megan said hesitantly.

"We sign a bond to work for a number of years. We are not free to leave until we fulfill our time but our employer can sell the bond, and we must work for the buyer until our time has been served. Like gangly Simon, I shant be free for years."

"That's not fair! For how long were you bonded?"

"To pay my passage, I was bonded for five years. Fortunate folk who pay part of their passage sign for two or three years, but I had no money. Five years did not seem much when I was fifteen in England. I dreamed of strolling like a squire in boots with silver buckles between my own forge and a cottage. In England, we knew only sooty drudgery. We were lucky to avoid a plague or a cutthroat. The average age at death in England is thirty-four so this was a chance at a new life."

"If you're twenty and you signed up for five years at fifteen, you must be almost done. I am almost done high school now that I'm eighteen. I'm Megan, by the way."

"Since I call myself Mark, so may you." The smith pulled the glowing bar from the fire and faced the anvil. His hammer sliced the air and flattened the malleable glowing metal. "Almost five years have gone by and three more to serve." Clink!

"On the voyage we had stormy seas. We clutched the rail to save ourselves from going overboard and had bouts of puking over the side. At times, we wished we could die to end the awful pitching of the ship. Lying down on the berth made it near bearable. The food had maggots. We had no appetite and got by on hard biscuits and water. The sight of a coastline relieved us. We crossed the Chesapeake to see forests and farms to portside as we approached Norfolk." Clink!

"We staggered onto the wharf, small sacks holding all we owned. The quay was not moving which made it hard to walk. Imagine that! One fellow, though sober, staggered to the edge but dropped to his knees to avoid falling into the sea."

The metal faded to ruddy brown. Mark put it in the fire, added a scoop of coal at the edge, and raked coke toward the center. "Megan is it?" She nodded.

"I worked three hard years at an ironworks northwest of here. We heard of free land in Georgia for debtors and other unfortunates. So one night, emboldened by rum I tried to escape. I clambered along a river bank, keeping out of sight for two days. On a road by the river, I jumped into the woods when I saw a pair of Redcoats. My behavior was suspicious and they seized me. When I confessed they laughed. 'Georgia is to the south you dullard. You are scramblin' west on your way to losing your scalp to the Indians!'"

The smoke began to sting Megan's eyes so she stepped to the side.

"I was not afraid of Indians, I worked with them. But I ran without knowing where to go. That added a year to my contract. Another was added when I was found in a barn in the Carolinas. By then I knew which way was south. My contract was sold to the owner of this forge. One night at gaming cocks, I made a desperate bet with my owner for a year of service and lost. Eight years in all I have to serve. I may be worn out before I am free."

"You can be bought and sold like that?" Megan asked incredulously.

"Just like African people, but they are owned as property their whole lives while our bond just seems eternal. Now Simon has run. I hope he has coins. I sometimes go over in my mind how I would do it better now."

He pulled on the bellows. A column of fine ash and smoke puffed into the air; then the draw of the chimney pulled the wisp in. Mark paused to watch the curved white line as it disappeared into the chimney. He placed the tyre on the anvil.

"It's not fair that you can't come and go. Do you like being a blacksmith?"

"In three years, I will be my own man. That would not happen in England. This forge is the best situation I have known. I like making things and here I eat every day. Back home, getting enough to eat is a problem for many." Clink!

"You are like a slave and slavery is not right!"

"In the Southern colonies many are in servitude. On the frontier, others struggle in bondage to clear the land. Most will work away their lives in poverty. They are called squatters because they have no chairs and eat squatting on the ground."

"Dutch sailors brought the first Africans to Jamestown. People put them into indentured servitude until they worked off the cost of their purchase. Now Africans are enslaved for life. I agree slavery is wrong. A planter should set his slaves free after their work has paid for their cost. But few people pay any mind to what is right." Clink!

Megan was stunned to realize so many were owned as property. She had no idea what life had been like early in the long struggle for human rights. "What will happen to Simon? Those were very bad men chasing him."

"If the Pamunkey Indians find him, they will help him get to the Carolinas, maybe to the Cherokee. He may find a new life. In those hills, they do not like the rich landowners of the coast. Some escaped themselves years ago. But the fighting in Massachusetts may sweep away the life we know today." Clink!

"Mark, I'll be here for four days. May I visit you again?"

"I would enjoy that. Thank you for not giving Simon away."

Megan curtsied and stepped into the sunlight. She wondered about Mark. "He's cute, but uptight about something." She resolved to find out what it was.

20

Day 1-7:   Lunch in Shields Tavern

Megan hurried up the steps into Shields Tavern, a white building with black shutters, and a row of gables protruding from the roof upstairs. She saw Peter and her parents being seated at a table with a hurricane lamp on it.

"You can have brunch or order from our lunch menu," said the hostess.

"Leave both menus and we'll figure it out," said Susan. "We're a family with a wide range of firmly held opinions... speaking of which," she waved to her approaching daughter. "Hi Megan. That's a lovely apron."

"Thanks, Mom. What happened at the Capitol?"

"In a short time we learned a lot we didn't know before," said Susan.

"Like what?"

"Like if we don't order quickly I'm going to starve," Peter exclaimed.

The server stepped up. "I'm sorry. I didn't see you were ready to order."

"We're not," said Megan. "We have an impatient teenager among us."

"I'm twenty-one and look who's talking!"

"I'm not stalking!" Megan laughed.

"Kids, our waitress is busy. Let's order a Shields Sampler to share as appetizer and I'll have the chicken," said Susan quickly, hoping John would not lose patience with the kids. "What are the salsify and sippets appetizers?"

"Those were common in colonial times. Sippets are rectangles of dried bread like a cracker. Salsify is a root—whitish yellow like a parsnip. It's very good pickled."

John looked up from the menu, "I'll have cornbread-stuffed quail. Peter, do you know what you want? We'll give Megan a moment to decide."

"I'll have the crab cake."

"Have you had time to decide, Miss?"

"Yes, thank you. I'll have the pecan waffle and sage sausage."

"If the pig were so sage, she wouldn't be sausage," said Peter.

When the server left Susan asked, "Are you enjoying this visit so far, Megan?"

"I'm learning tons of stuff. Many white people in Virginia were indentured servants. I've decided to write my paper on that."

"We heard at the Capitol that the American Revolution was maybe not for the reasons what we thought. The Burgesses weren't concerned about taxes but about something called the Quebec Act."

John scowled, "They got it wrong. Everyone knows the Revolution was over 'taxation without representation.' It says that on Washington DC license plates."

Susan persisted. "Maybe public sentiment was whipped up for a senseless war that generated profits for some people. If people could see what motivated their leaders and what war looked like, they would not send their kids to war."

"Always the protester, Susan," said John.

"How come you never talk about your time in the Army, Dad?" Megan asked.

Susan winced. Perhaps John's testiness was a reaction to talking to the soldiers.

"I went where they sent me and did what they told me to do. Peter, you heard the sergeant say it's not glorious. He was right." John was grim.

"Amen," said Susan. "The woman by the Capitol was troubled by war."

"She's a reenactor, Susan. She could be upset about something or maybe she's nervous about playing her role right." John shook his head.

"I don't think so, John. Did any of you notice anything strange this morning?"

"Like what?"

"In the Capitol I smelled tobacco, candles, and wool, but no one was smoking."

"That's just your immersion into the experience," said John.

"Oh, I didn't tell you!" Megan blurted out. "Something scary happened after I left you. A skinny indentured servant man ran by me chased by two guys."

"They stage events like that all the time around here," said John.

"Why put on a show when no one is there to see it? One guy pulled a knife from behind his back. I got a bad feeling about him. His friend called him Dagger. They wouldn't let someone work here who didn't shower. He was scary and he stank!"

"Honey, be polite. We're in a restaurant!"

"Why were the blacksmith and Indian relieved the skinny guy got away, Mom?"

"What blacksmith and Indian?"

Megan told them about the blacksmith and what she learned about servitude."

"Was he cute?" Peter teased.

"I didn't notice, and it's none of your business. Oh, another thing — in the yard behind the blacksmith shop I smelled pig manure like when we drove past those hog farms last year."

"Pig manure? Nice — what's strange about that?" John asked.

"There weren't any pigs anywhere, Dad. That's what's strange."

"How about you, Honey? Did you notice anything unusual?" Susan asked John.

"Not really. Maybe the reenactors practice on that back street, Megan."

"It was real, Dad. I saw the knife. I would have been less scared if you'd been there."

Peter thought the slave woman was not acting either but he kept that to himself.

"Your victuals have arrived," announced the server.

As the hungry quartet dug in, Peter asked, "At the Capitol they talked about Wilkes and the 45. Were they like the Seven Samurai or the 300 at Thermopylae?"

"I never heard of Wilkes," John said. "Let's look it up."

Day 1-8:   Peter Meets Annie

Outside Shields Tavern, the Sinclairs agreed to meet at five. A poster invited one and all to give Peyton Randolph a rousing sendoff to the Continental Congress. "What if it's crowded and we can't find each other?" asked Susan.

"Mom, we'll call each other on our phones! I'll say 'I'm in front of the tree' and you'll say 'I'm so pretending I'm in the past that I forgot I had a cell phone...'"

John grew irritated. "If we don't connect at five, we'll meet at six at Christiana Campbell's Tavern where Megan made reservations, OK?"

Susan saw something was bothering John and she watched him for a moment. He was not often this short with the kids.

"OK, bye." said Megan as she left on her shopping quest.

"That girl can be rude, Susan."

"She'll grow out of it," Susan assured John. "I did. Did you hear her say she'd have been less scared if you had been there when the guy pulled out a knife?"

John nodded. "She hasn't said anything like that to me since she was eight. I guess she was really frightened of those reenactors."

Peter followed John and Susan past the front of the Powell House where he tried not to be obvious glancing between buildings for a sign of his new acquaintance. They turned left on Nicholson Street and strolled to a brick house with three chimneys and few windows. Beyond it ran a high brick wall with a large sturdy door. They were greeted at the gaol by the woman in the green dress Peter had seen in the morning picking up food at the Powell House. As his parents entered, Peter said to the reenactor. "I've come to turn myself in."

"What horrible deed have you done?" asked the woman.

"I urged a slave to run away."

"That is a serious crime! Slaves are far and away the leading families' most valuable possessions, more valuable than all their land and buildings combined. Helping a slave escape is stealing, like helping horses or silver candlesticks escape. It would end badly. You could hang on that gallows." Behind the jail on a barren rise, three stark columns were joined with beams forming a triangle at the top. The grisly form and its function unsettled Peter.

"My husband is the gaoler and I can tell you that a quarter of those convicted of a felony here are hanged. If they committed hideous crimes, their bodies are put in cages called gibbets hung on posts by the road into town. Buzzards and crows picking at the corpses warn others to avoid their crimes and their fate."

"They actually did that here? It's an awful bird feeder."

"Aye, it inspires awe of justice and fear of transgression. When people see the wicked become a meal for vultures, they resolve to resist the Evil Tempter. Until dry bones remain in the gibbet, people entering Williamsburg cover their noses."

Peter asked, "How does a slave find churches that would get him to freedom?"

"Escape to where? In 1775, slavery is legal and a pillar of the economy of British colonies. I know of no sanctuary since the Floridas became British in 1763."

"You said 'the Floridas.' Are there more than one?"

"There is East Florida on the Atlantic and West Florida is on the Gulf of Mexico. In northern colonies some people help slaves improve their lives, but I never heard of churches helping slaves escape."

Peter was disheartened to learn the Underground Railroad did not exist in 1775.

The gaoler's wife continued, "A judgment by Lord Mansfield in 1772 declared slavery not to be within British law and slaves on British soil were freed. However, the British own slaves in their colonies. Getting to England is near impossible for a slave. Some run west into the wilderness where they risk death or capture. Demand for slaves is great, and some Native tribes trade in slaves."

"But slaves are human beings! How can a slave get a chance for a better life?"

"Most people in this world are not free. Many here are indentured servants. In Europe, most people are serfs or tenant farmers to the princes and dukes who control the lands. As for Africans here, perhaps one in a hundred is free."

"But..."

"The few Africans who obtained freedom were rewarded with manumission because of extraordinary service to their owners or they saved money to buy freedom when their owner had a desperate need for money. Most slave owners believe slavery is the only hope of saving themselves from ruin. There is no excuse, but it is their view of the world."

"You say 'There is no excuse.' What do you think about slavery?" asked Peter.

The woman looked into Peter's eyes and ignored the question. "Slaves trained in carpentry or other trades are more valuable and have better living conditions than field hands, so learning a trade helps them."

Peter listened carefully. "If slavery is legal and supported by people here, why are you telling me ways that slaves might improve their lives or obtain freedom?"

She lowered her voice. "You are perspicacious. My parents were servants. Pa was so worn out by servitude he could barely put food on our cracked plates. When he died, Ma did washing to get salt and meat for the soup. She taught me to pray for all children in bondage, including African children.

"There was a school for Africans in Williamsburg, set up by the British Society for the Propagation of the Gospel. After Missus Wagner, the director, died last year, it closed. Lord knows what those twenty-four children shall do now."

Peter grew discouraged. "Was there no way out? Maybe I'm wrong to think a problem can always be solved."

"There is that one chance in a hundred," suggested the gaoler's wife. "A slave having a strong desire to be free would need to watch for opportunities and seize the moment. He would also need help from God." They stood in silence.

"Would you like to see the cell they will lock you in if you help a slave run?"

24

"Will they let me back out? I'm still an innocent man — so far."

"Aye, they all say they are innocent men. The gaoler will release you if you follow the law and behave yourself while you are in there." The woman smiled.

Peter walked up the steps into the gaoler's house. His parents listened to the gaoler near the hearth in the tiny front room.

"They really kept mentally ill people in here?" a young visitor asked.

"Yes, until the Public Hospital opened, insane people were locked up here if they were a risk to others. It must have been frightening for the gaoler's children to scurry past the cells in the narrow hallway each night to get to their bedroom. Over the years, this gaol held thieves and murderers, pirates, debtors, Loyalists, and runaway slaves. The accused waited weeks or months for their cases to be heard."

The visitors moved through the house into the bare yard behind high brick walls and stepped into one of four cells. It took a moment for eyes to adjust to the shadows. Walls of hardwood planks were securely anchored by great bolts. The cell had a toilet seat on a wooden box held in place by iron straps and rivets.

"You wouldn't want the toilet to escape," someone suggested.

"This cell must have reeked. I don't see any showers."

"The prisoners got a blanket and meals of corn mush and occasionally, dried salted meat," explained the gaoler. "Prosperous families might bring a relative clothing, blankets, food, or even liquor. But most people would be unable to offer an extra blanket or food when they lacked these things themselves."

"Looks like the prisoners slept on the floor."

"Yes, but a cover of straw made it softer, warmer, and easier to clean out. It seems like rough treatment when you know this is not punishment, but just waiting for trial. Three of the four cells have no window for ventilation."

Susan pointed. "Look at those chains and leg irons!"

Peter did not notice his father shudder.

"At least there was no torture," John murmured. He rubbed his thumb, once dislocated when he was hurled into a gully by an exploding shell. He had snapped it back himself. He remembered the stab of pain, but he was ready for battle — for ten more minutes until he was taken prisoner by four bearded mountain herdsmen pointing rifles him. He was chained in a hut for twelve days until a Special Forces team parachuted out of the night sky to rescue him. He forced his focus back to the present. He walked behind Susan and Peter out of the cell into the sunlit yard, through the heavy door, and out to the street.

On leaving the gaol, Susan saw a woman in colonial dress approaching carrying a basket. She seemed distraught. "Are you all right?" Susan asked.

"Yes, praise God. The Lord has provided food to bring to my husband. He has been here two months but I pray not much longer. Forgive me, Missus, but I must hurry in. It has been five days since I last found food for my husband to add to the thin gruel and dry bread he gets here."

As the woman reached the door, Susan called out, "Why are they holding him?"

"When he was called by our Lord to preach His Word, he answered the call!"

Susan found this puzzling but she turned to catch up with her husband and son. As they strolled, she chatted but John was silent. Peter was preoccupied. If there was no Underground Railroad for years to come, was there any hope?

They came to the cabinetmaker's workshop beside a stream. Peter heard the gurgling water. A young black man in a beige vest and gray knickers opened the door for customers. John and Susan moved into a hallway flanked by finely made chairs, china cabinets, and a handcrafted harpsichord. Beyond was an ancient workshop where tools hung on pegs: saws, C-clamps, a large compass, and a set square. Tables were cluttered with tools and finishing rags stained many shades of brown. A bin by the wall held boards and dowels. The windows were large and the walls and ceilings painted white to reflect the light needed by the artisans.

Peter paused by the door when he noticed a big black woman sitting on the far side of a small pasture. She worked on something in her lap with a wooden bowl in front of her. "Who is that woman sitting up there by the white fence?"

The man at the door looked surprised. "She be Annie, a free African."

"She's free?"

"Yes. A free black be rare and Annie be rarer still."

"May I talk to her?" Peter was eager though gaol and gallows crossed his mind.

The man hesitated. "She don't bite but best to talk to her when no one around."

Puzzled, Peter approached the large woman with short-cropped curly hair. He glanced behind to be sure he was not followed. He had a feeling of stepping across a threshold. Annie diced a soft white cube into her bowl beside a cloth spread on the grass. On the cloth were piles of wild garlic, dandelions, and other greens.

"Excuse me. Are you preparing food?" What a stupid question, he thought.

The woman studied his face with a kind expression. "I'm Annie."

"I'm Peter."

"Well, Mister Peter. I'se surprised you came to see me and ain't much surprises me." She gave him a long look. "I'se cuttin' up pork fat for tonight. We don't always get to flavor corn mush wit' smoked salt pork belly like this."

"What's happening tonight?" was what Peter asked, but what he thought was, stop beating around the bush and get on to what you need to ask her.

The woman paused as if to not interrupt his thoughts. "If we speakin' out loud, nuthin's happenin' tonight. Slaves ain't s'posed to gather 'cept in church. But if we speakin' jus' me and you, can you keep somethin' secret?"

"Well, to tell you the truth, Ma'am, I've been here half a day and I already am."

"Thank you for that. White folk don't call me Ma'am." Then she whispered, "You already am what? Keepin' secrets?"

"Yes. The man at the cabinet shop says you are free. I'm curious to know how."

26

"I was born free."

"My family is visiting the shop. Since I can keep a secret, may I help you pull the stems off those greens while you tell me what you're preparing the food for?"

"You don't give up easy, do you?" Annie chuckled. "Sit by this bush so folks walking in the street don't see you talkin' wit' me. You can tear them leaves and stems into pieces. I'se makin' food for a gatherin' of African folk tonight in a wooded hollow. We call it a Hush Harbor. Free blacks not 'sposed to help slaves come together."

"I have questions but I'm afraid to ask you."

"What you 'fraid to ax me?"

"I was talking to someone at the Powell House about running north to get free. Now I'm troubled to think people could live in slavery with no chance of freedom. You were born free. Can you tell me of paths to freedom for people born slaves?"

Annie tilted her head slightly to the left and studied Peter. Then she smiled. "So you was over at the Powell House? That Evie is a handsome woman ain't she?"

Peter blushed. "Well, yes she is. Until now I didn't know her name was Evie."

"You didn't know her name? Why does you want to help her get free?"

"She is there against her will. Her two sons are slaves. That's not right."

"It ain't right that's true. There be a whole lot of 'ain't right' in the world and slavery is an abomination. But, it ain't fully against her will. If she does what she do and don't do somethin' else, there be will in that. And if she has a hint of somethin' she don't understand and she don't look at it until she figures it out, there be will in that."

"I don't understand."

"I gonna say it slow and you listen careful. Sometimes there be a chance for somethin' we don't see 'cause we is so sure things is the way we think they is and sure they can't be otherwise."

"Is there a way for people to get free they are not seeing?"

"Most people don't see what is there to see. I can say more when we meet again. 'Most everybody who look like me is owned by somebody who look like you. When I was a girl in Africa, I was catched and brought over the sea. It was many years before freedom and I found each other again." Annie sighed. "Many people is sufferin'. Here we sit, a white man in strange clothing, talking wit' me about helpin' a slave get free. Tell me why you interested in helping Evie."

"She could choose where to go and what to do. I have confusing feelings about her. She is beautiful. It feels like we're family." He was startled by his own candor.

"Well now, that be the truth Mister Peter. But most people 'round here of any color ain't free. Middle-sorts planters be chained to their land and work wit' no end. Better-sorts gentry got big houses but most be hidin' the painful truth that they burdened wit' debt. Burgesses meet only a few weeks a year because they got to rush home to struggle to keep they lands. They be called free but they feel tied up by the strong rope of they situation just the same."

Annie sliced another cube of fat. "Living life free ain't bein' a feather floatin' in a gentle breeze. There is always somethin' each of us needs to be gettin' on about. Sometimes we choose it and sometimes it comes to us. We is free to choose what we think and what we pray for. We struggle, rejoice, and grieve as we go along."

"I think that's true—but I don't like the idea that somebody can own you and make all the choices for you. Owners can even hurt their slaves. You are free. Do you care about freedom for others?"

"Yes, I talk to folk 'round here, and a mother at the Powell House is one. If I see a way they could live a better life, I give a seed of advice on a small step to take. They hear it or they don't. They might take up the seed or not. That also be a kind of freedom. I been free for years and there is people who never once done axed me about freedom for they self.

"You ask how folk can find freedom. You could ask how to let freedom find its way into folk 'cause it always be right here. Sometimes a massa give manumission like I got, but most times the massa's children gets the slaves when he die. Sometimes slaves work all night for money at tobacco packin' time, when the massa fear bein' late would bring ruin. They work Sundays off the plantation if they allowed. Once they get money, some buy and sell things to make mo' money to buy theyself. Some take a dangerous path and run."

Annie shook her head. "Slaves who run into the forest can die if they don't know how to get along. If a slave pay a ship captain to carry him away, the captain might sell him to a sugarcane plantation. People in the islands feel more whips and shackles than in Virginia and life is short. We can't get a ship back home to Africa. Folk who come from Africa say wars and slave catchin' goin' on more than ever."

"Can you give me advice on how I could help?"

"My advice is be careful about what advice you give people. Your care for Evie is true. I see danger but my caution ain't likely to scare you off. Better not grab the first answer that comes when you ax a question. Sit patient wit' the question. Maybe it gonna get clearer or ideas come into you head that change the question and a deeper answer come. In time, a door may open."

"Peter!" Susan called from the porch steps. Peter was embarrassed.

"Don't be shy 'bout your mama callin'. Many folk don't got a ma no mo'."

"Annie, I hope to see you again."

"You will. You saw me in the first place so you is bound to see me again."

Peter caught up with John and Susan. They did not ask about Annie. At the bend in the path he looked back to see that she had already gone—bowl, cloth, greens, pork belly, and all.

Day 1-9:   William's Bricks

As they entered the Brickyard, a tall, black man smiled and called out, "Come on over folks! You know why they call me William? 'Cause that be my name, that's why. Massa hired me out to the owner of this brickyard to do what? To make mortar and bricks that's what. I does that all day and part of the night if we is busy as we oft times am," he grinned.

"You know why I likes mortar and bricks? Because they ain't tobacco fields in a cold rain, and they ain't a stable full of horse manure that needs cleaning out on a hot summer day, that's why. We make what this town is made of, that's mortar and bricks. That's right! You all know 'burg' mean town, don't you? Williamsburg mean William's town and William's town made from William's bricks and them bricks is made here by William. That's me."

Susan wondered how a slave could be traded like that. Peter wondered how a slave could enjoy himself so much. John wondered how William could keep that routine up all day.

"Bricks and mortar is born right here. Let me show you how, startin' wit' mortar. Yesterday this fire burned a pile of oyster shells taller than me. Them oyster shells was changed, which ain't no surprise. You and me would change if we was burned in a hot fire all night. Once they cool, they crumble. Don't touch them because what do you get when you burn shells? Quick lime, that's what Massa say to a man from Scotland who was lending money. I don't know what quick lime is 'cept that's what we reduce shells to. Yes, we do."

William picked up a bucket. "We shovel burned shells into troughs and pour on water. We get what I heard is a comical reaction wit' water and shells. We push it back and forth like this to make mud and add sand and animal hair to bind it together. It becomes the mortar to lay the bricks. But you can't be stickin' your hands into that mortar even when it cools."

"Is it an acid?" someone asked.

"Massa told me quick lime is the opposite of acid. They call it basic. Maybe they call it basic because basically it can burn your skin right though. Yes, it can.

"And besides mortar, what else do you suppose we make here in this brickyard?"

"Bricks!" several people called out.

"I am happy to see you is learnin' the finer points of a brickyard. We make bricks out of clay and you can see we been cuttin' some raw bricks just over there."

"Do you dry them in the sun?" asked Susan.

"In Spanish colonies wit' hardly no rain to soak brick walls and weaken them and no frost to crack them, people dry bricks in the sun and reinforce them wit' straw. The Spanish call sun-dried clay 'adobe.' Do you know why? 'Cause that be the name in Spanish."

John laughed aloud, surprising Peter who did not hear his father laugh often.

"Sun-dried bricks ain't good where winters are cold enough to freeze water in a crack and break 'em. Here we fire bricks to make them hard enough for all kinds of weather. I heard that over in Europe, there are brick buildings standing after a thousand years."

"We stack bricks in that kiln and fire it up day and night for a week. That ain't half-baked is it? We make the bricks to build Williamsburg. Did you see any bricks that look shiny blue on the end? Why might that be?"

"The ends of bricks used as blue headers were next to the fire in the kiln. The heat gave them a glaze-like finish," said John who had paid attention on the tour of the Capitol. "Why don't you stack some bricks sideways toward the fire so you get blue stretchers as well?"

"That's exactly right, Mister... who?"

"John."

"Mister John, you know a header from a stretcher. Stack 'em sideways to get blue stretchers? We don't because... Huh, we may have to try that someday. Thank you all for comin' by the brickyard. If you want a wagon load, I can load up your wagon for you."

Susan asked John and Peter, "Would you guys like to look in some shops? I need a hat now that the sun is out." She hoped to talk again with the woman she met at the Capitol and felt an urge to move on.

"I think we'll stay around here and visit another tradesman," John said, to Peter's relief.

Day 1-10: Susan at the Milliner Shop

Susan felt restless as she left the brickyard. In the window of the Margaret Hunter Milliner Shop, she saw a man with spectacles and bushy eyebrows, sitting cross-legged on a platform, hand sewing a hem along a bolt of brocade. His breeches were the color of pekoe tea with milk, buttoned tight below the knees. Susan nodded to him and he nodded back.

As Susan entered, the tailor looked up from his work. "Good day, Madam."

Susan noted the fine stitching of his waistcoat and the lace edges of the loosely tied white cravat. His long hair was tied at the nape of his neck. "You are sitting in what my grandmother called the tailor position. Do tailors really sit that way?"

"I sit next to the window to get light for sewing. I spread the cloth around me on the tailor's board to keep it off the floor where it might be soiled. Customers such as I hope you might be, see me in the window and may give us their custom when they note the quality of our materials and our work. This manner of working is typical of a colonial era tailor."

"What is that beautiful fabric you're working on?"

"This fine brocade was imported from Belgium by a Scottish factor. I will make a formal gown to be worn to a ball at the Governor's Palace. Please have a look at the other garments we fashion here for better-sorts people."

"Were richer people actually considered better?"

"The names better-sorts, middle-sorts, and lesser-sorts suggest that. I have great expectations of having my own shop one day to finally attain the middle." He smiled. "I was a foundling, abandoned in a basket one winter morning in a pew at Coventry Cathedral and raised in a church school where orphans were fortunate to learn a trade. I learned tailoring and by sailing to Virginia, trebled my earnings. I wager the poor woman who left me under a blanket did not have the opportunities life has given me. I am grateful for what I have and don't complain about what I don't have."

"That's a great attitude. Tell me about that navy blue cape with the exquisite gold embroidery along the hem."

"I fashioned that mantua myself after a French design. It is for sale for eight hundred dollars. Had you dropped by in 1775 you could have purchased one for a few pounds."

"It's tragic I'm so late. You called it a mantua?"

"Yes, it is common in fashion to use French and Italian words. The word millinery comes from the textile city Milano. Mantua is from the town in Italy by that name."

"What about those hats?"

"The brimmed straw hats with ribbons are for fashionable attire, and the mob caps that tie beneath your chin are undress caps for ordinary wear at home."

"I'd like a dressy hat." Susan tried on several hats in front of what the tailor called the looking glass and chose one trimmed with a wide blue satin ribbon. She paid the tailor in colonial currency. As he thanked her, his eyes twinkled.

Outside the store, she paused in front of the Golden Ball jewelry store. "Hmmm, that was a strange urge, wasn't it, to buy a new hat? I'll resist the temptation to buy jewelry."

At the end of the street, she walked to the Secretary's Office behind the Capitol. With stone floors and brick walls, it was designed to protect public records from fire. She stepped into a bookstore. Next to books on religion, she brushed against the only other customer who asked, "Are you interested in religion in the colonial period? I am giving a sermon on that subject tonight at the Bruton Parish Church."

"Are you an interpreter?" Susan asked.

"We're all interpreters of something aren't we? I am James Walker, an Episcopal priest. Tonight I'll talk on the faiths of our forebears."

"Hello Reverend Walker, I'm Susan Sinclair. I will get tickets for my husband and me. You said you are an Episcopal priest. I thought only Catholics had priests."

"The Church of England kept the term priests when we broke with Rome. After the American Revolution, we were called ministers in the U.S., but we are now priests again."

"See how little I know? I look forward to your talk." After the priest left, Susan got tickets for the sermon. As she put them into her bag, her restlessness subsided. She felt impelled to follow an invisible trail. A trail toward what she was not sure.

Day 1-11:   Megan and Indentured Servitude

After leaving Shields Tavern, Megan walked west to the Mary Dickenson Store. At the array of colonial costumes — stacked straw hats with colorful ribbons, aprons and pretty dresses on a rack, and hooded capes hung on pegs. She decided to plunge into her research by dressing in costume. She tried on a blue print dress with tiny yellow and white daisies and did not take it off. She crammed her jeans into her daypack, paid for the dress, and stepped outside.

She marched straight to the blacksmith shop. As she entered, she saw the Indian in the deerskin jacket again quietly speaking with Mark. "Am I interrupting?"

"You are welcome here."

"May I ask about indentured servants? I'm going to write a history paper."

Mark frowned. "Nothing I have done is worthy of being called history. Why not write about Peyton Randolph, George Mason, or other great leaders?"

"Who were they? First, I'll introduce myself to your friend. I'm Megan Sinclair." She reached out her hand.

"Megan Sinclair. I am Standing Elk. When I worked in the iron foundry, they could not pronounce my name in my language. What does Megan mean?"

"It was my great grandmother's name. I don't know what it means. You worked at a foundry? Do Indians do that?"

"Some of us have done that. That is where Mark and I became friends. In the early days of settlement, my ancestors attacked foundries because whole forests were cut and burned to make iron. I worked there to get money to buy back land for my people."

"Do Indians still live around here?"

"My people are of the Algonquin group, which we call the Anishinaabe. We are related to many tribes from the Micmac in the Northeast, to the Ojibwa at the headwaters of the Mississippi. Tribes nearby are the Pamunkey, the tribe of my mother and the Mattaponi, the tribe of my father. Time has passed since elk were here, but this Elk is still standing." He tapped his chest.

"I had no idea elk once lived in Virginia. Where did they go?"

"For countless generations we hunted elk and wood bison in the eastern forests as did the wolves and big cats you call cougars. We were all in balance."

"There were bison here too?"

"I saw them grazing in meadows west of here when I was young. Settlers cleared the forest home of the animals. They got harder to find in a hunt then they were gone. Life is out of balance." Standing Elk looked out the open door. "I remember crystal winter nights when I was a boy lying in our wigwam, listening to wolves calling to the moon over the lake. My son and daughter have heard them only on a long hunting trip west of the hills. Their children may never hear them."

Megan responded, "We still do that. We cut all the trees, eat all the fish, burn all the oil, use up soil and fresh water, and poison everything. If we keep it up there'll be no forests or fish anywhere, just like there are no more bison in Virginia."

"My father named me Standing Elk to remind me of that danger so I would live in balance. He was a medicine man who joked that the white man calls it 'history' because it is *his* story. You want to talk about indentured servitude. That is *his* story." He pointed to the blacksmith.

"Mark, you told me you signed a contract. How did you sign if you can't read and how did you know what you were agreeing to?"

"They handed me a quill and showed me where to put an X. I surprised them as I printed the letters M-A-R-K." He smiled enigmatically. Megan did not detect he was withholding a secret. "They read the good parts to me. We learned the bad parts when we got here. Standing Elk helps me see beyond my troubles."

Megan reread the notices offering rewards for runaways. Most described the clothes they wore. Standing Elk spoke furtively to Mark, nodded, and left.

"He didn't say goodbye."

"He nodded and looked into my eyes. Words are not the only way to talk."

"Would it be rude to ask what were you and your friend talking about?"

Mark tightened. "It would not be rude to ask, Megan, but not safe to answer. 'Tis kind of you to show interest in bonded laborers. The original peoples of this land also suffer much. There is danger in making your concerns known."

"But...?"

"Sorry to be abrupt but I hope to protect people, including you." He returned to hammering then paused, "Thanks for coming to visit again."

Megan left more curious than when she arrived. She explored historic sites and when she met indentured servants, peppered them with questions: How long was their contract? Did they have plans for when they were finally free? Did they know former servants who prospered?

She discovered only one in three servants eventually succeeded by the humble standards of the day. Life was particularly harsh for unskilled laborers unable to earn enough to sustain themselves once free. They often took another term of servitude for the meager food and shelter it offered. Others got small land grants and wandered unprepared and ill equipped to the West. Many perished.

An educated man, brought over from England to tutor a Burgess's children, explained that indenture began in feudal times. Rising population and enclosure of common land into private ownership by wealthy families displaced rural people. Migrating people desperate for work were called the *mobile vulgis*, or mob. Many among them grasped at a chance to sail to a new life.

Megan sat on a bench, her mind racing. So many people were stuck in poverty. Was it possible for them to improve their lives? It was time to meet her family.

Day 1-12:   Peyton Randolph Leaves for Philadelphia

Leaving the brickyard, John and Peter strolled a few blocks west to the Deane Shop. Working at a bench was the sergeant they had seen by the Capitol.

"I knew we would meet again," he said.

"Good to see you, Sergeant."

"Does it take patience to cut and sand wood day after day?" Peter asked.

"A day has twenty-four hours whether we hurry or not. When our hearts are in a craft, 'tis satisfying. A wheel made by these methods is sound for more years than a man has to live. 'Hurry up' is neither the best nor the fastest way."

John and Peter looked around at work in progress on sawhorses and workbenches, glue pots incrusted with layers of ancient resin, and tools neatly arranged on racks. John had helped Peter on school projects using Grandpa's old tools so they recognized the wood planes, chisels, and brace-and-bit hand drill the wheelwrights used. Spiraled shavings from the rhythmic sliding of the wood plane had been swept into leather pails. Each shaving showed the grain pattern of the board from which it came and each exuded the wood's perfume.

John inhaled the scent. "I should work here. I love the smell of wood."

"As long as I wake up in the morning to draw breath and drink a good mug of coffee, I'll want to come here to savor these fragrances. I joke that coffee sparked the Great Awakening."

"Dad, it's almost five and we should get over to Market Square."

"Good timing," the wheelwright said. "Today Peyton Randolph, the first President, sets out for the Second Continental Congress. He shall come out of the red house on Nicholson Street. Get close to the house for a perfect vantage point."

"He was called President at the Capitol," John recalled. "How is he President?"

"Titles such as 'Your Highness' or 'Your Majesty' remind us of the hierarchy that gives us problems, so at the First Congress they called Randolph 'President' because he presides over the meetings. Our second President, Henry Middleton of South Carolina, serves while Randolph is in Virginia. The Virginia Militia calls Randolph the Father of his Country."

"Does George Washington know about this?"

"He would call him that himself. Washington was a colonel in the Virginia Militia. To hear the President's farewell, you had best be over there promptly."

They walked to Peyton Randolph's house where a crowd was gathering. A footman cleared the way for a coach-and-four pulled by a pair of white draft horses with magnificent manes and tails, followed by a pair of handsome coal black horses. John spotted Susan. She waved and signaled she would join them. "Your Mom is working her way over to us, but I don't see Megan yet. Oh well, she can't get into much trouble in the Historic District."

Peter, already concerned about getting into trouble himself, did not respond.

Peyton Randolph, President of the Continental Congress, came out carefully, following two men down the steps. An extremely portly man, his fine clothing trumpeted his wealth and station. He wore an expensive white human hair wig and carried a gold-trimmed tricorn hat under his arm. His royal blue coat, fashioned in London, hung regally to his knees. The open coat revealed a goat-hair waistcoat trimmed in brocade, highlighting silver buttons. His cravat covered his triple chin. He stepped onto the running board of the coach with the help of an assistant. The sergeant of his security escort, needed because of the British warrant for Randolph's arrest and execution, called out, "Huzzah for the President!"

"Huzzah!" shouted the militiamen.

"Thank you for seeing me off on this long bumpy journey to the great city of Philadelphia." Peyton Randolph was accustomed to public speaking. "Over the next few days, these bones shall be shaken along the rutted way. To hasten the end of this tedious journey I must begin it, so my words will be brief. I would like to announce that the Continental Congress is about to name a third President.

"We chose John Hancock of Massachusetts, a man of renown. This signals our support of our beleaguered brethren in Boston. With Hancock as President, I shall better attend to the needs of Virginians. If I clung to power, what would separate us from the corruption and mendacity of the Royal Ministries? I pray that future Presidents relinquish the post when their terms are complete. Who in his right mind would cling to such a burden rather than attend to his farm and family?

"I am happy to say Georgia is now represented in Congress. We expect all colonies from Newfoundland to the Floridas will join us in time. Our descendants may speak of the 'Twenty Colonies' with reverence. I like the sound of that.

"We should avoid the tragedy of wider war. On this note, the *Gazette* berated my brother John Randolph, who remains loyal to the Crown, as 'defective as a friend and insignificant as an enemy.' I suggested he ignore the insult. We call the Tories 'Tories' and they use that name themselves, but we gain no benefit by insulting them. As when Governor Dunmore seized our powder, I urge moderation in speech and comportment. We were reimbursed for the powder without making widows. I admit the threat of retaliation from Patrick Henry and Hugh Mercer, and the militias they gathered, accelerated payment. Henry, under my guidance, did not fire a single shot and Mercer stayed in Fredericksburg.

"To stop the spread of this malignant war we need good men with the ear of the King and his Ministers across this ocean of disagreement to build bridges to a peaceful resolution. Save your feathers for pillows and your tar to mend your roofs. Not long ago we shared the Tories' view. If we changed our minds, so might they. And now, I bid you all farewell."

People standing nearby heard Peyton Randolph wheeze as he stooped to enter the coach. Was that a groan as he sank into his seat? The coach pulled slowly away to another trio of huzzahs. No one knew as they waved goodbye that in three months Peyton Randolph would be dead of a stroke in Philadelphia and his return would be in an oversized coffin.

Day 1-13:   Dinner at Christiana Campbell's Tavern

Megan heard Peyton Randolph's farewell from the back of the crowd. As her family moved across Market Square, she found her way to them. Her father was fretting. "I think the reenactors are improvising. I've never heard of many of the things they're saying."

Twice they moved to stay clear of oncoming horses as they walked past the Capitol to the broad front porch of Christiana Campbell's Tavern. Making a reservation had been a good idea. They were shown through the crowded restaurant to their table by a window.

Susan opened her menu. "What a strange vacation! Much of what I thought about the founding of the United States seems to be wrong."

"I doubt it, Susan. I want to find a library. When I got home from Central America and... other places, I was shocked the press accounts were so different from what we witnessed." He refrained from talking more about his secret wars.

"I didn't know Randolph was the first President and 'Father of his Country'."

"I'm learning strange stuff too, Mom, and something is bothering me."

"What's wrong Pete? Got the bubonic plague? I'll move to another table."

"Thanks for your support, Meg. I'm bothered that ordinary people here saw slavery as normal. I think that if you are in a bad situation, you can find a way to change it, walk away, or at least wait it out. But imagine you were a slave in 1775. There is no Underground Railroad, no boat home, no way out—maybe no change for the better for four generations until Lincoln's Emancipation Proclamation. It's hard to accept that people were trapped for their whole life."

"We still have millions trapped in poverty and a few very wealthy people who put their own interests first," said Susan. "More than one in a hundred of us are in prison, more than any other country. We are far behind many countries in how we take care of our elderly, our mothers, and our children. The Bible says 'Thou shalt not kill,' but we almost constantly make war, often killing innocent civilians."

John looked at his wife. "Susan, it may be true we're not attentive to the needs of many, but some of us think people should be taught to take care of themselves."

"Not easy when we underfund education and parents are underemployed."

"We don't hang a quarter of convicted felons or keep slaves," said Peter.

Megan jumped in. "I talked to servants today. They worked until the cost of their passage was paid for. If they screwed up, more years were added to their bondage. Most got bad food, one set of clothes, and poor places to live. Our ancestors were probably poor here or serfs in Europe. Why did nobody tell us? Were our grandparents ashamed about how uneducated their grandparents were?"

"I don't think they were ashamed," Susan suggested. "Surely our ancestors were proud of the first person in the family to read. There is no shame in that. We're all slowly learning."

Peter turned to his sister. "Meg, you said things here seem real. I've had that feeling. Mom and Dad, remember the woman I talked with behind the cabinet maker's shop?"

"I saw you walk down the hill but I didn't see you with anyone."

"Wow! She was hard to miss, Mom. She was quite... uh wide, an African-American in a multicolored print dress, sitting beside me next to the fence."

"I guess we weren't paying attention," said John.

"That's weird because I was about to say she seemed to be really in the past."

"That's what good actors do, Peter," said Susan. "They use their imagination to bring characters to life. I like going to a good play. On-stage, the transformation of an actor in character can be astonishing. What did you talk about?"

"It seemed real. She must be a great actor. We talked about uh... the food she was preparing and how a slave might escape."

Megan looked at her brother intently. "Did you guys have anything weird happen this afternoon?" she asked her parents.

"I had a sense something was calling me. It faded when I got tickets for a sermon at the Bruton Parish Church tonight. I didn't think you kids would want to go."

Savory food arrived in abundance. Part way through the meal Megan asked, "Mom, a guy asked me what my name means and I forgot."

"Megan was my grandmother's name, honey. It means great or powerful."

"Did you hear that, Pete? Great and powerful!"

"I heard 'grate' like when someone gets on your nerves!"

When dinner was over and they were making their way to the door, Megan whispered to her brother, "Are you thinking about how you could actually help someone escape, Peter?"

Peter said "Yes," before he could catch himself.

"Me, too."

Day 1-14:   Peter Meets Evie's Family

The Sinclairs stepped through the door of Christiana Campbell's Tavern to the porch banister. The sky was a deepening blue and the sun gilded the edges of the billowing cumulus clouds—a radiance of pink, mauve, and orange. This porch, this town, and the whole Earth on which it stood would turn and turn eastward all the way around and return, to about this angle to the sun late tomorrow, and people would count the passing of another day.

A gentle zephyr coaxed a rustling in the leaves of the giant hardwoods, deeply rooted for centuries in their places between the tavern and the Capitol. Susan took John's hand. "It's a timeless evening. Those clouds have a magical quality."

"A billion prisms—we seldom pause to look," John marveled.

Megan, standing a few steps from her parents, murmured to her brother, "Mom is wondering what's going on. Dad doesn't see it but he mentions his time in the army. He never does that, so maybe something's happening with him too."

"It's confusing. Sometimes I'm right here and sometimes... there."

"Yeah, Pete. I'm talking to someone from a long time ago and snap—I'm on a trip with my family. Do you think we could get lost or stuck?"

"I don't think so. It changes without us doing anything."

"Right Peter, it's just like that."

"Meg, knowing you're in it, too, makes me feel better. At least I'm not crazy."

"I'm your sister. Maybe it's inherited and we're both crazy."

"Do you plan to be a psychologist with that reassuring manner?"

"Right now, I'm thinking about being a historical activist. Do you get a feeling there is something we could do here? Like help somebody for real?" Megan asked.

"Maybe—we can see where it leads." Peter turned to his parents. "I'm going for a walk to explore. I'll see you at the house."

"We've only got two keys, Peter," said John.

"I'll stay out until you're back. Leave the door unlocked so I don't wake you."

"That sounds good. See you guys back at the house."

Peter walked to Powell House and found it dark. He looked into the garden. Seeing no one, he leaned on the fence, sorting out his experiences. He had never met anyone like Annie. It was strange that neither of his parents noticed her. He walked into the lane. At the gate by the kitchen, he heard a child laugh. Two African boys played in worn canvas pants too large for them, rolled up at the cuffs. They were close in age, one about eight and the other six. The younger light-skinned one threw a stick into the air and caught it after it flipped end over end.

"Good catch, Dilli!" the older one called out.

On the next throw, Dilli threw the stick behind him in a high curve. The boy ran to catch it with an irregular gait, his left foot stepping forward and his right swinging around to the side, scuffing a curve on the ground where the foot dragged. The stick flew over the fence and Peter caught it. "Good throw!" Peter said. "Here it comes back." He tossed the stick in a slow arc toward the boy who caught it in both hands.

"Thanks, Mister! Are you here to see Massa Powell?"

"I..." Peter broke off. The boy looked strangely familiar.

"Who you talking to, Dilli?" A woman's voice came from around the corner.

"A nice gentleman be here at the gate, Mama."

Evie stepped from behind a wall, faced Peter a few yards away, and stopped. Peter's right hand moved involuntarily in a wave.

"Oh!" she said. "Good evening, Sir."

Peter looked for words but those he found were meager. "Ma'am, I heard the children laughing. It reminded me of playing ball when I was a boy."

"Dilli don't have no ball, so he catches that stick."

"Evie, I hope I'm not disturbing you. I notice the house is dark."

"The Powells went to sup wit' friends. I lights the lamps 'fore they come home. The girls is in bed. You came by this mornin'. How you know my name is Evie?"

"Today I spoke with Annie about slavery and free Africans. She called you Evie."

Evie's eyes widened. "You saw Annie today? You talked wit' her? Where?"

"Behind the cabinetmakers' shop. She was preparing food..."

"... for a gathering," finished Evie. "She said my name? What be your name?"

"I'm Peter."

"'Scuse me, I got to sit. Boys, fetch us water. Mister Peter, please come through the gate lest a neighbor think you fixin' to steal something valuable." Evie sat on a bench patting her chest and taking deep breaths. Peter sat on the steps next to her.

"I apologize for just showing up like this. There is a lot going on here that I don't understand." He heard a splash as the bucket hit water at the bottom of the well.

"You called me ma'am in front of my boys, which they never heard a white man do, then you apologized to me, which nobody do. You was talkin' wit' Annie. I never knew someone like you talked wit' her. I don't understand neither."

The boys came back each carefully carrying a cup of water. The older boy gave one to his mother. Dilli presented a cup to Peter. "Here is water for you, Mister."

"Thank you, Dilli." Peter turned to the older boy who stood barefoot holding his mother's skirt. "What's your name?" The boy looked up at Evie.

"Go ahead and tell him your name, son. Do like you do after church."

"I'm James. Pleased to meet you." He looked at her. She nodded approval.

"I'm pleased to meet you boys, too." Peter extended his hand. Dilli smiled and shook his hand but James held his mother tighter.

They sipped water as the sky gradually darkened to blue-black. As they talked, the first few stars directly overhead were slowly joined by others, one by one, then by tens, then by hundreds until they were too numerous to count.

Peter exhaled slowly. "I made mistakes today," he began. "I was careless when I suggested you run away. I see it would be hard with two little boys especially..."

"'Specially when one is lame?"

"That could make you easy to identify, but that's not what I meant. I learned that people who might help are not around here, at least not yet. My timing was off."

"Mister Peter, I thought a lot about your visit. Even thinkin' that runnin' wit' my boys be crazy, a feelin' stuck' wit' me. I felt I knowed you. You said bein' free would be better. Why should you care about us?" Her eyes searched Peter's face.

"I saw you in the garden and realized you're a slave. It may seem strange, since you live in a time... I mean a town where there are slaves and that's normal, but I think slavery is wrong. All people deserve a chance to find their own way."

"That be what Annie think. Some say Annie knows your mind better than you do. When Annie say somethin' I think about it and pray about it. She is deep like the salty sea. You must be blessed. She don't show up and talk to just anybody."

"Whenever I was thinking, she stopped speaking, as if she were waiting for me to finish. I heard she was a free African and I wondered how she got her freedom." He stopped. "I went to her because I wanted to find a way to help you."

"What we think when we wit' Annie matters. Why was you thinkin' 'bout me?"

"You are the first slave I ever met and I don't like the idea that you're not free."

"You never met a slave before? You must live in a strange place."

"How long have you worked for the Powell family?"

"'Bout fifteen years. I was the size of James when I was brought here after Mama died." James looked worried and hugged her. Dilli leaned against her leg. "Boys, don't worry. My mama was older and she ain't had strong boys to help her. I ain't gonna die until you is old, and by then you gonna have your own families."

Peter figured Evie was two years older than he was. "Annie said she'll tell me how she got free. If I find a chance for a better life, would you think about going?"

"I am dizzy wit' you carin' about us and talkin' wit' Annie. We's lucky to have the Massa we does. I don't know a better life than the one we got here."

They listened to songs of birds nearby and looked up at the distant stars. "Them stars over the pine tree look like a ladle. Is that what you was talkin' 'bout today?"

"Wow, there it is! That's the Big Dipper. That's great Evie, you found it!"

"Stars move slow across the sky. How can that bright star always be north?"

Peter thought a moment. "The stars aren't moving across the sky. The Earth turns to the East so the stars seem to be moving. The North Star is above the line around which we turn, so it's always to the north."

"What be up north? I heard they be slaves in New York and Boston has war."

41

"You heard right. I made a mistake this morning. This is not a good time to run."

"You know a star that tells which way is north. Do you know a star that tells what be a good day to run or a good day to stay put?"

"Sorry, I don't, but if you are OK with this, I'll see what I can learn about ways to get freedom. Annie knows more than she has told me, I am sure."

"I am sure she do. What is 'okay'?"

"OK means all right."

"Mister Peter, I'se afraid. When the Powell girls marry, my boys might get sold away. Tell me if you hear a way to get to a good place. Annie could help me see what to do." At the sound of feet on gravel, Evie held a finger to her lips. They sat quietly as two men passed the house. "Ain't no good reason we could say for you bein' here. I had best get the boys to bed and light lamps. The Powells comin' home soon. You is a kind man. Maybe I gonna hear more from you by and by."

"I hope so, Evie. Good night, boys. Mind your Mama and get your rest."

"Good night, Mister Peter," said Dilli, as James clung to his mother.

Peter had walked barely a block when a carriage passed him going the other way. A lantern shone from the porch of the Powell House as it pulled into the lane.

Back at the house, Peter opened the unlocked door and found Megan in the living room reading by the light of a hurricane lamp and two candles.

"Hi, Pete! Did you find anything interesting?"

"I talked to a slave family at the Powell House—amazing! Then a carriage passed me on the way here. But the reenactors have been off work for a couple of hours."

"It's strange around here when weird stuff starts to happen, isn't it?"

"You can say that again!"

"OK, I will. It's strange around here when weird stuff starts to happen, isn't it?"

"How did that little bundle in the pink blanket get to be such a smart-ass?"

"I studied with my brother for years. He shared everything he knew, and then I learned lots more from other sources."

"Not bad. Megan, I admit you're kinda funny. I think I'll go for a run."

"It's dark out there. There are hardly any street lamps. There's no electricity!"

"Wow! This is amazing. But there's a half moon so I can run on the paths."

"I'll look for brighter light to read by. Maybe I'll run into George Washington or Benjamin Franklin and they can explain the reasons for the Revolution to me. Oh wait, Franklin was from Pennsylvania. So bumping into him would be strange."

Megan watched her brother jog down the road and then she set off carrying two history books under her arm on a quest for reading light.

Day 1-15:   Megan Studies by the Fire

Megan passed closed shops and taverns with dimly lit interiors. One inn to the south had brightly lit windows. She entered to see an array of lamps on the mantel over a blazing hearth and sat in a massive wing chair. She looked up topics in the index of her text and jotted notes. Before the Revolution, there were many indentured servants in Southern colonies. More than half of early English, Scottish, and German settlers in the South served a period of indenture to pay for all or part of their passage.

A man in a well-pressed waistcoat approached. "Would you like a chocolate?"

"A chocolate? Can I order a hot chocolate?"

"All chocolate is served hot, isn't it?"

When the man returned, with a large mug of hot chocolate on a tray, Megan handed him her last twenty-dollar bill of colonial currency. "Oh my, I rarely see a note so valuable!"

He returned with four pounds and nine Spanish dollars, two half crowns, ten shillings, one with the edge obviously shaved to take off silver, and many sixpence coins and large pennies. "Keep all that money tucked away, Miss, and don't let the transitory people see it. The chocolate was four pence. We are forbidden to keep sterling so I gave you all the British money we had. I hope you don't mind."

"No, I don't mind. Can you can tell me how many people in Virginia are indentured?"

"I do not know, Miss. Virginia has many indentured servants. I heard there are two hundred thousand slaves, more than twice the number in any other colony. Owners prefer the life-long bond of a slave to a contract that ends in a few years. Owning slaves is for the very rich. They say only one white family in twelve owns even a single slave."

"What happens when a servant escapes?"

"Please, we should not talk about that. Running is a bad idea. Sorry, I must get back to work." The server left hurriedly.

Megan read what she could find in her history books about indentured servants then spent an hour reading about the events leading to the Revolution. She reviewed her notes, first looking for easy connections like the edge pieces of a jigsaw puzzle, and then for other associations. She closed her notebook and drained her mug. "This might upset people when I get home."

Megan stepped outside and began to walk toward home. A man approached from the shadows ahead of her. She veered to the right to avoid him but he stepped right in front of her. "Where are you going in such a hurry?" he probed.

Megan stepped to the left but the man blocked her way. He was shabbily dressed. "Excuse me, I am going home," she insisted.

"You ain't got to be in a rush. Can you spare a coin for a new friend?"

Megan stepped backed a step.

"Maybe 'tis best if you give me all your coins and I'll have no need to hurt ye," said the man moving closer. "You are a pretty one."

Megan tightened and decided to run.

"Away with you!" A strong voice came from behind her. The man ran away.

Megan looked behind and made out a tall silhouette she recognized. "Oh, Standing Elk!" she said, relieved, "You came just in time."

"Miss Megan, I saw you leave the tavern and followed you at a distance so as not to startle you. You should not be out alone."

"Is this a dangerous neighborhood?"

"All neighborhoods are dangerous. Many desperate transient people take what they need when it is not theirs to take. Remember the man with the dagger? The gallows here is busy and yet hungry ones make the mistake of stealing or worse."

"Thanks for watching out for me. I'm still freaked out."

"You are safe now. I will walk you home and we can talk as we go."

"Phew! I wasn't sure I could outrun him. That was just as scary as the man with the knife."

They walked in silence for a block as Megan calmed down, and then she said, "It's a coincidence you should show up to help me. I was reading about your people tonight, Standing Elk. I read about the Proclamation Line of 1763 in which King George declared... just a minute, I may be able to make out my notes in this lantern light... here it is:

> "...the Nations or Tribes of Indians with whom We are connected, and who live under our Protection, should not be molested or disturbed in the Possession of such Parts of Our Dominions and Territories as, not having been ceded to or purchased by Us, are reserved to them as their Hunting Grounds"

"I have read the King's' proclamation many times."

"How did you learn to read? Do Native Americans go to school?"

"I studied at the College of William and Mary here in Williamsburg. Those who show promise or are related to native leaders are brought here to study in the hopes of cooperation and to civilize us. I am happy to say I remain quite uncivilized to this day."

"Standing Elk, is it true that the King wants to protect the tribes and nations and keep land west of the Appalachian Mountains as Indian Territory administered by Quebec?"

"England was almost bankrupt from war against the French. The King made that declaration in 1763 to ensure peace on the frontier. Last year, he gave control of the land west of the line to Quebec because French fur traders travel the West to trade with Indians and do not clear land or bring settlers."

"Is it working?"

"Not at all. Powerful people here and in England anonymously formed land companies to settle the Ohio Valley far west of here. Some of His Majesty's governors are investors. Those companies claim land the King reserved for Native people. Besides that, many land grants given by the King to the soldiers who served in the war are the lands reserved for us."

"Everything I learn about the history of your people in this country does not make a happy story. I'm sorry. Is there anything I can do to help?"

"Few care about Indians, but this is too risky for a young woman."

"I don't mean to be bold, but where I come from women assert their ability to be a part of whatever is happening. Some of us are leaders and some even go to war."

"I have seen war and I pray you never do."

"Well, if I stick around here for long, I probably will. If I can help, please let me know."

"Miigwech for your persistence and courage."

"Meg Witch? Do you think I am a witch?"

Standing Elk chuckled, "Are you? I think you are powerful, like women warriors in our legends. No, Miigwech means 'thank you' in our Anishinaabe language."

"I asked my parents the meaning of my name today. It means great or powerful."

"Your parents named you well."

"Miigwech, Standing Elk. How do you know Mark?"

"I have known him for years. We became friends working at the iron works."

"He is a good man. I'm sorry he is not free."

"We all have to work in different kinds of weather, some that is not favorable. He is now doing well in his situation. Anderson the blacksmith is not unkind to him."

"I hope it gets better for him. That's our house. Miigwech for walking me home."

"You are welcome. Today you helped Simon escape from pursuers. I have sad news."

"What happened? Did they catch him?"

"No, Megan, they shall never catch him. Simon slipped in a ravine and struck his head. Two men from my village found him alive but he died this evening. He did not suffer much and died as he lived, smiling. We shall bury him in the custom of his people. Only his friends will know what happened. Those who owned the rights to his labor and those that pursued him for a reward will think that he has escaped forever. And in truth, he has."

"Oh that's terrible! He was not a reenactor?" Megan asked mainly to herself.

"He was not a what?"

"I'm sorry. This is upsetting news. I didn't know Simon but I was hoping I helped him."

"You did, Megan. My people and his friends have already heard how you helped Simon on his last day in this world. Good night. Our paths will cross again."

"I hope so. Good night." Megan entered the house to find she was the first home. Troubled, she lay awake in bed thinking about poor Simon's smile, the man with the knife, and how Standing Elk saved her from the man blocking her way.

Day 1-16:   Peter at the Hush Harbor

Peter ran beyond the buildings through cleared land. By the light of the moon, he followed a trail into the woods, dropping into a steady rhythm. He shuddered at the memory of the car spinning on the highway and of how close they had come. It was strange they had been so calm. As he jogged, his mind slipped into a reverie listening to the rhythmic crunch of his feet on the path. Suddenly a shriek tore through the other forest sounds. "What the...?" He spun and ran back along the path. Who knows what might be out here?

After a few minutes he stopped. It had sounded like a small animal. What was he afraid of? He jogged back to where he had heard the cry. It did occur to him that perhaps the small animal had encountered a larger predator but he pushed ahead up a rise. On the down slope, he saw flickering light through the trees ahead and he slowed to a walk as he heard voices. A group of Africans sat around a fire set in a shallow pit. High above, lashed at the corners, a piece of canvas blocked the firelight from shining into the treetops. The people gathered in this hollow did not want to be spotted from a distance.

Peter approached quietly. Two men lifted a stout spit and rotated a small feral pig a quarter turn. It had not been over the fire long. Peter concluded the squeal had been the pig's final statement. Next to the fire, two pots simmered — one full of grits and one with greens in salted water.

Old growth trees of enormous girth towered high above the clearing. He moved closer in the shadows and saw Annie sitting next to someone on a mossy patch set back from the circle. She looked across the fire directly at him and subtly signaled him to be silent and come closer. Peter sat against a tree without being noticed by anyone else.

Peter recognized the voice of William the brick-maker holding forth on catching pigs in the woods between plantations. "Early spring be a good time to catch a pig, yes it is. When the acorns is gone, there ain't much for pigs to eat so they's hungry. You set a snare wit' a loop of cord and put two apples from a fruit cellar in that snare. A pig ain't smelled apples since last year's wild fruit rotted away. Best you wash yourself and hide up a tree else he will smell you and run off snortin'. You sit quiet and that pig gonna come into your snare for the apples and you'll be settin' by a fire tellin' stories 'bout how you catched a pig jest like I is tellin' it."

Peter smiled and rested his head against the tree. How does this guy have so much fun while living as a slave? Peter closed his eyes and listened to the banter as the drippings from the pig crackled on the fire. The scent whetted his appetite.

Opening his eyes, Peter was startled to see Annie listening to Evie but looking intently at him. She moved her fingers slightly to beckon him closer. He circled the group and sat a few feet behind Evie to her left. No one other than Annie reacted to his presence. He had a thought that sounded like his own voice but strangely seemed to come from Annie: "Listen to the questions of others and your own answers will come quicker."

Peter wondered what it meant.

"Hush and listen," another thought came to him.

"There is so much to think on, Annie," Evie said. "I can't help Dilli not be lame. James be so shy he hardly speaks. A gentleman came today, talkin' about us bein' free. Then he came back and say he made a mistake. If they ain't no place to go, how is bein' free better than the life we livin'? The Powell's is kind, they don't beat us, and they give us old clothes, but they ain't gonna give manumission like you got."

"Why you try to carry them problems, child? Take them to the Lord. When you got no idea what to do, do the best you can and learn from what happens. Evie, some things like your boys growin' up takes many years. Say you want a sorrel plant so you have sour greens. If you pull that plant instead of lettin' it grow, you gonna have a little bitty plant in your hand and no greens tomorrow. The Lord will fix them problems over time."

Evie was not convinced. "There is big things like my boys gettin' sold away or I never knowed what happened to James' pa. And little things, like ol' Rosie complain all the time. The Lord and his son Jesus watch over me and my sons even when life be hard. We gonna be in heaven but how can I make life here better for my sons? Don't the Lord want that?"

"You can do somethin' wit'out all that strain." Annie looked at Evie and tilted her head to the left. "You seen children rollin' a hoop, hittin' it wit' a peg?"

"Yes, Annie."

"Take a good look at how they play that hoop. Happenin's in your life is like a hoop rollin'. Some things in the hoop ain't just about you but about many folks, like many people is slaves or a country has peace one year and war the next. Sometimes there be a drought and sometimes rains come in a flood and everybody got to run to higher ground. You know what I'se talkin' about?"

"Yes Annie, many troubles ain't 'bout me but about sufferin' everybody got."

"Well, child, if you stand in front of that big hoop rollin' wit' all those problems, it can roll right over you. It too heavy to lift and you can't help by gettin' in the way, unless you want to make you-self into mashed potatoes and gravy."

Evie put her hand to her mouth to cover a laugh.

"It be funny but ain't you doing that? Standin' in front of a problem is danger. To wish it gone be a waste of your mind. If you run alongside and tap like children do, you may help the hoop roll left or right so it don't fall on you. When you is alongside you knows which way the hoop goin' so you stay out the way. Leave the weight of your burden to the Lord."

Evie closed her eyes. "Annie, I see them problems like a hoop rollin.' I gonna stay out the way. I pray the Lord gonna help me roll it right."

"Do you have patience to wait for slow things to grow and big things to change?"

"I gonna do my best, Annie."

Peter was not prepared for the shock of Evie walking past him, her skirt brushing against his knee, without her noticing his presence in the slightest. As Evie walked to the circle, two people moved toward Annie. A light-skinned man sitting close joined her and the other sat nearby to be next. Clearly, people respected Annie and left distance for others to talk in confidence. Peter wondered if he was intruding but Annie nodded at him to stay.

"Hello, 'Gustus," said Annie to the light-skinned man. "Did that cut foot heal up good?"

"Yes, Miss Annie. The poultice took down the swelling. It don't hurt no mo'. I got no problem to ax about. I want to thank you for teachin' me how to heal my foot."

"You gonna remember how to crush them balm-of-gilead poplar leaves to make the poultice and how to boil white oak bark until the water is dark then mash it and gently put it on a wound to slow bleedin' and avoid festerin' and pus?"

"Yes, I will."

"How you know what is white oak?

"The leaves has round ends, not points like other oaks. I wash my hands good in boiled water before I put a poultice on the cut. If I cuts my foot again I can do it."

"Good, 'Gustus. How else can you use a poultice besides if you cuts your foot?"

"Do you think I'se ready to make a poultice for somebody else? I could help them not swell up or poison they blood like you told me. Annie, I ain't done physic for nobody 'cept water when they was thirsty wit' fever. It will be good if I can help other folk. Would you teach me more things to do? People get into more kinds of trouble than just cuttin' they-self."

"I will, if you want to learn, 'Gustus. There be someone you can help right now."

"Who is that, Miss Annie?"

"Dilli is your son, and James is his brother, and Evie was your woman."

"She wasn't my woman 'zackly, Annie. We never jumped the broom. My massa had me stay in Massa Powell's back in '68 when he worked on that hospital."

"It was just before Christmas."

"Yes'm. It was cold and Massa sent me to the kitchen to sleep. I climbed into the loft and lay next to Evie to keep warm. She was learning to be a washer woman back then and wit' the cold night and one thing and another, she had herself another boy and that was Dilli."

"The boy Dilli knows you be his pa. He might like to see you."

"I never knowed my daddy 'cept I know he was a white man like Mama's daddy was so I has light skin. I thought I already done what a daddy was 'posed to do. Anyhow, Dilli is lame and I ain't got no way to fix that."

Annie grew stern. "We is all lame in some way, 'Gustus. Dilli be lame in his leg but he ain't lame in his head or his heart. He be a shinin' light of a boy. Tell Evie you is happy to see her and give her somethin' for the boys. Don't worry 'bout what to say. Ax how they is doin' then hush and listen. People feels better when someone care about them. Don't you visit me sometimes just to be heard? You learned the poultice and you can learn to listen to folks."

"That sounds good, Annie. Even if I can't get there much, I gonna ax her tonight how she and the boys is doin'. I will bring them somethin' sometime. You right like usual, Annie."

"'Gustus, be helpful to folk. Lord knows we all need kindness!"

"Phew," breathed Peter. Annie looked up at him and suddenly an idea came to him that it was not for him to listen to the next conversation. Annie had invited him to hear about Evie and her family, but now it was time to step away. He sat in view of the fire. Peter's interest in Evie's freedom had begun with no idea of her situation, but now he had much to sort out. He looked into the luminous dance of the flames.

Day 1-17: Evening Service at Bruton Parish Church

"It's an hour before the sermon begins," Susan said after Megan and Peter headed off. "I'd like to get a good seat but we can take our time to walk over."

They strolled past the Capitol and along the main street of Williamsburg. When they reached Palace Green, it was still early, so they turned to the circle at the front of the Governor's Palace. John looked at the regal brick mansion, and down the broad boulevard.

"Shopping for real estate?" asked Susan.

"Our house doesn't convey this kind of authority. I'm getting ideas for an extra story, a cupola, plus east and west wings to make a stronger statement in the neighborhood."

They meandered to a pond beside the Palace where a pair of wild ducks fed near the grassy bank. "I wonder if their ancestors cruised on the Governor's pond," mused Susan.

"That would have risked a special appointment to the Governor's platter."

Walking slowly down the west side of Palace Street, Susan looked into the windows of the stately homes. "They've got wild wallpaper but I like the furniture. I want to visit these houses." Susan was enjoying the evening, happy seeing John less stressed than earlier. Relaxed moments like this had become too rare.

They arrived at Bruton Parish Church, in use since 1715. The steeple, made of darker bricks than the rest of the church, was added sixty years after the building was completed. It had three square stories with tall arched windows, and above that two hexagonal stories and a conical roof. For colonial parishioners — living in two-room cabins made of rough boards nailed to posts imbedded in the earth — this steeple stretched toward heaven.

Inside the church, Susan was struck by the elegance of brass organ pipes and candelabras gleaming in evening sunlight streaming at a low angle from the windows. Plaques on pews named distinguished families, including Washington and Jefferson, who once sat there. Floral arrangements appeared poised to greet a bride at the altar. The Sinclairs found seats near the pulpit with its wooden canopy inlayed with a 32-point Radiant Glory.

James Walker, the Episcopal priest, mounted the pulpit steps. The rumble of conversation ebbed to a few coughs. "Good evening, friends. Welcome to historic Bruton Parish Church. We will begin with a hymn sung here for centuries, the Doxology known as 'The Old Hundredth.' Psalm 100 calls on us to make a joyful noise unto the Lord and come into his presence with singing!" The organist played a verse and the congregation rose and sang:

"Praise God from whom all blessing flow; Praise Him all creatures here below;
Praise Him above, ye heavenly host; Praise Father, Son and Holy Ghost."

"In colonial times, that hymn was one of a few sung throughout the year. They were sung by heart, for many were illiterate. The hymnal in your hands would not

51

have helped them. Religion was a central pillar in settlers' lives. Today, polls show three-quarters of Americans believe in God and half the rest believe in a Universal Spirit, percentages much higher than other advanced countries. Tonight we will explore the roots of our faiths in the Virginia Colony.

"We think of early America as a haven of religious tolerance where Pilgrims and others sailed to escape persecution. We are told Maryland was a refuge for Catholics from religious wars in Europe. True, compared to Catholics and Protestants burning each other at the stake in Europe, there was relative tolerance here. But tolerance is more than refraining from killing people of other beliefs." The priest looked around. "At least, for those of you who aren't Episcopalian like me, I hope your standard is higher than that."

There were a few chuckles in the congregation.

"Colonists, like many people the world over, thought their form of worship was blessed in the eyes of God and perhaps the only true way."

Susan noticed movement in the empty balcony upstairs to her left. Jane, the woman from the Capitol, quietly took a seat and stared directly at the priest.

"Colonial Virginia had no separation of church and state. The Church of England was the official state religion or 'Established Church'. Virginians were obliged to pay taxes to that church and to attend services once a month or pay a fine of five shillings or fifty pounds of tobacco. Those in other denominations were called 'dissenters'. Some Revolutionary leaders called for disestablishment of the Church of England. Although re-establishment of my church would be lucrative for our organization, I do not support antidisestablishmentarianism as Patrick Henry advocated for a time. And you thought you'd never hear that word in a sentence!"

Some in the congregation smiled but Susan noted that Jane did not move.

"Maryland was founded by the Calvert family as a colony where Catholicism was legal. In 1649, Governor William Stone, a Protestant, signed the Toleration Act. Under the act, if you insulted someone's religion you could be fined. If you spoke ill of the Virgin Mary or the Apostles you could be whipped or jailed. The penalty for not believing in the Trinity was death. How's that for tolerance?"

Susan saw Jane brace herself putting her hands on the rail.

"When Thomas Lord Fairfax and his second-in-command Oliver Cromwell defeated the Royalists in England, Maryland became a Puritan colony. Former Governor Stone gathered an army and attacked the Puritans at the Battle of the Severn in 1655. The Puritans won, took Stone prisoner, and executed four Catholic prisoners on the spot in a religious war fought an hour's drive from our nation's capital. No wonder we prefer to forget some of our history."

John shifted in his seat. The thought of war at home in which religious fundamentalists executed prisoners made him uncomfortable.

"In 1691, the Church of England became the established religion of Maryland. When Maryland was returned to the Calverts in 1715, Benedict Calvert was a converted Protestant. Catholics were forbidden vote and masses were banned but secret masses were held in homes, sometimes by Jesuit priests who married, owned land, and maintained their faith.

"On this side of the Chesapeake, the seating in this church reflects hierarchy. Members of the Governor's Council and Burgesses in the front pews had status clear to all. Middle-sorts then lesser-sorts people sat in remote pews. In the back benches were servants and visitors from the hills. Slaves and free blacks sat out of sight in the empty North Gallery up there." As attention turned to the North Gallery, Jane sat still as a statue.

"Every Sunday saw readings from the Book of Common Prayer, a few hymns, and a sermon. Four times a year parishioners were offered Holy Communion, taken mainly by the elderly as they faced their impending end. Peter Pelham, an organist here, was also the jailer. To some of you the practices might resemble a spiritual jail but there was benefit in the repeated rituals.

"In a *Short History of the Book of Common Prayer*, William Huntington, Rector of Grace Church in New York, wrote, 'For the origin of liturgy... go a long way back; beyond the Prayer Book... beyond synagogue worship, ...to that dimly discerned groundwork we call human nature. Where three or two assemble for supplication, some form must be accepted if they are to pray in unison. When the disciples came to Jesus begging him to teach them how to pray, he gave not twelve forms... but one. 'When ye pray ...Say Our Father.'

"The Book of Common Prayer guided Bible readings, baptism, communion, visitation of the sick, and many aspects of life in this community. Last week, on the fifth Sunday after Easter, congregants would have heard from Deuteronomy 8:

"For the Lord thy God bringeth thee into a good land, a land of brooks of water, of fountains and depths that spring out of valleys and hills. A land wherein thou shalt eat bread without scarceness... a land whose stones are iron.

"That verse would have encouraged people who scraped sustenance from the land. At evensong service that same Sunday in 1775, they would have heard:

"Hear, O Israel: Thou art to pass over Jordan this day, to go in to possess nations greater and mightier than thyself, cities great and fenced up to heaven.'

"That may have given the Founding Fathers courage to rise against Parliament. This coming Sunday, the reading will be from Deuteronomy 12:

"Ye shall utterly destroy all the places, wherein the nations which ye shall possess served their gods, upon the high mountains, and upon the hills and under every green tree.

"What would annual repetitions of this passage mean for native peoples?

"For some, rote practice is unsatisfying. You have heard of the Great Awakening? Charismatic preachers from Britain and New England were called 'enthusiastic', which in those days meant fanatic. The passionate preaching, singing, and body movement were unlike the sedate rituals of the Established Church in Virginia. The Great Awakening may have arisen from the longing for direct spiritual experience that calls people today.

Susan wanted to join Jane in the gallery. She felt after their encounter at the Capitol that they had experiences in common. The invisible trail she was following had led her to Jane. She gave a little wave but couldn't catch Jane's attention.

"The Bible is the main vehicle through which Christians hear the word of God. For most of the time Christianity has been practiced, most believers were illiterate. Although Christians now can read the Bible, we differ in where we place authority to interpret it and to define beliefs and practices. I can only hint at distinctions among churches to help us understand the paths of others. The names of each denomination give a clue.

"Do you remember Simon bar Jonah, the Hebrew fisherman? Jesus said to him, 'You are Peter, and on this rock I will build my church.' Simon Peter traveled to Rome to found the Catholic Church. With a small 'c,' catholic means: broad-minded; liberal; universal; pertaining to the whole Christian body or church. With a capital 'C' Catholic means pertaining to a theology declaring it possesses the only, true, and universal church with unity, apostolic succession, and sanctity. Not the same meaning is it? In the Catholic Church, authority rests with the Pope, heir to the apostle Peter."

Susan hoped Jane would look down, but she was absorbed in the sermon.

"In the 1500s, the Reformation sought to reduce corruption in the Church. In England reform merged with other desires of King Henry VIII who wanted to divorce Catherine, daughter of Ferdinand and Isabella of Spain, in order to marry Ann Boleyn in hope of producing a male heir. He got the Pope to accept his choice for Archbishop of Canterbury; then separated the English Church, placing the Archbishop in charge. The Church *in* England became the Church *of* England, born of reform, nationalism, and the King's desire to remove limits to his power. This was the religion of over half the Founding Fathers.

"'Episcopal' means of the bishops. The Archbishop of Canterbury leads the Church but there were no bishops in the Colonies. Each Virginia county had two parishes governed by a vestry of landowners who chose their own members. Burgesses and militia commanders were usually elected from among vestrymen. So wealthy, slave-owning landowners put themselves in charge of the religion, military, and government. Most middle-sorts did not aspire to change this system. The ambitious among them sought to rise within it.

"There were four thousand people in Virginia for each Established Church clergyman so access to services was limited. The gap was filled by the arrival of other sects. Presbyterian ministers came from Scotland. Authority was in the hands of a 'Presbyter' or Council of Elders. Presbyterian ministers worked in areas where the Church of England was not established. When they entered parishes, they needed a license or faced being jailed.

"German and Dutch Protestant denominations were known as German Reformed, Dutch Reformed, and Lutheran after Martin Luther the German reformer who founded that Church. German ministers preached to their communities here in their own language.

"A group originated in the Church of England, derogatorily called Puritans by others for seeking pure worship and less worldliness. They wanted to eliminate bishops and revise the Book of Common Prayer to emphasize Christ and individual holiness. Some separated from the Church or were ejected by the bishops. Later many called themselves Congregationalists placing authority in the congregation. This resonated with levelers in New England, who boldly contended that all men were created equal. The very idea threatened established hierarchies. Puritans were unlikely partners for the Established Gentry of Virginia.

"Methodists also originated within the Church of England through the teachings of John Wesley and others. As their name suggests, they emphasized method and experience over doctrine. Methodist missionaries rode circuits from county to county, preaching in houses, barns, taverns, and fields.

"Baptist preachers also called for experience of Spirit. If illiterate, they quoted scripture from memory. They brought solemn customs and austere dress, and called each other Brother and Sister. Their name shows the importance placed on baptism, immersing adults in water as did John the Baptist, to signify rebirth in the spirit. Some Baptists opposed slavery and attracted slaves and free blacks into their fold. When followers gave 'testimony' to how Christ worked in their lives, they were respected no matter how humble their station.

"The Society of Friends, known as Quakers, did not emphasize the Bible but believed that in silence, an Inner Light can inspire us and express itself through us. Virginia's establishment worried that a religion without hierarchy would lead to a breakdown of society. In New England, Quakers were hanged for preaching by the Puritans a century before the Revolution."

Susan saw movement in the Gallery, glimpsed the back of a hood, and Jane was gone. She whispered to John, "Something scared her. I've got to go outside."

"Scared whom? Can't you wait until the end of the sermon?"

To stand up in the front row and leave before the sermon was over would be awkward, so Susan resigned herself to wait.

"How did we move beyond such intolerance? Young Thomas Jefferson attended the Classical School of Reverend James Maury, son of a Huguenot Protestant who escaped persecution in France. Maury taught that people had a right to worship in their own way if it did not interfere with others. Five of his students signed the Declaration of Independence and three became American Presidents. Since Jefferson lived with Maury and his family, he surely was influenced in those formative years.

In June 1779, the month he was elected Governor of Virginia, Jefferson introduced a 'Bill for Establishing Religious Freedom' despite other priorities at the height of the Revolutionary War. By the time the bill passed in 1786, he was Minister Plenipotentiary to France. We call that Ambassador today.

"How significant was this bill to Thomas Jefferson? At his request, his epitaph lists three accomplishments: author of the Declaration of Independence, founder of the University of Virginia, and author of the Bill for Establishing Religious Freedom. These were more important to him than serving as President.

"I hope I said nothing here that offended you. I did not include all faiths, just Christian denominations prevalent in the Virginia Colony. The Native Peoples and Africans had their own approaches to spirituality, about which I am learning. Freedom of religion is a gift our Founders gave us. Let us close with a prayer.

"Dear Lord, we are all brothers and sisters in your great family of life. Please guide us to open our hearts to all people and open our minds to your infinite gifts as we walk the paths of our lives. May our individual paths lead all your children to You. Amen. Thank you for coming. God bless you and God bless America."

As the priest left, Susan jumped up. The entry to the North Gallery was chained and locked so she hurried outside.

When the aisles of the church were clear, John walked outside to find her breathless. "I ran a block in each direction but couldn't find her."

"Who?"

"That woman from the Capitol left early. I need to talk to her."

"You are bound to run into her tomorrow. Why do you need to talk to her?"

"I think we have something in common. Maybe we can help each other."

John waited for Susan to explain further but she said no more about it. They walked to their little colonial home and checked on the kids. Megan was asleep, but Peter was not home yet, so they left the door unlocked and went to bed. John dropped off to sleep immediately and Susan lay awake a few minutes, away of the faint familiar sadness.

Day 1-18:   Many Colors in the Glass

At the sound of Annie's voice, Peter came out of his reverie staring at the flames. He had a clear view of her standing on the other side of the fire. "This be a good gatherin'," Annie said, "but somethin' goin' on here that ain't good. Who got a bottle of Jamaica rum?" The circle around the fire got quiet. "I need that bottle to 'splain somethin' to you all. I'se gonna close my eyes and cover them wit' my arm. You all do the same and don't peek. I want that bottle to git over to the earth in front of me right now!"

There was a thud and gurgle as a half-empty bottle landed in the pile of soft soil dug up to make the fire pit. Annie pulled the cork from the clear bottle with her teeth and poured the contents into a bowl. "That be a pretty white shirt, William. You wear it on Sunday?"

"Yes'm."

"Come on up here beside me and let the people have a look at that fine shirt."

"It ain't my rum, Annie, I swear!"

"I know, William. We need your white shirt to show somethin' to the folk. We also need you not to talk for a bit." As William moved up next to Annie, she placed the bowl filled with rum next to a pile of dry pine needles. She then scraped the edge of a metal bowl under the broiling pig to catch liquid fat in the bowl, and she placed it next to the bowl of rum.

"William, you hold this bottle near your shirt facing the fire like so, so folk can see behind it. You folk across the fire, move to one side so you can see his shirt behind the bottle. Don't watch me and don't watch the fire. Watch the shirt. Some of you gonna see what I'se showin' and some ain't." She looked around the circle. "Which is you gonna be?

"'Gustus, sit by William and pick up handfuls of pine needles. When I says 'Now!' throw them over the fire." Augustus shuffled over, gathered up needles in both hands, and watched the fire intently as Annie took the bowl of rum in her left hand and the drippings in her right.

"Now!" shouted Annie, and Gustus threw the needles as she threw the liquids into the fire. Pine, rum, and pork fat ignited in the air above the fire in a dazzling flash. Peter watched William's shirt. For an instant, light shone through the bottle and cast bands of red, orange, yellow, green, blue, and violet light onto the white shirt. It was there and gone.

"What did you see?" Annie asked the circle of faces.

"I saw a bright light."

"They was a little bitty rainbow on William's shirt."

"Anybody else see colors?"

"Uh- huh, they was there but just for a blink."

"That's good. William, hand me back that bottle. You and 'Gustus sit over there. Thank you both for helpin'. Robert, Claudius, and Samuel, please come on up here by me." The men were not in a hurry to come forward, but after some fumbling, they sat in a row by the fire.

"Samuel, did you see the colors on William's shirt?"

"Yes, Ma'am, I did."

"Good. Now, tell me how that bruise got on yo' fo' head?"

"I... I ain't gonna trouble you wit' how it got there."

"Robert, what did you see when the fire got bright?"

"I saw colors and 'den white again... maybe yellow since the fire is yellow."

"That's true. Can you tell us the truth about how Samuel got a blue spot?"

"He got that bruise while I was defendin' myself." Robert stared into the fire. "It ain't his fault. I tol' him if he did not go to church, he goin' to burn in Hell. I was tryin' to help him."

"Did you share this bottle that I used to do this ceremony?"

"I don't want to make trouble. You said drinkin' spirits ain't in the Spirit."

"Claudius, Robert ain't havin' an easy time. Can you help him out?"

Claudius looked downcast. "I was at the dock last month unloadin' cases of rum. One fell and broken glass was all over and bottles rolled into the river. The overseer made me jump into that muddy water and feel around for bottles. It was so cold my teeth was clickin' and my lips was blue. I got eight bottles and the overseer called me out. They gave me a mug of hot water so I would not die on them, least not 'til the work was over."

"How did this bottle come to be wit' you, Claudius?"

"Wit' this gatherin' comin' I hoped they was a bottle in the river for pourin' libations. So I snuck into the water, which was not so cold like last month, and felt around beside the dock. Sho'nuff this bottle was stickin' up in the mud. I bet they is more down there."

"Well, that ain't stealin' but still dangerous and could get you whipped. Claudius, you said somethin' 'bout libations"

"Yes Annie, my Mama was Yoruba. She learned Old Ways from her Daddy in Africa and wanted to teach me libations and such so I could pass it on to the young ones. When I got sold away, I forgot what she taught me. Spirit gave me that bottle to pour libations to honor my ancestors like Mama done, but I drank some and shared some. I feel bad."

"What do you remember of what she said, Claudius? You people listen to this."

"She say there was Spirit in everything. She say that be hard to understand, so people names Spirits in mountains and animals and trees. There be Spirit that help us and Spirit that stop us when we doin' bad. Spirit be like light shinin' inside everybody. People tell stories 'bout different spirits to help them slowly, slowly see somethin' that be hard to see. She told me her Daddy was a story teller and singer called a gri... a gri..." He stopped.

"A griot, Claudius, you say it like gree - oh. You done a good job tellin' us 'bout your wise Mama. You be the grandson of a griot and you can learn those ways. I can tell you more 'bout libations if you want."

"Now, Samuel, how old was you when you was catched up?"

Samuel sat on the ground, his arms around his knees. "I was a boy, Annie. We lived in a town, big as ten Williamsburgs, with markets and many places to pray."

"How did you pray in your town?"

"Every mornin' at first light they would call us from a high place like a steeple. The first time was at dawn and they called that Fajr. And at noon we prayed again and they called that..." Samuel struggled.

"The high place called a minaret and the noon prayer is Zhuhr." Annie's voice was comforting.

Samuel looked up at Annie surprised, "Yes, Zhuhr." Tears came to his eyes. "I didn't think I would hear them words again. On the horrible ship, I prayed every day. But here, nobody knew and time went by. I fell away."

"Samuel, when you was a boy what was yo name?"

"My name... there are too many dead folk back there."

"Remember them wit' love and thanks, Samuel. They knew you by what name?

"I was Abdul Latif." He began to cry and put his head down.

"Abdul Latif, you raise your head up and look out at these people." Firelight reflected in the salty streams down his cheeks, his wet eyes radiant. "Did you go to school and learn to read when you was young?"

"Yes, Annie, until the war came, five years after I started school." He wiped his nose on his sleeve and turned to her. "It wasn't supposed to be like this, Annie."

"I know. Everyone here had a life stolen from us and has pain inside. Our hope comes from findin' what is left of our old path and goin' ahead on whatever road the Lord gives us now. None of us is forgotten, I promise you all."

"I read a book called the Koran and helped in my father's shop. He sold fine cloth; some silk was carried from far to the East. The letters was different. I can't read the writing here. I got no kin and no Holy Book. Robert says I'm going to Hell," he said with anguish.

Robert interrupted. "Annie, I tol' you I was defendin' myself, but I hit Samuel and he was defendin' his self. He did not hit me. I is sorry, Sam."

"That be the truth, Robert. When did you get here, Abdul Latif?"

"'Bout twelve years ago, Annie."

"When you was catched as a slave did people die?"

"A big war came and many people died. My father, my uncles, and big brother died with their... how do you call them... swords in their hands."

59

"When you was on the ship loaded tight like fish in a salt box, did people die?"

"Maybe one in three died before we got to 'Napolis."

"All them people had names, had plans and dreams, and people they loved and we should remember them in our prayers, shouldn't we Claudius?"

"Yes, Annie, we should." Claudius was captivated by the story.

"Did you die, Abdul Latif?"

"No, Annie. Many times I thought dyin' was better than livin', but I did not die."

"What was you doin' all that time on the trail and in the ship?"

"I prayed to God to save us, Annie. I sang to the Merciful One and prayed to the Compassionate One. I spoke the three tongues I learned from my father and told people that like good times end, bad times end, too. If we got through this, it could be the worst we would ever see. I prayed in the dark and cold to be close to God, and I prayed we would have a life again if that was God's will."

"Insh-Allah," Annie said. "If God wills it. And he did."

He was startled and stared at her. "Yes, Annie, Insh-Allah."

"Where are the people from the ship now?"

"I don't know, Annie. In 'Napolis we was sold off and I never saw them again."

"I want to tell you all somethin' important. Six months ago, I was at a Hush Harbor in Maryland, and folk was testifyin' how Jesus came into they life. Robert, is you listenin'?"

"Yes, ma'am, I know Jesus do miracles. I told Samuel I was tryin' to help him."

"At this Hush Harbor, one woman told us she was wit' child on the ship. It looked and smelled like Hell and people wailed like she heard they do in Hell. She was scared her baby would be born in Hell. Then she heard a young man prayin' in the dark. He said somethin' like 'in Shalla' and she think the boy come from Shalla or Shalla is Heaven. She think, a boy who pray so much can't be in Hell.

"The baby came four days before they got to 'Napolis. They hollered up to the men who took the mama and baby and washed them. If they could get that woman to auction lookin' healthy, the baby would be worth money too and they had lost many slaves to sickness. So they gave her food and used a sheet for a dress and she felt better when they got to port.

"A Catholic planter who hid his religion, went to 'Napolis to buy field hands. When he saw the woman up there wit' a sheet to block the sun from her child, lookin' like Mary and baby Jesus, he took it as a sign and bought them. He was sure the mother and child would help his wife at the house."

Abdul Latif was sitting upright. "She is alive? And the baby girl?"

"They live in Maryland. The woman cooks at that good home, and she teachin' her girl to cook. She got two secrets. She be Catholic like the family where she live. They pray to God, Jesus, and Mary over and over wit' beads like you used back home, Abdul Latif. Her other secret is she go to Hush Harbor meetings and tell folk that Jesus sent a holy boy to save people on the ship and wit'out that miracle she and her beautiful daughter would be dead. Her name be Esther now and she named her girl Sally after Shallah in the boy's prayer."

"Praise Jesus!" said Robert, "That's what I'm talkin' about. Jesus do miracles!"

Annie looked at him. "That's true, Robert, but you was only half listenin'. That holy boy was Samuel Abdul Latif who helped that woman on that ship."

"He was? You was workin' for Jesus, Samuel?"

All eyes turned to Samuel. Tears again streamed down his face, but they were tears of joy. "Annie, I am ready to serve the Most Kind One again. I am sorry I lost my way for so long."

"Samuel, you got through Hell and came out alive wit'out a bitter heart. If all you done was forget for a while, you done good. If you want to read English letters, I can show you."

"Annie, I want to learn."

"Please stand and face these people." He stood up. "Listen, everyone. Samuel lost his way and tonight his way found him. Don't call him Abdul Latif because that could make trouble wit' his massa. Call him Sal and if anybody ax, say it be short for Samuel. Look here." Annie picked up a stick and traced the letters S, A, and L in the earth. "S be for Samuel, A be for Abdul, and L be for Latif. S-A-L is for little Sally saved by a miracle through you and now in a home filled wit' kindness. Samuel in the Hebrew tongue means 'His name is God' and Abdul Latif in the Arab tongue means 'Servant of the Kind One'. When we call you Sal we callin' you by all your names."

"How do you know the meaning of my name?"

"When I traveled wit' the Fulani, we traded in towns wit' mosques built around 1000, a long time before 1775. Later Muslim slaves here taught me some of the hundred names of God. Sal, if I find a Koran, I'se gonna bring it to you. I learned to read this book." She reached into her sack and held up the Holy Bible.

"Robert, when you is down, do Jesus and this Holy Bible lift you up?"

"Jesus helps me every day and wit'out that Holy Word I might be dead."

"Do you see how God came through Sal to help Esther and Sally? Do you think Claudius could help folk through the spirit of his griot grandpa in his heart?"

"Yes, Ma'am."

"Do you know how to read, Robert?"

"I know some letters like R and S. Somebody showed me once."

"I believe that was the time I spelled R, O, S, and E in the sand on the beach."

"Oh, that's right. You said roses looks and smells beautiful even fenced in a garden. We can feel the warm sun and breeze like roses do and love one another and remember the Lord be smilin' on us until someday he open the gate for us to be free."

"Good, Robert. You was listenin' that day. When Sal learns to read English, would you like to ax him to teach you to read Bible stories? That might help open the gate in your heart."

Robert was shy about asking. "Samuel, I mean Sal, I'se sorry I said you was goin' to Hell. If you teach me how to read the Bible, I will be thankful my whole life."

"I will learn the letters and teach you," Sal answered. "The Bible tells about Jesus, and Mary his mother. They are also in the Koran. When I hear about Jesus and Mary here, it comforts me that they led me from Africa through Hell to Virginia. Like Annie says, I was not forgotten."

Annie smiled. "You men did well. It be late now and that pig is 'bout cooked."

"Please, Annie, tell us about the colors on William's shirt," Augustus called out.

"I showed you colors on William's shirt and then Claudius, Samuel Abdul Latif, and Robert showed you the colors again. Who knows what I'se talkin' about?"

Claudius spoke first. "Spirit is like that bright light when you put pine and rum and fat on the fire. When Spirit shines on us it be like light comin' through the bottle. One white light make many colors, like sunshine make a rainbow. Each color is somebody's way home to the white light of Spirit."

"That is a good way to say it, Claudius. You have the soul of a griot. I don't need to add nothin'. Should we respect the ways of others as they go up the road?"

"Yes, we should," said a number of voices.

"Anyone else?"

"All the colors come from the bright light in they own way," Robert added.

"I is happy you all listenin'."

"Claudius, some warm night carefully fetch another bottle by the dock and hide it. Next time we gather I can show you how to pour libations and give thanks for your Grandpa the griot and all who went before like Jesus, Moses who led the Hebrew Children out of slavery, Sal's Prophet Mohammed, and prophets in the Bible."

"Yes Annie, I will do that. I want to learn my Grandpa's way."

"Your Mama will smile down on you. Now let us celebrate all the colors. William caught us a fine pig and we is going to thankfully eat it ain't we?"

"Thanks, pig," said William. What he had witnessed touched him deeply. He placed succulent slices of pork on squares of corn bread and handed out portions to everyone. Most had not eaten so well since Easter Sunday weeks before. Annie took one to Peter. It was the best sandwich he ever had.

Peter heard the twang of banjo strings and the rhythm of a homemade drum began. The music went on for an hour as people took turns leading the call and response. Some songs were spirituals, and others so bawdy that folks laughed even without rum in their bellies. On the upbeat rhythms, people danced. Songs were sung in harmony, in sweet major keys and haunting minors. When the music ended, people looked into the embers, immersed in the glow of the moment. In spite of hardships, life had joy. They were renewed.

"Well," said Annie, "it be closer to mornin' than to last night, so until we meet again, help each other along 'Gustus, before you go could you step over here, please." He came close. "'Gustus, this be Mister Peter."

Augustus looked where Annie indicated and was surprised to see Peter. "Don't know why you didn't see him before what wit' that firelight shining on his white face." Annie smiled broadly. "Please show `Mister Peter the short way to Williamsburg from your quarters. You ain't got time to take him all the way yo-self. And don't let nobody see you together."

Peter was full of questions yet speechless. Annie made a little circle with her index finger that somehow told him now was not the time for questions and that she would talk to him another time. How does she say so much with just a move of a finger?

Men took down the canvas and filled the fire pit with the pile of soft earth as people dispersed into the darkness.

"Can you run fast and far, Mister Peter?" asked Augustus. "I ain't never seen a white gentleman run and we ain't got time to dally 'round here no mo'."

Peter winked at Annie. "Let's see if I can run fast. You lead and I'll follow."

Day 1-19:   Peter Running Home

Last week's heavy rain had left puddles and with the mud now dry, Augustus ran barefoot, stepping on smooth patches of clay and sand. The first hint of dawn lightened the sky above the trees. He kept a quick pace, lifting each foot high and placing it straight down like horses trotting. That way he would not trip or stub his toe badly, a lesson learned the hard way. As Augustus felt burning in his legs, he smiled at the reminder of the dancing. Recalling the drum added rhythm to his gait. Tokah Tam, Tokah Tam. That was some fun!

There was already too much light. He had to get to the quarter while everyone else was still abed. He heard Peter's footfalls behind him. Even as Augustus ran flat out, Peter kept up. Half a mile to go. That smell of wood smoke might be from the kitchen fire at the main house. Tokah Tam, comin' home, Tokah Tam, legs sore, Tokah Tam! He wiped his forehead with his sleeve. Hoo boy! He was going to make it home on time.

Augustus' world suddenly exploded in a burst in front of him. He cried out and fell flat on the road, palms down to cushion the fall. He saw the tail of the wild turkey he had tripped on disappear into the woods. His wind was knocked from him so he sat up to draw deep breaths. "Turkey!" He looked at his hands. "Ain't too bad." Peter helped him up.

Augustus panted, trying to catch his breath. "Whew! You can't find them turkeys when you hungry." His breath finally slowed. "I ain't never seen a white man run fast as you. Keep on down this road to town. I gotta cross to the quarters quick so they don't find me gone."

"Good luck, and thanks," said Peter. They ran another hundred yards and Augustus veered across the field to the slave barracks. He avoided the corn stubble that can puncture a foot and slowed to a walk. He opened the door and entered the rough cabin, stepping lightly across the dirt floor to the plank he placed beside his pallet so his feet would not touch cold clay on a frosty morning. He lifted the edge of the old blanket and sat on the straw mattress. He took an old rag and wiped his feet from the mud of the road. With a sigh, he lay back.

An hour later, the overseer called outside the door. "Up you get now! Get movin'! We got ourselves a big day."

DAY 2-1:   May 1775   Breakfast by the Hearth

Susan awakened early and quietly slipped from the bedroom. In her bare feet, she stopped and stared. The bathroom was gone. Gone… the discontinuity so complete her mouth opened but no words came. Fear arose and passed, leaving behind calm curiosity. Where a tub and shower had been the previous night, Susan stared into an open fireplace, coals still glowing.

She pulled a chair by the fire and gazed at the embers. A blackened wood-grain pattern was visible on the stubs of logs dwindling under yellow peaked tiny dancing blue cones of flame. What is this…? Susan wondered. Peaceful—I should not be afraid of this. Again she asked, "What is this?" Phrases moved through her awareness. She pulled a pencil and pad from her handbag and wrote:

> The extraordinary – extra ordinary, forever underlies the apparent.
> Beneath habitual, behind familiar, all form animated,
> All pattern emerging, resolving, and dissolving.

Susan lingered then, hung her robe, and pulled on slacks, sweater, and sneakers. Through a door that was not there yesterday, was an outhouse. That's convenient, she thought and crossed the yard to use it. In the trees, American goldfinches chirped over the rasping calls of grackles. Far away, a rooster crowed. Going back to the house, she looked into a brick well. The sky was reflected in the water below. A wooden pail with oak staves like a miniature barrel sat on the wall of the well.

I can do this. She lowered the pail by a rope tied to its handle. It struck the surface of the water, scattering the reflection of the sky into concentric circles of blue fragments. Water sloshed over the rim as she drew it up.

She carried water to the kitchen, added wood to the fire and put pots on the wrought iron rack at varying distances from the fire. "I'll warm one for washing and set this one over the fire to hurry along a cup of coffee. If I'm dreaming, will a dream of drinking coffee wake me up? Do I have any...?"

In the antique armoire were the snacks they brought. When the water in the first pot was warm, she half-filled the oriental-design porcelain wash basin, washed using a cloth as she did on camping trips, dressed quietly and returned to the kitchen to prepare breakfast. She arranged a platter with sliced cheese, apples, and muffins and called out, "Breakfast in ten minutes! I've got hot water on for a wash up and there's a big surprise out here!"

"Good morning, Hon." John emerged a few minutes later, a towel over his arm.

"No shower this morning. I've got hot water for the washing bowl."

"What the... What happened?"

"Maybe stealth remodelers came in the night? There's an outhouse in back."

"Good God!" John sat by the fire. "Unbelievable! How did this happen as we slept?"

"I don't know but I've had a peaceful feeling since I got up. We can go to the office and ask to change rooms; although this is pretty authentic don't you think?"

"I think I'm hallucinating. Why didn't we hear anything?"

Megan called out from her bed, "Do we really have to get up this early?"

"There's something here you should see."

Megan staggered into the living room rubbing her eyes. "Hey, there's the fireplace and the bathroom is still gone. I used the outhouse before I went to bed."

"That's not possible. The bathroom was here last night when we got back from the presentation at the church, and you were already asleep."

"I know it's not possible. It wasn't there when I was trying to read by the lantern light last night and it isn't there now. What's possible got to do with it?"

"How could someone remove the bathroom and put it back and remove it again just like that?" John asked, snapping his fingers.

"I guess it was just like that." Megan snapped her fingers.

"Ridiculous, Megan!"

"Peter saw it yesterday, too. He'll tell you." Megan knocked loudly on the door to Peter's room and opened it. "Time to get up, Peter! It's still going on."

"Unnh!" The sound came muffled by a sheet and a blanket.

"Come on, Pete. They can see the fireplace. Mom made breakfast. Get up!"

Peter sat upright. "Is it still happening?"

"Yeah, big time. Mom and Dad are out here staring at the fireplace."

"Wow! Give me four more hours to sleep and two minutes to get dressed."

"Forget the four hours," Megan grinned and closed the door.

After they washed up, they breakfasted around the hearth. "You guys say it was not just this house last night, but all over?" asked Susan.

"Yup, all over town," said Megan. "I walked to a tavern where everything was in the past. I read my history book and there are some things I can't wait to tell you."

"We'll go over to the office and ask what they did. I'll bet these houses are built to be converted suddenly like sets at a theater," said John.

"Yesterday, this seemed to go in and out, or we seemed to go in and out of it. Peter and I have projects to work on to really help some people!"

Peter shot her a 'shut up' look. "Yes, we both found topics for school. I am looking at slavery and Megan is working on—what, Megan?"

"Last night I learned the American Revolution was not about what we thought. There were secret deals among leaders in England and the colonies to take land from the Indians. King George reserved land for the Indians, but his governors granted Indian land in his name to soldiers who fought in the French and Indian War. Rich guys secretly bought up the land grants and sent servants who didn't know better into Indian country to clear the forests.

"Whoa there, Megan. It sounds like a historical conspiracy theory. Pick an idea for your paper and work on it, but do research to make sure it's true."

"But, Dad, I did research last night and I haven't even told you most of it yet!"

"First we have to figure out what happened to the bathroom!" John growled.

To calm the tension, Susan handed John a mug of coffee and changed the subject. "It was a good sermon last night. Before Jefferson advanced religious freedom, everyone in Virginia had to attend Episcopal services and pay taxes to that church or be fined. Jefferson helped make this a country where we can practice any religion or no religion."

"If Jefferson was really for freedom, why did Lincoln still need to free slaves ninety years later?" Peter objected testily.

"Pete's right. Over half the people in Tidewater were slaves, and many whites were bonded servants. Many free men owned no land so they could not vote either. Almost half the free people were women who did not get to vote for another hundred and forty years. Whose freedom were they fighting the revolution for anyway?" asked Megan. "And I want to show you something…"

Her father interrupted. "Wait just a minute! They fought for us! The American Revolution gave us freedom and gave birth to the greatest country in the world!"

"True, John," said Susan quietly, "but we did hear yesterday about taxes being repealed long before the Revolution. The burgesses mentioned that some leaders in Britain shared the views of our Founding Fathers. Maybe war was unnecessary."

"That's what I'm trying to tell you!" interjected Megan.

"Not now, Megan," warned John, controlling himself. "We'll get dressed and sort this room problem out. Later, if I find a library they haven't converted to a chicken coop, I'll do some reading myself."

"This sudden change is a shock. We need to find out what happened," said Susan. "There are other strange things. I saw the woman who talked about peace again in church last night and she was terrified. At the Capitol she looked around as if someone was following her."

Peter said, "I want to look for someone I think can help with this time problem."

"I don't know if it is a good idea for us to split up when…"

"When things are so weird, Mom?" Megan asked.

"I'll go to the office and demand an explanation," said John. "Peter, don't take reckless risks. Look both ways before you cross the street. Let's meet here at 12:30."

"See you then." Peter gave his parents and sister a hug and was out the door.

John was surprised. "He hasn't hugged us in a long time."

"There's nothing like the overnight appearance of a warm hearth to bring the family together, Honey," said Susan. "Did I just hear horses outside our door?"

"Mom, there's always horses on the street in Williamsburg. I'm going to go learn about servants and Indians and who was fighting who."

"Who was fighting 'whom'," Susan corrected.

"Yeah, that too. They were all fighting each other." Megan went to her room and came back dressed faster than her parents had ever seen her change. She was about to leave when her mother asked John, "Are we sure everything is safe out there?"

"I've been in bad situations," said John, looking at Susan's concerned face. "If I hadn't spotted dangers, I wouldn't be here. This feels safe. Let me finish my coffee, and then we'll find out what happened. Megan, you stick with us."

"What for!"

"We aren't sure what's going on here and if I hadn't been sleepy and stunned by the sudden remodeling, I would have kept Pete here, too."

"It wasn't remodeling, Dad. We have gone back in time," Megan insisted.

John saw his daughter's intensity. "Come on, Megan, that's impossible!"

"What if you're right, Meg?" said Susan. "You saw this change before we did, so you can help us figure it out. Let's stick together for a while until we understand what's happening."

The idea she could help appealed to Megan. She sat to eat the last muffin. "If this morning is anything like last night you won't find an office," said Megan.

Megan was right. The moment they stepped out the door their senses were assaulted by sounds and scents. From a porch that had not been there yesterday, a merchant's son called out a list of goods just arrived from the docks. As they walked, they winced at strong smells of smoke and horse manure, the reek of sweat, and the stench of urine in the lane beside a tavern. There were as many people on the street as the day before but everything was different.

"Everyone is in period costume," said John. "Old worn out costumes."

"These are smells I picked up on yesterday," said Susan, "but today it's really…"

"Up our noses, Mom!"

Most people wore faded rough garb: shirts of osnaberg—a fabric as tough as canvas—pants of worn leather, and coarse dresses. Those in carriages wore fine hats, linen shirts, wool trousers, or dresses. Ladies in carriages held handkerchiefs over their noses and mouths.

"This must be a once-a-year program," said John. "Why didn't they tell us?"

"A program? Maybe it's a Williamsburg version of *Brigadoon*. The town shows up one day every hundred years. Soon they'll start singing and dancing or…" Megan looked at the ragged people shuffling out of the way of horses and their droppings. "Or, uh, maybe not."

The Sinclairs walked toward the office amidst a rush of strange sights. They arrived at a building they had never seen. Where yesterday there was fresh paint and contrasting trim, they now saw weathered clapboards. Unshaven, unwashed travelers, some with more gaps than teeth, sat on steps near a board scrawled in charcoal: "NO MOR BEDDS TONITE."

John struggled to avoid an impossible conclusion. If he found himself alone back in time, he would have known post-traumatic stress had snapped him at last. But his family saw the same things he did. Looking around, he realized there was nobody to talk to about their shower. "We need to sit a moment." They walked away from the crowds to a garden in bloom. John sat on a bench, took a deep breath, then another. "Is this crazy or are we crazy?"

"Are there any other options?" asked Megan. "What flower is this, Mom?"

"Megan, those clusters of tiny pink and orange flowers are milkweeds, great for attracting butterflies. I think those pretty yellow ones on the stalks are wild indigo, past their peak."

"I thought indigo was, like indigo, blue-purple."

"For indigo dye, people used the leaves, not the flower. I saw a documentary. They soaked and fermented the leaves then dried the sludge and mixed in lye.

"Hey! Why are we talking about dye?" John challenged. "We have a problem!"

"We are getting settled, John. We need to be calm to figure out what to do." She recognized her husband's stress and put her hand on his arm.

"Yes we need to stay calm. Sergeant Sargon used to say, 'Stop, breathe, and get right here, because like it or not, right now we're nowhere else.'" He took a deep breath and exhaled slowly, looking at Susan. "This doesn't feel dangerous, but it's crazy. Megan, you and Peter had something like this going on last night?"

"Yeah. I came home to read but the lights and bathroom were gone. I found better light at a tavern that had a fire and lanterns. On the way home I ran into the Indian I met at the blacksmith shop. He said the servant I saw running away had fallen on his head and died. His name was Simon. That was not a program."

"There must be another explanation for this. We're in a place full of historical reenactments. I'm going to find out." John walked to the street. Picking out the best-dressed man, he asked, "Excuse me, Sir. Could you tell me what the date is?"

"Have you just come out of the wilderness? 'Tis May 13th, 1775."

"I was traveling and lost track of time, Sir."

Three men nearby were in a heated discussion. One waved a newspaper to make his point. "'Tis here in *The Gazette*. The British fired at Lexington and killed eight then advanced to Concord. Three hundred militiamen were waiting and opened fire. The Redcoats retreated to Boston being fired upon from behind walls for mile after mile. Some stopped to loot houses and were shot by farm wives as they filled their satchels. By the time they reached Boston, over seventy were killed and one hundred and seventy wounded. The Massachusetts militia had fifty killed and forty wounded. The militia laid siege to Boston the next day."

"Excuse me," interrupted John. "When did this happen?"

"April 19, 1775, about three weeks ago. The news came on a fast ship before fair winds. Some are calling it the shot heard round the world."

"Thank you, gentlemen." John walked slowly back to the garden.

"Williamsburg, we have a problem. It's partly cloudy and it's May, 13th 1775."

"Cool."

"Not cool. How do we get home from here or from then?"

"I don't know, Dad, I told you it goes back to normal by itself. It'll be fine."

"We don't know if it's fine. In battle, time seemed to slow down or almost stop. Sometimes there were flashbacks…" John stopped himself. "Megan, if this is real, we're in a time when a war is starting. This is a bad time to get hurt."

"Maybe this effect or whatever it is will pass soon, John. Megan and I will look around to find out what's happening. I want to find that troubled woman."

"And I could get first-hand information for my paper, although my teacher may flunk me if I say my sources were live interviews with real people in 1775."

"All right," said John. "Pete will meet us at twelve-thirty. We need to get back to our time whether we're imagining this or not. This may be nuts, but let's split up. You two stick together and find out what you can and I'll do the same. We'll let each other know at lunch."

"Oh, Dad! How much of that colonial currency do you have left?"

"I gave fifty to you and Pete and a hundred to Mom, so I have two hundred left."

"You're rich. I bought hot chocolate last night for pennies. Dinner for us all costs less than a dollar. Being in 1775 is not all bad!"

Susan and Megan walked back to Duke of Gloucester Street. "Mom, don't you think I'm old enough to look around on my own?"

Susan gave Megan's hand a squeeze. "Be careful, Honey. See you at home."

Day 2-2:   Peter Finds the Field Hands

Peter strode off the stoop and tripped on a brick. He stumbled forward planting his right foot deep into freshly dropped horse dung. "Shit!" He looked up and gasped at a team of horses bearing down on him. He jumped back—as the driver pulled hard on the reins to bring the carriage to a stop. The flank of a horse was one step from Peter's face and a large wagon wheel next to his right shoulder.

"Are ye all right?" asked the passenger tipping a gold-trimmed tricorn hat.

"He looks sound, Mister Mercer," the driver grinned, "but he messed his boot."

"Aye, I see that," said the passenger. "Glad ye are unhurt lad, but mind where ye step or ye could be run down and maimed. 'Tis good we were moving slowly."

"Yes, Sir. Sorry," mumbled Peter.

"I have not seen ye before. Your attire is foreign. What would your name be?"

"Peter Sinclair."

"Hugh Mercer." The man touched his hat. "You'll be fine. Mind ye look both ways when crossing the street." He waved as the carriage pulled away.

Peter took a deep breath. "Good advice at any time."

He wiped his shoe on the grass and hurried to the Powell House. No reenactors welcomed visitors. Past the kitchen, he was able to get a view of the garden and saw a woman stooping to weed between the rows with a hoe. It was not Evie.

"Excuse me."

"Yes, Sir?" Rosie the cook was startled.

Peter hesitated; a white man asking after a slave woman might arouse suspicion. "Evie asked about laundry soap, and we have it in stock now. Is she home?"

"Evie shoppin' wit' Missus Powell 'til noon." Rosie resumed weeding.

"Is that you, Mister Peter?" Dilli limped to the gate.

"Yes, I've been me since I woke up this morning, Dilli. Is that you?"

Dilli giggled. "I am me, too. I been waitin' for you. You been gone a week."

"Didn't I see you last night?"

"Mister Peter, you funny. That was a week ago you came by here."

"I'm glad to see you again. Say hello to James and your Mama, Dilli."

Peter was taken aback that a whole week had slipped by. Could Annie explain these time shifts? Ramshackle shanties huddled along fence lines near the roads. He came to the pasture where he first met Annie, but it was empty except for a pair of tethered sheep.

By the fence, a gentle draft carried trace scents of blossoms, fresh cut hay, and pipe smoke. The sound of a distant two-handled crosscut saw moving back and forth through a large log blended with the laughter of children in a nearby garden. Crickets chirped, a bird called, but absent was the hum of air conditioners, lawnmowers, and vehicles, the drone notes of the soundtrack Peter lived by. Now there was space between the sounds. Peter smiled, remembering how Annie paused when he was thinking. She seemed to know his thoughts as if they were part of the conversation. He would follow this path where it led.

He walked out of town toward where he had parted from Augustus. Beyond a pasture where Guernsey cows grazed serenely, the rustic huts of the quarter came into view. Skinny, dusty chickens, pecking for bugs in the grass, ignored him. "You lookin' for Mister Jack, I suppose?" called a voice behind the rail fence, where garden greens were past knee high.

"Mister Jack?"

"He in the fields wit' the boys." Molly stood from weeding to address this unusual visitor. She had taken off her apron and was in a long dress and yellow head wrap. "They ain't far today." She pointed, "Follow yonder road a quarter mile, go right at the fork 'til you see a gang workin'. He'll be there."

Peter was intrigued. The next steps seemed to open up as clearly as a trail marked with chalk on trees. "Look both ways and don't take any reckless risks," he muttered.

He retraced his steps up the road he had run on after the Hush Harbor a week before. Before the woods obscured his view of the quarters, Peter looked back at the barracks. Each building was seven yards by five yards, made from boards nailed to upright posts, chinks filled with mud and straw to keep the wind at bay. Wooden clay-lined chimneys were separate from the building so when a chimney fire broke out, slaves could pull the chimney away to save their house. Peter shook his head. What a life those slaves endured! He turned and set out up the track.

*   *   *   *   *   *   *   *   *

In the barrack a week earlier, the morning after the Hush Harbor, the fires below the chimneys dwindled to warm ash and glowing embers. Outside the door, the overseer shouted, "Up you get now! Get movin'! We got ourselves a big day."

"One more day 'till Sunday." A voice sounded in the dark barrack. There were coughs, sniffs, and scuffs of bare callused feet on the dirt floor followed by an intruding burst of light as the first of the five slaves in the hut opened the door.

Augustus opened his eyes. Lines of light from cracks stretched across the clay floor. At the foot of his pallet, a box held his simple belongings: a small knife for whittling and skinning, a ball of twine, one brass shoe buckle found by the road, and a rough osnaberg canvas shirt, not torn like his work shirt. He had won this prized possession in a foot race.

"We don't know what we're doin' today or what we'll be standin' in," Robert said from the far end of the barrack. "I ain't wearin' my boots to stand in muck."

"I ain't putting no boots in shit neither," Claudius declared.

"You ain't got none, mister barefoots. I'se goin' for grits while there's grits to get." Robert laughed as he and Claudius jostled at the door. Augustus followed them out.

Jack Read, the overseer, stood next to Molly the cook at the head of the line. Augustus held back. "If he catch me for gettin' back late, no breakfast today," he breathed to himself, trying to look like he was just waking up rather than dragged out from dancing and running. He kept his eyes down but his ears told him there might be nothing to fear.

Jack reminded Molly, "Mister Carter says a special portion of mush and cube of sow belly. You all want to be hardy today. We got work to do."

Confidence rose as Augustus held out his wooden bowl. "Good mornin', Mister Jack. Mornin' Molly."

"Mornin', 'Gustus." Molly plopped a ladle-full of corn mush from the iron pot into his bowl and rapped the edge of the ladle handle on the side of his bowl so the dollop on the back plopped in. She placed a cube of salty bacon fat on top. With a ration of two gallons of corn meal a week and a bit of meat, fat, or fish only three times a week, this was a treat.

"Thank you, Mister Jack. Thank you, Molly." Augustus ambled to the large logs alongside the quarters where the other men sat eating.

"Must be some heavy work' today." Robert spoke with a mouthful of corn.

Augustus bit into the bacon fat, eating quickly, more from fatigue than hunger. He would need strength. They ate breakfast in ten minutes. Augustus swiped two fingers over the bowl and licked them. Jack called out, "Put your bowls away and grab a hoe. We're heading to Partridge Quarter to put tobacco in the ground."

Partridge Quarter was a hike northeast across the York County line. The winding road passed lands owned by several better-sorts men who were called Gentlemen, not planters. Planters were middle-sorts who owned land but no slaves or very few. They did the hard physical work of tending fields themselves.

Robert muttered as they walked to the pile of tools Jack had laid out. "It be too late in the season for pullin' up hills."

Claudius was thinking about it too. "I guess hills was washed out. We got to hoe then plant 'cause they needs to get crops agrowin'. This gonna be a hard day."

Up the road trudged five pairs of callused bare feet and four pairs of worn boots. Two men pulled a cart filled with tobacco seedlings from seedbeds, carefully covered in wet burlap to keep the moisture in. Upright sticks protected the shoots from being crushed. The men had ragged shirts and pants torn at the knee. Some wore tattered coats and some had rags around their neck as a scarf. A few stalked opportunity, guarded eyes scanning for any chance to improve the narrow pens of their lives. Others were bent, their eyes retaining no light of hope for a better life.

One pair of feet was warm in black wool stockings darned at the heels inside leather boots with brass buckles and thick new soles. Jack Read had a second pair back at his cabin, with small silver buckles. He wore them with pride to church and on rare visits to the main plantation house to signal his first step up the long ladder of society. He also had a better waistcoat for those occasions. He got few such invitations but gentlemen did show favor to their overseers from time to time to motivate these agents of productivity on the plantation.

Jack's britches were fastened at the knee with five buttons a side, each punched from horn and hand-drilled for the thread holes. The bottom buttons had a habit of popping open, so Jack added leather lacing outside the knee band on each side to take the strain. The oversized hunting shirt kept him warm and his white shirt clean. His tricorn hat would have fallen off his head were he as stooped as the slaves his age, but he carried his head high.

Hoes over shoulders, each slave carried a ball of corn mush wrapped in a rag for lunch. They passed the cornfield Augustus had crossed at dawn and then tobacco fields on the right and woods on the left. The sun was behind a pall of low gray clouds. The damp air clung to their skin.

Tobacco crops had saved the struggling Jamestown Colony 150 years before but tobacco wore out the land after several seasons. Plantation owners accumulated up to ten times as many acres as were under cultivation in tobacco at any one time. The slaves trudged past a patchwork of tobacco, cornfields, and a few parcels still forested. There, semi-feral hogs rooted and ate acorns in season and were roasted and eaten themselves. Newly cleared land could yield sweet Virginia tobacco. As the soil tired, owners would put cattle out to graze and renew the soil with manure. Tobacco from those fields was bitter and of an inferior grade.

Augustus followed behind an older slave, a good tactic since an overseer would often yell at the man in front for setting too slow a pace. He looked down and rested as he walked, and did not notice the deer in the woods to the left, alert and ready to leap away from the men on the road. Nor did he notice Mister Jack drop back from the front to walk on his right.

The deer suddenly bolted and Augustus looked to his left.

"How ya feelin', 'Gustus?" The words from so close gave him a start.

"Wha? Oh, Mister Jack. Sorry, Mister Jack, I... I didn't see you."

"'Gustus, this morning when I stepped out of my cottage, I saw someone run across the field to the barrack. Did you see anybody come in before rising time?"

"Uh, no suh, Mister Jack."

"Maybe it was just a dream about a fast black buck and a young white buck running next to the road through the corn stubble."

Augustus became very worried.

"I thought it was a dream, but walking by the cornfield, I saw two sets of fresh footprints. One set led to the quarter and the other stayed on the road to town. So then I thought, maybe 'twasn't no dream at all. But 'twas not light enough to see clearly who either of them was. How long have you been at this quarter?"

"'Bout twelve years, Mister Jack."

"How long has it been since you had any kind of trouble, 'Gustus?"

"Well, I got a bad croup last winter and that infected foot a while back,"

"You never did nothin' that needed a whippin'? I don't recall givin' you one."

Augustus felt the threat. "Oh, no Suh, Mister Jack, I does what I s'posed to do, and I don't do what I ain't s'posed to do." He tried not to show fear but he began to sweat. Last year he and other slaves had been forced to witness a slave get a savage whipping from an overseer at a nearby quarter. Tiny knots at the tip of the lash tore the man's back open and he screamed and bled until he fainted. Augustus threw up in the trees when it was over.

"I suppose runnin' back to the quarter ain't near as bad as runnin away from it."

"No, Suh. You want me to ask around to find out who might have been runnin' in the dark wit' the son of a gentleman?" Augustus' voice was too shaky.

"A young gentleman eh? No 'Gustus, Nobody will tell anything but stories. You know how people make up stories when they think they are in trouble."

"Yessuh."

"'Gustus, we got to hoe up hills to get plants in the ground before a rain comes." He looked at the sky. It was not getting lighter. "We'll pray the rains ain't heavy."

"Yes, Suh."

"I need the boys to work hard today and no leanin' on the hoes, you hear? I need a strong boy to stay out front and help me keep everybody moving. If we get all the hills planted, I could forget that dream I had. What do you think 'Gustus?"

"We gonna work strong, Mister Jack. The fried pork belly will keep us hoppin'."

"That's good, 'Gustus. I brought more with me and if the morning work is done well I can cut off a piece for every man here to have with his corn at mid-day."

Jack moved to the head of the column moving up the road. "Step quicker now," he barked. "We ain't carrying a casket! Not today."

Augustus let out a slow breath. "Ran into a snare and out again wit'out gettin' skinned," he murmured.

The slaves and their overseer were on a long quick hike before starting the work. As he walked barefoot, Augustus thought about the long loop of the seasons. Three months before, in February, he had shivered as he sowed tobacco seeds in beds hoed, raked, and picked free of stones. When the seedbeds were threatened by night frost, slaves covered them with straw. The straw was pulled back by day to give sun to the seedlings.

In early spring, fields were prepared for transplanting tobacco seedlings and for planting corn and wheat. Wheat was planted in rows, tobacco and corn in mounds a yard apart for drainage. Large plantations had thousands of mounds, hoed, raked, and planted by slaves. The backbone of the plantation economy was a multitude of backbones, stooped in servitude. The gentry saw slave labor as the key to prosperity. For each good field hand five acres could be worked. This gang walking down the road could raise over forty acres of tobacco.

Augustus did not look forward to May, when tobacco seedlings were transplanted from seedbeds to waiting mounds. He recalled the never-ending strain on his back, bending over the hills, making holes with a stick, inserting a seedling and filling the hole. He did not look up at the other men or women with mud caked past their knees, streaking their faces and matting their hair. They would wipe their eyes with the backs of their arms; spit grit, and keep their heads bent, from early morning to sunset as the ache of muscles increased through the day. The owners had learned to give them water to avoid fainting or worse from dehydration.

Augustus preferred planting corn. He stuck the pointer finger of his left hand into the earth to his second knuckle to set a constant depth, made a design of holes, and dropped a kernel into each hole patting it shut. He was the fastest planter in the quarter, which partly explained the lack of whip scars on his back. Even when he felt sad or angry, planting corn brought him peace.

He carried a piece of canvas to kneel on to reduce the pain of hours of stooping. He focused on the pattern of holes and the rhythm of dropping a seed in each hole. When two dropped, he would say, "Friends," pat the hole shut and keep planting. He knew how big a handful of seed to grab from the hemp bag tied at his waist to go quickly without spilling. He recalled the preacher reading, "As ye sow, so shall ye reap." As he put seeds in the ground, knowing corn would come made him happy. Sometimes he had nothing on his mind but the smell of soil. Planting corn made him feel at home and this was the only home he knew.

Augustus saw the owner and overseers watch the fields like hawks hunting mice. What they saw determined the slaves' tasks six days a week, nine to twelve hours a day. If they spotted an attack of the tobacco fly, the slaves would rush to cover the plants with straw until the danger passed. Heavy rains brought orders to dig drainage ditches and replant washed out hills. Drier weather brought weeds the slaves would hoe or pull.

If rains were right and worms scarce, Augustus found the hot days of summer less grueling. Slaves girdled trees or cleaned tobacco and horse barns. When there was drought there was little to do but hear the planters pray for rain and complain the rest of the time. In church when the preacher said, "Give us this day our daily bread," Augustus pictured abundant yellow corn bread. He believed the easier days of August, with the varied work of mending fences, hauling firewood, and walking fields looking for worms and not finding any, were a gift in the month that carried his name.

When worms were spotted, the field gang stooped all day, picking caterpillars off tobacco leaves and crushing them between thumb and fingers. It was easier to lie on the ground to spot worms under the lower leaves. When slaves were lying down, they had to put the worms in a canvas bag to show they were not resting.

76

In late August, slaves cut tobacco as the owner decided which fields were ready. They chopped stalks with a half a dozen leaves each and left them to wilt in the sun. Then the stalks were carted to tobacco houses, placed on long stakes, and hung high in the beams. While tobacco dried, slaves harvested corn. It was stored in cribs with gaps between the boards where breezes passed through to dry the corn for grinding. Augustus enjoyed husking in a circle with the others. They chewed on corn kernels so they were never hungry those days.

The slaves planted rye, barley, and wheat. After the first frost, another burst of work occurred as tobacco was covered to "sweat" or ferment the leaves. The stalks were stripped and women tied leaves in bundles or "hands." These were prized, which meant packed into hogsheads in presses weighted by stones to squeeze more tobacco into the four-foot barrels. Fully prized, a hogshead weighed half a ton. Overseers gave meat or coins to slaves to prize barrels all night in an excited, exhausting rush when a ship was due at the wharf. The seductive smell of tobacco that Augustus liked on his fingers was the fragrance of prosperity to his owners. To a few slaves, the extra rewards of packing tobacco provided a scent of freedom.

The men skirted a swamp to arrive at Partridge Quarter. Dead trees girdled the previous year stood in the field, lower branches stripped for firewood and the rest reaching out gnarled fingers on blackened dead limbs, foreboding silhouettes against the cool slate sky.

Jack stepped into the field. "Listen well, boys! The rains washed these hills out bad. We'll hoe them up then plant seedlings. Leave the pebbles on the sides of the hills. We ain't got many big stones, but if you find any, throw them into piles carefully. Don't knock each other senseless. Some of you ain't got sense to spare. We'll start here... here... and here." Jack dug his heel into the soil of the first three hills then he pointed. "Work up that rise. Hoe them fine but hoe them fast. Show 'em what I mean by fine and fast, 'Gustus."

"Yessuh!" Augustus stepped to the nearest heel mark and swung the blade of the hoe down through the cover of twigs and leaves blown in from the woods. The hoe imbedded itself into the earth with a thunk. He pulled the clod of earth over, and as it fell from the hoe, he swung the hoe up and hurled the blade down into the earth again a hand-span to the left. He pulled each clod toward him, bending to toss a large twig to the side.

"'Gustus showed you how. Now, show me you saw what he did! Get to it!" The slaves moved to the hills and began to hoe. Jack assigned Robert to separate the seedlings. "Don't poke each other with the hoe handles. Them hills are close but I don't want nobody hurt so bad they can't work. Poke enough to stay awake!" Jack laughed and watched the quick movements aimed to impress. "Settle down, boys. Keep it smooth and steady so you last all day. How about a song, Claudius?"

Claudius began. "Hmm, hah! Hmm, Ho! Lord, show me the way. Hmm, hah! Hmm, yes! Lord, show me today." The 'Hmm' on the upswing and 'Hah' on the downswing to chop the earth masked the groans of toil. 'Hmm, Ho!' was for pulling the clod of earth over and the melodic prayer line marked a momentary rest after the pull. Other men joined in, first in unison, then branching into harmonies and syncopation. Claudius sang to help men find a flow and to ignore the pain of sore muscles and blisters. Sometimes the songs passed on messages or stories the overseer did not understand.

Jack walked thirty paces to a stump and sat to load his pipe. A peaceful smoke was a morning ritual. He was far enough away to see all the slaves and appeared to be paying attention. No slave dared look at his eyes closely enough to know.

Augustus sang along. When the soil was chopped, he pulled the hoe back and forth to flatten the hill and made cuts for the seedlings Robert brought. He placed a seedling in each cut and patted it closed. He stepped up the rise two paces to the next mound and began again with a swing of the hoe. "Hmm, Hah!" His legs ached already. It would be a long hard day and a long hard summer. He moved with the hoe and the soil and the song. He would sleep tonight.

       *   *   *   *   *   *   *   *   *

A week later, Peter heard the singing as he approached a field close to the quarter. He slowed his walk as he saw the slaves pulling weeds. He witnessed how hard the men worked, stooped under the gaze of a white man sitting on a stump smoking a pipe. He figured the white man must be Jack the overseer and decided to stick to his story of being a trader from a northern colony. Peter boldly walked into the field toward the overseer. As he got close, he recognized Augustus, Claudius, and Robert at work, but knew he could not say anything to them.

"Hello Mister Jack. Someone told me I could find you here."

"Hallo." The overseer took off his hat assuming from Peter's confidence and strange but fine clothing he was at least middle-sorts, perhaps better-sorts, but certainly a strange sort.

"I'm Peter Sinclair." Peter extended his hand. "We don't grow tobacco up in the northern colonies, but we do enjoy a pipe-full of sweet Virginia now and again."

"Jack Read." The overseer chuckled with pride and shook Peter's hand.

"I walked out to trouble you to see that miracle of Virginia tobacco done well."

"No trouble, Mister Peter." Jack smiled. "Today they are cleanin' up them hills pullin' weeds around the young tobacco plants." Enjoying Peter's interest, he explained the cycle of how tobacco is sown, grown, cut, cured, packed, and the barrels pulled down the rolling roads to the docks. Barrels were hitched to a horse and rolled like a giant wheel.

"Those are fine field hands. How would I buy two for my farm up north?"

"Slaves are mighty expensive and these hands ain't for sale. There are auctions on market days and you can buy what's up on the block. You can buy them in Williamsburg or go to a port like Norfolk or Alexandria and buy them next to the ship for less money. But those don't speak English and sometimes they get sick and die before you can say 'wasted money.' You could make a private arrangement with an owner, but that could be more expensive I reckon."

"Why more expensive?"

"A rich man might like money, don't you think? An owner can bargain hard if he don't care to sell them slaves. He might name a high price as if they are good slaves and they might be or they might not. He would know which, but you wouldn't."

Peter smiled at the bargaining advice. "About how much does a slave cost? Ready money, since no one here would be likely to sell me something on a note."

"I reckon not, Mister Peter, no more than they would give me credit, a man with no land to forfeit if I couldn't pay. A slave costs from twenty-five to one hundred pounds sterling depending on age and skill. That is more than I earn in several years. For these good field hands without a trade, you might pay forty pounds for the young ones, and twenty-five for the older ones, who have less time left to work. Slaves cost much more than virgin land to the west where I hope to buy someday. Even if you have money to buy a slave, you have to feed him, give him blankets and heavy shirts so he don't freeze to death on you, and you must have him build himself a quarter. You give him boards, nails, and the time to do it. All that costs money, too, and I don't have any."

"And what if I needed a cook or say, a laundress, how much would that cost?"

"A good cook costs more than a field hand but less than a man skilled in wood, stone, or brick. A laundress, who could keep you alive with her cooking, could cost 30 pounds. A wench costs more if she has a pretty look, easier to get her bred and increase the slaves you have," Jack winked and did not notice Peter wince.

Talking about people as property was distasteful but Peter needed information so he pressed on. "Some Africans are free. Can we hire one for a wage?"

"Yes. When Master Carter has work like fancy plaster for the parlor or new windows at the main house, the work is done by an undertaker with a gang of men under hire. Some are free black men or slaves hired from others. One African joiner had his own slave working with him on a window job."

Jack pulled on his pipe and they fell silent and watched the slaves put tobacco plants into the hills making slow, steady progress, singing in syncopation and harmony. Peter hummed a few notes along with the gang and Jack looked at him, surprised.

"Catchy tune, isn't it, Jack?"

"They can have their ways as long as they get the work done."

When Augustus turned, he saw the young white man who had run with him last week talking with Jack Read. "I wonder what they talkin' 'bout." Augustus returned to work. He was grateful that today was Saturday and he had heard that tonight Jack would bring the slaves home early so he could clean up and put on his good waistcoat and shoes with small silver buckles for an evening with the better sorts.

"By the way, I heard an African woman named Annie comes 'round these parts. Do you know her?" Peter asked.

"I heard of her. She cheered up some of our slaves when they were dejected. Some slaves kill themselves when they get like that. She is a kind of preacher. Like I said, they can have their ways if they get the work done. She don't cause harm nor stir them up or nothin' and the field hands can't get the work done if they kill themselves."

"Good to meet you, Jack. I must get back to town now."

"Mister Peter, you could get sunstroke wanderin' around with no hat on."

"Good idea. I'll get a hat." Peter started down the road thinking about the irony of an overseer with a touch of sympathy for dejected slaves and strangers without hats. He watched Augustus working as he passed.

Day 2-3: John in the Taverns

John felt urgency to solve his "time-zone problem" but had no idea where to look. He pushed his way past men arguing on the stoop of a tavern and entered a room filled with loud voices, smoke, and more men than chairs, some stood with bread and coffee or beer. Those who had a coin to spare breakfasted on a meat pie or bowl of stew. A sudden cheer came from a table near the back where a roll of the dice had just changed one man's month for the better and made this a dark morning for three others.

Seeing no spare seats John threaded his way through the crowd, barely avoiding beer spilling on him when a serving girl swerved to avoid the intrusive hand of a drunken patron. Men slept upstairs in the tavern, several to a bed or on the floor. A few had splashed water on their faces but none washed to the standard John was used to even when camped in a jungle or desert. He heard threads of conversation as he made his way through the crowd.

"We may soon see if ye can stay calm enough to shoot a bright red coat as well as you shoot a squirrel. Unlike squirrels, Redcoats will shoot back at thee."

"Tobacco prices are down at the Liverpool docks, so I canna offer ye more."

John looked for breathing room and saw space by the window. He was taller than most men in the room so he could scan the room without obstruction.

"Here's a toast to Liberty, Wilkes, and the 45!" Even at ten-thirty in the morning, twenty men stood and raised their glasses.

"There's a rumor the King will offer George Washington a title and lands in England. He is so ambitious I wager he will take the bait. That would dampen the firebrands among us."

"Washington does not need a fiefdom from the King. He has lands aplenty here in Virginia, and some say he has much more land west of the Proclamation line."

"No one heeds that Proclamation of '63 or the Importation Agreement. The lucre from tobacco shipments brings fine china to tables and a fine lining for pockets! Imports have risen during this non-Importation Agreement. It is an agreement few wish to keep."

"We sent petitions to the King. Some towns are casting lead statues of His Majesty to honor him in hope he comes to his senses and ignores the bad counsel of his governors."

"We might have to use the lead to make musket balls. Those royal statues may melt away."

John felt dizzy. He disliked crowded noisy bars, even after a beer on a Friday night, and this was cold sober in the morning. He left the tavern and crossed the street to a bench. His mind was full of questions: If we considered ourselves Englishmen and had friends in Parliament, why did we start a war? Why did we get into the wars I fought?

He noticed he was sitting near the Raleigh Tavern and went in. It was cleaner and less crowded than Wetherburn's. In the large Apollo Room, he found an empty table in the rear corner and ordered a cup of coffee. Five men near him were playing a game of cards for high stakes, but they were more refined and quieter than their compatriots across the street.

Suddenly a hush swept over the patrons as a trio of men walked across the room. The patrons whispered. All eyes were on the young men taking seats at the vacant table next to John. One of the men was six feet tall and had a long face and prominent forehead. He wore an ill-fitting brown wig tied at the nape of his neck with a brown ribbon, his auburn widow's peak showing. The second man was taller, John's height, bony with a gangly posture. He wore no wig, and with his freckles and long red hair tied back, he would stand out in any crowd. The third man was not much older than Peter.

A man stood and doffed his hat, "Good morning, Mister Jefferson, Mister Henry," giving a respectful bow. "I thought this morning would find you in Philadelphia."

Patrick Henry pushed his spectacles to the top of his head, almost dislodging his wig. "You are correct. The Continental Congress began a few days ago. I depart after this farewell breakfast with my friends."

"Do you think we will have a war, Sir?" called out a man at a nearby table.

Burgess Henry stood to reply. "Our brothers in Massachusetts are at war. The distinctions between Virginians, Pennsylvanians, New Yorkers, and New Englanders are no more. I am not a Virginian, but an American! So, Sir, we have no election. It is now too late to retire from the contest. There is no retreat but in submission and slavery! Our chains are forged! Their clanking may be heard on the plains of Boston! The war is inevitable and let it come!"

"Just so!" called out a vestryman. "We were not subdued by unjust taxes. Neither shall we accept port closure, quartering troops, or giving land to Catholic Quebec."

"What about the Olive Branch Petition to the King?" asked another.

"It is natural to indulge in the illusions of hope," Patrick Henry replied. "We are apt to shut our eyes against a painful truth and listen to the song of that siren. Is this the part of wise men, engaged in a great and arduous struggle for liberty? Are we disposed to be those who, having eyes, see not, and having ears, hear not, the things which so nearly concern their temporal salvation? For my part, whatever anguish of spirit it may cost, I am willing to know the whole truth, to know the worst, and to provide for it."

Men in the tavern applauded. John recognized some of Henry's words.

"William Pitt told parliament that the colonies are 'equally entitled to all the natural rights of mankind and the particular privileges of Englishmen'. No man in Britain would lay down his rights or liberty voluntarily or under duress. Then should we, gentlemen?"

"No!" called out a dozen men in chorus.

"A year ago, Burgess Jefferson and I, and ninety others met in this room when Governor Dunmore suspended the House of Burgesses. We planned a Day of Prayer and Fasting to protest closing the Port of Boston. We resolved to call other colonies 'to meet in general congress, at such place annually as shall be thought convenient, there to deliberate on those measures which the united interests of America may require'. The place chosen was Philadelphia in the midst of the colonies from north to south. The Continental Congress is now a reality, so no one should doubt our capacity to triumph in our cause!"

"Huzzah for Patrick Henry!"

"Have you heard Pitt's words to Parliament four months ago?" Henry asked without losing his rhythm. "Lord Chatham, to use his title, addressed the Ministers, 'The whole of your political conduct has been one continued series of weakness, temerity, despotism, ignorance, futility, negligence, blundering, and the most notorious servility, incapacity, and corruption!'" Patrick Henry paused and looked around the room. "Now why did he not come forth and say openly what he thought of the ministers and their policies?"

The roomful of men, including John, laughed.

Patrick Henry pulled a folded paper from his vest pocket and opened it. "A few days later when Parliament decided to send more troops against us, Liberty's friend, John Wilkes…"

"You mean our libertine friend?" called out a regular patron of the tavern.

Henry laughed. "Indeed. Wilkes admits he uses his sense of humor to befriend as many women as are willing to tolerate his homely face. In order not to have anyone mistake his words for mine, and hang me for it, I will read his words to Parliament received in a letter."

"In the great scale of empire, you will decline, I fear, from the decision of this day; and the Americans will rise to independence, to power, to all the greatness of the most renowned states, for they build on the solid basis of general public liberty."

"These words of Wilkes resound with truth about our future. Thank you, Gentlemen."

The men in the Apollo Room cheered. "Huzzah for Patrick Henry!"

"Let us hear from Mister Jefferson," called out a portly man in an expensive wig.

Thomas Jefferson stood, obviously uncomfortable to be called upon. He kept both hands on the table causing him to look stooped. When he spoke, all but those close to his table strained to hear him. John could scarcely believe he was seeing the young Thomas Jefferson — barely over thirty.

"Other business keeps me from departing for the Congress until June." He stopped, as if looking for something else to say. "With regard to the adversity in Boston, I agree with Mister Henry. The spirit of resistance to government is so valuable on certain occasions that I wish it to be always kept alive. It will often be exercised when wrong, but better so than not to be exercised at all. What country can preserve its liberties if its rulers are not warned from time to time that their people preserve the spirit of resistance? There will be differing views. I say in matters of style, swim with the current; in matters of principle, stand like a rock."

"Huzzah for Thomas Jefferson!"

"I shall present my friend and neighbor from the Piedmont who serves on the Committee of Safety for Orange County, Virginia, Mister James Madison. I believe he will contribute to the governance of our country some day." Madison, at twenty-four hoping his wig made him look older, stood and nodded to the patrons of the tavern as Jefferson quickly sat down.

"What think you of our Congress, Mister Madison?" called out a militia officer.

"If men were angels," Madison responded, "no government would be necessary. If angels were to govern men, no controls on government would be necessary. In framing a government, which is to be administered by men over men, the great difficulty lies in this: you must first enable the government to control the governed, and in the next place oblige it to control itself. A dependence on the people is, no doubt, the primary control on the government, but experience has taught mankind the necessity of auxiliary precautions."

Patrick Henry applauded. "If our struggle for liberty takes us on an independent path from Britain, perhaps Mister Jefferson's friend, Mister Madison could write a Constitution."

John was sure that he had read some of those words of Henry, Jefferson, and Madison in high school. If I ever get home, who will believe that I actually heard them say those things in a tavern before they included them in speeches, he wondered. Would I dare to tell anyone?

Day 2-4: Susan at the Wig Maker and Milliner

"You are here to sell your hair? Do you speak English, Meine Frau?"

Susan nodded, somewhat puzzled.

"Did you come to sell those long lovely auburn locks? I can give a fair price. We have gentlemen customers who can afford a wig made from human hair. I know a lawyer with auburn hair who wears a brown poorly-fitting wig. I might be able to persuade him to invest if I had your tresses to work with." The wig maker was a petite, prim, middle-aged woman.

"No Madam, but if I ever cut it short, saving it for a wig is a wonderful idea."

"Terribly sorry, Missus, I mistook you for a new arrival. You never know what those Germans, Swedes, or Dutch will be wearing. They often have no funds to begin their new life and the women folk sell their hair. But your fine speech shows that you are a lady of the better-sorts."

"Please forgive my clothes... uh, for the voyage. I will hurry to buy something more appropriate. Where I live, I'm a middle-sorts wife, so no need to be deferential."

"If you would like hair dressing, we are happy to serve you. My husband imports perfumes and soaps we can offer you. Most of our goods are not from England, so we are not interrupted by the non-importations agreement, which we ardently support, of course."

"Of course you do. We all do!" a woman joked from a chair, where she was getting her hair powdered with a product rowed ashore by Dutch smugglers.

"Are you here to prepare for the Governor's Ball tonight?" asked the wig maker.

"Governor's Ball?"

"Yes," said the woman in the chair. "Even as we hear rumblings of war, there remains a place for social graces. I hope higher culture will prod men loyal to the King and supporters of the Congress to settle their differences, rather than scrap like wicked schoolboys. The ball may be the idea of Lady Dunmore, the Governor's wife, who wishes the stubborn men of all sides to take the pot off the fire before it boils over."

"Hush, Amanda. You may offend the lady."

"I'm not offended," Susan assured them. "Like you, I'm troubled our leaders resort to war when war is usually worse than what provoked the fighting. We proudly wave flags and pray for victory. Our enemies do the same thing to their people. On both sides, people get rich selling arms. We fight for years, and many people die. Oh, sorry! I made a speech."

"You speak well. Are you a preacher's wife?" asked the wig maker.

"No, my husband is not a religious man."

"Madam, if you wish to have your hair prepared for the ball, we can help you now. This afternoon we have promised the time to several ladies."

Susan chose to go to the ball on the spot. "It will be lovely to have dressed hair."

"I can give you delightful ringlets with your beautiful hair. I can't write your name but my husband likes me to put the first letter of the name in the book."

"I'm Susan with an S. I could write the whole word in the book if you like."

Susan wrote her name imitating the printing the wig maker used for the initials.

"The name Susan reminds me of sunshine," said the woman in the chair.

"The name has been in my family for a long time."

"My daughter is expecting her second child. I don't want to be an interfering grandmother but if it is a girl I shall gently insist she name her Susan."

"I heard you called Amanda, which is a lovely name. May I call you Amanda?"

"Yes, Susan, if we are prisoners together in these chairs we can use our personal names. Can you extend my stay, Charlotte? 'Tis a respite to be out of the house."

The wig maker laughed and peeked at her book. "Most days, you could linger, but Missus Byrd is next. She was not pleased I could only take her at eleven."

"And by what name might I call you, Madam?" Susan asked the wig maker.

"She is Charlotte, like our Queen," said Amanda.

"And my husband is George, like the King. We are the not-royal couple."

"Charlotte, speaking of the Queen, have you seen her portrait?" Amanda lowered her voice. "Some say she is an octoroon and the portrait makes plain her African features. The gossip is that she has connections to black lines of Portuguese royalty. Others say her painter is an abolitionist and the image promotes the end of slavery. 'Tis three years since slaves were set free in England," she added.

"Were there troubles and uprisings when the slaves were freed?" Susan asked.

"None I heard of. They became servants and received a wage and that was that."

"Perhaps slave owners fear violence because they know in their hearts that slavery is wrong," Susan said.

"You're not an abolitionist, I hope," declared Amanda. "I'll remind you that slavery is still legal in the British colonies and British commercial houses thrive in the slave trade. We own but one slave and treat him well. If we set Caesar out on his own, where would he go? How would he eat? We don't confine him yet he chooses to stay with us."

Susan forced herself to keep her mouth closed in spite of the urge to counter what to her were outrageous ideas. She decided not to provoke an argument.

Not meeting resistance, Amanda admitted, "We made it through hard years without slaves and we have only one now. At prayer meetings, Africans are among us singing hymns. It no longer seems right to own another soul in bondage."

"But Amanda, you have other servants in bondage. You bought their contracts."

"Yes, our servants are Scots. Ethan is free now and has a small cottage with a glass window and he gets a wage. Mattie has time left on her bond and cooks and washes at our house. They have clean, warm beds, we feed them well, and when they have paid off the sum we gave for their contracts, we give them money so they can start out on their own. Mattie may continue working with us for a wage, maybe to marry Ethan."

Amanda continued, "I try to live as a Christian each day, not just on Sunday. My parents lived hard lives under selfish masters and both died when I was fourteen. I worked to feed myself until my husband married me on my seventeenth birthday. Knowing what unkindness feels like, I want to be kind. Perhaps we should begin to pay Caesar a small wage and give him manumission when we pass on."

It was almost impossible for her not to comment, so Susan changed the subject. "Do you both go to Bruton Parish Church?"

The women looked at each other and Charlotte shrugged, "Amanda and I differ on religion. I attend Bruton Parish Church every Sunday."

"My husband and I come once a month to Williamsburg." Amanda explained. "We shall go to Bruton Parish Church tomorrow. We have friends there like Charlotte and her husband but we draw spiritual sustenance from the Presbyterian Meeting House. We obey the law. Our minister has a license to preach given to him at the courthouse here in Williamsburg."

"Amanda and I agree on many points. 'Tis wrenching to see families torn asunder and preachers beaten and jailed. Not all preachers are sincere and some are deluded. A man was brought to the gaol for preaching without a license. His wife sits outside the gaol crying or begging because she has naught to give him."

"What about those who practice no religion?" Susan asked.

"Without redemption they are doomed to perdition. I do not take it upon myself to judge their blindness. They are in God's hands," Amanda pronounced.

"Charlotte and I disagree and can still be friends. Men seem feeble on that point, because they have never been mothers. What Church do you attend, Susan?"

Susan, not a churchgoer, thought a moment. "I believe in tolerance and trusting the wisdom of Spirit to beckon us all to the Divine on the path that is best for us."

"You are not a preacher's wife, but you heard many a sermon haven't you?"

"Yes, but my path is a personal one. I support giving space to everyone."

The women looked puzzled. "You are not a Quaker are you?" asked Amanda.

"No, I'm not. I meant I think we should give each person the opportunity to find inspiration that is meaningful for them." Susan decided the less said the better.

The women sat quietly as Charlotte and her helper worked. Amanda took her leave and said she looked forward to seeing Susan at the ball. Charlotte held up a hand mirror for Susan to see the hair piled above her head and the ringlets beside her face and on her neck.

"I like it very much. My husband will be surprised. How much do I owe you?"

"I'm afraid our costs have gone up. It is ten pence without the powder."

Susan pulled out a smaller bill of colonial currency. "Can you take it from this?"

Charlotte looked at the bill. "Yes, we were paid in ready money for a wig this morning. She counted out the change coins carefully, checking twice, and wrote the total in the book, slowly, one digit at a time, biting her lower lip. "There!" She exhaled after the effort.

"Thank you, Charlotte. Will I see you at the ball?"

"Yes, this is my first ball. With the tension, there has been no ball at the Palace for months and until recently; my husband and I were too poor to be invited."

The door opened and Missus Byrd glided into the shop.

Susan walked slowly looking into faces of people in the street. Each had a story, a struggle. She wondered if any were her ancestors. Perhaps she had her hair done next to a relative.

Entering the Prentis Store, Susan gazed at felt hats, powder horns, prints, baskets, wooden mugs, weights to close garden gates, flasks, and fringed hunting shirts of coarse blue-green osnaberg. There were whale products from New England: whale oil for lamps, candles made from spermaceti, a wax from the head cavity of whales, strips of whale bone for corset stays, and ambergris to retard evaporation of perfumes. At the back of the store, she eyed women's clothing. Next to a rack, two women spoke about the man in the gaol for preaching without a license. She recognized one as Missus Powell. A slave woman stood behind them, well practiced in being non-intrusive.

Susan looked over the dresses and picked a pink one she liked for everyday wear but saw nothing for the Governor's Ball. Then it occurred to her that if they were stuck there for a while, she should get something for John and Peter so they fit in better. She looked at men's clothing and picked out hats and hunting shirts.

Loaded down with packages, incongruous for a woman with such elegant hair, Susan made her way down the street toward the Capitol and home. "Hi Mom!" Megan appeared from a shop door. "Wow! What... an amazing hairdo! Are you going to the Academy Awards tonight?"

"I'm going to the Governor's Ball tonight and got my hair done. I have tickets for your dad and me. I thought you'd prefer not to go. I've done some serious shopping following your example of dressing to fit the times. You always told me I was living in the past."

"I had no idea you were so good at it. Can I help carry those packages?"

"That would be nice, Honey. There is another favor I would like to ask."

"I'll do anything short of actual help."

"I'm hunting for a bargain on a gown and I have a hunch where to look. Would you buy us lunch and meet us all back at the house. I'll give you the money."

"Getting lunch will be fun. Let me treat using the colonial currency Dad gave me."

"I'm glad I had children." Susan hugged Megan and hurried to the milliner shop. There in the window crossed-legged on his board was the bushy-browed tailor. She was excited to see him and tapped the window. He waved back and she entered.

"Hello again. I'm happy to find you in."

"You might find me here at any time," said the tailor with a knowing look. "During the high season we are open seven days a week during business hours."

"Good. I have a problem and I hope you can help me. I'm going to the Governor's Ball."

"That does not seem like a grave problem, Madam."

"The problem is I need a dress and I remembered you were working on a gown for someone to wear at a ball. Is that gown already promised to someone?"

"No one has come forward as yet. Perhaps, Madam, I was working on that gown for you. It is not completely finished so if you would like it, you may try it on for a final fitting and I can have a perfect fit ready for you in about five hours. Would you like the mantua to wear against the brisk evening air and stun the overly proud ladies of the large estates?"

"Oh, that beautiful cape with the embroidered trim! I can't afford it." She stopped as the tailor smiled. "Oh. You said if I had come in 1775, the mantua would cost a few pounds."

"I did — six pounds to be exact. It has been waiting for the perfect customer."

"I'll take the gown and the mantua. I have bills and coins of several countries."

"Rather inconvenient how the British attempt to increase our dependence on them by forbidding us to have our own currency and limiting the supply of theirs to a trickle. It makes commerce difficult and ingenuity inevitable."

"I agree and I have a question for you."

"I am a tailor and do not know physics, mathematics, or time and the like."

"My question is, what is your name? I am Susan Sinclair."

"Ha! 'Tis my turn to be surprised. I find my name embarrassing."

"Why embarrassing?"

"Alwyn means 'friend to the elves.' I was short and other children teased me. Taylor means tailor. It seems my height and my trade were preordained."

"Alwyn Taylor is a charming name. Speaking of charm, I have another question. Since you became a tailor as a result of your last name, did you become a friend to the elves because of your first?"

"Susan. I have yet to meet my first elf, assuming of course you are not a tall one. You could be a tall elf. It is a rare thing to meet a customer at this time."

Susan smiled. The tailor was mum about the mystery of being in the past, and probably did not know how it worked. Nevertheless, it was a relief to know that she had seen him in her time and now in the colonial era and he was clearly enjoying it.

Alwyn smiled. "I'll take a break from being the window dressing to alter the gown for you." He measured Susan and then marked the gown with a chip of soap and pinned the fabric, which he called tissue, in a score of places. "I'll have it ready at five."

"In what year?" joked Susan.

"Today, in time for the ball, I promise."

"Alwyn, I have another problem."

"Oh dear, Madam Susan, you certainly seem to be beset with them today."

"Yes, it's been dreadful! This time it's my shoes."

The tailor looked down. "Ah yes, verily you have an acute problem there but providentially one that has a ready solution. Three blocks down is a shoemaker's shop. Alas, George Wilson died last fall, but Elias, his Scots-Irish journeyman and a capable cobbler, bought the shop from George's widow. Tell him I sent you."

"Thank you Alwyn. Goodbye until this afternoon."

"God be with you, too."

"I forgot goodbye means that."

Day 2-5:   Megan at the Market

As Megan approached Market Square, her thoughts turned to Mark the blacksmith. She expected he was getting ready to escape again and guessed Standing Elk would help him. She veered suddenly to avoid walking head long into a man carrying a wooden crate of fresh eggs. Dodging him, she collided into a woman holding a basket of vegetables and a leather pail half-full of fresh milk. The woman cried out in surprise and dropped the pail splashing milk on both their dresses and the pants of the man carrying the eggs.

"I'm terribly sorry!" Megan squatted to grab the leather pail before it was completely empty, saving a ladle or two of the milk. "I was not paying attention."

The woman looked stricken. "Oh, I spilt the milk! My children hav'na had a cup for days. My husband just spent six days cutting firewood. He will be displeased."

"Your kids are hungry?" Megan had to do something. "Sorry, it was my fault. Let's go back to where you bought the milk and buy more."

"But my last coin was spent on wilted vegetables."

"I'll buy the milk. I bumped into you. I've... been fortunate and I have coins."

"But your dress, Madam and your pants, Sir..."

"We'll give them a rinse," the man holding the box of eggs assured her. "Don't worry, Missus. 'Tis kind of the young miss to buy milk for you. How many children have ye?"

"We've three, Sir, three living."

"Both my hands are full with this box but Missy could you take six eggs for the Missus, one each for her husband and children, one for her and one for the pan."

"Oh, no, I couldn't, Sir!"

"Missus, it will take me more than six eggs to repay the miracle of my angel mother feeding my brother and me in a hut after our pa was killed. Please accept and help me happily make this payment on my debt."

"God bless you, Sir. You are a kind of angel yourself."

Megan carefully put eggs into the woman's basket.

"I must be off to the inn, and Missus, we are not stealing eggs. My master told me to buy a shillings worth of eggs. I struck a bargain for a dozen extra. My master is getting half a dozen more and he will be happy. Farewell, ladies."

Megan took the woman's arm and they pressed into the dense crowd in Market Square. Holding tightly to keep from being separated, she muttered, "Did absolutely everybody forget their deodorant this morning? Somebody ought to tell them to wash!"

The market ran every day but Sundays and holy days. Live sheep, pigs, and cows were tethered to stakes, chickens and ducks squawked from baskets as hawkers shouted. Slaughtered animals hung from tripods—quarters of beef, sheep, and pigs. Megan was revolted by flies gathering to drink at the bloody spots until vendors waved them away. Plucked chickens hung by their feet, heads swinging. Live oysters from Chesapeake Bay, dried fish, fresh fish, and, by the odor, not-so-fresh fish, wrinkled carrots, potatoes, and beets stored all winter in root cellars were piled on rough tables. Eggs that had been carried in boxes of sand to keep from breaking over rough roads were neatly stacked.

Megan and the woman came to a stall where milk was ladled into whatever container the customers brought. Megan greeted the dairywoman. "We had an accident and I would like to buy more milk for this woman."

"I remember you, Ma'am. Seven ladles wasn't it?"

To Megan, prices were low and she could help this woman and her family for pennies. "There are still about two ladles in there — let's buy another seven ladles to give her more."

"Shall we make it eight for the price of six? She has hungry ones at home."

Megan surveyed the goods on the table. "Very kind of you, Madam. I'll buy her some butter and two packets of cheese curds. She will be making eggs."

The poor woman's eyes showed surprise. "Bless you both for your kindness."

"I shall tie a piece of twine tight around the neck of the leather bag using a slip knot you can easily undo," said the dairy woman. "If the pail falls again you won't lose the milk."

Megan thought about lunch. "I'd like two packets of the cheese myself. There will be three hungry mouths to feed at my house."

"Remarkable for one so young," the dairy woman marveled.

"Yes, I'm young. And even more remarkable, those hungry mouths are older than I am. This is lunch for my mother, father, and brother."

A smile found its way to the thin woman's face. "You are a kind daughter."

Megan paid for the milk and cheese and walked with the woman to the edge of the market. Getting over her aversion to the crowds, noise, and smells, she looked closer at the faces of the sellers and buyers. "Are you and your husband bonded servants?" she asked the woman who still held her arm.

"No. I wish we could find a station having shelter and food we could rely on."

"How did you get to the Virginia Colony?"

"I was born here. My Ma died at my birth and Pa died when I was fourteen. He finished his servitude, but had no luck as a planter. My man, I should not say but you are kind, came to North Carolina as a prisoner at fifteen for stealing bread for his widowed mum in Brighton. His master took him to clear land in the Piedmont near the Great Wagon Road. After he served two years, a gang of men killed his master and his wife while my husband was off searching out a lost pig. They burned the house, shed, and his cabin and left.

"My man found the bones of the couple in the ashes and buried them with what prayers he could remember. They were almost the only folk he had seen for two years. He cried and stayed there a few days. He wanted to tell someone but folk would not believe a former convict and he feared suspicion so he wandered off. When he came into the Tidewater, no one knew him and there was no record of his bond so he was free. He took work as he could find it.

"He found me after Pa died. I was fifteen and he was eighteen. We picked worms together alongside slaves in the fields or worked at drying time for food and a place to sleep. When our first baby came, we built a shelter but our baby died. We had other babies. My man has not abandoned us these five years, providing as well as he can. God bless you, Miss."

Megan worked her way back into the crowded market. Some vendors were animated and engaged with the passersby. At those tables was a sense of abundance and activity. At tables holding only tired root vegetables or spring greens wilted beyond freshness, the sellers were not hopeful this late in the market day. Megan sensed desperation.

She purchased biscuits, smoked ham after sniffing the meat, a jar of wild mulberry jam, and carrots with life left in them. From a vendor with a heavy German accent, she bought a bottle of "apfel cidah." From a wiry man who reminded her of the runaway, Simon, she bought an earthenware pot of honey sealed with beeswax. She felt a deep disquiet. What will happen to the people who don't sell much? They will eat their own stuff but they have no money to buy other things. Who will help if they fail completely? She had never seen deep poverty before nor thought much about it. Now it was right in front of her.

Megan came to a table displaying nothing but dusty root vegetables. A woman stood up with a spark of expectation on her tired face. Megan thought the woman was younger than Susan, but life had been hard. She pulled out two coins. "What could I get for this much?" she asked, showing the woman the money.

"For ready money, Ma'am, I can give an ox bone for stock, and greens to boil."

"Thanks, that will be..."

"Parsnips, radishes to pep it up, a beet, potatoes, and salt to make it savory."

"You have just given me the whole recipe. I will take all those things."

The woman wrapped the goods in a sheet from an old gazette and tied a piece of string around the bundle. "Thank you for your custom, Miss. I put in an extra beet root for ye."

On the edge of the square, a woman sat on a worn blanket by a pile of wild green onions. She had acorns in another pile and some dried mushrooms. Where the last woman had seemed tired, this one seemed frightened. She was skinny, her skin dry from sun and wind, and about Megan's age. "What would be good in soup?" Megan asked her.

"This wild onion gives flavor. I shelled and soaked these acorns in ash water for three days to get out bitterness. The mushrooms are from fallen trees and dried in the sun. An Indian woman taught me how. These tiny leaves from a pond are duckweed. All are good in soup."

Megan offered a small coin. "How much could I get for this?"

The vendors were used to customers with no cash. They bartered one foodstuff for another or exchanged what they had for a candle or a spoon—whatever the person had. Megan's coin got her a small bundle of each item and brought a rare moment of relief to the woman. "Are you a servant?" Megan asked.

"No, I am my own person. I have not found a master."

"Where do you live?" Megan asked.

"I live where I am, Ma'am, as best as I can. I hope to find a station. Last winter was hard."

"I have more carrots than I need. I'll give you two for your lunch. I wish you well, Miss."

On the way home, Megan passed a skinny horse and three shorn sheep foraging on sandy ground in a fenced yard. She tossed the most wilted greens, carrot tops, and half the duck weed over the fence. The animals approached and immediately began to eat her offerings.

Back home she got a pot of water, made a fire, rinsed the ox bone and put it into the pot to start simmering as she washed and cubed the potatoes, parsnips, carrots, and beets.

Day 2-6: Picnic Lunch at Home

"Hi, Mom! That's an amazing hairdo. Looks like you've done some serious shopping." Megan was busy in the kitchen. I bought ham, cheese, and biscuits and I'm making soup. I boiled the bone, salt, root vegetables, and acorns then moved it away from the flame to let it simmer. I'll add the green stuff just before we eat it."

"Sounds great, Megan. Where did you get the recipe?"

"A woman in the market sold me ingredients and told me what to do. Remember the story of the soldiers and the stone soup? We're having stone-free soup!"

"Good. Now I can go off duty in the kitchen and you can take over."

"Mom, that guy I met, Mark the blacksmith—he didn't seem to be reenacting."

"The indentured servant—I remember you mentioned him. How is he doing?"

"I haven't gone over there, yet. I think Mark was planning to run away. Hardly anyone makes it. People without work can have a harder time than servants."

"Mark is his name?"

"Uh-huh."

John came into the house. "I just saw Thomas Jefferson, Patrick Henry, and James Madison today in the Raleigh Tavern. Wow... that's quite a hairdo!"

"I hope you like it. I wanted to surprise you. I got tickets to the Governor's Ball tonight. We have not danced in I don't know how long. How many had you had when you saw those Founding Fathers, Honey?"

"I had a second cup of coffee before they walked in."

"In college I drank coffee while studying for history exams. Founding Fathers appeared then, too. Did you learn anything about how to get back to our time?"

"No, did you guys?"

"Not yet, John. Megan was telling me about the blacksmith she met."

"Yeah. This guy, his name is Mark, may run away. Runaways usually stay close to home to get food or help from friends. They usually get caught."

"What about his contract? If someone paid his passage, Mark owes him money."

"I don't care if it's legal or not. It's wrong. You condone indentured servitude?"

The door flew open and Peter stepped in. "What happened to you, Mom?"

"Good to see you too, Peter." Susan walked to the door. "When you left this morning we did not realize we were in 1775. How did you get along?"

"He's fine." Megan persisted, "Why do you think it's fair for Mark to be stuck as a servant even though he's had years added to his term as punishment?"

"Mark who?" asked Peter.

"The blacksmith I told you about."

"Megan, people should not have to work involuntarily and maybe the contract was unfair, but if you help him escape he could get into a worse situation."

"I'm worried he might run away and get caught or get killed like the guy who ran past me yesterday, Dad. I'd like to help him not make a big mistake."

"That's a worthy goal, Megan. Who knows why we're here? However, we should not change the course of history."

"If we change something we might go home to find Sylvester Stallone never was elected Governor of Pennsylvania." The others stared at Peter. "Just kidding."

"Megan made ham and cheese sandwiches, and the soup is ready."

Peter opened the back door. "Let's have lunch in the garden."

John and Peter moved benches and a table near the well. "Dad, I saw a gang of slaves in a field this morning watched by an overseer. It was depressing."

"It took a big struggle to get rid of the abomination of slavery in this country," John said. "Some people have willful blindness to injustice."

When they all sat down, John used a pocketknife to pull the cork from a bottle. "Whew, this is potent stuff! What did you buy?"

"The guy called it 'apfel' cidah. Wouldn't that be apple cider?"

"Yes, but it's fermented like strong wine. Do we have anything sweet?"

"I bought honey at the market, Dad."

John poured a little cider for everyone and added a bit honey and lots of water.

"This drink is refreshing," said Susan.

"What are these little leaves floating in the soup?" asked Peter. "They're good."

"Duck weed. I fed half to animals on the way home. Who knew it was good? I made a poor woman happy by buying her stuff."

Susan pulled out her surprises and handed John and Peter the tricorn hats and hunting shirts. "You guys are embarrassing Megan and me. This stuff should help you fit in if we're stuck here a while." She pretended she was not worried.

John and Peter changed shirts. "Now we won't scare the neighbors," said Peter.

Megan decided that even though her dad was less stressed than he had been in the morning, she would not bring up what she had learned about the taxes.

"This afternoon I need to find a way to get us out of here," John said. "I felt time slow down in wars, but never anything like this. I don't understand it."

"Don't forget the ball at the Governor's Palace tonight. Wait 'till you see the dress I bought. The tailor is working on it. Here is the cape. It's called a mantua."

"It's very nice."

After John left, Megan said, "Dad seemed in a hurry to get out of here. He mentioned the army more today than I ever heard him in my life."

"He's fine, kids."

"OK, Mom, I'm ready to take off. Did you find the lady you worried about?"

"Not since church last night, Megan. I need to find her."

Day 2-7:   John at St. George Tucker House

John explored the streets of Williamsburg for an hour, hoping to unearth a shard of understanding about their inconceivable slide into to the past. In Market Square, bustling earlier in the day, a few tired vendors tended their sparse tables. The barter and banter had dwindled as farmers, craftspeople, and merchants dispersed toward home or, if sales had been good, to join friends in a nearby tavern.

He lingered near groups of people, listening for any hint that would make sense of this impossible situation. In front of a store, men in a crowd shrouded in a cloud of tobacco smoke complained about the non-importation agreements. "If our smithies are so damn good, why is there almost nothing on Greenhow's shelves where iron goods should be?"

"And who can afford whiskey?" asked a man who stitched harnesses.

"I don't drink away my money," scoffed a man in fine wool jacket.

"He brought money from England, that one," a man beside John muttered, "enough for a horse, a pair of oxen, two slaves to clear his land, and the contract of a woman to cook and wash so his wife won't harden her hands."

"How did he do that?" asked John.

"He is the third son of a landed family. The first son will inherit the estate and the second went into the church. The old man gave this one a sum as a wedding present to start life here. They plan to ship tobacco to England to increase the family fortune. However, as a recent arrival, he could only find a large tract of fertile land far above the fall line where the river is not navigable to the sea. He has the added expense of transporting tobacco to the ships."

The man shook his head. "My old man died coughing when I was nine, and when me mum died five years later, I shipped over here in Pa's old clothes to find my fortune. My auntie sewed ten shillings into the waist of my trousers. 'For your future wife and baby,' she told me. Though I shall never see her again, I am grateful. My uncle paid half my passage and I got a bargain of two years service to pay the balance. I was free at sixteen, better off than most new arrivals. Did your father leave you land or lucre?"

"My dad is eighty and still fit."

"Astonishing! A rare bit o' luck. I wish you the same longevity."

"May you also live long and prosper."

The voice of John Randolph, Attorney General of Virginia, boomed from a porch next door. "Gentlemen, let us not be rash. In the House of Lords, William Pitt proposed withdrawing British troops, and recognition of the Continental Congress's authority to levy taxes. The Intolerable Acts would be suspended. When this proposal wins in Parliament, we'll have our rights without war."

"Dear John," another voice resounded, "we respect thee as we do thy brother Peyton. At your Tazewell Hall, we admired the tones of your violin. But Pitt's motion failed and more troops are under sail. They cast the die and we are resolute. Our grandchildren may shake their heads in sad wonder of how we came so close to resolving this in peace. We pray they will be wiser than we."

The Attorney General answered, "If we threatened each other wielding knives, friends would pull us apart. However, nations taken by similar madness send young men to kill the youth of another nation. All march to a charnel ground under the arrogant misconception that to negotiate signals weakness. How do sane men become so mad in groups? After great loss to the people and great wealth to those who sell cannon and black powder, nations build monuments to the sacrifice of fallen heroes and praise God for triumphs that brought misery upon others. Those monuments represent the failure of leadership.

"My friends, if not reversed, that defeat of Pitt's motion will live in history as a failure of civilized man. I will close Tazewell Hall and sail to England soon with my family to do all in my power to seek a peaceful outcome. I will correspond with Thomas Jefferson and others here. I pray we can untie this knotted problem."

"Three cheers for John Randolph," called out a man. John noted the huzzahs were less spirited than the cheers for Peyton Randolph.

Even under his tricorn hat, John felt dehydrated. He rested in the shade of a large sycamore north of the market. "Maintenance of the objective." He reminded himself to seek a way to his own time. The walk along hot, sandy streets evoked veiled memories and he grew edgy. He had been nineteen, barely older than Megan. He squinted at the sun, "At least you didn't take us to the desert or tropics.

"Enough of this!" He stood up. "I'm going back to my own time to get a lemonade." On the north side of Nicholson Street, he glimpsed someone entering a house on a broad lawn enclosed by a white picket fence. A small sign by the gate read St. George Tucker House and John assumed it was a tavern. He opened the gate and walked up the path.

He stepped through the door. A woman looked up. "It certainly is hot out there."

Looking down at his disheveled state, John realized the woman was wearing modern clothing, and suddenly he was as out of place in this air-conditioned place as he had been on the street. He weakly returned her smile. "Uh... yes it is. Pardon me, but is there a rest room here?"

"The Tucker House is a rest stop for donors to the Colonial Williamsburg Foundation. We have sitting rooms, refreshments, and a library. Are you a donor?"

"No, but I would like to support this place."

"Well, when you get back from the restroom you can sign the registration book."

John hurried to the men's room where he splashed water on his face, looked into the mirror, and struggled to get oriented. Returning to the entrance, he made a contribution. The woman directed him to a salon. "Would you like lemonade?"

"Amazing! I mean, thank you."

He looked over the books interspersed on shelves with reproductions of colonial period porcelain. He chose two books and sat in a comfortable chair to skim them, occasionally shaking his head in disbelief at his experiences this morning.

He read that at sixteen, George Washington found a benefactor in a distant cousin. Thomas Lord Fairfax, the Sixth Earl of Cameron, had a domain of over five million acres in Northern Virginia when he employed young George as a surveyor. The only British Lord living in the colonies was a rare mentor for an ambitious young man at a time when land ownership was the path to wealth and power.

Lord Fairfax's predecessor and namesake, Thomas Lord Fairfax, the Third Earl of Cameron, commanded Parliament's army against the Royalists. Parliament worried that King Charles I sought absolute power so they overthrew and beheaded him. Four months later, the third Lord Fairfax put down a mutiny by 'Levelers' who had the audacity to declare all men were equal! He then retired with a generous pension. His second in command, Oliver Cromwell, became the Lord Protector. What a perfect role model Lord Fairfax was for young Washington!

In the French and Indian War, Washington rode with Braddock to the terrible defeat by the Indians in the Battle of the Monongahela. Washington had several bullets through his clothing and said he was saved by the "all-powerful dispensations of Providence." John smiled at the irony. Survivors of a battle might believe they had Divine protection, but if some of them were killed a week later in another firefight, survivors of that engagement thought the same thing. John shuddered. He could have been face down in the field and Danny Adamson or Sergeant Sargon could be here sipping lemonade, trying to figure out a flashback to the colonial period – maybe thinking about him.

A man in a sweat-spotted blue shirt and button-pulling paunch sat down hard in an armchair beside him. "Warm out there! I'm too old for hiking in the sun."

"I got hot and parched myself." John wanted to read but he was being polite.

"I'm from Shepherdstown, West Virginia," said the man proudly. "It was chartered in 1762, here in Williamsburg. My ancestor William Crawford came here on business just before the Revolution. We have a letter that mentions a GW. Grandpa told us GW was George Washington."

"What was the business?"

"Land. He was registering claims. There was something secretive about it – maybe rival claims. There were no problems at the home farm – it's still in the family. I brought the grandkids here to show 'em where William Crawford, their great-great – I don't know how many greats – grandfather, came so long ago."

"It's good you were able to keep in touch with your family history."

"Yeah. I'm in real estate just like my ancestor, so it's in the genes." The sweating man welcomed a glass of sweet iced tea from a volunteer. "I sell vacation homes along the Shenandoah. It's not easy to get permits near the George Washington National Forest but William Crawford had trouble with claims, too. History around here was all about real estate."

"I'm starting to get that idea."

"In the old days, surveyors used a rod sixteen and a half feet long. Four rods make a sixty-six foot chain. A tract two chains by five is an acre. People know there are 640 acres in a square mile but no one remembers what an acre is. Did you know George Washington made a fortune surveying land before he married a rich widow and doubled his holdings? Our Founding Fathers knew rods and chains."

"Sounds like they did."

The man continued, "Bees make hives, birds make nests, and people make buildings. I ought to hang a rod and a chain over the fireplace since they've been good for my family. Well, I should go make my grandson let his brother out of the stocks."

"Good talking with you."

John read that at the end of the French and Indian War, in the 1763 Treaty of Paris, Great Britain gained Quebec and French territory west of the Appalachians. From Spain, Britain won East Florida on the Atlantic and West Florida, on the Gulf Coast of what are now Florida, Mississippi, Alabama, and Eastern Louisiana.

He felt a presence and looked up. "Hello, Ma'am."

A thin dark-haired woman smiled at him. "Oh, Hello, I'm Frances."

"I'm John. Sorry, I did not hear you come in. Are you a docent?"

"I am a caretaker. You are reading about land in the West. You know the second half of that interesting story but maybe you never knew the first half."

"I would like to hear it."

"The house closes soon. I am afraid there is no time today. Can you come back?"

"I will. I'll use your plumbing again before going back to colonial times."

"There has been progress. Williamsburg these days seems miraculous to me."

When John stepped onto the street outside the gate, he was back in the Virginia Colony in 1775. "I've got to figure out how this works," he said to no one.

It was almost supper time. John absorbed the sights, sounds, and scents of clothing on the lines, shacks, and shanties on every side street, smoke curling from chimneys, and a metallic odor as he passed the blacksmith shop. Recalling the kindly woman in the St. George Tucker House and her smile, he was less tense, knowing his family was not stuck in the past.

Day 2-8:   Susan at the Shoemaker and Randolph House

Susan and Megan strolled along Duke of Gloucester Street to the shoemaker's shop. Inside, a young bearded man worked on a pair of men's shoes. He greeted them. "A pleasant afternoon to you. How might I help you this fine day?"

"A fine afternoon to you as well. Would ye be Elias, then?"

He was surprised by Susan's accent, "Are ye Irish? How do ye know my name?"

"My name is Susan Sinclair. Me grandmother was from Belfast, and both me grandfathers descend from the Scots-Irish. Alwyn the tailor said you might solve my problem regarding the Governor's Ball." She pointed to her shoes.

"And who is this lovely colleen here, your sister?"

"This is my daughter, Megan. But no use saying you thought she was my sister because I've already decided to buy shoes even before you resorted to flattery."

"You caught me. I have three pair of ladies shoes made. I hope one fits, as there is no time to make a pair. I promised the shoes I'm working on to Carter Braxton for the ball. His old ones gave him bunions. See, I've got them stretching on a last a half size larger than his regular shoes. Braxton hopes the soft deerskin lining will make him a better dancer."

"Oh, Elias, I need a pair of magic shoes that make me a better dancer!"

"I'd love to sell you a pair, but alas, no leprechauns are here to make them."

When the shoemaker placed the three pairs of fine ladies' shoes on the floor and Susan slipped off her sneakers, it was obvious one pair was too small and another pair too big, so she tried on the remaining pair. "These fit perfectly. I'll dance in them at the ball."

"Wonderful. Shall I wrap them?"

"No thanks. I'll carry them in this bag." Susan paid for the shoes and the shoemaker picked up an awl and with a smile, bent to his work on Carter Braxton's dancing shoes.

Strolling along Nicholson Street past the St. George Tucker House, Susan and Megan were unaware that centuries later, John was inside drinking a second glass of lemonade. They came to the red house from which Peyton Randolph had left for Philadelphia. A woman at the gate said "Welcome, Ladies. Are you here to join Missus Randolph for a chat?"

"Mother..." Megan used that appellation for the first time in months, "I have errands I need to do. I will see you back at the house before dinner."

"You'll probably get to the shops in time to find some real bargains."

"I hope so. See you later."

Susan entered the Randolph House and with other guests, was given a tour of the elegant home. The hall and main stairwell were decorated with bold wallpaper in a pattern of columns, arches, and belvederes bedecked in garlands and large flower filled vases. Upstairs, in dark wood-paneled bedrooms, large four-poster beds had fully curtained canopies to protect against drafts and mosquitoes.

Downstairs, Susan admired the dining table, set with fine china and silver. She peeked into Peyton Randolph's office. On a worktable were candles, spectacles, a quill pen, and a long clay pipe lying there as if he had stepped away a moment rather than for eternity.

In a large salon were portraits of Randolph and his wife Betty Harrison Randolph. Susan thought the reenactor yesterday and the costume and makeup people had created a close likeness of Peyton. She was taken aback as two ladies entered the room. Betty Randolph looked as if she had stepped out of the painting.

"Lovely to see you, ladies." Betty Randolph was a study in poise. "May I present my niece, Lucy Randolph Burwell. I hope you enjoyed your tour of our home. My husband inherited this house from his father, Sir John Randolph, the only native Virginian knighted by the King. 'Tis lonely when my husband is at the Congress in Philadelphia. You may have noticed he occupies considerable space, so without him here we have more room for guests."

"Will you be going to Philadelphia to visit him, Missus Randolph?"

"I should like to see Philadelphia. My husband says it is twelve times bigger than Williamsburg and the third largest city in the English-speaking world. Alas, the affairs of this household are too burdensome to leave for any length of time, what with servants and supplies to manage and meals to oversee."

One of the guests asked, "Missus Randolph, I heard a Baptist preacher is in the gaol and will be tried in court for preaching without a license. What are your views on religious tolerance and the new practices some call the Great Awakening?"

"This problem concerns me. Too much freedom to express whatever comes to mind leads to chaos, as I am sure you agree. Unschooled men are saying the Lord called them to preach. They incite servants and gather up people's money. They are called more by their purses than by the Lord. Maintenance of order and prosperity are important. The man in gaol will be treated fairly and his punishment will serve as a lesson to others that the Church of England provides the proper way for English people to worship."

Susan was shocked by Betty Randolph's views on religion. The Established Church helped keep power in the hands of those who already held power and privilege. Susan's musings were interrupted by the Randolphs' niece, Lucy.

"Dear Aunt Betty, I am unsettled by the discord in our community. I listen to Uncle Peyton, Uncle John, and my husband endlessly debate about it. We, who are established, hold power and economic privilege in one hand, while in the other hand we withhold freedom and prosperity. The poor face danger and sometimes lack food for their children. Is it surprising they seek emotional expressions of their relation to God? The Established Church and established society bring people outside the establishment neither prosperity nor comfort. Were not our grandfathers rough-hewn like people coming on the ships?"

"Lucy, those rough-hewn men educated their sons and their sons began to educate their daughters so they could be articulate in their impertinence. We provide work for freemen and bondsmen. Our commerce sustains countless families here and in England. Our husbands are leaders. Many of those men of integrity now gather in Philadelphia to ponder affairs of all the colonies."

"Auntie, our families have contributed and our efforts have been compensated, but the word 'integrity' does not portray all acts in pursuit of prosperity."

"Whatever do you mean, Lucy Burwell?"

"Well, we could begin in 1766 with the death of John Robinson, long-time speaker of the House of Burgesses and treasurer of the Colony of Virginia."

"We don't speak of him any longer, Lucy!"

"He was a close friend and we need to understand unseen currents underlying today's instability. Robinson took a fortune of £100,000 in currency due to be burned by the treasury and lent it to his prominent friends in the Tidewater."

"Lucy!"

"I won't mention all names, but I can say the Burwells, of which I now am one, and many others, secretly owe large amounts to Robinson's estate."

"Lucy, you are talking about a horrid scandal that is behind us now since John Robinson died nine years ago, may he rest in peace."

"And important families are grateful he rests in discreet silence. The affair is not behind us. Many well-known Virginians still have burdensome debts to the Robinson estate, which in turn is in hopeless debt to the colony. William Byrd III, of the Governor's Council, had a debt of £15,000. Archibald Cary, a member of the very committee formed to resolve the Robinson estate, borrowed £7,500 so he is more interested in keeping the problem quiet than in solving it."

"Lucy, stop!"

"This is important, Aunt Betty. The corruption is kept secret or the leaders will lose their positions. The people abhor such hypocrisy. The men at the pinnacle of Virginia society were aware the money should have been burned. I grant that Richard Henry Lee with his debt of twelve pounds and Patrick Henry who owed only eleven may have been innocent of complicity, but it will be another fifteen years before the large debts are cleared."

"How could you possibly know such things, Lucy?"

"A member of the committee to resolve the debt often visited Kingsmill. When he over-drank, which was on every visit, he strutted like a peacock displaying a fantail of gossip of the underbelly of our society. He had dipped his hand into the public coffer. Last year, after gambling away his family fortune trying to clear his debt, he took an overdose of laudanum to escape his failures in the oblivion of death. His shamed and penniless widow lost the plantation."

"That is quite enough, Lucy Burwell. Our guests must think the subject tiresome. I surely find it so. I don't understand currency or operations of the treasury."

To the contrary, Susan found it shocking that leading Virginia families benefited from embezzlement and covered it up for two decades. As their carriages rolled past the shacks of hungry people, could the gentry not see? A network of cousins and friends held the reins of government, church, and economy. It was a puzzle to Susan how our democracy was born from a culture with so much injustice woven into its fabric. We have not solved the problem in our time either, she thought. Missus Randolph would be relieved to know that centuries later almost no one knew of the secret corruption and those who took the money have streets and schools named after them still.

Betty Randolph was obviously displeased and brought the salon to an end. Lucy would get a stern talking to when the guests departed even though she had not mentioned the Randolphs. The shameful secret gnawed at the security and privilege of this family as well. Missus Randolph feared worry over this matter would kill her husband. Had nervousness not contributed to his gluttony? When she learned the secret, she had tossed in bed and kicked at her covers. If it became public, they would be humiliated and, if forced to pay promptly, bankrupt. The specters of shame and ruin constantly pressed her like a vise.

Lucy stepped to the door to say goodbye to the visitors.

"I learned a lot from your account, Missus Burwell."

"I am afraid I badly overstepped the bounds of social correctness."

"Being socially correct is not as high a calling as having the integrity to tell the truth, however uncomfortable that is. It is a challenge to know when and where to say what must be said. You made your aunt uncomfortable but you gave us the truth and I thank you."

"I am grateful for your frankness. May I ask your name?"

"My name is Susan Sinclair, and it is a pleasure to meet you, Lucy Burwell."

Susan stepped out with time to spare before supper. She shook off her reaction to the scandal and focused on happy things including a fine gown waiting to be picked up. She had not been this excited about a dress since her wedding. She spotted a woman in a brown cloak walking at a distance, quickened her pace, and dodged people coming the other way. This was her chance! Losing ground to the woman in the cloak, she veered into the street, looked to see no carriages were coming, lifted her dress to her shins, and jogged a block to catch up.

"Excuse me! Jane?" The woman turned. It was the gaoler's wife.

"Oh, I'm sorry! I thought you were someone else."

"At times I wished to be someone else but I'm me and shall make the best of it."

"We may as well be who we are," panted Susan. "Sorry to bother you." She continued to the milliner's shop to pick up her gown, wondering if she would ever encounter Jane in 1775.

Day 2-9:   Peter at the Library

Peter took a different road north toward the quarter where Augustus lived. Looking down a street to the right he was surprised to see the opening of a tunnel. He could see a path through trees at the other end and felt compelled to walk through. The path beyond ran by a stream and a copse of trees. He followed it into bright sunlight. He squinted and heard a screech. He jumped back and gasped, "A car!"

The car was only going ten miles per hour at the entrance to a parking lot when the driver hit the brakes. He opened the window. "Are you all right? You had good reactions there."

"I'm fine. The sun was in my eyes and I didn't see you, sorry."

The driver did not guess the extent of Peter's surprise. "I'm afraid the library is closed on weekends. Is that where you were going?"

By the entrance, a sign read John D. Rockefeller Jr. Library Parking. "Uh... yes, the library."

The driver thought Peter might be in mild shock. "Look, I've got to do some work and there's a group in there in a workshop. Why don't you come in and read while I work."

"Great!" said Peter brightening up. "I would like to research slavery," he added.

"Give me a second to park and I'll let us in the side door. I'm Joe, by the way."

"Peter."

Joe let them into the building and led Peter to a reading area. "Soda, juice?"

"Do you have any orange juice?"

"Sure, I'll get you a can from the machine. What do you want to research?"

Peter was confused to find himself in his own time. "I'm... researching slavery and would like to know how slaves got manumission. Also, since there was no Underground Railroad in colonial times, how could slaves escape?"

"Have you heard of Dunmore's 1775 Proclamation? All slaves and indentured servants belonging to owners in rebellion were freed if they took up arms on behalf of the King."

"Wow! I would be very interested to read about that."

"I'll get your juice and help you pick out something. That will give me ten minutes to procrastinate before finishing off this budget I need to complete."

Peter looked at the bookshelves. Filing cabinets held information on the history and contents of each building managed by the Colonial Williamsburg Foundation.

Joe came back with two cans of juice and pulled a book off a shelf for Peter. "You'll find much of what you are looking for in here. The men's room is down the hall and if you need anything, I'll be in my office—the one with the open door."

"Thanks, Joe."

Peter sipped cold orange juice as he read that John Murray, Earl of Dunmore, the last British Governor of Virginia, abandoned Williamsburg in June, 1775. From a ship off Norfolk, he ordered attacks on rebel towns. In November, he issued what became known as Dunmore's Proclamation. Peter was excited to read:

> " I do hereby declare all indentured servants, negroes, or others, (appertaining to rebels), free that are able and willing to bear arms, they joining His MAJESTY'S Troops as soon as may be, for the more speedily reducing this Colony to a proper sense of their duty."

Men, women, and children from rebel and loyal plantations had streamed toward Norfolk seeking freedom. "That's it!" Peter said aloud. However, he read on to learn that the real British intent was not freedom for slaves but rather, to break the revolutionary leaders economically. The fate of most slaves who joined the British was tragic. Many died of illness or fighting. Some were captured and sold. Some voluntarily returned to their masters because they had nowhere else to go. Despite those dangers and snares, of one hundred thousand escaped slaves, as many as ten thousand made it to freedom in Europe, Africa, or the northern colonies.

Peter reflected on the risks of altering the past. "I could change one thing and that might mean I was never born, or the Continental Army lost the Revolution." He took a sip of juice. "Maybe it's safe to help people do what they want to do. I won't persuade Evie to run if she doesn't want to." He heard Joe walking up the hall. "I made progress on my budget. How is your research going?"

"I'm learning lots! I hope you don't mind that I took copy paper for notes."

"Not at all. Glad this was helpful for you. I'll be ready to go in ten minutes. Just leave the books on that trolley and a librarian will put them away Monday morning. They're careful around here about getting history in the right order."

Peter said goodbye to Joe in the parking lot and walked to the opening of the tunnel under some railroad tracks. He stopped. Now that he had knowledge of Dunmore's Proclamation, would he return to 1775 through the tunnel or stay in his own time with only a memory of strange experiences? He felt a pull toward the tunnel.

"What do you want?" He heard his own voice within. He clearly wanted to return to 1775 and help Evie and her sons find a way to freedom. The pull to the tunnel became insistent. He stepped out of the sunlight and strode to the other end of the tunnel, where the scent of wood smoke immediately struck him. Two men rode horses across his path fifty yards ahead. He walked into town without looking back.

Day 2-10:   Megan Shops for Contraband

Megan thought her mom's Irish accent was cool. While they looked at shoes, an idea suddenly came back to her that she grew impatient to act upon. She decided to shop in several different places so no one would see all her purchases.

She left her mother at the gate of Randolph House and hurried to the John Greenhow store, then the Prentis Store before taking the packages home. She started again at the other end of town at Tarpley's Store and continued on to the wigmaker. "Oh-oh! Sticker shock."

"Pardon me?" asked Charlotte, the wigmaker.

"Oh, sorry. Do you have wigs cheaper than these? My uncle is not a fancy man."

"Yes, of course. Those human hair wigs are expensive. You remind me of a woman who came this morning who had beautiful auburn hair. I first took her for a foreigner, but she was an educated lady. Miss, we have several good middle-sorts wigs made from horse hair."

Megan chose a distinguished-looking white wig with a black bow.

She dropped off the second batch of packages before returning to Market Square where vendors were loading their wagons for the bumpy ride home. Megan studied the men loading the wagons and spotted one in a nice waistcoat.

"Sir, I have an offer to make to you."

"Lovely. Would you like honey or corn meal? I have not packed those away."

"I see you're a man who appreciates a fine vest."

"A fine what?"

"Sorry, a waistcoat like the one you're wearing. The Prentis Store has new ones with carved buttons made of deer horn—very stylish and only two pounds."

"Oh, you are seeking customers for Mister Prentis, are you? Well, I like my waistcoat fine and 'tis but a year old. My wife bought it didn't you, Maggie?"

The woman packing up the next table looked up. It was the milk and cheese woman. "Oh, hello, Miss. Did your friend get home with her milk all right?"

"I hope so. I walked her out of the market. You were kind to give her extra milk."

"Bartholomew and I try to help where we can. We were often hungry ourselves and rose from a lowly station to a life of sufficiency for which we are thankful."

"You two know each other? Maggie, this miss wants me to buy a waistcoat at Prentis store but I am satisfied with this one you picked for me last year. She says the new ones have horn buttons," he winked, "but two pounds is a bit rich for us."

"I'm not selling waistcoats. I'd like to surprise someone with a waistcoat to cheer him up. I like yours, and I'll give you the two pounds to buy yourself a new one."

"An astounding offer! Why not buy the new one for your friend, Miss?"

"I'm Megan. My friend is in a situation where he might draw attention to himself if he wore a fancy new waistcoat. People might be hard on him for putting on airs."

"He's a bonded servant, I would imagine."

"I'd rather not say. It's a surprise."

"I understand. This is the strangest offer I've heard in seventy Saturdays, but if you think it to be a good idea, Maggie, I shall do it."

Maggie looked at Megan. "Bartholomew, Megan was kind to a poor thin worried woman this morning. She did not haggle over prices. She is all right. This is to help someone, I reckon. Megan's offer is beyond fair. Give her your waistcoat for one pound fifteen shillings. We can pay the balance of the new one."

Bartholomew helped count out Megan's diverse collection of currencies taking two shillings less than his wife suggested. "I shall bargain them down at the Prentis Store." He unbuttoned his waistcoat and gave it to Megan.

"Thank you so much!" Megan left them to their packing and returned home to lay out her treasures. She yanked the top sheet off the bed. Wrapping everything in the sheet with a loose knot at the top, it looked like a laundry bundle and that would attract no suspicion as she walked. "Perfect!" she declared.

Day 2-11:   Mustering the Militia

On the north side of Market Square, men mustered for an infantry drill. John recognized the sergeant in charge as the man from the encampment and the wheelwright shop. He now wore a blue double-breasted tunic with bone buttons, giving a formal appearance most citizen soldiers around him lacked. They wore old red coats from the French and Indian War or fringed pullover hunting shirts. John moved into the shade to watch.

The sergeant called to bystanders, "If Tommy Redcoat comes marchin' in, ye best move as an army rather than a herd of goats rushing a pile of corn husks, or worse, dashing at the first sight of the enemy like rabbits from the shadow of a hawk. Step up, lads, and muster as part of the Second Virginia Militia."

He got louder so the crowd could hear. "The Virginia Militia Law calls for an annual muster in each county. We humbly demand all able-bodied males from sixteen to fifty to step forward. The Virginia Convention prepared a Plan for a Militia, drafted by Thomas Jefferson, a good man with a pen. It specified a Virginia infantry company to have 68 soldiers commanded by a captain, two lieutenants, an ensign, four sergeants, four corporals, and a drummer who also bears the colors. Do ye see 68 men here? Neither do I. Step forward and be lively about it."

To the gathered men he shouted, "Company, fall in! Form ranks!" The men in uniform shuffled quickly into ranks; the newcomers fell in behind them. "Dress right!" The experienced men in the front rank raised their arms to the side, turned their heads, then shuffled forward and to the side until their arms almost touched the shoulder of the man beside them. In seconds, the row was straight. The men in the front rank carried a mix of flintlock rifles and muskets while the men behind had no arms. Two corporals distributed oak broom handles to the men behind.

"To the front, face! Attention!" The militia looked forward and stood straight.

"All right ye future sharpshooting, quick marching, seeds of a Continental Army. Listen carefully. If you do not know what to do, follow the man in front of ye. The front rank has done this many times, and every man-Jack one of 'em lived through the worst war had to give. If ye pay close attention, so might ye."

"Port arms!" The men in the first rank held their muskets in front, their right hand on the butt and their left around the narrow end of the stock near the trigger. The following ranks fumbled for a moment to get the hands in the right spots and the formation became still again, their weapons in almost the right position.

"Shoulder arms!" The men brought their muskets to their shoulders. "LEFT shoulder arms unless the sergeant in command says otherwise, you newborns!"

"Do it again, but this time don't lay the baby in a cradle. Do it with a snap. Port arms! Left shoulder arms!" Even broom handles went crisply to the left shoulders.

"Company, forward march!" Onlookers in front of the formation scurried out of the way but there was no hurry, for a second later the sergeant shouted, "Company, halt! Have ye ever heard the words 'Left right, left right' in that order?

If you set out on any foot you like, you will trip and land on your snouts while bayoneting the bottom of the man in front of you. That is bad for morale and gives aid, comfort, and entertainment to the enemy! Lead with the left foot, shall we soldiers? Company..." he paused and looked along the ranks, "Forward march!"

Again, a noticeable difference occurred as the company moved forward in unison. As they marched past the tree, John recognized Peter in the fourth rank. He stepped out to fall in beside him. "Hello, soldier."

Peter was surprised but kept the pace. He could hardly wait to tell his father that they were not stuck in the past. "You'll never guess what happened!"

"Silence!" shouted the sergeant. "Company, halt! Take the terror off your faces, lads. We drill and fight as a unit. Failing to work together makes ye less effective and puts ye in grave danger. Grave danger means danger of being put in your grave. Be calm. No one is shooting at ye. In battle, enemies will be shooting. By then ye will know what to do."

"Company, forward march!" John hoped his son marching beside him would never have to kill, see his friends die, or die violently himself. He was relieved his family was not stuck in the past permanently but he felt the pain of foreknowledge that many of these young men would be killed.

Peter was happy to march next to his dad and eager to tell him about the tunnel and library. He began to whistle "Yankee Doodle" and others picked up the tune.

"Stop that whistling," ordered the Sergeant. When they arrived at the Magazine, the sergeant called a halt. "Ye'll be good soldiers before long, men. Ye have done well. The corporals shall collect the weapons. Company, dismissed!"

Peter and John walked toward the house. "Dad, I've got something huge to tell you. We are not stuck here. I walked into our own time this afternoon and after a couple of hours in a library walked back to the past again."

"Were you at the St. George Tucker House?"

"No, I went through a tunnel and almost got run over by a car. I learned amazing things in a library and was surprised I could walk back to this time."

"This is a weird situation, Peter, but I'm not worried. It seems we can leave when we want." He was not as surprised by the news as Peter hoped he would be.

Chowning's Tavern was to the east of Market Square. "Hey Dad! We talked about having dinner here tonight. We could book a table now." They were told there were no inside tables until eight but a table in the garden would be open in twenty minutes at six o'clock.

John frowned. "Peter, this experience is bringing memories back. I need a walk. I can catch a bite later if I am hungry. Go ahead and book that table for three."

"Don't you and Mom have the Governor's Ball tonight?"

"Oh, that's right. I'll take a short walk while you get the girls."

Peter jogged back to the colonial house, his concern about his father eclipsed by his excitement to tell Susan and Megan about his walk through the tunnel.

Day 2-12:   Dinner at Chowning's Tavern

The Sinclairs were led to their table in the garden of Chowning's Tavern, and Megan and Peter paused in their conversation as they looked over the menu.

Susan ordered the Welsh rarebit. "I'll have one of those, too," said Megan.

"And what about you, Sir?"

John was looking over the fence. "Me? I'm not hungry. I'll have today's soup."

"Did you have a nice walk before dinner, Honey?" asked Susan.

"It was all right."

"Peter walked through a tunnel to our time for a couple of hours. I am relieved we're not stuck. I'll bet we can find our car in the parking lot and drive home."

"I'm sure we could, Mom. In a library, I read that later in 1775, Governor Dunmore is going to proclaim free all slaves willing to bear arms for the King against the rebels. The British freed as many slaves as the Underground Railroad!"

"Slaves were freed by the British long before Lincoln's Emancipation Proclamation? I never knew that. How was the day for you, John?" asked Susan, concerned about his mood.

"In a donor center library I found myself back in the 21st century."

"You found a way back to our time, too?"

"More like an island in time than a way out. I learned that young George Washington worked for Lord Thomas Fairfax whose predecessor and namesake overthrew the king. Fairfax may have influenced our revolutionary general."

"John, I learned that leading families borrowed currency stolen from the Virginia treasury. Being found out would have led to scandal and ruin, so they kept the debts secret as they slowly paid them off. The pressure of those debts led to several suicides. It seems the financial mess of the large estates tempted them to throw off the authority of the King."

"Mom," said Megan, "there was lots going on around here we didn't learn in school. Indentured workers sent west to clear Indian land didn't know that their greedy employers ordered them to do illegal things that could get them killed."

"Megan, be respectful of our Founding Fathers. They created this great country."

"I am respectful, Dad. But don't you see that for people to keep freedom we need to understand the reasons behind the actions of our business and government leaders? The Revolution was not about taxation. You guys said I should learn something. I'm learning if we don't pay attention, we deserve what we get."

"Everyone knows the American Revolution started because people were against taxation without representation. You can't just make up stuff about history."

"I'm not making this up, Dad! I did research and took notes! Parliament passed the Stamp Act in 1765, but the colonies resisted and it was repealed the next year — 1766. In 1767, the Townsend Duties Act was passed and repealed in 1770. No taxation without representation? Would you go to war over taxes repealed five years or nine years earlier?"

"Of course not!"

"Well, neither did they, Dad! Almost all unpopular taxes had been repealed. Who would fight about something already over for several years? No one would risk their lives, fortunes, and sacred honor for that. It had to be something else!"

"Where did you get this information, Megan, a conspiracy theory on the web?"

"No, the history books I brought—one of them won a Pulitzer Prize. The truth is easy to find if you look. The outbreak of war followed implementation of the Intolerable Acts, passed in 1774. That should give us a clue. What was so intolerable? The Boston Port Act closed the port. I wrote them down... here they are. The Administration of Justice Act allowed extradition for trial in England. The Massachusetts Government Act took rights away from Boston citizens. The Quartering Act put British troops into taverns and empty houses, but people were told they would have soldiers in their homes. And the big one—the Quebec Act was about who controlled land west of the mountains."

"Hey, just because somebody wrote a history book does not mean it's the truth. Why are you arguing against what everybody knows to be true?"

"Rich families needed new lands as they depleted their land with tobacco crops. The leaders persuaded people it was for their benefit. Sound familiar? Listen, Quebec was far away and had only sixty thousand people compared to two million in the thirteen colonies. By having Quebec manage the western lands, the King tried to stop settlement and avoid more war with the Indians. Virginia and Pennsylvania land developers did not want to be prevented from taking more Indian land. Ordinary people didn't know what the real fight was about!"

"You don't think a war was necessary?" Susan's eyes widened.

"No, everybody misled everybody. Peter told us the British freed slaves and servants. That was not because the Brits cared about the slaves—they tried to ruin the disloyal slave owners. There was rotten stuff everywhere!"

"Why are you riled up, Megan?" asked John. "I don't think you've got it right, but people don't usually fight about history over dinner."

"It goes on in our time! Wealthy individuals and giant corporations hire lobbyists to draft laws and push tax cuts in their favor. Rich talk show hosts support even richer guys and companies by telling people it benefits everyone and they call opponents nasty names. The government bails out big businesses when they fail and taxes ordinary working people to pay for it. Follow the money, Dad."

"Now just a minute Megan..."

"You know who you remind me of, Megan?" interrupted Susan.

"Who?"

"A young man I met a long time ago who is always ready to take a stand for justice even at personal risk. His name is John Sinclair. Now let's enjoy dinner."

112

Day 2-13:   Annie's Journey from Africa

Peter left Chowning's Tavern, more determined to find Annie. He walked only half a block when he passed a great oak tree. There on the other side of the tree Annie sat on a wooden crate – her back against the trunk.

"Oh!" Peter was startled. "I was looking for you, Annie."

"Looks like you found me waitin' for you. We found each other by me feeling where you was comin' from and you feelin' where I was waitin'."

Peter was perplexed. "I didn't notice feeling you waiting. Mind if I sit down?"

"Try it and see if I mind." She broke into a warm smile. Peter got another crate.

"Move 'round behind the tree, Peter, so no one see us talkin'. I know you confused by what you seein'. Most folk be confused even though they don't see much at all. They don't know they's confused. Somebody comin' here soon so I gonna tell my story like I promised and you ax me 'bout other things after."

"That would be good, Annie."

"I came here as a girl. I pulled weeds and washed pots. Later, I cooked.

"I was born in West Africa of a Bambara-speakin' mama from grasslands. Folk lived by rivers and grew rice in the sun. Daddy spoke Dogon and came from the forest. They lost three babies 'fore I was born so they held me close and talked 'bout how good life was, prayin' I would be healthy and not die like them other babies. I started talkin' 'fore one year and my folks forgot somethin' important."

"What was that?"'

"If babies talked early, the tribe s'posed it possessed by a dead relative or a devil. Some said clever children might grow up smarter than the chief but folk 'fraid to say that very loud. Fo' whatever reason, bright-eyed babies who talked too young was taken from they mamas and sacrificed in ceremony for the good of the tribe."

Annie took a long breath. "One day when I was two, the head man came by to visit. I talked with a doll Daddy carved for me. Mama said to hush but the chief kep' lookin' at me.

"When Daddy came home, Mama cried into the night. Next mornin' Daddy took me wit' him far up river. In a month we found the camp of Fulani people who move cattle wit' the seasons. His cousin married a Fulani man and Daddy told her I was a year older than my real age. He axed her to take care of me for a few years. She wouldn't have no trouble if I was short, but talkin' too soon was dangerous.

"Auntie was good to me. The Fulani is nomads wit' herds that graze on pastures so wide it takes months to cross. Gazelles, a deer wit' straight horns, live on them grasslands. A big cat called a cheetah chases the gazelle fast-fast-fast, and the gazelle can leap and race off in another direction when she land. Nothin' here, not even a gallopin' horse, be as fast as a cheetah and a gazelle.

"We saw long-necked giraffes hunted by lions. The she-lions disappeared and the male stood high on a mound so the giraffes could see him. The giraffes stared to see what that golden lion was gonna do. All of a sudden, the she-lions ran from a gully to snatch a giraffe still starin' at the male lion. When lions was near, men herded the cattle into a circle. Men stood outside wit' spears, and women and children stayed together behind the herd.

"We camped near towns wit' people of many colors and tongues. I spoke Fula wit' Auntie and learned Hausa words used in town markets where we traded milk, yogurt, cheese, and meat from our herds. I milked cows and goats. I got cow pox like all the women do. They joke the marks left on they skin makes them prettier. We say we is leopard ladies.

"In dry times we moved the herd south into forests to forage. We could not swim in rivers 'cause bama was in there. Bama is Bambara for crocodile. There was big animals we called mali and you call hippopotamus. They look funny but they be dangerous. A mali can kill a crocodile. The men watched out for mali and bama before they drove a herd across a river.

"One night we was sleepin' by a dry river when men wit' spears attacked. Our men was surprised and some was killed. The rest of us was tied wit' leather strips around our necks and made to walk many days down the river bed wit' little food.

"We reached water in the river where they done hid canoes and we floated wit' the men pushin' on long poles. I heard men speak Dogon and the words of my daddy came back. The men thought I was Dogon taken as a slave by Fulani.

"After two weeks the little river flowed into a wide river through forests. On the bank many men sat by cookin' fires. We stayed two days while they ate and drank, pointed to us, and argued. Auntie told me we was bein' sold to work in rice fields. When the tradin' was done, the new men took us by straps bindin' us together at the wrists and dragged us into canoes. We drank from the big river called the Gambia so we was not thirsty, but we got only enough food to keep us alive.

"When I prayed, I felt Spirit movin' in the water. The men pulled on paddles and kept to the middle of the river. Men wit' spears watched the shore but they was too worried to be huntin'. Maybe somebody was huntin' to steal us. When we camped, half the men stayed awake while the rest slept and two nights we slept in the canoes driftin' past sleepin' villages. We could feel the danger. They kept arrows in they bows and watched the huts."

"A month after we started down the wide river, we came to an island wit' a big stone building called Fort James. Some weak folk was stabbed and they bodies thrown in the river. I was so sick to see it I threw up. We was taken to rooms wit' iron bars over the holes.

"After three nights a few of us was pulled out of the big rooms and men grabbed me away from my auntie. I cried and she screamed and prayed. That was the last time I saw her. Outside I saw a big boat wit' white cloth rolled on long beams they call spars hung across high masts. The men on the boats looked sick 'cause they was paler than the lightest skinned North Africans in the markets of Timbuktu. A few wit' fancy shirts and hats was pale as better-sorts ladies here. They put iron rings on our ankles and pushed us down into flat wooden racks inside the boat. I thought they was blind in they heart. They had no feelin'."

"The next day they brung us on deck to move and we got an awful surprise. The banks of the river was gone and everywhere was rollin' water. The boat moved like magic wit' nobody padlin'. I wondered if the pale men was magic, but no light shone in them like in magic people. I saw the wind moved us by pushin' on the white cloths. I was scared, hungry, and thirsty, but I felt Spirit in the wind pushin' us over the waves and heard it in the sails. It whispered in the dark water below, 'Everythin' is deeper than you see, prayers is always heard.'

"People cried and moaned. The smell in them wooden racks from pee and shit would make you gag. Every day they splashed the racks wit' buckets of sea water but people got sick and died and was thrown into the sea wit' no songs or words. Some folk tried to jump but they was chained to people who wanted to live so no one was able to kill they self. When a bad storm came, the pale men was too scared to bring us up top or feed us for three days. The boat bounced so hard two people broke bones from bangin' against walls. A man on the ship set the bones, but he was not kind and smelled like fermented grain.

"Finally one day a man up high in the ropes pointed and shouted and we saw a green line in front of the ship. We was comin' to land again. At Annapolis, we was washed wit' fresh water and fed to look better at auction. At the sale they stood us up naked so people could see if we had sores or wasn't well and strong"

Annie looked down the street. "Yonder come 'Gustus. You say hello. Then I gonna finish my story when he gone."

"Hello, Annie," called out Augustus. "The overseer sent me to town on an errand and I been lookin' for you."

"Looks like you found me waitin' for you," Annie winked at a fascinated Peter.

"Say hello to Mister Peter, 'Gustus. You 'member him from the Hush Harbor."

"Hello Mister Peter. You the best runner I ever seen for a white man. I saw you again this mornin' talkin' wit' Mister Jack.

"I was learning how to buy a slave into freedom. I don't have enough money."

Augustus looked astonished. "Is that a fact? Well, the gentry all talkin' 'bout freedom. It must be good or they would not do somethin' dangerous to get some. So I gonna try to get some freedom myself. Annie you is the only free African I know. What do you say?'

Annie tilted her head to the left. "Runnin' away be very dangerous."

"True Annie, but stayin' be dangerous, too. My life be more than half over, and if freedom be so good, I want a taste 'fore my life be done."

Annie took another long look at Augustus. "Maybe wisdom comin' to you, 'Gustus. You want to try for freedom even though it be dangerous and you ain't sure you can succeed?"

"Yes, Ma'am"

"What do you think be the chance your massa might set you free some day."

"Annie, Massa don't know me 'cept my name on a list of his property. The chance he gonna set me free when he alive or dead be betwixt none and not any."

Annie sat quietly then asked Peter, "What would you say if 'Gustus axed you?"

"I don't know."

"You need knowin' when you don't know or you gonna waste a very long trip."

"Well, Augustus, freedom is worth working hard for. Even so, life is precious and you can help people using the herbs as Annie taught you. So I say be patient, do your best, and watch closely for a better chance to be free than we can see now."

"You think somethin' will happen to make it easier to run to freedom?"

Peter felt restraint new to him. "I wouldn't be surprised. You're a good runner, but you need a good path. Remember how the wild turkey tripped you?"

"Yes, I do. Well, Annie always told us to be patient until a gate opens. I can do that. Maybe I is a slave you be plannin' to buy, Mister Peter."

Peter paused. "There are several people I would like to help but slaves are very expensive, precious actually, and sadly I don't have enough money to buy them."

"That be sad, Mister Peter. I will watch for chances. Please don't tell nobody."

"I promise I won't."

"I'll be hoppin' past a gibbet on just one foot! A white gentleman makin' me a promise! I never thought I would hear that. Annie, you got wonderful friends. Well, I got to get back. Thanks for the good words, Annie. You too, Mister Peter. I wish I had a massa like you."

"Didn't you say you wanted to be free without a master?"

"Oh, that's true. I need a new kind of wishin'." Augustus was off, running.

Annie tilted her head to the left to take a long look at Peter. "You done well. I have a feelin' the path is not what you think it is. Now I'se gonna finish my story.

"I got bought as a slave by a planter who worked tobacco and corn four days' walk west of here. I cleaned and helped in the kitchen and garden. His wife taught me English. As her eyes got weak she taught me to read to her from her Bible.

"After Massa died, his widow grieved and despaired of runnin' the plantation. I read her the Bible, and when she felt prayerful, I told her she treated folk kindly and they could work wit'out bein' forced. It was they home too and they had nowhere else to go. The Missus looked at me wit'out a word. Saturday she had me make up a big meal for all the field hands. She told them she did not want to sell the plantation and break up the families. Death broke up her family and she knew how bad it felt.

"The Missus had some good years. She let folk keep gardens and chickens and gave us meat when a hog or calf was butchered. Folks got food and more free time.

"I had watched what Massa did when slaves was sick. I learned 'bout herbs used by the Pamunkey Indians, and healin' ways African folk remembered from home.

116

When a doctor came, I watched what he done. I looked at Massa's books on physic and read papers that came wit' powders from the apothecary shop. I axed questions and like you do, I kept them in my mind and watched and listened until I got an answer wit'out axin' out loud."

I do that? Peter thought.

"Yes, you do." Annie smiled and continued, "I helped people when they got sick and folks from nearby plantations came when they needed help. The Missus got sick two times, and two times I healed her. Because she was kind and generous, the field hands never made no trouble when she was feelin' poorly. I gave instructions and everythin' hummed along like bees on a flower-bush."

"How can you tell what I am thinking?"

"That ain't part of this story, but I can say they ain't no walls betwixt people's minds 'cept what they put there they-self."

"But...

"The second time I nursed her, she was so grateful I kep' things smooth on her plantation she said she would give me manumission in her will and testament."

"I heard the word manumission yesterday. What does it mean?"

"Manumission is papers that say the slave is free. They own themselves like white folks do. I told her slave or free, I would help her because she been so kind to me and taught me to read. Well, this good woman cried. 'Annie, I would have lost everything and died if not for you. You would stay if you was free?'

"I said, 'Yes Ma'am, this been my home for thirteen years.' And she told me, 'You came to us when you were little. I never had children and you was like a daughter.' She went to Williamsburg and did the manumission. It don't happen often. I served her two more years 'till she was taken wit' a fever I could not cure.

"I grieved for her and so did the other folk, even 'fore they learned she freed them all in her will. Maybe she freed them because she had no children to pass the slaves to, or maybe the plantation had no debts to be paid by sellin' slaves, but they was freed just the same. I think her hearin' the Bible in my voice helped her see wit' her heart. In Africa, my family still prays for me and I pray for them. Maybe the missus felt them prayers.

"Some slaves was worried, but her brother might break the promise to set them free. He was happy to inherit the land wit' no debt, 'cept for the twenty acres apart from the rest which she left to me. It had a small quarter on it and was on a creek. I grew food and kept chickens. Some folk stayed in their quarters even though they was free. They was paid for their work in his fields and kept gardens. Later, I sold my land to the brother. He paid a good price to have me gone. I was scared to venture out alone but grateful to be free at twenty-two years old.

"I talked' wit' wise people wherever I found them. I met folk who could cure people by prayer or kindness in they hearts whether they was Christian, Indian medicine woman, African, or some other path. I met a Dogon man captured by the

Yoruba in a war. He told me the wisdom of our ancestors." Annie paused. "Is there anythin' you want to ax me?"

As Peter listened to Annie's story, he thought a lot seemed to depend on luck. "Annie, you were kind to your Missus and she was kind to you. I wonder what Evie might do to be free. I don't know how I got here but I have a feeling I'm supposed to help her and the boys."

"That may be why you be here, Mister Peter. Maybe somebody was prayin' you would come. But Evie ain't made a choice in her heart to be free."

"But if she was prayin' someone would come to help..."

"I did not say Evie was prayin', I said maybe somebody was. I ain't gonna guess who, but if you feel somethin' callin' you, you should follow that call."

"How are you able to tell what I'm thinking? I don't understand that."

"I said there ain't no walls betwixt people's souls. Somehow, you came a long way here to do somethin' that looks impossible. The path may be hidden. If you don't pay attention you ain't gonna see it." Annie looked at Peter and suddenly her eyes got wide. "You already found a way to help slaves get free ain't you?"

"Well, earlier today I went through a tunnel under the train tracks and read in the library. Later this year, Governor Dunmore will issue a proclamation freeing slaves loyal to Great Britain who are willing to take up arms."

"See what I mean? You done gone through a tunnel that ain't there to a place that ain't there and read about somethin' that ain't happened yet! Those must be powerful prayers brought you here. Keep lookin' for a way and you gonna find somethin', but it might not be what you expect. Now, I got to wander off to be useful in another place and a woman this big don't wander fast," Annie grinned and stood up.

Peter thanked her and started up the street. When he turned around, she was already gone. Again! How does she do that? Peter had forgotten to ask Annie about the shift in time. He decided to go to bed to make up for the lack of sleep the night before.

Day 2-14:   Susan and John at the Governor's Ball

The reception line at the Palace moved slowly as Susan and John approached the Governor and Lady Dunmore. As she was introduced, Susan curtsied and said she hoped peace would return soon to all the colonies. Lady Dunmore complimented her mantua and her new shoes. "Are those from Europe?" she asked.

"Thank you, Your Ladyship. They're made by a tailor and shoemaker in town."

They entered the ballroom to chamber music played by a string quartet and harpsichord. Elegantly dressed couples from prominent families were enjoying the dance. It was coming to an end, so Susan did not coax John onto the floor.

The first violinist stood to welcome everyone. "It is an honor to play at the Governor's Palace. Tonight we have contra dances, which are European versions of English country line dances. You will hear familiar music by Vivaldi and Scarlatti. As a special treat, we shall play two minuets by the young Austrian composer Wolfgang Amadeus Mozart. At nineteen, he has been popular in European capitals for several years. The sheet music for these works arrived last month from London and we practiced ardently to play them tonight in their Virginia premiere."

"Mozart is nineteen? The whole world is in 1775!" whispered John.

"This is 1775. We are the strange ones here," Susan whispered back.

John surprised Susan when he squeezed her hand and took her onto the floor for the next dance. "It would be a shame to wear that beautiful dress for nothing and how often do we dance at the debut of a new minuet by Mozart?"

A diminutive man gave a brief minuet lesson. He took a portly woman by the hand and went over the steps. "That was perfect, Missus Byrd," he gushed. He asked each couple in turn to try a few steps. "Well done Mister Braxton!" He flattered an elderly awkward man in soft new shoes with a deerskin lining.

"It's one thing to encourage people, but this fellow is obsequious," Susan said quietly. She took a dislike to the man. "There's a slithery insincerity about him."

As the ensemble launched the minuet, several couples who had not joined in the lesson were surprisingly good at it, evidently having danced at many such events before. Susan noticed Charlotte the wig maker and her husband George near the edge of the floor, not masters of the dance but doing their best.

"When is the last time we danced together, Susan?"

"I don't remember but this is our first minuet. Isn't that romantic?"

At the end of the dance, the first violinist called for a short break. John went to the restroom and Susan took a glass of apple cider from a side table. The dance instructor approached. "Good evening, my lady. My name is Randall Weaver. Forgive me, but I do not think we have met before. You and your husband dance nicely. Are you recently arrived from Great Britain?"

"I'm Susan Sinclair. I live to the North. This is our first visit to Williamsburg."

"At a Governor's Ball on your first visit? You must be from a renowned estate."

"My family prefers restraint, Mr. Weaver. We are happy to be unknown."

"That is refreshing, Lady Sinclair." He lowered his voice to a conspiratorial level. "One finds the pretentions of the so-called great houses here in Virginia to be tiresome, doesn't one? I often miss the refinement of real gentry back in England."

A middle-sorts planter at his first ball at the Governor's palace was standing next to the dance instructor and asked, "What is so different in England?"

"Sir, this house which people call a palace would not be called such in England. This is the only residence worthy of the name 'house' in this colony. The dwellings of these so-called 'gentlemen' do not compare to the hundreds of elegant great houses of England. Most are grander than this palace.

"And palaces? Compare this humble building to Blenheim Palace in Oxfordshire built for John Churchill, Duke of Marlborough, after his victory over the French. Such architecture, statues, elegant gardens! People here would faint at the sight. That stately palace shall inspire leadership in the Churchill family for generations to come. We shall not bother comparing this place to the least of the royal palaces.

"The Governor puts the best face on it," Weaver allowed, "but this village must feel like an isolated outpost to him. Just think; there are two thirds of a million people in London! Compare that to the mere two thousand in Williamsburg." Susan grew increasingly uncomfortable as the dance instructor mocked the people from whom he earned his living.

"When are you planning to return to England, Mister Weaver?" Susan asked.

"As soon as I gather up a decent purse from these rural pretenders for a comfortable existence in my native land, I will hie me thither to civilization again."

Good riddance, Susan thought as she smiled thinly and wandered across the room to where John was standing.

He took her aside. "I liked dancing with you but I need a walk to work out some memories this is bringing up. I'll walk you home first." He took her arm.

"I understand, John. Dance one more dance with me." They stepped onto the floor for another dance but Susan could see that John was preoccupied. When the contradanse was over, Susan said, "I would like to stay a bit longer, you go ahead."

"Are you sure you will be all right? You should not walk alone."

It's only a few blocks to the house and I will walk with others. I'll be fine." For the first time in years, John gave Susan a kiss on the cheek in public.

"He'll be all right," she whispered as she watched him edge past people gathered near the main door, each vying to catch a moment of the Governor's attention.

She walked to the wigmaker, who was standing next to her husband just beyond the dance floor. "Hello, Your Majesties. You look elegant tonight, Charlotte."

"Hello, Susan." Allow me to introduce you to my husband, George. George, this is Susan Sinclair, the woman I told you about."

"I am George, no relation to the King," he said, bowing awkwardly.

120

"Oh Susan!" Charlotte exclaimed. "I saw you and your husband on the dance floor. That is the most beautiful cape. Fit for a queen it is!"

"Alwyn, the tailor across the street from your shop made it."

"Maybe someday he will make something for me in barter for a fine wig."

The men standing near them grew loud. "Quakers were traitors in time of war."

"They are not fighters and will remain on the sidelines. I am more concerned about those German speakers in Pennsylvania. Will they remain loyal to their fellow German, King George III, or will they follow the dreadful Leveler's ideas that claim all men to be equal?"

An elegant woman walked across the room to Susan. "Madam, that is a most stunning mantua. Wherever did you find such a masterpiece?"

"Alwyn Taylor, here in town, is an excellent dressmaker. Excuse me, but I saw you today at the home of Peyton and Betty Randolph. You are Lucy Burwell?"

"Oh dear, yes! You witnessed that unfortunate conversation I had with my aunt. You offered frank but kind words to me as you departed. The secret has troubled me for years, and I felt I would explode if I did not finally share it. Thank you for not judging us harshly."

"There is nothing to judge, Missus Burwell. We all have our crosses to bear."

"Please call me Lucy. And your name is Susan?"

"That's right, Susan Sinclair."

"You don't live in Williamsburg, Susan. I would have noticed you. Oh dear, my husband is signaling me to meet a new Burgess. Can you write your address in this booklet so I can invite you to a party at our plantation? It is refreshing to meet someone of an unpretentious nature and like everyone living in the countryside; we are hungry to welcome visitors."

Susan wrote her local address. "How do you know I'm not a horse thief?"

Lucy laughed. "You are the only person here able to say such outlandishly funny things without blushing!" She crossed the ballroom back to her husband.

A man nearby exclaimed, "Virginia will stay loyal to the crown. Even when Cromwell was in power, Virginia stayed in the hands of the loyal Cavaliers and ruled itself for a period."

"They did until the first British ship arrived. We think the Cavaliers were sympathetic to the Papists," muttered Charlotte's husband George.

"They are Loyalist, drunk, opinionated, and intolerant," Susan commented.

Charlotte's husband whispered in her ear and she nodded. "Susan, we are ill at ease here. 'Tis wonderful to see you looking so beautiful, but we are going now."

"I understand, Charlotte. It has been wonderful to see you at the ball. I am ready to leave as well. Let's make our dignified exit and we can walk together."

Day 2-15:   John and Bruce Wallace at the Tavern

The walk had done him good. John put his elbows on a table in Shields Tavern, rested his chin on his fists, and stared at the candle in the hurricane lamp. The flickering flame entranced him. He took another sip of beer.

Susan had said during their courtship that his emotions were bottled up. "You're a wonderful man," she told him, "but it's not easy to touch your heart." What did that mean? He talked it over with an Army psychologist on his return from the First Gulf War. Having a lid on his feelings was not a problem. It was self-control. He did not want to blow up. Anyway, she married him, didn't she?

John did not think about the wars and that was best. He had experienced combat in sweltering Nicaraguan jungles and cold, dry Central Asian mountains. He knew the heart-pounding rush of adrenalin, the surreal focus, and the slowing view of rapid events seen through the borehole of intense concentration.

There were places in the world he had gone before he married, places he could not talk about because the United States had not officially sent combats troops. His clothes, weapon, and gear had not been American and he carried no American ID or currency. Had he been killed, even a field examination would not have confirmed his nationality. With his dark hair and tanned skin, he could be from any number of places. The army would have declared him lost in an accident. He was told it was in the national interest and he had volunteered.

Like places he could not admit to having fought, he had places in his mind he did not venture. Stress? Yeah. Post-traumatic stress? No, he was sure he was fine. Sure, there was pressure at work but he was running again and doing Tae Kwan Do. Not the combat martial arts he learned from Uncle Sam, but it was relaxing and kept him fit. Punching a heavy sack was a good release — release of what?

The beer was bitter, like the beer in Malta on his weekend off before he was dropped into the desert. Don't even think about it. No one knows we were there.

"May I join you?" The voice had a Scottish accent.

"Sure, have a seat." It was the wheelwright who today was the drill sergeant on Market Square. The uniform jacket was replaced by a woolen waistcoat.

"Lass, I'll have an ale with my friend here," he called out to the serving-girl.

"I'm John Sinclair."

"I'm Bruce Wallace. Sinclair? Are ye a Scot then?"

"My ancestor came from Nova Scotia to Ohio and married a German widow."

"I dinna know settlers were in the Ohio territory long ago but Nova Scotia has many Scots." Bruce raised his glass for a Scottish toast. "Here's tae us, wha's like us? Damned few and they're all deid. Slainte!"

"Slainte!" John knew the toast.

The serving girl came back to take their food order and set a basket of warm corn bread on the table. John asked for the Yorkshire beef and cabbage pasties.

Bruce was a regular. "I'll have my usual shoat pâté. Liver peps me up.

"We spoke at the militia camp, John, and in the wheelwright shop. I learned me first trade back home in Glasgow, apprenticed in the shipyard. When I came to Virginia, I grew fond of working with wood. Maybe I saw too much iron in battles..." He paused. "I built my own cabin and then made a cart. Making a good wheel was the hardest part. I made money from fur, firewood, and timber. Once I had my cart, I was my own transporter, so I saved enough to buy a wee cottage on the edge of town and some land beyond. Then I found a good woman. Now as wheelwright, I work in both wood and iron. What is your work, John?"

"I install things more than make them."

"You are a joiner or a wright then?"

"Not exactly. I send out... wrights to be sure machines are installed properly." John changed the subject rather than attempt to explain to a wheelwright in 1775 the work of an information systems integration manager. "You were right when we spoke yesterday. Like you, I was a soldier. Where did you serve?"

"In 1742, as a boy of fourteen, I fought in the Highland Rangers under James Oglethorpe at the Battle of Bloody Marsh in Georgia. Do you ken Bloody Marsh?"

"Do I ken... no, I don't know of the Bloody March."

"That would be 'Bloody Marsh', John. I am surprised you have'na heard of the victory. It is why we still speak English in Virginia. Fifty years before the English came, the Spanish destroyed a French fort in Florida and a colony in the Carolinas and hanged the prisoners for being Protestants. Two centuries later, they planned to crush the Protestant English colonies one by one. An invasion force of fifty ships filled with soldiers set out to start at tiny Fort Frederica on St. Simons Island.

"We were six hundred Redcoats and a small militia of new arrivals in the Province of Georgia. The colony was a new chance for people down on their luck and their militia was ready to fight to keep that precious chance alive. Do you know of James Oglethorpe, then?"

"No, I don't know much about the history of Georgia."

"As a Member of Parliament, Oglethorpe envisioned a new province to help debtors and others in difficult straits that would be a buffer between the English and Spanish colonies. He named the proposed colony "Georgia" to win endorsement from King George and the tactic worked. Oglethorpe was Governor of Georgia for years before returning to England.

"As a junior officer, Oglethorpe was in the successful siege of the Ottoman Turks at the White City or Belgrade as they say in their Slavic language. From that experience, he knew we could not hold Fort Frederica against the Spanish, so he took a bold gamble and had most of us leave the fort to lay an ambush along the trail from the sea. 'Twas a noisy day and as a soldier ye ken my meaning. With few losses on our side, we defeated the Spanish at the outset of their campaign to conquer the British colonies. A piece of Spanish armor still snags a plow blade in the fields now and again to remind us how close we all came to oblivion. Only later did I begin to think about the mothers, wives, and children in Spain and Florida waiting in vain for their men to come home."

Although it was a pivotal moment in American history, John had not heard of this threat before. "You had an important victory." They clinked glasses.

"Johnny, I tasted defeat as well and seen my friends' wives widowed. After Bloody Marsh, I returned to Scotland and Oglethorpe returned to Parliament in London. Three years later at seventeen, I joined the Rebellion supporting Bonnie Prince Charlie. You've surely heard of him?" John nodded. "Good. I am named Bruce Wallace after Robert the Bruce and William Wallace, so 'twas my natural choice. Do you know who they were?"

"Yes, I saw *Braveheart* the movie..." John barely caught himself. "I mean I know the moving story of brave Wallace and Robert the Bruce."

"In a bad spot at Culloden chosen by O'Sullivan, the Prince's adjutant general, we formed lines on an exposed moor betwixt stone livestock enclosures. Other officers complained, but Prince Charlie did not overturn the order. We were tired, hungry, and soggy. Many men were out foraging and did not hear the call to battle. Disputes among clans led some to leave and others to refuse to charge when the fool order came.

"Lowland Scottish clans ranged against us on the English side and the artillery under Major James Wolfe hit us as we waited for an attack, but it never came."

"The same General James Wolfe killed as he defeated Montcalm at Quebec?"

"Aye, the same, he was not a general then. Our men were cut down like oat stalks by artillery on the hill and muskets behind stone walls. The Prince ordered the first line to charge. As those reaching the British line raised their broadswords, the Redcoat to their right, bayoneted each man under his sword arm. 'Twas the first trained use of the bayonet in history and a lake of Scottish blood was spilled.

"In the second line we waited for an order to charge or retreat but if 'twere given, I never heard it. Musket balls, cannon balls, and rain fell upon us, and men turned to run. The British carried out their orders to kill even those who surrendered.

"Some things we do not talk about when we return home, but I see in your eyes you know battle, so I will tell you 'twas the gift of Robbie McDougal's last thoughts and prayers that saved me. He stood forward to my right when a cannon ball swept away his head leaving his body to fall limp to the ground. I was showered by a horrific splash of brains. I wiped my eyes and turned to run when I felt a sting in my leg. The whack of falling to the stony ground saved me from being shot again.

"From where I lay, I saw the Redcoats bayoneting Scottish wounded. When a bayonet got stuck in a man, they fired a round so they could pull back their weapon. I lay 30 yards away, not bleeding much from my own wound but with Robbie's brains on my face, I looked deader than most dead men and no one checked me before they moved back to refresh themselves and celebrate their victory. Too many men died there, John.

"I heard the whistles of musket balls sentries fired at men attempting to crawl away in the moonlight. I slowly pulled the arm of a dead man over me face, the folds of his wool cape over me chest. Lying amongst the dead and dying I carefully sipped water from me flask. The wound on me leg was not serious. I prayed for me mother and sister and the soul of me father already passed on. I prayed for clouds to cover the moon but none came. In the morning, the soldiers camped far from the stench of corpses. When the moon passed behind clouds the next night, I crawled away. Two thousand Scots were slaughtered at Culloden and the victors butchered people in the highlands. They plundered food and livestock and burned buildings. Many survivors of the massacres starved.

"I was taken to Hugh Mercer, a doctor for the Scottish forces. He saved my life by disinfecting and sewing me leg. He asked if I would come to the colonies. 'I've been in the New World' I told him, me at seventeen being the one with experience.

"I heard that Major General James Oglethorpe led four cavalry companies at Culloden. One company proudly bore the name Georgia Rangers. I found it, how do they say, ironic."

John asked, "How did you get back to the Colonies?"

"With the help of sympathetic Scots, including many who had not joined our cause, hundreds of us made our way to the Hebrides Islands as did Bonnie Prince Charlie, helped by Flora MacDonald. The Prince took a boat back to his exile in France but we found ships carrying refugees to Nova Scotia, Pennsylvania, and the Carolinas. Flora went to North Carolina with her husband Alan MacDonald.

"Mercer moved to the western frontier of Pennsylvania where he fought in the French and Indian war. Wounded, he was left for dead by his retreating mates. He found his way home, moving alone for weeks through Indian country dressed as one of them. Mistaken for an Indian, he was almost shot by sentries as he limped toward a fort. He became known for his adventure and accepted Washington's invitation to move to Fredericksburg, Virginia, to open an apothecary shop.

"Like Mercer's, my life has settled. I am 47 and happy as a wheelwright. I am also a cooper. I like coaxing soaked hardwood to bend into wheel rims and barrel staves. If I push too hard, the wood snaps just to spite me. Johnny, tell me of your service to Mars the God of war. How did it come to be I am supping here with ye and not your lonely widow?"

"Well, Bruce, I served in more than one war."

"You speak like a man who had schooling. Were you an officer?"

"No, I was a sergeant like you. I went to college when I came home."

John was stirred by Bruce Wallace's stories and for the first time, he told his without naming the countries where he fought. American advisors to the Contras in Nicaragua were not officially in combat. Nor were men inserted into Afghanistan to support the Mujahedeen in the fight against Russians in the eighties.

John told Bruce of losing his friend Danny to friendly fire in the Gulf War. "Our own cannon took him down. As Danny lay dying, our sergeant, we called Sargon, was furious as Hell. He saw Danny blown open and he jumped up to wave off our guns—a bad mistake. A round from an enemy sniper took him through the head. Like your friend Robbie, Sargon was dead before he started falling. That moment I became acting sergeant. I yelled at the men to drop down and crawl among the rocks closer to the enemy to get out of the target area of our artillery. I ordered them to cease firing to avoid drawing enemy fire and we wriggled forward like salamanders. When we neared the enemy, we lay still. They pulled back to avoid the artillery fire which was finally landing forward of our position."

It was good medicine for John to open up to a seasoned warrior with graying temples like his. Bruce understood the sudden loss of close friends. "Who was it you fought? And what is a sniper?" He looked at John with curiosity.

"A sniper is a crack rifleman. In Central America we fought uh…the Spanish and later I battled Russians in the mountains of Asia."

"'Tis strange I have'na heard about your wars. 'Tis not easy to defeat people on their own territory. We wonder why we are there. How did the wars end?"

"We won most of the battles but our leaders got tired of the dying and expense and we were brought home. Years later we made peace with our former enemies."

"Maybe the English will win most battles here until they get tired and go home."

"Maybe so."

"Well, John, we are living quieter lives these days although perhaps for not much longer. People on both sides of the ocean seem eager to offer up the lives of young men to win an argument. Are ye planning to be in Williamsburg long?"

"In a few days, I'll return to where I come from."

"Well, since ye will be here a few days let me warn ye about taverns around here particularly at crossroads outside town. They can be as violent as a battle field."

"What should I watch for, Bruce?"

"There are bad apples baiting drunken buckskins from the frontier into a fight for money against a man who has stayed sober. They gouge and dismember. They might pluck out a man's eye or tear off his privates as the betting crowd cheers. Pay special mind to a pair called Dancer and Dagger. Dancer fawns upon the better-sorts with dancing lessons. He also talks young men into fighting Dagger."

"I heard the name Dagger before. My daughter met him when he was chasing a runaway servant for bounty. I hope for their sake I don't run into them."

"Stay sober if ye mean that. Ye shall need your wits and skill. He's a wily one."

"We are closing the tavern now," interrupted the serving girl.

"It's time to go home, John. I have enjoyed your company."

"Likewise, Bruce." The former sergeants made their way to the door of the smoky tavern and set off in opposite directions in streets dimly lit only by oil lamps on a few porches.

126

Day 2-16:   Megan at Mark's Hut

Megan picked up the bundle of clothes she had prepared. Wary from her experience walking alone the previous night, she waited until two couples came by on foot and fell in behind them for safety. She looked back several times to be sure no one was following her. When the couples turned down a side street, she walked near two women until she ducked down the walk to the blacksmith shop. The forge was locked and dark. She recalled that indentured servants lived near their place of work so unless Mark was locked in she guessed he was probably close by. The large house in front of the forge was too fancy a place for a servant to live.

She crossed the yard past piles of coal and cinders. Nothing at the back of the forge looked like a dwelling. She walked toward the back gate, careful not to trip or make noise. She smelled pigs as she had her first time in this yard and stopped. Grunts and tiny high-pitched squeals came from beyond the fence where a large sow lay on her side as six new piglets squirmed past and over each other to vacant teats. "You're so cute," she whispered.

She stealthily opened the gate. It squeaked loudly. She froze before easing it closed behind her. In darkness she edged down a path, feeling her way one step at a time, worried about bumping into a stranger. Sudden, savage barks of a large dog burst out beside her. An image of angry fangs leapt into her imagination, and she let out a cry, stifled by her own hand as she realized the dog was behind a fence. As a chorus of dogs began, she rushed along a hedge fearing something big would bite her and hoping she would not trip on a stump.

Around a corner, dimly lit by a lantern, two men stood up from a quiet conversation. Standing Elk chuckled. "I think this is the screech owl we heard frightening the dogs."

"Oh, it's you! That was scary! The dog was right next to me and..."

"'Tis all right now," interrupted Mark. "Please sit here and I shall give you water." He indicated a log standing on end, its bark removed and its top sanded smooth. He flung water from his mug into a bush and refilled it with water from a clay crock. He handed the mug to Megan. "Cool and fresh from the well."

"What brought you out again alone?" asked Standing Elk. "I told you 'twas dangerous."

Megan was breathing too hard to respond. After a moment, she handed Mark the sack. "Here's a present."

Mark placed the bundle on the log beside him. "If you have finished your water, would you like a cup of broth?" he asked.

"Yes, please."

Mark stepped into a lean-to set against a wall and was back in seconds with steaming chicken broth. He filled her cup. Megan sipped on the salty broth and her breathing and heart rate slowed down. No one spoke for a few minutes. Crickets chirped and a few cicadas out early in the season added a rhythmic rasp that reminded Megan of summers past.

"Shall I open your present, Megan?"

"Sure, go ahead and open it. Standing Elk may be able to help you with what's inside." As Mark looked over the clothes, Megan explained her idea. "Mark, the wanted posters describe runaways by the clothes they wear. There are no drawings of their faces. If a person were away from his own town in different clothes, no one could recognize him from the description. I bought things separately in each store so no one knows the whole outfit."

"Why did you do this, Megan?"

"You have worked so long and have more years left, so I wanted to help. With new clothes you have a good chance of getting away."

Mark shuffled through the clothes, the likes of which he had never owned. He studied the white wig. He was moved by her generosity but awkward about expressing gratitude. "This is most convincing. No one would suspect a bonded blacksmith to be so well attired."

"Are you happy with the outfit?"

"These are fine clothes, but I don't know..." He hesitated.

Megan sat quietly. A crow squawked from a roost beyond the wall. Green katydids high in the canopy joined in with the cicadas. Megan tapped their rhythm on her knee.

Standing Elk broke the silence. "Megan, do you have an idea that Mark should run away?"

"I thought he was planning to escape. Isn't that what you two were talking about so secretively?" Mark looked at Standing Elk. They did not answer.

Crickets carried the conversation. Slivers of cool moonlight filtered through the bows of a tall pine. Looking up, Megan saw the glow of fireflies high above them. "Look up there!" She pointed. She noticed repeated pulses of lights moving among the outer boughs of the tree, tracing dots when they hovered and dashes as they moved. "It looks like many fireflies but there are five. You can trace their paths by their flashes. There's a pattern behind the twinkles."

Standing Elk nodded.

Mark cleared his throat. "Megan, your generosity and the gifts you offering to me are... well, even with these clothes, the success of an escape is not guaranteed."

"You have to take a chance to make a change. You're not happy stuck as a servant so I want to help." Megan hesitated. "I know a secret. My brother Peter found out that Governor Dunmore is going to issue a proclamation to free slaves and indentured servants who are willing to take up arms on the Loyalist side."

"How could your brother know such a thing, Megan? We have not heard this."

"My brother is smart and knows lots of people. I'm not sure how he heard."

128

Standing Elk studied her. "There are currents and eddies in the river of events these days and anything could happen. Mark has never seen such a gift Megan, and it is not easy for him to find the words to thank you. I am sorry we seem secretive, but danger is afoot. I'll tell you something that may explain why Mark and I are concerned.

"To the west of the fall-line, up-river beyond where sea-going boats can pass, the land has long been filling up with settlement. Since the end of the French and Indian War, new arrivals and freed servants have moved even farther west seeking unclaimed land that is almost free. They have new land titles in hand, or often none. Brigands attack settlers moving along the trails. They steal everything and make the massacres look as if we Indians were the perpetrators. This leads to more fighting even though my people and yours hunt down the cutthroats. Along the frontier, Redcoats and militias still skirmish against Indians twelve years after the end of the war. Escape for anyone in that direction is not easy.

"Now in many places, Loyalists and patriot rebels have begun to fight, sometimes settling scores with old enemies that have nothing to do with politics. These are not good times to set out into any violent areas."

"What are you saying, Standing Elk? Should Mark work until he earns his freedom? Should he accept the coming Proclamation and get free by being loyal?"

"Megan, I live in a small Mattaponi village not so far north of here. We have gardens and animals, fish in the river, and live in peace. If my people become entangled in the rage sweeping the colonies, we could be swept away even if we pick the winning side. Just as we must be careful, the gentry, settlers, servants like Mark, and slaves all face difficult choices in the months ahead."

Megan wondered why Mark did not respond himself to the suggestion he run away. Maybe Standing Elk was trying to distract her. "How did you manage to keep your lands during the French and Indian War? Weren't people afraid that you would fight on the other side?"

"Since the mid-1600s we have paid an annual tribute in deer skins and other bounty to the Governor of Virginia. We stayed out of the last war, which took place to the north and west. Some people worried about us but we did business with local people and were as friendly as possible. It did not hurt that many in our village are part European or part African or a mix of all three. When times were tense, it is embarrassing to say, but to protect our families we went into town looking as much like the other people as we could or we stayed home. There is too much suffering in our history to risk breaking the peace now."

Megan turned to Mark. "Something is troubling you, Mark. I don't want to make your life more complicated. The clothes and wig are a gift whether you decide to run away or not."

"Thank you, Megan. This means more to me than I can say."

"You're welcome." Megan hesitated, "Mark, don't think I'm pressuring you for a relationship or anything. If you ran away as I thought you were going to, I knew I would never see you again. Besides, I live super far from here."

"Megan, you are the most honest, direct woman I ever met. We have not heard of a proclamation freeing servants and slaves but if the condition for freedom is taking up arms, I have never killed anyone and I hope I never shall."

They slipped again into silence. The cricket and cicada songs sounded new to Megan. She noticed that an individual creature sent out each chirp or rasp. The fireflies high above were beautiful and signaling each other. She was absorbed by the rhythm in the sounds and patterns in the flashes of light. "Wow!"

"You have strange words. What do you mean?"

"Sorry. The insect sound and light show is beautiful. I have been mean to them. Bugs have short lives and they are doing the best they can."

"They are born into the same world we are, Megan. They share this day with us."

"I'm beginning to see we share this world. These are hard times. Settlers need land and take it from Indians. The King has tried to stop the fighting by reserving land for the Indians but the plan is not sincere. The rich use the poor, and people kill each other because they think the others are wrong or they are afraid of them. They don't see what you call the gifts of the Creator, Standing Elk. They don't notice that it all fits together — them and the other, their side of the argument and the other side.

"Mark, you told me to be quiet about your meeting Standing Elk because it was dangerous for me and you might be hanged. I was not listening, but now I think that you and Standing Elk are talking about something big, about how all the problems fit together. I don't want to put you in more danger but I hope you don't mind that I will pray for you to be safe."

"Megan, I..."

"Better not tell me." Megan stood up. "This is a special evening for me. I'm learning how to notice what is happening and not just see what I want for myself. See you again, I hope."

Standing Elk rose. "You shall see Mark again, Megan. I will walk you home."

Megan and Standing Elk stepped into the darkness and found their way as their eyes adjusted. Mark sat quietly. After a minute, he heard barking of dogs but no shriek.

Day 2-17:   Home for the Night

As Susan got to the door of their house, she was startled by a figure hurrying up to her.

"Hi, Mom! I recognized your luminous cape in the moonlight."

Putting a hand over her heart, Susan relaxed. "Oh, you scared me, Megan! Did you have a good evening?"

"I learned how little we know about history, especially Dad! How was the ball?"

"We made history. Your father danced the minuet with me. He left early to go for a walk. Don't be mad because he didn't accept what you learned about the taxes. You are saying different things from what we were told all our lives. If what you say is true, it will take him time to work through it."

"If it's true? Mom, don't you believe it either?"

"I'm adjusting to a new way of looking at things. We are all learning here. I believe you."

Inside the house, Megan headed to her room and Susan looked in on Peter through his open door. Tired from the gathering at the Hush Harbor the night before, he had fallen asleep on the bed with a book beside him and the oil lamp still lit. She gently placed a blanket over her son, put out the lamp, and smiled, thinking how fast twenty-one years had gone by.

She lit a candle and started a small fire in the fireplace. As the kindling crackled and three small logs began to burn, John arrived and she could tell he had had a bit to drink.

"Hi, Honey," she welcomed him. "Did you have a good walk?"

"I met the sergeant again. It was good to talk with an old soldier."

Susan saw that the conversation with the sergeant had a salutary effect on John. Something in him was loosening up. She gave him a hug and he returned the squeeze. She was disappointed when he slid into sleep within seconds of his head touching the pillow.

Day 3-1:   November 1775

"Rise and shine! It's time to get up!" Susan called to Peter.

"What time is it? I mean what year is it?" Peter yawned loudly.

"It's still 1775 but it's chilly. Megan and I got coffee and scones at the Raleigh Tavern bakery. She took hers and went off to study her notes."

At breakfast, Peter said, "I won't take food for granted any more. Virginia had hard beginnings. Fifteen years after the founding at Jamestown, only two thousand people survived of fifteen thousand that landed since 1607. They faced starvation, disease, fights with Indians and each other—lots of disasters. A ship from Bermuda saved them at the beginning, and later, tobacco provided income."

"Two out of fifteen surviving is worse odds than a battle or an outbreak of bubonic plague." John said as he sipped his coffee.

"I'm praying our survival rate is four out of four," said Susan.

"This is not the 1620s. We'll survive," Peter assured her, hoping it was true. "But slaves and servants are poorly fed and settlers moving west try hunting and gathering, but many don't know how to hunt or what to gather."

"Megan says the local Indians are friendly and that helps," John added, "but soon His Majesty's Royal Artillery, Infantry, and Grenadiers will be very unfriendly. This is a much more violent society than the one we live in." John finished his breakfast. "Let's meet here at noon. How will Megan know?"

"One of us is bound to run into her. This is not a big town."

Day 3-2:   Peter sees Augustus off for Norfolk

For an hour, Peter read notes from his visit to the Rockefeller Library. It was not going to be easy. Over the course of two generations, the Underground Railroad led tens of thousands of slaves to freedom mainly into Canada. The British freed a hundred thousand in six years — but rarely helped them. Only ten per cent of those who ran during the Revolution made it to a new life.

The downside could be death for Evie or her sons. Was it worth the risk? Knowing the British were going to lose, a slave's best chance seemed to be to get to loyal colonies, Britain, France, or Africa. He would tell her Dunmore's Proclamation was a rare chance for freedom and she could make up her own mind.

Peter stepped into morning air so chilly he went back inside to put two T-shirts on under his hunting shirt to keep warm. As he walked to the Powell House, he grew excited that Dunmore's Proclamation could be a way for Evie to escape. She would have to beat the one-in-ten odds of success and the consequences of failure. By a tavern, he learned he was not the only one excited.

On the porch a citizen called to passersby, "A week ago on November 7, from his ship, Governor Dunmore proclaimed slaves who join the British cause to be free. He ordered attacks on rebel towns and plantations. We have war in Virginia as in Massachusetts. What a calamity if slaves attack their masters! Make haste to spread the word lest the news reach the slaves first. Prepare to defend yourselves."

"November? No wonder it's cold." It did not matter if Peter told Evie about the proclamation because it had happened already. Farther on, Augustus marched toward him, a canvas sack on a pole slung over his shoulder like a musket.

"Hello Augustus," Peter greeted him in a failed attempt to avoid startling him.

"Oh, Mister Peter. I ain't seen you since we was wit' Annie in the spring. It turned out like you said. I waited a few months and then this proclamation came."

"Are you off to Norfolk?" asked Peter.

"Please don't say nothin' to nobody. If I leave town beyond the College and walk down the road like I does when I'm fetching something for Massa, and don't look scared like a rabbit, then I'se hopin' nobody will ax me my business."

"That sounds like a good plan, Augustus, but planters and the county militia will be watching the roads to Norfolk like a big owl eying a rabbit hole, and you could be their rabbit. The closer you get to Norfolk, the more you should keep to the tracks through the woods and fields. Would you like help?"

"I would, Mister Peter! I'se tryin' not to look like a rabbit, but inside I'se jumpy."

"Is freedom worth this danger?"

"Yes, Sir! If Annie and you is free and Moses freed the Hebrew children, then the Lord who delivered Jonah from the whale and Daniel from the lions can deliver me! If I is free, maybe I can do somethin' for Evie and them boys. I could come back here someday and steal them away or buy them or somethin'."

"Sit on this bench, Augustus. I have an idea." Peter took a piece of paper from his wallet and wrote, "The bearer of this note is my trusted servant, Augustus. I gave him five Spanish dollars to take to his former master, my cousin George, near Smithfield, to buy medicine for his sick wife. Augustus will return directly to me at Williamsburg carrying a package." He dated it and signed it with a flourish.

"What do it say?"

"It says you're taking this money to my cousin near Smithfield to buy medicine."

"Is he sick?"'

"I have no cousin there, Augustus. The money is for you and the note shows anyone who stops you that you have a reason to be on the road. Smithfield is across the James River toward Norfolk."

"I can't take five whole dollars of your money!"

"I saw you become a healer, and now I see you setting out courageously on a challenging journey. Augustus, you can help others with the money and with your healing skills. Don't try to get to a boat to Norfolk. The militia could stop you or the boat owner may sell you. Instead, go up river toward Richmond until the river narrows, and then find a bridge or place where you can swim it."

"I can't swim."

"Find a shallow ford if there's no bridge. Hopewell is south of the James. From there keep to the woods and head east, the direction of the sunrise, to Smithfield then Norfolk. If someone stops you, find out which side they're on. If they are Tories, say you're joining the forces loyal to the King. If they are colonial militia, show them the note. Pretend to be stupid. Maybe they won't shoot you. If they point a gun at you, don't be nervous. It will make you look guilty."

"Don't be nervous? I'll die of nervous 'fore they shoot me even once! But I been pretendin' to be stupid all my life. That be easy for a slave like me."

"You're not a slave anymore, 'Gustus. Not because I say so, but because you say so. You just ran away, remember? You are a free man running to stay free from slave owners. Slavery is in their minds, not yours."

"I hear that and I believe it be true. Praise God! I'se a free man!"

Peter reached out and shook Augustus's hand. "Good luck, Mister Augustus."

"Mister Augustus... *Mister* Augustus! Thank you, Mister Peter. I will always remember this." He set off down the road.

Peter sat watching Augustus disappear around a far corner. Suddenly it occurred to him that it might have been a bad idea to sign his name to the paper Augustus carried. Too late to do anything about that now, he thought. As he stood to walk to the Powell House, two militiamen and a man in a cloth cap man ran up to him

"This is the fellow!" The man in the cap pointed at Peter.

"Halt right where you are," said one of the militiamen brandishing his musket.

Peter stood still and raised his hands. "Did I do something wrong?" he asked.

135

"This fellow says he saw you talking to a slave. He says you gave the slave a note and some money. What did the note say and what was the money for?"

Peter worried Augustus had been captured.

Peter took a chance. "He went to buy a hammer for his Master and I asked him to buy a leather holder for it as a gift from me. I wrote a note to Mister Carter."

"Why would you do that?"

"I want to thank Mister Carter for a favor he did. I am leaving town today."

"We have a lot of trouble with slaves running away these days. It ain't right you talking to another man's slave like that. Are you sure he ain't running away?"

"I hope not. Then Mister Carter will not get the gift or the hammer."

"You hope not? You gave him money and with that, he could go farther away and feed himself until he was long gone. We can't have that going on."

"Before he leaves town, let's put him in the pillory or stocks to teach him to be careful about the slaves," said the other militiamen.

They each grabbed one of Peter's arms and marched him to the nearby courthouse. There was already a man sitting with his legs in the stocks outside the building so they called for the bailiff who opened the heavy upper board of the pillory and placed Peter's head and hands into the holes and locked him in.

The soldiers and man in the cap left Peter in the pillory, standing bent over in an awkward position. "What did you do?" asked bailiff.

"They saw me talking to the slave of a friend. I guess that was the wrong thing to do." Peter did not want to get in any deeper.

"Well," said the bailiff. "Those militiamen are short tempered these days." He pulled out an old pocket watch. "I don't want to go against what they said so I'll keep you here only an hour. I hope no more young ragamuffins come by to throw rotten fruit or dog shit at you. Time in the pillory or stocks can be dirty."

The man in the stocks said, "Look what the ruffians rubbed in my hair this morning! Can you let me out in an hour too?"

"Not 'till sunset, Alfred. The merchant you insulted was sorely angry at you." The Bailiff walked back into the courthouse.

"I apologized for what I said," the man in the stocks called out.

If what Peter did for Augustus were known, he could be sitting in a cell and facing a questionable future. He bent his legs slightly to take the strain off his back. After a few minutes, he grew extremely uncomfortable. He hoped no one would come to harass him during his hour in the stocks. His hope would not be fulfilled.

Day 3-3:   John at the Magazine and Masonic Hall

John approached a noisy spontaneous assembly near the octagonal powder magazine. "When Dunmore seized our powder and threatened to cancel land grants to veterans, he almost provoked insurrection!" a man shouted. "Patrick Henry called up militiamen and Hugh Mercer prepared to ride from Fredericksburg with a company of light horse."

"But Peyton Randolph negotiated a settlement. Dunmore paid for the powder and maintained the grants."

"Settled poorly!" shouted a third man. "We need powder more than money! Let's march to Norfolk, sink Dunmore's ship, and chase the Redcoats off!"

"We should not widen this conflict! Britain is the world's strongest military power and does not fight alone. Do you want to fight the Loyalist militias of the Floridas, Southern Maryland, Nova Scotia, Quebec, and loyal counties in New York, New Jersey, the Carolinas, and Georgia at once?"

A man in the back of the crowd called out, "There is news up North from whence I sailed. Benedict Arnold and Ethan Allen raided the British at Fort Ticonderoga and captured cannons to fire at the Redcoats in the siege of Boston."

"No wonder our King declared those colonies in rebellion! His forces will thrash them!" exclaimed a man from across the Chesapeake. "Our Maryland legislature began its recent session with an oath of allegiance to His Majesty. Last year, John Adams said we do not want independence. We want our rights as Englishmen just as our forefathers in Britain struggled for their rights since the Magna Carta!"

John wondered how the Founders kept people together and how they survived years of fighting. The chances were slim. With so many links to Britain, was the war necessary? Were my wars necessary? His mind spun. It seemed simple in school. We were the good guys and they were the bad guys. This was more complicated.

He wandered away from the rancorous group and found himself in front of the Masonic Hall feeling a strong urge to bang the brass doorknocker. No response, so he tried the handle. Locked! He turned to leave when the door opened behind him. There in colonial dress was James Walker, the Episcopal priest. "Oh, it's you!" he stammered, "I'm John Sinclair. I was at your sermon Friday."

"You were in a front pew next to the woman I met in the bookstore. The Hall is closed but step in for a moment. I'll be getting out of my costume before church."

"Your costume?"

"Yes, the Lodge hosted a breakfast this morning."

"I... I am confused about the time. The reenactments seem so real that..."

"I understand. We conduct our lodge in colonial dress. Sometimes I imagine we are in colonial times. One gets used to it. This is an active Masonic Hall but we occasionally have public tours. I'll give you a quick look around." They climbed the stairs to the Lodge Hall where Reverend Walker pointed out highlights in the room including the intricately carved Master's Chair, a gift of Governor Botetourt in the 1760s. "If his successors had been Masons perhaps the colonists and Britain could have settled their differences without a war."

"Who is the Master today?"

"I am — for three more months, and then I'll be a Past Master. In Freemasonry we rotate through the chairs, moving up gradually so many can take responsibility when they are ready."

"You called this a Masonic Hall. I've heard it referred to as a Masonic Lodge."

"Technically, the building where we meet is a Masonic Hall or Temple and when we're in session that's a Lodge, but lots of people get that confused."

"How did you become a Mason?"

"To join, you ask a member of a Lodge to invite you. You'll be welcome if you believe in a Supreme Being whatever your religion, or even without a religion."

"Can an Episcopal priest be a Mason at the same time?"

"Yes. The Reverend James Madison, a cousin of the President, was a member here and later became the first Episcopal Bishop in Virginia. In the 1920s, W.A.R. Goodwin was rector at Bruton Parish Church and a Freemason when he enrolled John D. Rockefeller, Jr. into restoring Williamsburg. Many luminaries were members — Peyton Randolph, President James Monroe, St. George Tucker..."

"St. George Tucker? I was at his house reading and staying out of the sun."

"They have a good library. You may meet a wise woman there named Frances. She knows local history and seems to know something about intuition."

"She does? I met her there. I will go back this afternoon to talk with her. Reverend Walker, I have heard the Masons were involved in the founding of America, that they know deep mysteries, and that some of their symbols are part of the Great Seal of the United States. How much of that is true?"

"Many Freemasons helped form the nation including George Washington and Benjamin Franklin. At least nine of the 56 signers of the Declaration of Independence were members and probably more. However, many Founders, like John Adams and Thomas Jefferson, were not Masons.

"There are abundant myths about Masons. I could lower my voice and speak of a Divine Plan to bring forth a New Order of the Ages. Some talk of secret crypts hiding treasures or ancient scrolls. I could whisper those things but as a long-time Freemason and Master of this Lodge I have not run into such secrets while studying Masonic traditions or participating in our ceremonies. In my experience, men in the Lodges learn to work together, become more virtuous, and contribute to their communities. A popular Masonic slogan that sums up the point of our practices is, 'We take good men and make them better.' I think we do, with support from each other and from the Supreme Being, whatever name we use for it.

"We do use symbols in ceremonies that we don't make public. Why not? Realization of the meaning of symbols or parables is a personal experience. We prefer not to weaken the effectiveness by talking about them. If someone learns a new concept without experiencing the deeper meaning, a new obstacle is placed on his path. He thinks he knows the truth because he has a new belief. That false certainty gets in the way of observing the depth and value of the practice in his life."

"Is the Great Seal a Masonic symbol?"

"You can see the Masonic, Egyptian, and Hebrew symbols on the Great Seal of the United States on every dollar bill. The final design of the Seal was done in 1782 by Charles Thomson, Secretary of the Continental Congress, who was not a Mason. Some design elements were suggested by three earlier committees that included Masons and non-Masons. As a young man, Thomson was adopted by Delaware Indians. Perhaps the tribe provided the idea of the eagle that for many native peoples is a carrier of their prayers to the Creator."

"So what really was the Masonic influence on the birth of America?"

"One third of Washington's Continental Army generals were Masons — I think it was Freemasons' confidence in each other that led to those promotions. There is a spiritual quality to all we do at the Lodge and in daily life. Divine secrets are around us and within everyone. They are secret because we do not pay enough attention to notice. No one was keeping radio waves secret when Moses led the Israelites out of Egypt or when Christ preached the Sermon on the Mount; we just did not notice radio waves then. Radio waves are still invisible but they are not a secret anymore.

"I would also say Freemasons' ideals and aspirations supported the Founding Fathers' commitment to liberty. Whatever their status outside the Lodge, whether a Royal Governor like Botetourt who lived in the Palace or a jailer like Peter Pelham who lived at the Gaol, as 'Brethren in the Craft' they met as equals. They called it 'on the level' and respected each other as men rather than ranked by their titles, wealth, or station."

"I heard men talking about 'levelers.' Is that related to 'on the level'?"

"Not directly, but men who grew accustomed to treating each other 'on the level' might well begin to wonder about pillars of society such as the Divine Right of Kings and hereditary rights of nobility in Europe and of the wealthy landed class here in America. For the very wealthy those are revolutionary, dangerous ideas."

"Revolutionary, indeed! Reverend, I know you have to change for church. I'm still confused about the imagination at work around here but talking with you helped."

"Good to see you again, John."

John stepped back into the street amidst the smells of wood smoke and horses.

139

Day 3-4:   Susan Visits the Public Hospital

Susan set out to search for Jane. She stopped at the millinery shop. "Ah, Lady Sinclair, I have wondered how the dress and mantua were received at the Palace."

"They were a big hit, Alwyn. People assumed I came from a highborn family in the North. And my husband danced with me for the first time in a long time."

"A long time you say. It is not easy to keep track is it?"

"No kidding. It seems like yesterday I bought that mantua. You are a tease, Alwyn! I'm sure you know more about time than you are letting on."

"Susan, I work in Williamsburg in the midst of history. I have an active imagination and on rare occasions, I meet someone who experiences the same things I do. Not a good explanation, but it's all I know about it, verily."

"That's a bit helpful, Alwyn. Do you happen to know a woman named Jane who wears a hooded cloak and speaks about peace? I'm anxious to talk with her."

"I don't know her but I have seen her many times in public places."

"Thanks for everything, Alwyn."

Susan carefully crossed the street avoiding the horse droppings, and entered the wig maker's shop. Charlotte turned around and gaped.

"Hello, Charlotte! It was wonderful to see you at the Ball. Today is the first day I have been in town since then. I don't know where the time went. How are you?"

"Lady Susan! I worried all these months." She hugged Susan then stepped back. "Oh, Milady! Forgive my impertinence!"

"I told you I'm a middle-sorts wife like you." Susan smiled.

"Susan, my husband and I are fearful of the war. We have friends on both sides ready to hang each other. George says everyone has gone mad. I pray your family is safe. A customer is coming for her hair trimming, so I can't chat long."

"I understand. I just dropped by to say hello. Do you know a woman named Jane who wears a cloak and has light brown hair tied in a bun?"

"I know who you mean, Susan. I sometimes see her walking to the Public Hospital. We all have worries but that place gives me the shivers!"

"There are many people in distress. Thank you, I may look for her there."

The door opened as Charlotte's next customer stepped in. "Thank you for visiting, Susan. In topsy-turvy times 'tis nice to have friends."

Susan walked past the church and her thoughts turned to Jane as she followed the path to the two-story brick building topped by a cupola and weather vane. By the door, a sign read "Public Hospital for Persons of Insane and Disordered Minds." She paused at the entrance wondering if they would let her in, then smiled. More importantly, will they let me out? She knocked on the heavy door using the fleshy side of her fist. A key turned in the lock, and a slave opened the door a crack. "Are you here to visit Doctor John de Sequeyra?"

"Uh, he's not expecting me. I am Susan Sinclair. What's your name?"

Surprised to be asked, he said, "I am Sal. I will tell the doctor you be here."

Susan felt a shudder as the great door closed behind her and the key turned in the lock, but Sal's kind manner put her at ease.

A man with his hands pressed together walked by, slowly repeating a phrase. Susan could not make out his prayer until she realized it was not English. *"In manus tuas commendo spiritum meum. In manus tuas commendo spiritum..."* his murmured prayer faded down the corridor.

Sal returned to say the doctor was doing a ducking and she could follow him to see the doctor at work. They passed heavy doors with barred windows and the murmuring man going the other way, *"In manus tuas commendo spiritum meum..."*

They came to an immense barrel full of cold water. A chair was suspended above by a chain running over pulleys into the hands of a slave. In the chair, restrained by leather straps, a patient, gagged to keep her from biting her tongue, attempted to kick her bound legs. Her wet hair matted to her head and her eyes were filled with rage. "No more, cold!" Susan made out through the woman's gag.

A dark-haired man in a linen shirt and woolen waistcoat, standing beyond the range of splashing, nodded to the slave who lowered the chair into the barrel.

"No, no!" The woman's shouts became a stifled bubbling as she was immersed.

My God! Susan thought, do they think this woman is a witch?

The man in the linen shirt nodded again and the slave raised the chair.

"What do you think, Missus Jackson?" the doctor asked. "Enough for today?"

"No more! Cold, cold!" coughed the bedraggled woman in the chair.

"Well done! When you stop shouting all night there will be no more ducking." He nodded to the slave. "Daniel, you may lower Missus Jackson. Sal, escort her to her room where Rachel can dry her. Do what you can to calm her." The man turned to Susan. "Welcome. I am John de Sequeyra, the doctor here."

"I'm Susan Sinclair." Susan gathered herself after what she had just witnessed.

"It is damp here," said the doctor. "Let us adjourn to my office." Susan followed the doctor, surprised at his relatively kind manner with Missus Jackson. On their way to the office, the praying man passed them again.

In Doctor de Sequeyra's small office Susan sat where he gestured. "Thank you for coming to the hospital. I rarely get visitors. How can I help, Missus Sinclair?"

Susan started with a new question. "What is the man in the hall praying about?"

"He is repeating in Latin the last words of Jesus Christ according to the Gospel of Luke. Jesus was quoting the 31st Psalm, which is better known to me than the Gospel. It means 'into your hands I commend my spirit.' He may be a secret Catholic but he never talks about it. If so, it may be safer for him in here among the insane than out there with so-called sane people who could kill him for his beliefs. His prayers have a calming effect on other patients."

The doctor smiled. "You appear to be of sound mind. No troubled person knocks on our door of their own accord. Oh, except for one woman. We are the only such hospital in all the colonies. A need was noted by the Council of Burgesses and we were fashioned after the Bethlem Royal Hospital near London. Its nickname 'Bedlam' has come to mean chaos and madness. Did you come to visit a patient?"

"Thank you for seeing me, Doctor De Sequeyra. I am a teacher and mother from Northern Virginia. I came to ask a question and to look for someone. But first, can you tell me the benefit of the treatment you administered to that woman."

"The four humors, Earth, Air, Fire, and Water, make up our bodies. Air is represented by blood, Fire by yellow bile, Water by phlegm, and Earth by black bile. That woman has too much yellow bile as evidenced by her anger and shouting. We duck her to douse the fire and encourage the phlegm to balance those humors. With the coming of winter's own damp, that should not be needed."

"I see. For her sake I am glad of that."

"It is for her sake that we administer the treatment. She shows signs of recovery. I suspect the insane manage problems by retreating into unhealthy states of mind. We use compassionate restraint so they cannot hurt themselves. We use tulip tree bark to reduce fever, lavender flowers as a sedative, and rosemary to stimulate blood flow. We bleed patients to reduce pressure on the brain."

Susan winced, she hoped not visibly.

"Besides sparing these people the cruelty of being chained in barns or smothered by those who fear madness is demonic possession, we release one in five back to their families. We hope to cure more of these troubled souls."

"Doctor de Sequeyra, I have a question about problems of ordinary people. I am a schoolteacher. What can you advise for a person who is agitated or depressed?"

"I see such patients in my practice on the high street. I administer laudanum to relax them or prescribe a ration of brandy, but since you teach children, I shall share a professional secret. Humors have cycles, and moods change with circumstances. I find good results come from simply listening to what a distressed soul, young or old, wishes to say. When people share their burdens, adverse feelings begin to fade. I may suggest herbal tea or walks in nature. If they are devout, I suggest they pray for support in their travails. Are you religious?"

"I'm an infrequent churchgoer. Are you a member of the Established Church?"

"Like everyone in the colony, I pay taxes to the Church of England and attend services once a month or face a fine. But that is not the faith of my fathers. I am most familiar with the Old Testament. I am the only Jew I know of living in Williamsburg. We call the first five books of the Old Testament the Torah."

"There are no other Jews here? How does an eligible Jewish doctor find a bride? Where I come from, many young women would love to marry a Jewish doctor."

"I must live in the wrong town. I join Jewish families in Richmond or Norfolk for the Day of Atonement or Passover. I gave slaves here names from the Torah:

Rachel, Samuel, and Daniel. A few months ago, Samuel renamed himself Sal, which he says reminds him of his youth in Africa when he was free. At Passover, we Jews remember our Exodus from the wretched condition of slavery in Egypt, which is also in Africa, so I am happy that his name reminds him of freedom. He is skillful at caring for the hard to reach and he recently learned to read."

"As the only Jew in Williamsburg, you didn't spring from a burning bush. Are you from Pennsylvania? You have a slight accent that reminds me of German."

"I was born in Holland where my Sephardic ancestors moved to escape the Spanish Inquisition. I came here to experience the New World. Speaking of experience, do you care to walk through the hospital? Many of our patients are restrained but some walk in the halls, and help by cleaning or by serving food."

Susan walked beside the doctor past the twenty cells of the hospital. Through barred windows, she saw some patients in chains tethered to a ring embedded in the wall. Others lay arms and legs akimbo or in a fetal position on a straw mat. Two were restrained in leather straps and a head brace to prevent them from biting themselves or others. The cells were cleaner and better lit than those of the gaol.

A patient shuffled toward them with eyes at once piercing and vacant. His voice demanded and pleaded, "I don't want to be stuck for eternity. Day after day, it stretches forward and backward in time. I cannot remember when it was not nor can I see how it could cease. It is frozen but not cold. I am locked in a scream that has no sound." He opened his mouth in an expression of anguish and stood motionless.

"Ask the Lord to help you, Nathan."

"I don't deserve help!" he snapped. "None of you know a thing! You are as lost in eternity as I am. You believe religious fairy tales that disperse like steam from a kettle when you are frozen or lost! Day after day it stretches..."

Sal returned from escorting Missus Jackson to Rachel and put his hand on the patient's shoulder. "Walk wit' me, Nathan, to the end of the hall and back three times. Swing your arms when you move your feet and you won't be frozen all day. Listen for the heavenly music again. You know it is never far away."

Nathan looked confused and startled by the physical contact on his shoulder. Without another word, he set off slowly swinging his arms just as the praying man came past again, *"In manus tuas commendo spiritum meum."*

"He certainly has a way with patients," Susan noted. "Doctor, I am looking for someone." At that moment, a cell door opened and Jane emerged, carrying a basket with a soiled blanket. "Oh, I was going to ask you where I might find Jane."

Jane was startled to hear her name, "Doest thou know me?"

"We spoke by the Capitol the day... I mean a few months ago. You said you lost your family in a war. I told you my husband was troubled by his war experience."

"Forgive me. I speak to many people. I don't remember thee."

"Jane Harding, this is Missus Susan Sinclair," the doctor said. "She came to learn about the hospital. Please take a few minutes outside in the fresh air to explain to her what you have learned here."

"Oh, I would like that very much," Susan said, seeing Jane's hesitation.

"Go ahead, Jane. The fresh air will be good for you both. Oh, look! Here comes Sal with Nathan. He can open the door and you two can have a chat."

Sal opened the door. Nathan continued past swinging his arms and humming heavenly music. "Rachel will launder the blanket and you can come back to help another day," said the doctor.

Susan set a slow pace down the walkway from the hospital. She judged it would be better to walk in gardens rather than crowded noisy spaces. "Jane, it is kind of you to help at the hospital. I am sure you ease the burden of the doctor."

"I strive to do what I can. There are so many troubles in this world that it is hard to know where to start, and there is no end. Sometimes it seems so dark."

"Jane, I care about the spiritual life. I know you work for peace and help the tormented. Are you a member of the Society of Friends?"

Jane tensed.

"I attended a Friends' Meeting House for a wedding and was moved by the spontaneous voices speaking after periods of silence," said Susan.

"Hast thou been to Meeting? Most call us Quakers. Yes, I was born into the Society of Friends, but I have not been at Meeting for years. If I seek Inner Light, fear and loneliness come upon me. Friends were willing martyrs when Puritans hanged them for preaching after being banned. I fear losing my life, though it is not a happy one. I serve in small ways because I don't have a deeper service."

They came to a bench near an oak tree, boxwood hedge, and rose bushes that held a few remaining blooms. "Jane, let's sit a few minutes in silence." Leaves trembled in a light breeze. Their fallen brethren rustled on the path. Clouds soared slowly, shapes transforming and shifting. Jane sighed.

Susan recalled the deep calm the first morning by the fire. Was that months ago? She listened, watched, and felt herself slowing down. The words came to her again.

"The extraordinary – extra ordinary, forever underlies the apparent. Beneath habitual, behind familiar, all form animated, all pattern emerging, resolving, and dissolving."

Jane raised her hands in an attitude of prayer, put them to her face, and trembled. She sat in silence. Then words came:

"The Light within illuminates eternally through seeming darkness. Beneath the known, behind the dream, light causes all that moves, sustains all that is still: Source of all becoming and all slipping away. All come, all go. The Light is ever and forever so."

After several minutes, Jane looked into Susan's face. ""It has been so many long years. I was but a girl the last time I felt touched by the Light."

"You have been in pain a long time, Jane Harding."

"I wandered long in fear without solace. Thou gifted me, Susan Sinclair."

144

"We both received a gift, Jane. I have a pain I've never shared with my children." She drew a long breath. "Many years ago my older brother Richard was called up to war. He told me he was afraid to die or be maimed, but even more, he worried he would kill a young person who did not want to go to war either and was as afraid as he was. I was stubborn, naïve, and almost crazy from wishing I could stop the war. While my brother was in training, I joined protests on the streets of our city. When the time came, he went off to war... and he never came back to us."

"Did he die in the war against the French?"

"It was a far-away war, at another time. A week before he was to come home, there was an ambush in a forest. Men at the rear of his platoon survived and got back to their base. No one witnessed what happened to Richard and his body was never found. I think I married my husband partly to help a soldier like my brother. I saw my own pain in your eyes by the Capitol, and I looked for you."

"That was a great kindness thou did for thine husband. My grief led me to the edge of madness, and I visit the Public Hospital to help poor souls and seek peace. I witnessed what happened to my family. I have been alone since I was twelve."

"What happened, Jane? When you were in the crowd, what did you fear?"

Jane sighed. "This is not Pennsylvania, and sixteen years have passed. Doctor de Sequeyra told me many times that no one in Williamsburg wants to hurt me, but I never mentioned even to him that I was from the Society of Friends or those Paxton Boys who committed that horrible deed."

"I haven't heard of the Paxton Boys. Do you want to tell me what happened?"

Jane watched a squirrel harvesting acorns. "That squirrel is making ready for a hard winter. A hard winter is coming to us all. I don't know how I shall bear it."

"You said, 'The Light within illuminates eternally through seeming darkness.'"

Jane sighed. "During the French and Indian War, after years of our friendship with local Indians, a group called the Paxton Boys came west and slaughtered villages that had long lived in peace with us. People in the Society of Friends warned Indians they knew and urged them to escape over the mountains. My people sought to save lives but..." Jane took Susan's hand to compose herself.

"Rather than escape as the Friends expected, the villages were reinforced by Indians from the West. The Paxton Boys were ambushed, and some were killed."

Jane wiped away tears with her sleeve. "My father was one of the men who warned the Indians. Months later, after my mother died from fever, I was gathering berries by a stream a mile from home. As sunlight sparkled on the water, I felt my mother's presence and did not want to leave just yet. When my basket was full, I followed the path through the woods toward our house and saw smoke.

"When I ran home, I fell to my knees and wailed. My father and two brothers lay bloodied on the ground, their hair cut away as hostile Indians do. The roof of the house was gone and one of the burning walls fell in as I stared. I was horrified and ran along the wagon road to the east to get help from my uncle and his family.

"From a distance I saw their house in flames and men loading a cart. I crawled nearer through the bushes. They were five white men. One called out 'Let's ride lads! We have one more visit to treacherous Quakers today. I hope they are poor because we have no room in the cart.' They laughed, Susan Sinclair! Dead children lay on the ground and they laughed! Another said, 'Tis a tragedy the savages resorted to butchery. The militia will ride west to take revenge.' He cleaned a long blade on my auntie's apron torn from the line."

"I heard one say, 'Come on, Roger. You shall use your dagger again before this day is done.' The last of them mounted and rode away down the wagon road."

"I don't remember walking home. The shovel was gone but using pointed rocks, I scraped shallow graves for my father and brothers and covered them with stones as we did for my mother. Over the next days, I buried the poor souls at the other house and bathed in the stream where my mother saved my life by causing me to linger. That notion gave me comfort. I walked to southeast Pennsylvania finding food where I could. I worked as a maid for a German family. They were kind to me but after four years, I moved on.

"Where the Susquehanna empties into Chesapeake, I worked in a tavern. Men would not leave me alone, so I went to Alexandria and found a family that needed a maid. I was not bonded but I was not free from fear of the Paxton Boys finding me, so I moved on to Williamsburg. I thought my fear was silly because the bad men never saw me. But a few months ago, I saw the man with the long knife here."

"Fear is not silly, Jane," offered Susan. "My husband taught me courage is not the absence of fear. It is willingness to face that which we fear. I am inspired by the courage of the twelve-year-old girl you were. You and I seek peace so young people will not have such horrible experiences in the future. The Light was working through you all along. No need to call me Susan Sinclair. Call me Susan."

"In the Society of Friends we don't use mister and missus so we use the full name. Thou sayest the Light is always near. The Light came through now."

"Jane, I feel a calm that I have never felt. I feel my brother is at peace and I can be at peace about him. You and I experienced something wonderful together."

"I thank thee for this, Susan."

"Jane, my family and I have met wonderful people here. I can introduce you to them. With friends you might feel less alone."

"Wilt thou be my friend?" Jane hugged Susan and tears came to her eyes.

Susan hesitated. "Yes, Jane, I will. I live very far from here, but know that I will always pray for you and we will be friends from afar."

"Susan, there is a trial this afternoon at the Court House. I fear an innocent man is being persecuted, and I will be there to pray for him. Art thou free to join me?"

"I will join you at the Court House and we can pray together."

Jane took Susan's offered arm and they walked back toward Market Square.

146

Day 3-5:   Megan Sees Patterns in the Pasture

Fortified by her tea and scone, Megan found a path leading into a pasture and wandered to a spot in the sun among wildflowers. She sat on a log with her back against fence boards already warmed by the morning rays. Wrapped in a blanket she had brought with her, Megan began reading a history text and added to her notes. A trail into town passed on the other side of the fence.

She read her notes again and rechecked the history book. "Oh boy!" she exclaimed. "Wait till Dad hears about the Boston Tea Party!"

The sun shining through the thinning leaves of an oak tree reached her as a dancing mottled veil. She began to notice her surroundings. Bees were still at work in November. A lone swallowtail butterfly visited wildflowers, its open wings black with a patina fading from purple to light blue with vivid orange spots in a shimmering pattern changing with the angle of light. She saw a beetle moving along the ground. "Eeew!" but then she noticed colors in the sheen on the hard black shell and her aversion passed. Megan smelled grasses and soil, the aging wood of the fence, and fresh air carrying trace scents from distant fireplaces.

A birdcall heralded an approach on the trail. When the sound of footfalls was close, she looked up to see Standing Elk walking toward town. He smiled when he saw her and vaulted the fence. "Hello, Megan. It has been months. May I sit?"

"Sure." Megan put her book out of sight under the notebook. "It's been months?"

"It was May. This is November."

"How is Mark doing?" Megan asked.

"Doing well, still at the forge."

A minute went by. Standing Elk looked across the meadow to a line of trees. Megan was not used to silence and she spoke. "The scenery here is beautiful,"

"It is more than scenery. It is beautiful like the fireflies you saw in spring."

"What do you mean?"

"All we see moves like colors in the butterfly's wing. We are in it, and it is in us."

"What is *it*?"

"*It* is the breath of the Creator. All we see, hear, touch, and know. Everything."

"I remember how the pattern of the fireflies and the pattern of the sounds of crickets all fit together. We were part of that pattern as we sat in a circle."

Standing Elk smiled. "What do you see in those white flowers beside you?"

"Clusters of tiny white flowers with petals pointed up making cups with yellow at the center. The leaves are narrow and dark green at the top and drooping, curly, and silver gray near the ground." She felt a leaf. "Fuzzy underneath."

"We call it rabbit tobacco. Settlers call it 'everlasting' because it blooms into winter. We use it in tea to reduce pain or sooth coughs. We burn the leaves for aromatic smoke for purification. Mothers put it into pillows for a good sleep."

Megan broke a leaf in her hand and crushed it in her fingers. "Oh! That is a nice fragrance. It's… astringent, that's the word, like a persimmon that's not quite ripe." She touched the edge of the leaf to her tongue. "Yup, astringent like witch hazel."

"Good. You use all your senses. That shrub over by the sycamore tree is witch hazel. It still has a few unusual flowers, little green pots with five yellow streamers. We make a poultice of witch hazel bark for bruises and skin problems. The plant with smooth pointed leaves by your feet is Virginia Spiderwort. In spring, each purple blossom comes and goes in a day, a short beautiful life, but the flowers keep coming for two months."

"I'll bet you use that plant for something, too."

"Yes, we eat shoots as greens and when the leaves are old we boil them for a poultice for bee stings and mosquito bites to stop pain and itch. The tea is good for the stomach or kidneys. Mixed with other herbs it helps women on their moon. It was taken to England a hundred years ago. An Englishman told me that in spring, our purple friends are now in many English gardens. See those yellow flowers?"

"Those are dandelions!" said Megan. "We can use the greens in salad and children like to blow the seeds when the flower becomes a fluffy ball."

"Very good. Our children blow those seed balls, too. But our ancestors did not."

"They didn't blow on dandelions? Why not?"

"Dandelions were not here yet. Colonists brought them to eat as an early spring green. The flowers move west faster than the white man, and Indians who have seen not a white man now see dandelions. And we did not have honey bees before they were brought by Europeans.

"Megan, there are designs in the veins of leaves and wings of insects, and in the many mirrors of a dragonfly's eye. There are patterns you see, patterns you hear, and patterns you feel. Everything is part of moving patterns. You and I are part of the whole. We receive food and medicine from the Earth and warmth and light from the sun."

"I'm beginning to get that," said Megan.

"Bees, deer, flowers, and worms in the earth, we each strive to live and grow. Our bodies go back to the Earth. That is a flowing pattern, too. We feel solid and separate but we take in from each other and give out to each other or else we would cease to be. Most do not notice but you are waking up, Megan. What keeps people deaf, blind, and alone is that they do not listen, look, or touch. We live in closed worlds we imagine instead of using our imagination to explore the world as it is. You are moving outside that pouch to be open and to journey."

"I am?"

"Waking to the patterns of life may be why we are here. We learn from each other. My people receive both benefit and bane from the Colonists. Settlers sell us iron goods, muskets for hunting, and other useful inventions. And they buy from

148

us. South Carolina settlers get rich growing rice, but deer skins that native people trade with them are a major export of that colony as is the fur trade in the North.

"New plants, animals, and people can be good for this land, but some are greedy for more and hurt the life that was here before them. Colonists brought ivy that no animal here eats. The vines invade that land and kill trees by feeding on sap and blocking light. Some colonists are like that. Their hunger for land and the way they misuse it hurts all other life. They cut trees for iron works and leave land bare so rain carries away living soil to clog streams. Their tobacco depletes the soil. Much land in Tidewater is used up. Powerful families and new arrivals seek new land in the West to begin the destruction again by girdling trees."

"My brother told me about that."

"Take a walk with me and I will show you." He vaulted the fence, Megan climbed over, and they walked together.

"I told you my parents named me Standing Elk to remind me that the elk are gone but we are still here. Elk are not the only beings that vanished. Nearby are the Pamunkey and Mattaponi people, but other tribes are gone forever from the land you call Virginia. The Manahoac, Moneton, Nahyssan, and Occaneechi no longer tend their ceremonial fires. I feel sad to name tribes that are no more, though their blood flows in living people who remember a grandparent with love. We found a way to remain. In the Treaty of Middle Plantation, now Williamsburg, signed by Charles II, we agreed to pay a deerskin tribute to the Governor every autumn. We swore loyalty and kept small lands and the right to carry arms."

Standing Elk led Megan to a field where the trees had a ring of bark cut away, leaving dead blackening branches reaching toward the sun but no leaves to receive the light. Around them, mounds of soil with corn stubble were evidence of a harvested crop. "This is terrible," said Megan.

"Now look at the field over here."

"It's full of bare patches and weeds and has gullies that are washed out."

"Forty years ago that land was a forest. The trees were girdled by cutting a ring of bark and they died like these. The land was used for tobacco almost every year without letting it lie fallow. The soil was worn out and the crops failed. Now it will be barren for many years. These planters do not see the destruction because they are blind to life. When they ruin their land, they ruin themselves. This using up land cannot continue forever. However big this world, we will run out of land someday as more people keep coming. When the land, the game, the whale oil, and the fish are used up, all people and all life will suffer. But it happens slowly over generations and most people cannot see the pattern."

Standing Elk sighed, "This is a sad place. I struggle to find the will of the Creator behind this destruction. I know everything comes and goes but when whole tribes go and whole forests go, it is not easy to see purpose in the pattern. Maybe someday we will finally learn that what we do, what we say, what we think,

149

always comes back to us. Always. There will be great beauty when we all learn that. Let's walk to something else I want to show you."

They came upon a ravine and he pointed to a tree. "Here is a good thing Colonists brought. The white mulberry was carried to Georgia to feed silk worms. Black mulberries have been here forever but white mulberries are new to us. The berries are pink and delicious and come in abundance for weeks. They are something sweet for your people and ours."

"Do you think the people can learn to take better care of the land?" asked Megan.

"They might," Standing Elk replied. "Wiser land owners like George Washington and George Mason put manure, ashes, and bone meal onto the soil to replace what they are depleting. They let fields lie fallow alternate years to build up again. It helps their plantations remain prosperous, leaves a better estate for their grandchildren, and slows the race to use up the land Creator placed in this world for all creatures and people to share.

"But many owners are so squeezed by debt they plant every year until the crops fail and they abandon the land. New land beyond the proclamation line is being cleared against the command of the King. Secret investors in the Ohio Company and Vandalia Company send servants who do not know better to clear land in Indian country. Colonial leaders take land from the tribes because they ruined the land they took in the past. They think about getting wealthy quickly, not about tomorrow, and not even their own grandchildren. They give no thought to the future when there will be no new land to take. Megan, this is dangerous talk because many people are disturbed about it among both colonial leaders and the tribes."

"Taking that land is not only illegal but also unfair."

"It is unfair to us and to their grandchildren. They do not look deeply into the present so they do not see the shape of the future. We all have some of this blindness. Prayer and ceremony can help us see what is in and around us. When you saw the fireflies' paths that night, it was like a ceremony."

"I saw something I'd never seen before."

"Megan, today we are having a ceremony called a Spirit Lodge or Sweat Lodge. I would like you to come. You could learn about how people keep in balance in the face of challenges and how we practice seeing what is deeper but always here."

"Yes, I would like to come."

"Good. I must go to complete my tasks in town. Mark will come to the Lodge. Go to the blacksmith shop and ask him to take you there."

"But I..."

"See you tonight!" he called over his shoulder as he walked up the trail.

"Right! Back to Mark this afternoon." On the way to the house, Megan considered what to say to her father and how to ask Mark to take her to the Sweat Lodge.

Day 3-6: Lunch—Early Plans for Union

John and Susan ran into each other late in the morning and stopped into Charlton's Coffee House. Peter passed by just as his parents came out. "Peter!" his mother cried. "Are you alright?"

"Good God! What happened, Pete?" John ran to his son. "Where's the wound?"

Looking seriously injured with dry blood matting his hair, Peter insisted, "I'm fine, Mom and Dad. Some kids by the market poured bull's blood on my head."

"Why did they do that to you?"

"I was put in the pillory for an hour for talking to a slave. The kids played a prank. Two of us were locked in and they poured half the jar on each of us. The other poor guy has to stay like this until sunset. He may get other visits. I'm hurrying to wash up at the house."

They walked quickly. Peter wiped his face with a handkerchief Susan gave him.

"That's just awful, Peter. Who put you in the stocks?"

"A couple of militiamen told the bailiff to do it, Mom."

"I shouldn't have to tell you not to take reckless risks, Peter," said John.

At the house, Megan greeted them from her room. Susan laid out lunch. Peter rinsed off with well water outside before going to his room to finish washing up.

It was too cool to eat outside so they gathered to eat their sandwiches by the fire.

"Peter, you look better without blood all over your head. An injury or death can happen that suddenly. There are real risks here."

"I'll be more careful, Dad."

"This is a dangerous time," Susan said. "I learned a terrible thing from Jane, the woman I've been looking for. She volunteers at the Mental Hospital. I sat with her in silence like the Quakers do and it was beautiful. Then she told me her family was massacred by white men who made it look as if Indians did it. She was twelve when she found their bodies and buried them herself. No wonder she worried about war."

"War can do that to people," said John.

"What did you do this morning, Megan?" Peter questioned.

Megan was happy he asked. "I learned that getting rid of the Stamp Tax and Townsend Duties helped the colonies practice cooperation, but getting together was not a new idea. Way back in 1697, William Penn proposed a Plan of Union of English colonies for defense and business—like settling trade disputes or preventing people from running to another colony to avoid a debt or taxes."

"Nothing is certain, except debt and taxes," said Peter.

"Come on! That was death and taxes!"

"*That* was a joke."

"I'm trying to make a point. In 1754, an Albany Congress of nine colonies discussed common defense. Benjamin Franklin suggested a federation like the Six-Nations Indians had done. His plan was approved unanimously at the Congress, and then sent to London and the colonial assemblies. They all rejected the idea."

"So what about the taxes?" John persisted.

"That's the point I'm trying to make! The colonies were thinking about Union long before the problems over the taxes and they started the Revolution several years after the taxes were repealed so it was about much more than taxes!"

"What about the tax on tea? Everyone knows about that," challenged John.

"Aha! That's true, Dad." Megan was ready to spring a trap. "A small tax on tea was left when the Townsend Acts were repealed. The Boston Tea Party was in December 1773, more than three years after repeal of all but the tiny tea tax. The Tea Party was just a bunch of guys dressed up like Indians and it happened before the Revolution started. Here is the cool part. If the small tax on tea was there for way more than a thousand nights, why did those guys suddenly decide to throw that tea into the harbor that night?"

"I don't know, Megan — probably because of the non-importation agreement."

"Even some historians say that, but I don't buy it. Why that night? Look at what happened just before. In May of that year, 1773, the Tea Act was passed..."

"You see..."

"Yes, I do see! That Act was not a tax. It allowed shipments of tea by the East India Company direct from India to the colonies without unloading and reloading in England. It lowered the duties, which were much higher than the tea tax."

"What has that got to do with anything?"

"It had everything to do with it! The Tea Act undercut the price of tea brought in by smugglers rowing out to Dutch ships. Those British ships in the Port of Boston were the first to arrive carrying tea direct from India. It was due to be unloaded the very next morning and show up in stores at half the price people had been paying. That's a fifty-per-cent-off sale on a luxury at Christmas on an item ordinary people had not been able to afford!"

"So?"

"So obviously, it was the guys who made money from tea smuggling who threw the cheaper tea into the sea. Because it never reached the stores, the people never knew it was cheaper. They were told it was because of the taxes and they cheered. We still think it was about the taxes but it was not about helping the people, it was for profits! The Tea Party movement in our time got it completely backwards!"

"Hey! It's not so obvious, Megan. There was a non-importation agreement in place and a tax on that tea."

"Then why didn't the smugglers throw tea into the harbor a year before or two years before? I'll tell you why. Expensive tea was not a threat, but they were about to be put out of business by lower prices. They pretended to be Indians and pretended the reason was taxes. They would not get public support for throwing tea into the harbor to keep prices high, would they? We are not so dumb as to think Indians did it! So why do we still think it was about the tax? Why do people think the Boston Tea Party was a patriotic act when it really was a rip off of the people of Boston? Did someone give us all stupid pills?"

"There's no reason to get upset and call people stupid. We are those people."

"Yes, we are those people. I'm upset because we still are lied to in our time! Many laws about taxes or reducing environmental and health protections may cut costs for some industry but hurt working people, old people, and young people. How can we get a fair deal if we don't look behind the scenes? Follow the money, Dad!"

"The decisions were made by the elected leaders of the colonists. It was fair."

"No way! In 1775, there was no secret ballot. The vestrymen and burgesses for the county sat at the table when a person walked up to vote. An ordinary guy—I say guy because women couldn't vote—a ordinary free guy who owned property would have to be brave or dumb to vote against powerful rich men sitting right in front of him."

"We don't have a system that unfair in our time," insisted Susan.

"I agree it's not the same, but big money pours into elections on behalf of the interests of the donors. Like I said yesterday, guys on radio and TV tell the people what's good for them and mock anyone who disagrees. Listeners don't think for themselves but smugly think they're in the know when they hear the radio show!"

"You're upset for nothing! There's more to it than that!"

"You're upset, too!"

"I'm not upset but I don't think what you're saying is correct!"

"In Virginia it wasn't about taxes either. The King's proclamation ·that Indian land in the West would be managed by Quebec was a reason. The leaders wanted to take land from the Indians! How come we didn't learn that in school?"

"Maybe because it didn't happen that way!"

"Fine! I'll go do more research! I won't be back for supper. I've got an invitation." Megan jumped up and was out the door with half a sandwich in hand.

John went to the door to call her but she was already down the block.

"She'll be all right, John," said Susan.

"Do you believe what she was telling us?"

"It's not the history we learned, but she didn't make it up. We are finding out things we didn't know. The Burgesses talked about this our first day here."

"They were way off in their interpretation." John snapped.

"Based on what happened the next day, maybe they weren't interpreters."

Peter quietly ate his sandwich. Things in 1775 were not what he had learned either.

Day 3-7:   Peter and Evie on the Bridge

After lunch, the November air lost its chill. Peter found a sunny spot on a bench with views along Palace Green and Duke of Gloucester Street to watch for Evie returning from her errands. Was it his imagination or did the well-dressed people of Williamsburg look nervous today? How many slaves like Augustus were on their way to Norfolk already? He worried again about signing his name on the note he gave Augustus. At least no one knows who Peter Sinclair is.

"Good afternoon, Mister Peter Sinclair."

"Evie! You startled me. I didn't see you coming."

"I was behind you so 'less you got eyes back there it would be hard to see me comin'. Nice to see you, Mister Peter. I got to hurry to the post office on an errand."

"There are important things I want to tell you."

"Don't walk close. People will notice us talkin'."

Peter had learned a lesson this morning. He stepped back. "How's that? Better?"

Evie smiled and started walking. "Walk one step closer," she said without looking back. "If you far away you gonna shout and the whole town will hear."

"I want to tell you about Dunmore's Proclamation freeing the slaves."

"The Governor done made us free?"

"Not exactly. He proclaimed that slaves on rebel plantations will be freed if they go to Norfolk to take up arms for the King."

"Well, that don't help us 'cause we ain't on plantations and we ain't takin' up no arms. I could shoot my foot or my head off just touchin' one of them muskets."

"I know, but many are running to Norfolk, not just those who can take up arms and fight. This morning I ran into Augustus, running away. I helped him by sending him the long way around up the James River."

"Gustus ran away? Dear Lord, I hope no harm befalls him. He is my boy Dilli's daddy. Oh, maybe I should not tell you that."

"I knew that, Evie. Augustus is on a dangerous path. He will fight on the British side to get his freedom. He told me if all goes well, he'll help you and the boys."

Evie took a breath to calm down. "Here we are. I got to mail this letter for Massa Powell." Peter followed Evie in and pretended to look at quill pens for sale. The clerk weighed the letter, looked up the rate in a tattered folder, and carefully counted out the coins Missus Powell had given Evie. Peter left the post office first.

"Is this is a good time to get free?" Evie asked when she came out.

"It's a dangerous time. Soldiers are raiding plantations, and there is fighting in many places. Williamsburg is at peace so you and the boys are safe for now."

"I am 'fraid to run to an unknown fate. Did you talk to Annie?"

"I went looking for her and found her waiting for me. Can we look for her now?"

"We ain't goin' to find Annie just like that."

"I didn't say we'd find her. Just looking for her could help us think clearly."

"That be true, Mister Peter. We can take a back way home through a pretty place I go to be quiet. Follow until we get to where no one can see us." Peter watched Evie slip into a small passage past the grocer. He paused to look in a shop window then followed down a stairway and path into a beautiful miniature world.

A tiny waterfall splashed from a pipe to become a stream flowing over shining pebbles, past lilies, Queen Anne's lace, an ash tree with drooping boughs, and lush ferns in the damp rich earth. Peter heard bird songs and saw two squirrels chase one another on the roof of a press used to make paper for the printing office. Beyond, Evie stood on a little bridge over the stream and Peter joined her there.

They both jumped then giggled at the loud "Harrumph" of a bullfrog, wide eyed and alert on a sandbar. A stalking cat approached, interested in the birds but paying attention to Peter and Evie. The cat suddenly looked up and there was Annie coming down the path.

"Oh, Annie!" blurted Evie. "Mister Peter said to look for you, and here you be!"

The cat disappeared into the ferns seeking salamanders.

Annie was beaming. "I'se happy to see both of you, but let's get out of sight." They walked a short distance to a log bench well hidden behind bushes.

"Annie, what should we do? It ain't safe to stay and it ain't safe to run. Our lives was easier before these choices. If we run one night, death could take us by morning. My boys' life ain't so bad. They has food and clothes. Even shoes!"

Peter felt as if he had disappeared.

"Child, don't be so 'fraid about dyin'. We all die one day. You don't live by hidin' from life. You watch wit' your eyes and ears and mind open to which way everythin' movin' and not movin'. You 'member Old Julius? He stepped in front of horses and was broken up and gone by sunset. Maybe he stepped past the first horse and didn't see it was two horses, or maybe he didn't look both ways afore he crossed the street." Peter recalled his own near miss in front of his house.

"But how do I know the right thing to do? We could get found by Continentals and killed or brought back in chains. We could get die in the forest. We could be catched and sold to a bad Massa. We don't know if English soldiers will let us on a boat or how life might be if we go. How would we see anyone again that we love?"

Annie tilted her head slightly and studied Evie. "This knot has many threads, and to untie it ain't simple. Listen, child, you can't die seven ways on the same afternoon. You worry about so many things happenin' all at once. Someday you gonna die anyway so why fill your head wit' frettin'? Even if you die of one thing, it will save you from the other six that had you 'fraid."

"But that wouldn't help me!"

"It could save you worryin' every precious day about seven ways of dyin' when you could be prayin' 'bout ways of livin' well."

"I know you ain't wastin' breath, but I don't see the point in it."

"Listen. Every day you see them hoops the chillun' play wit' on the street."

"You taught me somethin' usin' hoops, about leavin' the burden to the Lord."

"Yes, child. Everythin' that moves and everythin' that stands still can teach us 'cause Spirit is in it. You remember when I told you some hoops in life is heavy, and you should not try to lift them or step in front like Julius did wit' the horses?"

"Yes, I remember."

"You roll a heavy hoop down the road wit' a tap-tap of a stick and run alongside as it rolls. Well, them hoops have more stories to tell and it be time you knew another. When you look at a hoop lyin' by the road how many hoops is they?"

"I don't understand."

"Child, this is the easy part. When a hoop is lyin' still, how many do you see?"

"One?"

"True. One hoop lyin' on the ground. When the hoop rollin' down the road how many hoops do you see?"

"One?"

"That ain't exactly so. You never ran beside a hoop to see how many. When the hoop goes 'round in a circle as it fallin' down, how many hoops is they?"

"I don't know what you mean."

"You don't know how many hoops because you never looked. This is a big choice you makin'. How things move and how they stop is how things come to be like they is, and you pay no mind to that."

"I don't understand, Annie, but when you tell a story I know somethin' is there."

"I want you to go home and heat up water and wash yourself all over like when you go to a weddin'. Pray for clear eyes and a clear mind to see a path through the brambles. Maybe you ain't got much time to choose a road for you and the boys. Then go roll a hoop and use wise owl eyes to look close as it rolls. Look close 'cause this world happenin' fast. You look when you hits the hoop and look when that hoop is fixin' to stop. You come and tell me what you seen, and we can talk about what to do and what to don't."

"Where will I find you?"

"Where you always do, right where I be and no place else." Annie walked off.

Evie stood quiet a long minute. "You know what she talkin' about Mister Peter?"

"She's saying it's complicated. You should look at a hoop. Evie, this is confusing to me, too. But I'll visit you with a hoop if I can find one."

"Will you come around tonight after dark to help? I gonna go to Nicholson Street and you wait 'til I'se gone to go the other way." She squeezed his hand and left.

Peter made sure he was alone and left the garden the way he came, pausing to listen to the water falling onto the rocks. He was about to have another surprise.

Day 3-8:   Megan Rides into the Countryside

Megan stomped three blocks up the road gripping the half sandwich. I'll just drop in on Mark who hasn't seen me for six months and say, 'Hi Mark, take me to a Sweat Lodge.' This is not going to work. She sat on a bench and finished her sandwich while staring at the ground. She wanted to prove her research had revealed something, but no — Dad's stuck on what he learned years ago.

She looked up at the slow drift of a cluster of cumulus clouds. Watching their lacy fringes dissolve into invisibility, she slowly cooled down. Standing Elk's words about struggling to see beauty and purpose behind a difficult pattern came back to her. There's a pattern here too, she thought. I blew up at Dad like I always do. All his life, he has known things to be a certain way. I didn't give him space to let in something new. I'll apologize when I see him next. But for now, I look scraggly and I'm in recovery from a hissy fit. It's not a good time to visit Mark and ask him to take me to the Sweat Lodge! This is part of a pattern too, I guess.

It was a short walk to the blacksmith shop. Framing and trusses were in place for a major building expansion. She sidestepped the construction and entered the shop. "Here goes..."

There were no customers and three smiths were hard at work as she approached Mark. He looked up. "Oh! Megan, you are a refreshing sight."

"I... thank you."

"When did you get back to Williamsburg? I have not seen you since May."

"I was away and uh, just got back today." For her, it was the truth.

"I've looked for you, Megan. I am grateful for what you did for me."

"I was happy to do it, Mark. What's all the construction here?"

"With the fighting, the shop is becoming an armoury to make musket barrels by the hundred for the militias. I am afraid we're going to be busy."

"I wish the war wasn't coming, Mark, I saw Standing Elk this morning."

"You did? So did I. He invited me to a Sweat Lodge. Will you go with me?"

"I..."

"Sorry to be so bold, Megan. You are probably busy doing something else."

"No. I mean, yes, I would like to go to the Sweat Lodge with you, Mark."

"Truly? Splendid! Mister Anderson is sending me to take a message to an iron works that is on the way. I want to stop for food for the feast, so we must leave in fifteen minutes. 'Tis an hour's ride from here."

"Fifteen minutes? An hour ride?"

"Yes. The Lodge will be this afternoon and we shall return not too late in the evening. I have to finish this quickly. Can you wait for me?"

"I... yes. I'll be back in fifteen." Mark resumed hammering and Megan walked to the street. There was no time to get home and change. She found a bench.

"Hi, Megan! I saw you come out that gate. How are you doing?"

"Wow! Hi. Peter. I'm in shock right now."

"Was the argument with Dad so bad?"

"It's not that. I should have realized that people can't let go of what they thought they knew the first time they hear something different. I want to apologize to him."

"I think you're right about the taxes."

"So do I but I don't have to be a rebellious teenager all my life, do I?"

"My, my. Little sister is growing up fast."

"This place is turning my head around, Pete."

"Mine too, Meg. I heard a strange riddle about a hoop today. 'When a hoop is lying still in the grass there is one hoop but when that hoop is rolling down the street and spinning around to come to a stop, how many hoops are there?"

"What's the prize?" asked Megan.

"The prize is freedom and the risk is disaster."

"That's a high-stakes game. I can find you a hoop so you won't have to guess."

"You can? Where?"

"Wait right here and I'll be back. I have two surprises." Megan hurried back down the walk toward the blacksmith shop.

Peter had waited only a few minutes when he heard Megan call him.

"Hi, Pete!"

He stood up, astonished to see his sister rounding the corner high on a white stallion, sixteen hands at the withers, behind a young man wearing a black leather jerkin over his linen shirt. She brandished a large iron tyre ring in her right hand.

"Here's your hoop, Pete." Megan held out the tyre. "Mark says you can borrow it to solve the riddle. Mark, this is my brother Peter."

"Good day, Mister Peter. Megan speaks well of you."

"Hi Mark. Nice to meet you." Peter reached up to take the hoop from Megan.

"Listen Pete, Standing Elk invited us to a Sweat Lodge an hour's ride from here."

"Who is Standing Elk? What should I say to Mom and Dad?"

"He's Mark's Indian friend. Please tell Dad I'm sorry I got mad. Tell the folks not to worry. I'll be with a group of people and I should be back before nine."

"We must be off." Mark nudged the stallion into a trot. Megan waved.

Peter watched his sister ride away. "In 1775, she rode off on a white horse behind a handsome blacksmith to an Indian ceremony. What am I going to tell Dad?"

At the edge of town, Mark cued the horse to the three-beat motion of a canter. Megan had ridden before but only at a walking gait or trot. They rolled in smooth arcs as the surroundings streamed by. "We're flying!" she called out.

They rode for twenty minutes on a dirt road; then Mark slowed the horse to a trot and turned down a long wagon track to a two-room log house. A neatly built livestock shed and corncrib stood behind it near a root cellar dug into the side of a hill. In the back was a huge pile of composting leaves. Mark dismounted and led the horse through a narrow point in the worm fence. "I want to buy a food offering for the feast after the Sweat Lodge. It won't take long."

Megan was happy to stretch her legs. She was surprised when Maggie, the milk seller from the market, stepped out next to her husband Bartholomew.

"Well, Mark, you brought a friend along. She is the kind young woman I met in the market in the spring. She got Bartie a nice vest."

"Hello, Maggie. Hello, Bart. Megan got a nice vest for me, too," said Mark. "I'm riding to the iron works on an errand, and then Megan and I are going to a Sweat Lodge at the Brown place. What have you got I can buy for the feast?"

"You've picked the perfect time to come, Mark," said Bartholomew, recognizing his old vest but not mentioning it.

"You say that every time."

"I do, because 'tis always the perfect time, Mark. We have corn meal, wheat flour, and salt for the fry bread the Indians like, butter or lard for frying, and we began pressing corn and sunflowers for oil. Maggie says it's good for our health."

"'Tis better for us than lard or butter," Maggie said.

"Animal fat makes us fat animals, I say." Megan added.

Ignoring Megan's comment and his paunch, Bartholomew continued, "I can kill a chicken for you fresh. Do you have time for us to blanch it to pluck the feathers?"

"They won't have time to cook a chicken. We will take the fixings for fry bread. What vegetables are left?"

"Carrots and cabbage and we have smoked sausages made this week."

"Good, I'll take sausages, a large cabbage, and some carrots."

Bartholomew went to the root cellar door and stepped down as he entered. He had dug the cellar underground into the hill to keep produce cooler.

A cow wandered from behind the livestock barn with a yoke around its neck. Fixed to the front of the yoke was a short wooden picket pointing forward.

"Why is that cow wearing a wooden tie?" Megan asked Maggie.

"Wooden tie? You are a funny one. That is a cowpoke. The cow cannot jump a fence when she is wearing it. I shall paint it like a tie in your honor."

Bartholomew came back with a bunch of carrots and the biggest cabbage Megan had ever seen. "Wow! How did you grow a cabbage that big?" she asked.

"Mother Nature's secrets child. Maggie and I labored many years to turn a sow's ear into a silk purse. Mark, do you have time for me to tell Megan our miracle?"

"Give the short of it, Bart. Standing Elk can smell sausages frying already."

"Well, Megan, the short of it is that Maggie and I were cheated into prosperity. During our servitude, she cooked food for a tavern for ready money. I became known as a capable wright. Owners of expensive tools were happy to pay good money when I repaired them.

"By the end of our bondage, we had saved money and we bought land in spring already sown with tobacco plants. Maggie was doubtful. She can smell a dead squirrel better than I can, but I saw those tobacco plants and got greedy. Within weeks, the whole crop failed. We lost five years of savings. We learned the same thing happened on that land the previous year and the owner left to go west. An agent without scruples bought the land for nothing and rented slaves to transplant tobacco seedlings into the depleted earth. He sold the land quickly to us at what seemed a good price before the truth became clear. We had no recourse.

"We cried and then set back to the cooking and repairs that gave us money in the first place. 'We did it once, we can do it again,' Maggie told me. Half my courage lives in her strong heart. We thought about why land that looks good can have nothing left to feed a plant. We heard that large estates put manure on their fields but tobacco was bitter in those fields. I spoke to planters and visited Standing Elk's village to learn about their gardens of corn, beans, and squash growing in the same field. I prayed in Sweat Lodges, as you will tonight. I prayed in church and I pondered while walking my land and in the forest.

"It was in a Sweat Lodge that a question came to mind that changed our lives: 'What did God put on the land that made it so rich before we got here?' I thought about it for days and answers kept coming. Animal manure, yes, but in small quantities. Ash from campfires and more from forest fires over the years. What else? What else? Then it hit me like the blue end of a brick. 'Leaves, Bartie, leaves!' Every autumn the ground is covered by countless leaves and twigs that rot into the soil. The trees give back.

"For two years I cleaned fireplaces and stables in town and carried ashes and manure home in my cart. I was paid to chop firewood and I brought home bark and chips. Some paid me a penny to clean out a ditch. The mud and leaves in the ditch were a banquet for our land. When I had no work, I filled my cart full of leaves. We covered our land acre by acre with the treasures in my cart and we planted clover to leave the land fallow for a time. The third year our miracle began. We planted grasses for the horse and cow and the next year beans, squash, and corn like the Indians grow."

"He said the short of it, Bartie," urged Maggie, wrapping a packet of corn meal.

"I'm done. We never planted tobacco, Megan. Only a third of the fields in Tidewater are tobacco anyway. The rest is crops for subsistence and for sale in the markets. We never bought a slave or bonded labor. At planting and harvest time, I hire people at fair wages including slaves on Sundays. We feed them well to let them know we appreciate them. We tell them how we succeeded so they find confidence to succeed someday themselves. Now that I know how to do this, I bought other spoiled land at low prices and we are bringing life back there, too."

160

"That's a hopeful story, Bartholomew."

"What do I owe you, Bart?"

"Nine pence, a low price to help with the feast."

"Here is a sixpence, I want to contribute, too," said Megan.

"But sixpence is most of it. I have to pay my share."

"You gave me the ride on the horse."

"'Tis Anderson's horse. You are generous, Megan."

Mark and Megan paid Bart and Maggie and they wished each other well. Then Mark rode out the wagon track to the dirt road. In half an hour, Megan saw black smoke billowing ahead of them.

They approached the source of the smoke, and long before they got there, Megan smelled charcoal and an acrid sharp odor. Air pollution that isn't horse poop, urine, or lack of showers, she thought. More like home, but I don't like this either.

Crossing a treeless wasteland, they rode beside a river to a row of buildings where chimneys poured out smoke. Wood was piled high next to what looked like cabin-sized beehives of brick and earth. Great piles of coal stood next to the river. Mark tethered the horse to a post upwind of the buildings and dismounted. Megan jumped down. "What is this, Mark?"

"This is an ironworks. Would you like to step through the gates of hell?"

"Not really. Will I come back out?

"That depends on what the Devil says."

Megan followed Mark through a wide opening and immediately covered her mouth and nose. The air was smoky and hard to breathe. Six shirtless men in the haze shoveled from three piles into an opening as tall as they were. Their skin glistened orange near a raging fire in a great stone furnace. They were streaked with black dust. Two were African, three European, and the youngest was Native American. One of the white men had rags around both ankles held in place by iron shackles joined by a chain. The fire roared and the spades scraped as the men shoveled from one pile then another.

Behind the furnace was a bellows much bigger than those at the blacksmith shop. It pumped air into the furnace and was opened and closed by a piston driven by river water flowing through a sluice. The creak of the piston, past due to be lubricated with whale oil, and rushes of air from the bellows added to the noise. "What's happening here?" Megan shouted near Mark's ear.

Mark stepped away with her toward a side of the building open to a yard. "This iron furnace is like the one I worked in. The men load the furnace with layers of charcoal, lumps of bog iron found in swamps, and oyster shells as a flux to separate out impurities. Molten iron flows through channels in the stone beneath the fire into sand molds to cool as pigs."

"Pigs?"

"Blocks of pig iron to be smelted into cast iron or better quality wrought iron."

"Why does one man have chains on his legs?"

"The man in shackles is a convict. He put rags there to keep the shackles from hurting his ankles. Convicts get longer bondage to begin with. The price for a convict's bond is less than for indentured servants. If he works well, he gets better food. If he tries to escape, more time is added and his life made miserable"

"Can we get out of the smoke?"

"Yes. I have to find the proprietor. He is probably upwind of the smoke. No one stands long near a furnace unless he must through bondage or need of money."

"What are these brick and dirt domes in a row? They're smoking too."

"These are charcoal ovens. The men stack wood over a fire then seal the doors. The heat bakes wood into charcoal since there is not enough air for wood to burst into flame. The moisture and impurities in the wood leave as smoke or drippings. The charcoal that remains burns cleaner and hotter than wood in the iron furnace."

"The word 'furnace' suddenly sounds like the word 'inferno'," said Megan

"Here is the owner. Hello, Mister Toliver. James Anderson sends a message."

"I saw the stallion and thought 'twas Anderson. You work at his forge?"

"Yes, I am Mark, a smith for Mister Anderson. He is occupied with building an armoury. He offers to buy triple the iron at a price suitably reduced for the increased volume. He would provide his own cartage. I am not authorized to propose a price. He asks if you will be in town over the next fortnight. If not, he will ride out to meet you here."

"I have news in return. The forests here are gone and nearby bogs low on iron so I will move the furnace. I have an agent riding north and south, looking for suitable property with access to bog iron and forests. Another reason to move is to get out of range of British naval guns. I suggest Anderson do the same. If the British come, he will make muskets for Redcoats or hang, depending on their whim. I am busy arranging this move. If Anderson wants to talk he should ride out here."

"I will pass on the message, Mister Toliver. On behalf of my employer and myself I wish you success and safety for your family in the coming difficult times."

"Thank you and the same to you and Mister Anderson. Congratulations also to you for having a comely wench sharing your horse. What is your name, miss?"

"Megan Sinclair."

"'Tis a pleasure to meet you, Miss Sinclair."

Mark and Megan mounted and rode away from the furnace and bad air.

"A comely wench?"

"He meant it as a compliment. The negotiations have begun. We shall be at the Lodge soon and you can sweat the soot off. This furnace reminds me of a hard time in my life."

162

Day 3-9:   John Hears the News from Frances

John signed the registry in the St. George Tucker House. Just as he settled into a chair he looked up to see Frances in the dress she wore the last time he saw her.

"Oh, hello, Ma'am. I'm glad to see you."

"Please call me Frances. It seems like only yesterday we met, but was it not in the spring on a hot day. I have been hoping you would return."

"Yes, it was in May. I find the passing of time to be confusing around here."

She smiled. "People have special experiences in Williamsburg."

"Frances, you had a story you wanted to tell me. Do you have time now?"

She sat on a chair across from him. "I have waited a long time to tell you. In the 1760s, the Ohio and Vandalia Companies surveyed land in the Shenandoah and Ohio Valleys. Investors included prominent citizens in Britain and the colonies, like Pennsylvania printer Benjamin Franklin and George Washington. Land in the West was cheap, less than two pence an acre. A wealthy person got fifty acres free as a 'head right' for every settler whose passage he paid. Those settlers worked in servitude to pay the passage, so investors got both land and labor as a return.

"In the Proclamation of 1763, the King forbade expansion west of the Appalachians but investors were unwilling to stop. The Indians knew the Proclamation reserved the land for them, so on occasion they attacked those cutting trees in western New York, Pennsylvania, Maryland, Virginia, and the Carolinas. Survivors ran crying havoc back across the mountains.

"The King sent Redcoats to keep settlers out of Indian Territory as much as to keep Indians on the other side of the mountains. Since the treasury was depleted by the long war against France, Parliament imposed the Stamp Act in 1765, followed by the Townshend Duties to cover the costs of protection and to assert its authority. You have heard the next part of this story.

"When the colonists shouted 'No taxation without representation!' the British were stubborn and stupid. If they had given the colonial councils authority to decide which taxes to levy, a main argument against the taxes would have melted away. Many in Parliament supported the colonies so after encountering resistance, most taxes were withdrawn."

"My daughter Megan told us the taxes had been repealed years before. I told her everybody knows the Revolution was over taxation without representation."

"Your daughter is wise. What 'everybody knows' is not always true. Sometimes we humans are no more clever than a weathered fence post. While colonists protested the Stamp Act and Townsend Duties, larger taxes gave more revenue to the Crown than all offending taxes combined. But no one noticed."

"What taxes were those?" asked John.

"High taxes were placed on sales of tobacco in Britain. The colonists did not see that those taxes lowered the amount of tobacco the British could afford to buy.

Why did the British use the Stamp Act that hindered every business transaction? Maybe because there was already a stamp tax levied in Britain without protest. The reaction in the colonies was doubtless a surprise to Parliament."

John agreed. "We still want low taxes but we want social security, Medicare, a large defense budget, and good schools. We don't look at the big picture."

"When the taxes were repealed, the British mainly left frontier settlers to defend themselves. Settlement continued beyond the line as did fights with Indians."

"What triggered fighting in 1775?" asked John.

"In 1774, the Quebec Act guaranteed Indians their lands west of the Proclamation Line by attaching those lands to Quebec and its Governor, Guy Carleton. Carleton ruled Quebec, not with an elected assembly as was normal in English colonies, but with a council of Catholic landowners that he appointed. A full survey of the line began. Investors in land feared Carleton would launch evictions. The Quebec Act threatened the fortunes of leading citizens."

"I'll be damned! My army friend Danny joked we were fighting for our lives, our honor, and the sacred fortunes of those who sent us to war. In the Revolution, sacred fortunes played a big role too? Why wasn't land mentioned in the Declaration of Independence?"

"Oh, it was." Frances pointed to a book. "Please open it to the Declaration of Independence." John did and she pointed to a section. "Read that."

John read aloud, "... *abolishing the free System of English Laws in a neighboring Province, establishing therein an Arbitrary government, and enlarging its Boundaries so as to render it at once an example and fit instrument for introducing the same absolute rule into these Colonies...*"

"The Declaration did not name Quebec nor make clear the significance of *'arbitrary government'*, or *'enlarging its boundaries'*, but fear of absolute Royal rule and enforcement of the Proclamation Line triggered fighting. 'Taxation without representation' was an old issue, but that victory gave the colonies confidence to try again against the Intolerable Acts."

"How do you know this story so well, Frances?"

"Staying in Williamsburg keeps me connected to my roots." She nodded to John and left as silently as she had come.

John read about the strength of colonial economies. A third of British ships were built in the colonies with plentiful white pine and skilled labor. That enabled Americans to launch naval vessels of their own. The combined colonies were a leading exporter of iron, tobacco, grain, and fish. Some years George Washington made more money from fish taken from the Potomac, dried, and shipped to the Caribbean to feed slaves, than from all other production on his large estates.

However, there were grave economic problems. A flood in 1771 destroyed stored tobacco and hurt prominent Virginians. Good prices in 1773 saved many from bankruptcy, but in 1774, a frost followed by a drought hit them again. They were desperate, John thought. With the survey of the Proclamation Line starting, they would be tempted to overthrow the authority that could take away their lands for debts and prevent them from expanding west.

John looked up John Wilkes, the English populist leader opposed to increasing royal power. Wilkes' first four elections to Parliament were voided, infuriating his supporters. There were parallels in Britain and the colonies. The Saint George's Day Massacre in Britain, a rallying point for voices for liberty, happened two years before the Boston Massacre roused passions here.

Other men in Britain supported the colonies. In February 1765, at the time of the Stamp Act, Colonel Isaac Barré spoke in the House of Commons in response to Charles Townshend, who later sponsored the Townshend duties:

> "...They planted by your care? No! Your oppressions planted them in America. They fled your tyranny to a then uncultivated and inhospitable country... they met hardships with pleasure, compared with those suffered in their own country, from the hands of those who should have been their friends.

> "They nourished by your indulgence? They grew by your neglect of them: as soon as you began to care about them, that care was exercised in sending persons to rule them, ...sent to spy out their liberty, to misrepresent their actions and to prey upon them; men whose behavior on many occasions has caused the blood of those Sons of Liberty to recoil..."

New England leaders took the name 'Sons of Liberty' from that speech by Barré.

American resistance waned once the onerous taxes were rescinded. What else sparked the uprising in 1774? What about New England where land was not the issue? John read that the arrival of ships direct from East India would have meant tea at half the previous price for this desired commodity. Megan was right again. Half price tea would hurt merchants including John Hancock and put more 'sacred fortunes' in jeopardy. How could we have gotten this so wrong for so many years?

John looked up the Battle of Culloden where Bruce was wounded. The Duke of Cumberland ordered massacres, but James Oglethorpe ignored the orders and called off the troops. Through his mercy, many Scots escaped. At a court marshal for disobeying, Oglethorpe was exonerated but Cumberland's reputation was tarnished for his brutality. Oglethorpe voted in Parliament against sending troops to crush the rebellion in America and supported colonists' rights. Significantly, he declined an offer to lead British forces to put down the Revolution. His decision left the post to less competent generals and was a big contribution to the American victory.

John wondered why Oglethorpe, Barré, and Wilkes were largely forgotten.

"They have not been forgotten in Wilkes-Barré, Pennsylvania." Frances startled John. "Nor at Oglethorpe University or in Oglethorpe County in Georgia."

"Oh! I didn't hear you come in. Frances, the last couple of days my family and I feel we are actually in the past. Reverend Walker suggested I ask you about it."

"He did? Well, imagination can enhance what we notice. You may be noticing more than usual without being practiced in how to sort it out. Consider it lucky. Did anything dramatic happen that might have opened up your perception?"

"Not that I know of. Oh. We almost had a bad accident on the way here."

"It can happen in different ways. I knew you were observant from the moment you saw me. Tell your family not to worry and enjoy it while it is happening. You will find that the meaning is in your experience and not in an explanation."

"Frances, I don't think about such things very often."

John turned to replace a book to the shelf. When he turned back, Frances had left. "She talked about it as if it were normal," he thought. "What did she mean she knew I was observant from the moment I saw her? Didn't she get that backwards?"

John left the Tucker House reflecting on how events happened in our lives without our understanding what underlies the circumstances. Danny and Sergeant Sargon did not know why they were fighting. It ended for them zipped into a body bag. "Follow the money," Megan said. She's smart, like her mother. But I'm not happy with what I'm learning.

Day 3-10:   Susan at the Court House

Susan arrived at the Court House amidst a gathering crowd. She scanned the faces, looking for Jane. To be sure to get a seat, she moved past the pillory where Peter had been held and edged toward the entrance. Near the double doors, a familiar-looking woman with a troubled expression stood with eyes closed, lips moving slightly, and hands clasped. When the woman opened her eyes, Susan asked, "May I join you in prayer?"

"Missus, many souls could benefit from prayer at this Court today. One of them is my husband, who will finally have his trial for preaching without a license."

Susan recognized the woman as the one she had seen carrying a basket to the gaol what for her was two days earlier. "But Ma'am, I saw you carrying food and a shirt to your husband at the gaol in May. This is six months later. Has he not had his trial yet?"

"No, Missus. It has been a long wait. The Lord knows why we endure this."

"I have a friend coming to the trial today. If you like, we will sit with you."

"I would appreciate your company. My husband has had his Bible and it gives him comfort to hold it when he prays." The woman began to sob and Susan put a hand on her shoulder as Jane found them in the crowd.

"Thou hast found another soul to comfort, Susan, as thou hast done for me."

"My friend Jane will join us today. I am Susan Sinclair. What is your name?"

"Dolly Cook," the woman sniffed. "I pray my husband Arthur will be freed."

The attorneys for today's cases, draped in robes and wearing their best white powdered wigs, pressed through the crowd. The public was held back until the lawyers and clerks were at their places, then the doors were fully opened.

Susan, Jane, and Dolly squeezed onto a bench halfway up the aisle and waited for the proceedings to begin. As three men in robes entered and took seats behind a wooden rail at the front of the courtroom, everyone rose. Susan assumed the man in the center chair was the lead judge, with the high stained-hardwood panel behind him, and the most imposing robe.

The first prisoners led in were two runaway convicts accused of stealing a cart on the Great Wagon Road and killing a family in a manner to make it appear Indians had committed the atrocity. They were spotted the very next day moving east in the ill-fated family's wagon.

Jane reached for Susan's hand, her attention riveted on the witnesses.

The deceased woman's brother testified that he recognized the wagon that day. He shot one man, who was holding a rifle, in the chest at close range. Then, as his wife pointed another musket at the other two men, he demanded their surrender. As their friend Billy twitched on the road beside the wagon and with their rifles under canvas behind them, they complied. The brother rolled the dying man into the swamp beside the road and the surviving brigands were brought to town, bound like cargo in the wagon they had stolen.

The brother identified the culprits. Another witness identified them as convicts from the docks at Norfolk. A third, also a prisoner in the gaol, swore he overheard the men expressing regret about the killings, not for their victims, but for their own predicament. The men were asked if they had anything to say.

One shook his head. The other blurted, "Billy killed them, not us. We should not be here."

Because this was a capital case, an appointed lawyer argued, "My Lord, these men risk hanging for this crime, so we suggest this trial should not be held here but at the Capitol."

The judge looked from one prisoner to the other after conferring among his colleagues. "You, your lawyer, and we judges agree that you should not be here. You should not have killed innocent people. You are convicts so your trial is here rather than at the Capitol and here today we decide your fate. We do not know how many others you murdered, but we can ensure you will kill no more. You are found guilty and sentenced to be hanged tomorrow at the convenience of the executioner. Then you shall no longer be here. Bailiff, take these men away!"

The two men were led from the court in stunned silence. Jane gasped. "Just five minutes and gone! The trial took less time than the murders," she whispered.

The next case involved a man accused of stealing a dairy cow. He had retained a lawyer, graduated from William and Mary, who explained that his client purchased the cow, and agreed to pay monthly for six months. His client paid the first three installments but, because of hard times, the fourth payment was late. He went to the bench to show hand-written receipts for the payments.

The Judge grew irritated. Speaking to the lawyer for the man who sold the cow he said, "This court does not take lightly wasting its time by bringing inaccurate charges. This is not a case of a stolen cow. It appears to be a partially unpaid debt."

"My Lord, my client did not mention the payments. I am learning of them now."

Addressing the defense lawyer, the judge said, "You have presented evidence of only four of the six agreed-upon payments. Do you have any other evidence?"

The lawyer whispered to his client who shook his head. "No, your Worship, my client has not paid the debt in full. He commits to do so promptly."

"This case should have been settled by the lawyers, not brought to add clutter to this court. We rule that the plaintiff is to be paid two remaining payments without interest because of the prevarications and exaggerations of his claim. The next payment is due in a fortnight and the final payment one month later. Next case!"

The next case was that of Dolly's husband, Arthur accused of preaching without a license. As he was led in, Susan slipped from her seat and spoke quietly with the young lawyer who defended the man who bought the cow. The lawyer responded and Susan nodded. Then she handed him something to him.

"Who represents Arthur Cook?" called out a clerk."

"With the help of God I will speak for myself," said Arthur hoarsely, and cleared his throat. Having nowhere to spit, he swallowed.

The young defense lawyer rose. "Your Worship and Mister Cook, I have been retained by the defendant's wife and friends to defend him in this case."

"Is that your wish, Mister Cook?" asked the judge.

Confused and happily surprised, Arthur smiled weakly at his wife and nodded.

"Mister Cook?" the judge repeated. "You have not spoken."

"Yes, Honorable Sir, I agree."

"When called upon, you may address the court as 'Your Worship' or 'My Lord'."

"Yes, my Worship, I mean Your Lordship, I agree to the lawyer speakin' for me."

"It seems that is a very good idea. Well then, let us proceed. You are charged with preaching without a license. Article 23 of The 39 Articles of Religion of the Church of England clearly states the following with respect to Ministering:

> *"It is not lawful for any man to take upon him the office of public preaching or ministering the sacraments in the congregation, before he be lawfully called and sent to execute the same by men who have public authority in the congregation to call and send ministers into the Lord's vineyard."*

"We cannot tolerate falsehoods in the name of God contrived to pass a basket and deprive the Established Church of funds needed to minister to the flock."

"Can they cite an Article of Religion of the Church of England as the basis for a charge in the public court?" whispered Susan.

"Yes, the Established Church and the Law are intertwined," Jane murmured.

"Heaven save us," said Dolly, a little too loud.

"No talking in the gallery," said the Judge, "or I will tell the Sergeant at Arms to clear that row. There are many standing who would happily take those seats!"

As quiet was restored the judge continued, "How do you plead, Mister Cook?"

"My Lord, my client pleads 'Not Guilty,'" said the lawyer.

"Not guilty," mumbled Arthur Cook.

The lawyer asked, "May I question my client to clarify the case for the court?"

"You may."

"Mister Cook, have you been to a seminary school of any denomination?"

"No, Sir, I have not."

"Has any man ever called you Reverend, or Pastor, or Minister?"

"No, Sir, none has."

"Do you own a Bible, Mister Cook?"

"I do. I pray over my Bible each and every day."

"Can you tell the court whether you are able to read your Bible?"

"I..."

"Mister Cook, have you ever learned to read?"

"No, Sir. But I spent Sundays in church and heard what is in the Bible."

"So you are neither able to read from your Bible nor write a sermon. Is that true?"

"Well, I don't write but I speak out powerful when the spirit moves me."

"I am sure that is so, Mister Cook. When the spirit moved you did you ever administer any sacraments such as baptism, first communion, or funeral rites?"

"Spirit has not called me to do that, and I have not learned how."

"How long had you been in this county when you were arrested?

"Two days, Sir. I was arrested speaking about the Bible at a crossroads."

"And how many people stopped to listen to you?"

"Well, my wife here and a few others stopped to listen for a few minutes on their way. I guess one of them must have gone to a constable."

"Did you pass a collection plate at the end of your talk?"

"No, Sir. I do not have a collection plate. I speak about the Bible because I love the Lord. When I finished it was only my wife and a boy and his dog standing there."

"That may have been an inspiring homily, at least for your wife who has stood by you these months while you languished in jail. The boy and his dog may have benefitted as well."

There were chuckles in court. The Judge held a handkerchief in front of his face.

"My Lord, I submit that Mister Cook gathered neither a flock nor contributions. He cannot read his Bible nor write a sermon. His unfortunate choice of a public place to speak put him in our gaol for eight long months. Surely, that is sufficient burden on the public purse and sufficient discouragement to Mister Cook. The prisoner's wife offers a fine of one pound to go to the gaol or the Church at the discretion of the court. Mister Cook apologizes for any trouble he has caused and agrees to leave the county if the court should offer mercy in this case."

The head Judge looked at the downcast defendant and at the three women praying. The one in threadbare attire was doubtless Missus Cook in the company of a better-sorts lady, one not to offend. He briefly conferred with the other judges then cleared his throat with a loud harrumph. "The noble bard wrote 'The quality of mercy is not strained. It droppeth as the gentle rain from heaven upon the place beneath.' Mercy may not be strained, but I am. We sent two men deservedly to the gallows, redeemed a milk cow oblivious to these proceedings, and we now release a misguided man who dwelt eight months in a cell for insignificant harm. The court directs the fine to be divided between the gaol and the Bruton Parish Church. Court is recessed for fifteen minutes!"

"That's wonderful!" whispered Dolly as they stood up. "But how can we pay a fine of one pound, and how can we pay the lawyer?"

"The fine is already in the hands of the Lawyer as is his fee." Susan moved toward the doors. "Here's ten shillings to help you and your husband get started when you get to a place more welcoming."

"The Lord surely sent you, Ladies!"

"He sent us all," Jane agreed. "May we be worthy of his purposes for us."

The Sergeant at Arms removed the shackles and sent Arthur Cook out of the Court House where he hugged his wife. She introduced him to their benefactors.

"Arthur Cook," said Jane, "some of my relatives met a worse fate than thee for preaching where they were not welcome. May the Light guide thee to do the Lord's work where it will be of benefit. Where goest thou from this place?"

"We shall walk to New Jersey where Dolly's sister is prospering on a farm. She will give us shelter and work until we find ourselves steady again. I will pray to serve without provoking anyone. Thank you, ladies, for what you have done."

They watched Arthur and Dolly begin their long journey north. Susan took Jane's arm and asked, "Would you like to join my family for dinner this evening?"

"Would I not be an imposition?"

"Not at all. I would like them to meet you, Jane."

A large carriage pulled by four horses approached from the opposite direction and stopped. A woman wearing a hat and a white scarf protecting her face from the dust of the road drew back the curtain. "Susan Sinclair, you are back in town." The woman removed her scarf. It was Lucy Randolph Burwell.

"Oh, hello Missus Burwell" said Susan. "I did not recognize you."

"Sorry about the highwayman's mask. The dust on these roads is dreadful. I am happy to find you through the lucky coincidence of coming into town for last-minute purchases. We are having a ball at our house tonight and I would be pleased if you and your husband could come and stay overnight at our house."

"Thank you but I don't know how to get there and..."

"Susan, I will send this carriage. Where can it pick you up?"

"We live near Christiana Campbell's, but my friend Jane is dining with us..."

"Please bring your friend. The carriage will be at Christiana Campbell's at eight. I apologize for being hurried but I must get back. I need to speak with you, so I look forward to tonight. Home, Obadiah!" The carriage driver uttered a single low syllable to the horses and the carriage was off.

Susan and Jane turned away to avoid the dust. "Jane, you are going to a party."

"I have never been to a great house before. I have no fine clothes to wear."

"You are my size, Jane. We can solve that clothing crisis when we get to my house. I have experience dealing with this kind of problem."

Day 3-11:   Virginia Militia Drill

Susan spotted John walking across Palace Green and waved him over to join them. "John, this is Jane Harding, from Pennsylvania. She will join us for dinner."

"It is my honor to meet thee, John Sinclair."

"Me, too."

Soon Peter came down the road. "Hi, guys. This is a tyre... for a science experiment." They shuffled to make room for Peter.

"Jane, this is my son Peter. Peter, say hello to Jane Harding."

"Hello, Jane. Dad, I saw Megan. She said to tell you she's sorry she got upset."

"She did? I want to apologize to *her*! She was right on the taxes. Where is she?"

"That's the other thing... Uh, she was invited to a Sweat Lodge by an Indian chief and the blacksmith gave her a ride on a horse. He's my age and a good guy."

"You let her ride out of town with a guy?" asked Susan. "How do we know she'll be all right? I thought when we leave here..." She stopped because Jane was there.

"I'm sure she'll be fine. She says she'll be home around eight."

The conversation ended as the sound of drums approached and high-pitched fifes began to play. "What's happening?" Susan asked a man standing nearby.

"The Virginia Militia is marching to fife and drum to put us in the spirit."

The music grew loud as the militia wheeled in straight ranks onto Palace Green. For generations, European men marched to martial music, which raised passion and muted fear. Susan felt exhilaration and foreboding.

The militia was unlike the rag-tag muster with broomsticks in May. These young citizen-soldiers had learned discipline. In uniforms of white hunting shirts, black tricorn hats, belts for cartridge pouch and bayonet sheath, most were younger than John was when he left for war. They would march against the best army on Earth. America needed to become independent but did we have to pay such a price? He wondered if there was a better way. He was startled by Bruce's voice.

"Soon many shirts will turn red with the blood of mortal wounds. God, how proud I used to be to march! Now I ask if we must pay such a price. I wonder if there is a better way. The young Scots and Englishmen in His Majesty's regiments drill like these lads and get ready for the sea voyage. Some will never go home."

"Bruce, this is my son Peter, my wife Susan, and her friend Jane. We are having dinner at a tavern after the drill. Would you care to join us?"

"Good to meet you all. My wife's sister ran from Norfolk to escape the fighting. My wife roasted a goose to raise her spirits tonight." Let us talk soon, Johnny."

"Not easy times for the few of us willing to think about it, Bruce. Be careful."

The Militia arrived at the Palace, no longer occupied by Governor Dunmore. It looked to John like a display of defiance and a claim of victory when the fight had just begun.

Day 3-12:   Dinner with Jane

Over dinner, Susan and Peter discovered it awkward to talk openly with Jane present, though it was not really an issue for John because he said little.

"I'm going to have the chicken soup and a salad of fresh greens," Susan said.

"That sounds just right." Jane closed her menu quickly, not embarrassed. In her world most women could not read.

After the waitress left, Susan said, "I hope Megan is all right."

"She's fine, Mom. She's in good company."

"Good company may not be enough if there's real danger."

Jane joined in. "These are difficult times. Many people shall be overwhelmed and it hurts me to think about it. Where is the light that illuminates the darkness?"

"Mom told me you're worried about the coming war. I know someone, a free African woman named Annie, who may be able to help. Have you heard of her?"

"I have not. I keep to myself for the most part."

"I'm busy with this hoop tonight but I'll look for a way to introduce you. She's very wise and kind and knows more about the Light than anyone I ever met."

Susan saw a change in her son.

The food arrived and there was little conversation. Jane enjoyed her meal. "I appreciate thy kindness John and Susan Sinclair."

"John, we've been invited to a ball and to stay the night at the Kingsmill Plantation, the home of Lucy Burwell. Lucy is sending a carriage and I hope you will come with Jane and me. It will be great to see a plantation. We'll be back after breakfast tomorrow, the day we planned to go home." Susan did not say more in deference to Jane's presence.

"Yes, we'll leave for home tomorrow," said John. "But thanks, but I won't go to the plantation with you. Tonight I want to go for a long walk to think things over."

"I'm going to excuse myself. I may be late tonight, too." Peter leaned over to John and said quietly, "Dad, I've got a set of keys with me. May I use the car?

"The car? Did I hear you correctly?" John whispered.

"I want to check roads to Norfolk to find the best route for an escaped slave."

"You can't go for a drive in our time, and see what is going on in 1775."

"I can't drive in 1775 but I want to learn the terrain today along the James River. I'm may have given bad advice and could do that again if I don't know the route."

John studied his son. "I know what it's like to get bad advice. Reconnaissance of the terrain is important. Peter. Here are the keys."

"Thanks, Dad. And I know you want to tell me not to take any reckless risks." Peter was shocked to get his father's permission.

Day 3-13:   Peter Takes the Hoop to Evie

Peter ran to the Powell House holding the iron tyre, slowing as he approached the side gate, trying not to crunch loudly on the gravel.

"There you are," said Evie from the bench in the shadows. I put the boys to bed early so we could talk." Evie had braided her hair and put on her Sunday dress. Peter caught his breath.

"Hello, Evie. You look beautiful. I brought you and the boys some cookies."

She opened the bag, inhaled the scent of oatmeal, raisins, and brown sugar. "Thank you, Mister Peter. The boys will eat these in the mornin'."

He found her voice beautiful too. "My sister found me something else," he said.

"You got a sister here?"

"Yes, and a mother and a father. We're staying not far from here."

"Your whole family came on this voyage? Why ain't you said somethin'?"

"Sorry. Uh, Evie, this is a family voyage. Maybe that's why I took such an interest in you and your boys because you are a family like us."

Evie was quiet a moment. "My daddy got sold away before I knowed him and he was long gone when Mama passed. I was brung to the Powell place as a girl." She sighed. "I ain't seen James' daddy but one day in my life. I don't know where he's at. Dilli's daddy, 'Gustus, stayed one night and along came Dilli the next year. 'Gustus didn't pay us no mind until that Hush Harbor meetin' in spring. You grown and you still has a mama and daddy. I heard only one slave child in three has two parents to raise them up. My boys and me is our family."

Evie pressed her sleeve to her eyes to absorb tears that had welled there. "I'se sorry, Mister Peter. I'se afraid 'bout this fightin' and folk runnin' away lookin' for a new life. I don't want to make a mistake and lose what life we got."

Peter put his hand on Evie's and she trembled. She leaned on his shoulder and he was quiet. She pulled out a handkerchief and blew her nose.

"That was done like a champion, Evie. You could play the trumpet with Gabriel."

Evie laughed. "Mister Peter, you is a kind man."

"Almost nobody calls me a man without putting 'young' in front of it, Evie."

"How old are you if you is so young?"

"I'm twenty-one."

"I is twenty-three and I got two boys, so twenty-one is a man, Mister Peter."

"Let me show you what I brought."

"I see what you brought. It be a tyre or a cooper's ring for a big hogshead."

"Evie, on an ordinary day, this would be a tyre. But tonight, it's a hoop we can look at to learn what Annie meant today. Do you have a strong, straight stick?"

"Let me run get one." Evie ran to the kitchen and returned holding a long-handled ladle. "Let's go!" She was more buoyant than Peter had ever seen her.

They walked to the end of the lane and made sure no one was around. Peter balanced the hoop and gave it a whack with the handle of the spoon. It fell over. On the next try, he shoved the hoop to get it rolling, and then they hurried beside and tapped it forward using the spoon handle. "It looks blurry when I hit it, Evie. Do you think that is what Annie meant?"

"Maybe so. When you hit it so it look fuzzy, we don't know 'zackly where it at."

"Now we'll let it fall and watch what happens!"

They slowed to a walk as the hoop slowed, and they jumped aside as it leaned to the left and rolled around in smaller and smaller circles. It leaned more as it rolled in place, wobbling faster and faster. For an instant, they saw in the blur of motion, images of many hoops falling away from the point where each image touched the ground. There was a final vibration as the many hoops came to rest as one.

"Oh! Lordie! They was so many hoops I could not count 'em, six or eight standin' out and goin' round and round as they fell and more dim ones in between. Ain't that Annie somethin'? And me tellin' her they was only one hoop!"

"But lying there is only one hoop," said Peter. "What do you think it means?"

"You is a strange gentleman, Mister Peter, askin' what I think."

"Evie, Annie gave the question to you. I'm just the guy who brought the hoop."

"Let's go back to the bench out of the street. I can ponder better when I ain't worried someone gonna catch me doin' somethin' I ain't supposed to."

"What aren't you supposed to do?"

"I ain't supposed to do much at all 'cept what I am told. I sure ain't supposed to be talkin' to you about runnin' away."

Peter sat next to Evie. She moved her hip and leg against his. He felt her warmth through her dress and his jeans. "Oh, God!" he said to himself. "This is not what this visit is about."

"I know Annie enough to know this ain't simple. When we goin' along in life it be like a hoop rollin'. But when a big change come like the hoop fallin' over, ain't no way to know which way it gonna fall. So you watch close, and pick what to do near the end when you see better how it gonna fall. Even then, be ready to change quick if it fall another way."

"How do women see so clearly sometimes?"

"Because we have babies we need to watch over real close, I s'pose."

"You're amazing, Evie. There are many ways this can turn out, so we should pay attention before making a move, and then choose. I hope Augustus is all right."

"I hope so too, Mister Peter. I hope he finds the freedom he wants."

Evie leaned close and Peter felt her left breast press his arm. "You bring me comfort, Mister Peter," she whispered. "When a man is nice to a woman maybe he want somethin'. Do you want somethin'? If you do, we can climb up to the loft. The boys is sleepin'."

Peter held Evie close. This was something he thought he wanted. He thought of Annie and what she might encourage him to do and his words surprised him. "Dear Evie, when I first saw you, I wanted to be with you so much I could hardly breathe. Annie knows about it. But you don't have to give yourself to me because I'm helping you. If I climb up in the loft, you might think I wanted to help just for that and it's not so."

"I know. But what about me, Mister Peter? I been lonesome a long time and scared since this fightin' started. You holdin' me brings a warm feelin'. You feel like you is part of our family, too."

"Evie, I can almost hear Annie in my head saying, 'Help her, but if your heart is true, help her find her own strength inside.' Evie, let me hold you here."

Almost lost in the pull he felt toward Evie, Peter held her tight and remained still for long minutes. The passion slowly ebbed and a deep warm peace came over both of them. She whispered in his ear "I think you came here from Heaven."

Peter sat back and looked at her. "Maybe we all came from Heaven and forgot."

"This, I won't forget, Mister Peter. I will remember this always."

"So will I, Evie, always. Now you get a good rest. You need to be fresh and alert to make good choices. I am going out along the river tonight to see what I can learn about the ways the hoop might land. Can you take this hoop back to a blacksmith named Mark over at Anderson's shop and armory when you get a chance? I don't know when I can get back."

"I will. First, I want to show my boys how the hoop rolls and how it falls. That will be a good teachin' for them. Bless you, Mister Peter. If you find a way to take me away, I want to go wit' you. If I'se goin' somewhere, come wit' me and the boys. I know you is our family, too."

"It's hard to understand, but I come from far away and I can't stay long. If you go away, I can't go with you. You and the boys can be my family another way."

"Please be careful tonight whatever you doin' and wherever you goin'."

"I will, Evie. Good night, mother of James and Dilli."

He felt her eyes on his back as he walked toward the tunnel with his hand on the car keys. He asked himself if he just missed an opportunity. No, he thought, I took the opportunity.

Day 3-14: Susan at the Plantation House

Susan and Jane climbed into the carriage Lucy Burwell sent to take them to Kingsmill Plantation. Four fast horses took thirty minutes to make the bone-shaking four-mile trip. Arriving at the plantation, the main house and all the dependencies—cookhouse, smokehouse, schoolhouse, chapel, stable, carpentry shop, distant tobacco houses, servants' and slaves' quarters, corn cribs, cattle barn, chicken house, and other buildings—looked like a village.

They walked through a groomed garden with chrysanthemums and trimmed, five-tiered topiary boxwood. The hedge on one side was twelve feet high and beyond, a stunning vista opened to an expanse of fields beside the James River. Jane gazed out at the faint lights of a house across the river. "Oh, see how wide the water is here!"

An herb garden was enclosed by a trimmed thorny hedge, dense enough to discourage rabbits. At the end of a broad footpath, at the large doors of the main house, Lucy Randolph Burwell welcomed them. "Oh, Susan, I am so glad you are here. This is my husband, Lewis Burwell. Lewis, this is Susan Sinclair, the wise woman I told you about."

Colonel Burwell bowed. "It is a pleasure to meet you, Madam."

"Colonel Burwell, I'm sorry my husband, John Sinclair, was otherwise engaged and could not join us. May I present my friend, Jane Harding."

"Welcome to our home, Miss Harding."

"Excuse me a moment, Lewis. I shall escort Susan and Jane to the refreshment table and show them the conveniences should they need them."

"Certainly, Dear."

Lucy took Susan's arm and with Jane following, moved through the hall with portraits of Burwell and Randolph ancestors gazing at them. "Susan, I see you lent Jane your elegant mantua," Lucy whispered. "You are a kind woman to lend your best. These gatherings are important to leading families in Virginia, and not only for proud display of our finery. We often feel isolated. Social occasions help us maintain a sense of community. We welcome travelers to learn of news from afar. Anyone recently arrived from London is particularly attractive as a guest for several days.

"I find a refreshing genuineness in you, Susan. You seem better educated than any woman in this county but you do not flaunt what you know. I went on about the false image that masks the great debt of most leading families but you are not judgmental. Oh dear, more guests have arrived, I must go back to greet them."

Susan and Jane used the facilities in a room off the hall. The toilet was a chamber pot under a chair with a hole in the seat. For this social occasion, a slave stood outside the door, his job to replace the chamber pot, empty the used one in an outbuilding, rinse it, and stand ready to replace the pot again. The Burwell's did not want to impose unpleasantness on their guests.

Reentering the ballroom, Susan felt instant unease when she saw the dance instructor Randall Weaver leading a group of guests in a contradanse. Weaver offered obsequious praise at every opportunity. He has an instinct of when to flatter, thought Susan. It was amazing to her that people did not see through him. He played in a practiced way to their vanity and lack of confidence learning the dances that were symbols of refinement.

The orchestra began an allemande in three-quarter time. Few guests were familiar with the new step. Weaver strolled to the side table to avail himself of the punch. Susan noticed him stop by the clock to check his pocket watch.

Suddenly, a man stepped in front of Susan and asked her to dance. She raised an arm to shoulder height and they set off circling the floor. "My name is Richard Henry Lee, back from the Continental Congress on personal business."

"My name is Susan Sinclair."

"I am charmed that you know the allemande, Missus Sinclair."

"Where I come from we call this a quick waltz," she replied.

"I see. I learned this dance as a student at grammar school in England. It is a surprise that this orchestra can play the music. Did you notice they include the cream of Virginia society showing off their skills? They include a Ludwell, a Byrd, a Randolph, two Carters, and a Marshall. The able violinist is Thomas Jefferson, also on a break from the Continental Congress."

"Congressman Lee, do your colleagues in the Congress think war is inevitable?"

"Congressman Lee! I like the sound of that. We can call a delegate a Congressman. Now to your question. Ah, yes, 'Is war inevitable?' That which is already happening could be called inevitable. We are already at war and the changes we seek are inevitable."

"What changes, Congressman?

"These subjects typically don't concern a lady."

"I understand the local customs and I mean no disrespect, Congressman Lee.

"I admit you did ask the question. We reject the alien system of an unelected Governor's Council, such as we see in Quebec, being imposed upon us. Giving Quebec and its Governor Carleton authority over all lands west of the mountains is an affront to free men and could ruin investors here and in England."

Susan assumed that Congressman Lee had visited the punch bowl several times to be so forthcoming. The illustrious orchestra went into a crescendo and finished the piece with a flourish. "I will return to my friends and endure less refreshing company. It was a pleasure and honor to dance with you."

"For me as well."

Susan walked toward the side of the dance floor when another man stepped in front of her. "You honored my older brother with a dance. Would you offer me the same charity, Madam? My name is Francis Lightfoot Lee. I am sure my brother wasted no time before informing you that he is a representative to the Continental

Congress. I will not be so vain. I shall wait a moment and then reveal that I am also in Congress." He and Susan laughed and she told him her name.

Lee was an excellent dancer, and Susan asked if that is where he got the middle name 'Lightfoot.' "You may withdraw that compliment, Madam, if one of my feet happens to alight on one of yours."

The dance ended and Susan walked with Francis to the edge of the floor. "Your brother is strongly against the Quebec Act. Do you agree with him?"

"We are all against the Quebec Act, Missus Sinclair, but our views differ on the best remedy. My brother considers independency as do some in Congress, but most people will not speak of it. They oppose the increase of royal power Parliament's usurpation of our right to decide matters here. Nevertheless, most consider themselves loyal Britons. As for me, I would consent to independency if we find no other way to remain free, but I remain in search of other means. Did Richard tell you our younger brother William Lee is Sherriff of London?"

"He did not mention that."

"Many work on these problems on both sides of the Atlantic. However, since the recent death of Peyton Randolph, who was a moderating influence, as is his brother John in London, I fear our options grow limited."

"Peyton Randolph is dead?"

"Yes, of apoplectic stroke in Philadelphia last month. His body awaits transport."

"He was Lucy's uncle. Poor Lucy!"

"Lucy is in mourning but this event was planned for months so she went ahead to have friends about. She is not dancing so soon after the news arrived."

Suddenly, there were cries from women across the room and Susan and Francis Lee saw that someone had fallen. They hurried over to see Lucy lying still. Colonel Burwell dropped to one knee and took her pulse. "She has fainted." He urged the guests to be calm as he hurried from the room and returned carrying his bag of supplies for administering physic to his family, servants, slaves, and animals. "This will return her to the land of the living." He opened a little bottle with a brass top and waved it near her nostrils letting the vapors waft in with her breath.

Lucy sneezed and awoke with a start. "Oh, what happened? I'm so sorry."

"Don't worry. You had a fainting spell. You can retire to your room to recover."

"I don't want to lie down and miss our guests," she protested.

"Perhaps you would like to get some fresh air." Jane offered her arm.

Lewis Burwell and Jane helped Lucy to her feet. Lucy saw Susan in the circle of concerned faces and asked, "Would you and Jane join me in the garden?"

"Yes, I would like that, Lucy."

Lucy's husband escorted them through the wide French doors to a bench in the sheltered courtyard beneath what in spring would be a magnificent wisteria arbor.

He instructed a slave to bring blankets to keep away the chill. "Very well, Lucy. I leave you in the care of Susan and Jane, who seem well able to put you at ease."

"Colonel Burwell, what did you use to revive Lucy so effectively?" asked Susan.

"It was spirit of hart's horn, Missus Sinclair. You look puzzled. It is also known as sal ammoniac or smelling salts. The whiff of ammonia stimulates a waking state. We distill ammonia here at Kingsmill from whittled flakes of deer horn. I shall attend to my guests and return shortly to see if any of you need anything."

"Thank you," said all the ladies at once.

After the Colonel left, Lucy sighed, "I am embarrassed to faint at my own party!"

"It's nothing to be embarrassed about, Lucy. I faint at every opportunity that presents itself, to have a quiet moment. Handsome men rush to my aid and I feel better," Susan said.

Lucy looked at Susan, then at Jane who covered her mouth to suppress a laugh. Lucy burst out laughing and none of them could contain themselves. They laughed until tears flowed. Lucy wiped her eyes with a towel the attentive slave had quickly fetched. "I have not had a good laugh for a long time. My husband thinks I am out of sorts because of the death of Uncle Peyton. I do miss him but given his age, girth, red face, and wheezing, his passing was not a surprise. He is in a better place I know, but I feel sad for Aunt Betty's loss."

"I am sorry for your loss and hers," said Jane.

"You two have empathetic hearts."

Susan put a hand on Lucy's shoulder. "You have the strength it takes to move through. I know from experience the unforeseen happens. We can adapt to unwelcome changes."

"I can say, Lucy Burwell," added Jane, "that all the help we could ever ask for is always right here waiting in patience for us to accept it."

"You two are so encouraging. I cannot linger because I must attend to the guests lest they leave early for my sake. I shall show you to your rooms in a few minutes so that you may retire when you wish, have a good rest, and join us for breakfast."

The trio returned to the ballroom and Lucy greeted her visitors to assure them that she was not ill. Susan noticed Mister Weaver, the dance instructor, again walking to the large clock to check his watch against it. He looked agitated and moved quickly toward the door where he bowed low to Colonel Burwell, excused himself, and left. Susan watched the door close wondering what it was about Weaver that she found so disturbing.

She saw Lucy take a seat near the windows and a slave bring her a small plate of food from the refreshment table. Two couples took their leave and moved toward the door. Soon Susan and Jane were shown to their guest rooms to sleep in canopy beds that had just been warmed by sliding a brass pan filled with hot coals from side to side between the sheets.

Day 3-15: Megan at the Spirit Lodge

Mark and Megan rode for two miles beyond the iron works before coming to the first tree of any size. Mark turned down a path into a valley through a copse of trees by a stream, to a two-room cabin. Twenty people were gathered near the house, some sticking long thin sapling poles into the ground. In the center of the circle, a young Indian dug a shallow pit. Standing Elk greeted them as they rode up.

"Hello, Mark and Megan. We are building the Lodge. If you wish you can help."

"I'll be happy to help," said Mark. "Why did you pick this place for the Lodge?"

"This place is upstream and upwind from where the foundry poisons the water and the air. There are no nearby neighbors and is only an hour's ride from Williamsburg. The Mattaponi and Pamunkey reservations are far up the York River beyond West Point. We need prayer and healing at this time, so we are holding the Spirit Lodge where more people can join us."

Megan whispered to Mark, "I'm hungry after that ride. Can we eat soon?"

"I'll wash some carrots for you. We have the feast after the Lodge."

"Great."

"Megan, my nephew Thomas has finished the fire pit. Now we bend the willow saplings to form the Madoodiswaan or Spirit Lodge in the shape of the womb of Mother Earth. Usually men make these but you can help. Stand with a foot against a pole to keep it from popping out of the earth while we bend it. While you do that, feel your connection to the Earth and pray that this Lodge will help people."

The upper ends of the saplings were bent over to the opposite side of the circle and pushed into the same hole as the base of the opposite pole and were lashed with leather strips to keep them in place. A wider space between poles was left on the east side for a door. Flexible willow saplings were woven horizontally at one quarter, one-half, and three-quarters of the height of the Lodge and the grid was covered with deerskins but for a small opening in the top for spirits to enter.

"I chose an east door today because the day begins in the East and British soldiers are also approaching from that direction. We pray the light will overcome the darkness and danger. Thomas will be fire-keeper. He built a low altar and sacred fire east of the door. He has chosen Grandfather rocks of the right size with no cracks or holes to cause them to crumble or explode. I will lead the Lodge and be the water pourer. We can go into the cabin for a few minutes to get ready."

In the cabin, Roweena, Standing Elk's half sister told Megan, "I have a loose-fitting dress for you. You will sweat so take everything off and put the dress on. It covers to your ankles and does not show your form. The Lodge is for prayer, not attracting attention. Men think making love is their idea, and we should let them think so. But in the Lodge, pray to Creator. Don't use your mind to attract men."

Megan changed quickly and joined the others outside the cabin. Thomas had started a fire by the altar of earth and stones and was placing large rocks onto the coals. Several people gave offerings of tobacco to Standing Elk.

"No more talking until we complete the Lodge," Standing Elk announced. "Begin to let go of everything that has been disturbing you. We will pray for purification, for healing those who need it, for all creatures in creation, and for progress on the spirit road. Did anyone take strong drink in the last three days?"

"I had wine two nights ago," admitted one Indian man.

"You know we do not take alcohol three days before a Lodge. We need a clear mind in there. You stay out here, pray with us, and help Thomas at the fire. The rest of you form a line, women in front, and men in back. Roweena will pass with cedar and sweet grass burning in a shell to smudge you. It is to purify you."

Megan watched people fan smoke over themselves with their hands as Roweena passed and she did the same. Roweena came back carrying a basket of shredded cured tobacco. Standing Elk called out, "Take some tobacco in your right hand, and hold it in your left because the left hand is closer to your heart. When you are clear in your mind what you are praying for, place the tobacco into the sacred fire.

"Now, staying in prayer, enter the Lodge by crawling through the door and go to the left around the fire pit. The first woman will stop before the door leaving room for the Lodge leader. Leave a space between the men and the women so you keep your mind on the Grandfathers and on Creator."

The first woman in line got down on her hands and knees on a woven grass mat, and crawled into the deerskin-covered dome. One by one, they followed her into the dark and veered left of the shallow pit in the floor. Sounds of shuffling told Megan where the others were. When the woman in the lead completed the circle, she sat and uttered a satisfied "Hmm." People sat in the dark. Megan slid her fingers forward to feel the edge of the pit a foot in front of her. Light came through the door once the last person was in.

Standing Elk took his place by the door. When Thomas closed the door flap, it got dark again. "We will do four rounds and bring in seven Grandfathers each time so it will be a hot Lodge," said Standing Elk. "Thomas will open the door after each round. If it gets too hot for you, breathe closer to the earth or ask me to send you outside to pray. You may come back on the next round. This Lodge is for healing, purification, and connection to Creator, not to show how tough you are."

Standing Elk asked Thomas to pass in the first seven Grandfather rocks. One by one, Thomas lifted a rock from the coals of the altar fire with a pitch fork. He reached through the door and dropped the hot rock into the pit. Standing Elk used a deer antler to arrange the rocks then pulled the flap closed and began to tap on a hand drum and sing a prayer to welcome the ruddy red Grandfathers. He sprinkled water on the Grandfathers and the steam in the small space made it hotter. Megan experienced why one name for this ceremony was Sweat Lodge.

"Now," said Standing Elk, "we will go around the circle. Say your name. Then out loud or in silence, say what you are here to pray for. Listen to the others and support them in your prayers. Say, 'Miigwech', or 'Thank you', so the next person knows you are done."

It moved Megan to hear people pray from the heart. Some spoke their native language and others prayed in silence. When her turn came she said, "I'm Megan. I pray for everyone who has pain, loss, or illness, and everyone feeling anger, fear, or sadness. I pray the invisible patterns behind what we see and hear give them comfort and strength. Miigwech."

The door was opened after each round, and each time, seven more Grandfather rocks were placed into the pit. Standing Elk prayed for Creator to open vision to see paths through the difficult times ahead. He put tobacco on the fire and prayed for all people. He prayed for all creatures that walk on two legs or four or crawl on their bellies, swim in the water, fly in the air, wriggle underground or stand rooted in the ground. He put water on the Grandfathers and the Lodge filled with steam again. "All that live are sisters and brothers in the Creator's family," he said.

The third time the Grandfathers were brought into the Lodge glowing red in the darkness, Megan had two realizations. When Standing Elk said, "Welcome, Grandfathers" as the rocks came in, Megan thought of her own grandparents and their parents and their parents in a cascade back into the distant past and envisioned her ancestors shedding their animal skin cloaks and sweating around hot rocks and coals in a cave in Europe. We did this too, she thought. The ceremony connected her to her own deep roots. If our fire had gone out in winter many would have died. There is no lightning in winter to start a new fire. The fire-keepers helped the clans survive.

Megan also realized that deep in the Earth beneath her, rocks were also red hot at this moment, down where the lowest levels of igneous rock glowed with the heat of the magma below and the great pressure from the rock above them. "These rocks were red hot millions of years ago and here they are glowing again. They really are our grandfathers!"

Standing Elk spoke. "On this fourth round ask a quiet question and sit in prayer to listen for an answer. You could ask 'What is the remedy for this problem?' or 'What should I do next to help others or to move forward on my spirit journey?' Then wait for what comes." He sprinkled tobacco on the Grandfathers.

Megan thought about the incredible journey to Williamsburg and sat quietly with the question, "Why did we come back to this time?"

The glow faded from the rocks in what might have been minutes or millennia. Standing Elk's voice seemed to come from the distant past and from a future not yet imagined. "If you wish, say what came to you."

"The path goes on and on. Don't ever stop," a man's voice intoned across the fire.

"Forgive, be kind to everyone, and be firm in truth," said a man to Megan's right.

"Thank you, Creator, thank you," a woman's voice said from near Standing Elk.

After a pause, Megan said, "Be present and be patient. The Unseen is here and Presence shows proof enough. The Mysteries are unveiled in Creator's time."

Standing Elk asked the participants to crawl out of the Spirit Lodge, out of the womb of Mother Earth, and stand in a circle around the fire and altar, leaving an opening between the fire and the door of the Lodge. He began his closing words: "Everyone, look into this sacred fire. Soil, seed, sunlight, moisture, and warmth together brought forth a sprout before English settlers landed at Jamestown. The sprout became a sapling then a towering sycamore until it was cut down last year. From firewood, to charcoal, to red glowing ember, to white ash, this limb from a tree standing tall a mile from here, dissolves before our eyes back into light and warmth, minerals of the Earth, and vapors going into the air."

Staring into the fire as it dispersed the elements that briefly had gathered to be a sycamore tree, Megan felt at peace with the mystery of moving through time.

Standing Elk thanked everyone for being in the Lodge, and Thomas for keeping the fire. They filed into the cabin where Roweena and other women laid out the feast on a long table. Megan and the other women changed out of their dresses.

In the front room, people were served venison and sausages, vegetables, fry bread and corn mush. Everyone was refreshed. Conversation began gently and gradually became animated. "I am happy to see Anishinaabe people, European settlers, and Africans here together in prayer," said Thomas the fire keeper. "There were times when we were not together in peace. Before the Europeans came, our people sometimes fought against the Iroquois Confederacy. When white people came, they started to fight against us. Can you tell us about that, Uncle?'

Standing Elk said, "The memory of the past can help us build a better future. When the first iron furnace was erected at Falling Creek, the Indians could see that settlers were cutting down all the trees and taking all the land, not just a line of farms along the water. On Good Friday 1622, my ancestor Chief Opechancanough led the Powhatan Confederacy in coordinated attacks on the Falling Creek iron works and almost every English settlement in Virginia and Maryland at the same hour. Every soul at Falling Creek was killed except two children. Two Christian Indians warned Jamestown and they closed their stockade and repelled the attacks but many other settlements were wiped out. A third of the colonists in Virginia and Maryland were killed that day. Our ancestors thought the rest would leave. Instead, more soldiers came to slaughter our people. The history is bloody so we seek peace for the years ahead. The Proclamation Line was the Indians' best hope in a century, but it is clear Virginia and Pennsylvania leaders will go to any lengths to get the land in the West, including rising against their King."

"Another iron works has opened at Falling Creek, Uncle," said Thomas, "just when trees have finally returned. Should we gather up people and attack again?"

"Our European and African brothers and sisters marry into our families and become our friends. This is what peace looks like. Native People in the Northwest are choosing to fight against expansion, but in our painful experience, there is no victory when many die on both sides. Instead of warriors, we need peace-makers:
184

strong leaders who have no need to prove their strength by harming others, leaders who listen to their enemies and search for common ground."

"I pray it is possible," said Mark, speaking for the first time since the Lodge began, "but I don't know where we will find such leaders on the settlers' side."

"Change the order of your words, Mark. First, know it is possible, and then pray we find leaders who can lead not on a warpath, but on a path of peace."

Megan and Mark listened to others sharing the experiences they had in the Lodge. "Everyone likes the sausages you brought, Mark," Megan whispered.

"We brought."

"I thought you were planning to run away, Mark," she said quietly. "Now I see that's not what you want. If there is some way I can help you, let me know."

"I know you want to help, Megan, and Standing Elk knows, too. I ran away before and it did no good. Standing Elk taught me that wherever Creator puts me, I can help people, help nature, and work for something bigger than myself. When I see a path, I can follow it. I don't have to thrash in bondage if my heart is free."

"Have you seen a clear path?"

"I can see part of it. Standing Elk's people near and far are in danger. Some are on the side of Britain and others stand with the Continental Congress. The colonists are also divided. Within colonies in rebellion, there are loyal counties. Even families are split. If fighting comes here, all men, women, and children are in danger. I choose to help people, the servants, the small planters, the native people, and the slaves. If I must support the King and the Proclamation Line, I will. If I must support the militia against an invasion of Hessians and Redcoats, I will."

"Will you fight?"

"Will I kill people to stop them from killing people? That is not an easy question. Several men loyal to the King have been hanged, and Loyalists attack those who support Congress. Standing Elk says it is best to settle the disputes without killing. If you want to help, help us find the seasoned warrior who can lead us in that."

"Don't give up hope, Mark."

"Your brother knew about Dunmore's Proclamation freeing slaves and bonded servants before it happened. Does he know of something else, Megan?"

"He says that someday the colonies and Britain will be friends again. Standing Elk's suggestion to help people while staying out of the fighting is a good idea."

As the feast ended, people hugged each other. Mark gave Standing Elk a packet of tobacco. Outside, as Mark and Megan mounted the white stallion, Standing Elk was suddenly next to them with a hand on the saddle. "Megan, your prayers lead to truth and depth. The Unseen is here and the veils are lifting for you."

"Thank you for helping us to see, Standing Elk," Megan said.

As Mark and Megan rode, the sky shimmered with a brilliant lattice of points of light. Megan stared up in awe. She imagined soaring into the dark empty spaces between the stars. She remembered that there were billions of galaxies, each with billions of stars beyond the range of her eyes in all those dark spots. "For each star we can see, billions more are out there. No, not out there—*right here!*" she whispered. Mark did not hear over the sound of the hooves and the wind.

Day -16:   John at the Walking Stick Tavern

Beyond the edge of town, the country road seemed to wind forever through fields, wetlands, and woods as John walked in the light of a hazy quarter moon. An occasional lantern in a distant window flickered through the trees. He hoped to step out of the past as Peter had done and find a bar where he could have a cold beer and think about the coming Revolution and his memories of war. He paused to listen and smell the air, scanning ahead and behind for any sign that someone was there. Keep yourself together, John told himself. This is not Nicaragua or Afghanistan. A sense of danger nagged him for the first time since arriving in Williamsburg and if there was an ambush, he was not going to walk into it.

After an hour, he came upon a tavern at a crossroads. The words Walking Stick were carved into a sign with a painted relief of a cane and mug. John pulled the heavy oak door open; the smell of sweat and rancid tallow lanterns immediately told him he was still in the past. In smoky, flickering light, he found a seat alone at a small table. Compared to taverns in town, this was a less crowded but rowdy roadhouse. Voices were loud, the floor dirty.

John ordered a mug of ale and watched the room; certain he needed to stay alert.

At a table across from his, a man with cruel lines around his mouth also sat alone, hardening the sharpened thumbnail of his right hand above a candle flame. He pretended to ignore what was going on in the noisy room. John knew this as a means to avoid drawing attention. The man slowly reached behind his back and pulled a large concealed knife from a sheath. Holding it in his left hand below the table edge, he sharpened the long cracked nail of the middle finger on his right hand then hardened that nail in the flame.

He's ambidextrous—this does not look good for somebody, thought John. He sipped from his mug and slowly scanned the room without turning his head. There! A noisy group of men played at dice and among them was a small man with cleaner, fancier clothes than most in the tavern. John watched him place small bets while he observed the other players, noting who among them carried a worthy purse. John recognized him as the dance instructor at the Governor's Ball.

"I'll be damned," thought John. "The ones Bruce called Dagger and Dancer. There is an ambush, but not for me." A shift happened in his awareness. He pressed more weight onto his left foot then his right. He put attention on his right hand as it held the mug and then on his left resting on the table. He slowly rotated his shoulders forward and back letting go of any tension he found in his neck. He breathed slowly, settling into a deep calm that would abide without fear in chaotic life-threatening surroundings. John's skills in karate and kendo, honed in hand-to-hand combat, had never been witnessed by his wife or children. And certainly, such fighting had never been seen in Colonial Virginia. He smiled. Like riding a bike, it comes back. He sat composed, vigilant, barely touching his ale.

Dancer switched tables and placed a few bets in a higher-stakes game. A few minutes later Dagger stood and walked to the table where Dancer was about to roll the dice and sat down across from him. I missed the signal, thought John, but there had to be one.

Ten minutes later, a young man next to Dancer stood up suddenly, swayed, and pointed at Dagger. The man was from beyond the Piedmont and the locals called his kind "buckskins" or "shirtmen" for the deerskin jackets and hunting shirts they wore. In the noisy room, John could not hear what he shouted. Dancer said something to the young man who took the bait and shouted again at Dagger, pointing to an open area in the room. Dagger stood and without a word walked to the open place.

The patrons heard the buckskin yell, "If you're so damn sure, put those coins you won on the table and I'll match 'em!" Dancer said something else and the young man shouted, "Give it to the inn-keeper and I'll give him the same, and the winner takes the whole purse out of here!" He swayed into a table and almost fell over.

The owner of the tavern cleared a table and counted the coins and notes in the leather bag Dagger gave him. Then he counted the money the young man was carrying for himself and four other families in the hills of western Virginia to buy tools and supplies. Dagger's purse was short so Dancer stepped up to cover the difference. The drunken buckskin struggling to take off his jacket did not notice.

"This is murder," John said quietly.

Two men held the buckskin back while side bets were placed around the room. The owner called for quiet. "Listen well. The man left standing will walk from here with both purses. If neither can claim his prize, the money will buy spirits for every man in the house." A cheer broke out. "Listen! When one of you is ready to give up his purse to save himself, he will follow the tradition and shout 'King's Cruise.' The winner must stop fighting or we'll stop you where you stand with that bludgeon." His brother held a wicked club in both hands doing double duty as he stood between the crowd and the shelf lined with bottles of beer, wine, and spirits. "Is that understood?" Dagger nodded. The inebriated buckskin strained at the men who held him. The owner shouted the instructions into his face. "Understood?"

"I don't care!" shouted the man.

"Did you understand you yell 'Kings Cruise' to yield and get hurt no more?"

"Yes, and I don't care. Let him yell what he wants!" That was enough for the owner's sense of fair play and he returned to his place at the table.

When the men released him, the young buckskin charged. Dagger stepped aside and slapped the man's face as he raced by. The drunk crashed into a table and fell to the ground, breaking a chair. Men grabbed the remains of a lantern from the floor and stamped out burning oil to avert a tavern fire.

The buckskin staggered up, shook his head violently, licked the cut on his palm, and rushed at Dagger again. This time Dagger tripped him and sent the poor dupe sliding across the floor with a yell as he picked up two splinters in his back. He would need help to remove them to avoid infection tomorrow, if he had a tomorrow. He came to rest beside John's table.

John helped the young man to his feet. He steadied him. "What's your name?"

"Luke."

"Luke, listen to me. Don't charge the wily old bastard. Go to him slowly and hit him hard." The young man nodded and spat.

This time Luke walked to Dagger and swung a wild roundhouse punch that Dagger dodged but the young man had been in enough fights to follow with a hard left jab that landed on Dagger's shoulder and spun him to the side.

Dagger stood still until Luke made a move to grab him but quickly turned and got Luke in a hold. John saw Dagger's right hand form a C shape with the two hardened sharp nails at the points. Luke from the mountains was about to become a one eyed man with no money.

John felt a surge of energy and shouted, "King's Cruise!"

The owner's brother raised the club and stepped forward. Dagger pushed Luke away but the young man lunged back before being restrained by two patrons. "I did not say 'King's Cruise,'" he shouted.

"No, but your second did. Give me the purse," Dagger demanded.

"I got no second!" Luke squirmed to get back in the fight.

"I didn't say 'King's Cruise' for him." John looked calmly at Dagger. "I said it for you. Innkeeper, please give Luke his purse." The innkeeper bit his lip.

Dagger's hand felt for the handle of the knife against his backbone. "That trick will win you nothing. Give me my winnings!" he snarled.

With slow, calm breathing, John stepped forward, his gaze fixed on Dagger whose hand was around the handle of the weapon that gave him his name. He sensed motion on his right as Dancer swung an iron bar at him. He ducked and shot out a kick that landed on the side of Dancer's knee placing fifteen pounds of pressure in precisely the right spot to dislocate the knee and send Dancer to the floor with a scream. The iron bar clanked against the edge of a table.

"You won't be teaching ladies the finer points of the minuet now, I suppose," called out John without taking his eyes off Dagger.

Dagger lunged and as quickly, John seemed to vanish and reappear to the left, slapping him across the face as Dagger had done to the buckskin. Dagger used every trick he knew, slashing the blade to the right and left with his left hand in arcs while seeking an opening for his right fist. He passed the knife to his right hand and moved in to jab without coming close to John, who taunted as he poked Dagger's ribs hard beneath his knife arm. "You're not good at this when your foe is sober. You need another line of work!"

Dagger roared and dove forward thrusting the knife. The knife found only air and Dagger got another slap across the face that spun his head to the side and raised a bright red welt. The crowd in the tavern was silent. The owner's brother stared with his mouth open.

"Yield now or face a gory gasping fate, you corpse in stinky boots!" roared John.

A shot rang out in the tavern as a lead ball from a .62 caliber single shot flintlock pistol tore through John's shirt between his chest and his armpit, embedding itself in a column. In the moment it took John to glance at the man across the room struggling to reload, Dagger slashed and John dodged too late to avoid a cut on his arm. He whirled to face Dagger again.

A thud from the stock of a weapon sent the man with the pistol crashing unconscious to the floor. A tall man with a black beard pointed the business end of an old blunderbuss around the room and shouted, "The next man to raise a firearm gets a belly full of bird shot. It's time we saw an even fight in this tavern."

"Thanks," John called out, "I've got Dagger hopelessly outnumbered."

That baited Dagger further, and crazed with rage he dove forward, making short slashes to keep the point of the knife between him and John. In an instant, he was spun around and immobilized in a lock with the knife still in hand. John dropped to one knee and held Dagger's wrist in a painfully tight grip with the honed edge of the blade across his throat. Dagger's left hand flailed helplessly in the air. It happened so fast that no one in the tavern could say how John had done it.

"One move and by your own hand your head will go east and your body west." John shouted in the loudest voice he had used in twenty years. "An old man like me with bare hands is no match for a seasoned fighter like you holding a knife."

Dagger moved and John pressed into his neck and with Dagger's own motion, the keen edge of the knife stung and started a trickle of blood on his Adam's apple.

In his rage, Dagger made another attempt to move. This time John twisted Dagger's hand to keep the knife away from his captive's neck but pulled Dagger's knuckles hard into his throat making breathing difficult.

"Why make a mess? Right, innkeeper? I said, Right, innkeeper?"

The innkeeper stared.

A local man with a large bet on Dagger slowly reached for his musket leaning against the wall beside him.

"Don't move!" shouted the bearded man. "If you touch it you won't live to point it. A second man with a pistol in each hand stepped out from behind the fellow with the blunderbuss. The local fellow put his hands on the table.

"All wagers are off," called out the innkeeper. "This fight is only for the purse." The patrons with money on Dagger visibly relaxed as did the man with the blunderbuss.

Dagger tried to twist free to no avail. John pressed hard and paralyzed his opponent. He could not yell, could not breathe. His eyes stared, his movements weakened. John eased the pressure and next to Dagger's ear threatened through closed teeth, "Stop struggling, or you'll never move again." Dagger nodded.

"What's your name?"

Dagger gasped for air.

"I said 'What is your name?'" John pressed his thumb.

"Roger!" He rasped.

"I'm no match for you, Roger. No match at all. But you like uneven fights, don't you? How do you think those men felt that you set up and cut down? Did they feel like this? Innkeeper, we'll take that iron bar Dancer found and stake Roger's head outside your door to attract customers. Once it rots away to a skull, rename the tavern Jolly Roger. No, that could ruin the pirates' good name. What about 'The Thirsty Skull?' Perfect! Men who prey on others will be dying to come in here."

Dancer, lying a few feet away moaned. "Be patient, Dancer. I'll end your pain when I'm done with Roger." Dancer moaned again more in terror than pain.

John saw luminous eyes looking at him from back in the crowd. Frances, the woman from the St. George Tucker House, was staring into him and praying. He could feel something else. Could that be Susan over there? No, maybe not. Where did she go, he wondered.

John drew a breath. "It was long ago," he murmured. "Danny and Sargon are gone. It's over." He stood up suddenly, snatching the knife and pulling Dagger upright giving him no freedom to move. "Roger, some people say I have a problem. Maybe I do. I get irritated by people who maim and kill for financial gain. What are your views, Roger? Does fighting make a good career? I've noticed it often ends badly. I don't like you — you hurt so many people."

John bellowed at the patrons in his sergeant's voice of command, "Stand up if you're one of the best fighters here!" No one moved. "You drunken gamblers just got bashful. Come on, haven't you seen a head come off?" Dagger twitched.

John nodded toward the men. "You there, and you, step forward. Innkeeper, you too! And your partner carrying the big stick—now! Or Roger's head comes off right here! I'll stain all your shirts red. You two big fellows at the table, who were betting on the fight, leave your musket over there and step up next to the others. Step closer!"

The man with the blunderbuss shouted, "Do as he says!"

John waited until the men were in a row. "You clever fellows figured out how to piss and how to blow snot out your nose, but you don't know much else. You own one shirt and you don't know what soap is. That's why you smell like a pig barn in July. If I swing Dagger's head by his hair, it will bloody up the only shirts you have. You will at least need to wash them.

"If you want to keep your shirts free of Dagger's blood and keep Dagger's head on his shoulders and not on an iron bar outside, raise your right hands." A few complied and after looking at each other and shuffling, all ten hands were raised.

"See, Roger? They love you more with your head on. Do you men swear that when baiting men into fights happens here, you'll keep the peace?"

A few half-hearted mumbles.

"Swear it you louts! Are you so blind you can't see that when the Redcoats come for you with fixed bayonets twice as long as Roger's dagger, you will need every smelly one of you and all the buckskins to be fit to fight? Those shirt-men can drop a squirrel for supper at ninety yards and you town folk can't hit a man at fifty when you are sober and the man is fat and standing still. You need the mountain boys to keep both their eyes! And no dismembering! In battle, you will need both your balls and then some! Now swear to stop these fights before they begin and spend your money on something sensible like land, horses, women, or whisky!

"Aye," a few men mumbled.

"I swear," said the innkeeper and his brother grunted agreement.

"And if one of you has a few tankards and forgets, the others remind him. I showed you some fighting, and now I want to show you something else."

With a jerk, John cut off the long hard nail on Roger's thumb and shoved him gasping to the floor at the foot of the line of men. John spun in a circle, putting the energy of his spin into the dagger, which he hurled into a beam above the door.

"Stand aside!" John shouted and he bounded onto a chair and the table nearest the door and leapt up to grab the knife handle in both hands. As he dropped back to the floor, the handle snapped off with his weight, leaving the blade imbedded in the beam, to remind patrons of this night until The Walking Stick burned to the ground eighty years later.

He stepped back to Roger, lying on the floor, and placed the carved antler handle next to him. "This is yours. What I'm showing you is called mercy. I lost too many friends in the big bar fights called war to put up with crap like this when I'm trying to have a quiet beer." With one hand, John grabbed Roger by the collar and pulled him to his feet. He walked him to the heavy door and shoved him outside. "Go far, Roger, or someone you hurt will finish you!"

John closed the door and exhorted the men in the tavern. "Whether war comes to you or you march out to meet it, stay sober, help your friends, and show mercy to your enemies. Today's enemies can be friends tomorrow."

John stepped over to Dancer who grimaced sweat-faced on the floor, his right leg at a painful, distorted angle below his knee. "No! Please!" he cried.

John spoke calmly "Let's fix that before it swells. You need not be crippled for life." John placed both hands around Dancer's knee and with a snap, relocated it. Dancer screamed at the momentary pain then looked down with relief at his leg.

"There was some tearing, so stay off it for a few days and bind it to give it support but not too tight. It will swell then begin to get better. What's your name?"

"Randall Weaver," Dancer whimpered.

"Randall, you'll be walking with a cane in a week, dancing with a limp in ten, and amazing the gentry with your recovery in half a year. Make an honest go of it." John looked back at the crowd but the women were gone.

He nodded to the tavern owner. "What do I owe you for the beer?"

"Nothing, Mister. I'll grant thee another if you have a thirst."

"No, thanks. I tend to get rowdy if I drink more than one. Please give our young friend Luke, his purse back and half of Dagger's purse. Use the rest to buy everyone a drink." The innkeeper complied.

"You won some money, but learn more sense," John cautioned Luke.

"I could have beat him myself!"

"No, Luke. Roger was about to gouge out your eye. Did you come on a horse?"

"Aye."

"I'll walk you outside and send you on your way. Wait! The splinters!"

"Barman, I'll take two shots of the strongest whiskey you have."

John tore off his bloodied sleeve and winced as he splashed whisky onto the cut and used the sleeve as a bandage. "Luke, turn around and hold the table." He complied and John pulled Luke's hunting shirt up past where the large splinters had pierced him. He pulled them out, and poured whiskey on the wounds.

"Ow!" yelled Luke.

"Done! That was so it would not get infected, Luke. Now you need to get far away from here. Good night, Gentlemen." John bowed to the stunned crowd and ushered the young buckskin out into the fresh night air. Roger was nowhere in sight.

Luke climbed onto his horse without help.

"Find a place to sleep and don't drink when you get there. If you make it back home, share the purse you won with the families that trusted you. Learn to read. They may elect you as their Congressman someday." John slapped the horse's flank and Luke was off down the road toward Williamsburg.

He turned to see the men with the blunderbuss and two pistols come through the door and a third man following behind them.

"Thank you for keeping the fight fair," John said.

"Roger maimed two of our friends last year," said the bearded man. "We came here to kill him but you saved us the trouble and perhaps saved us from hanging."

"I'd call that a good exchange."

"So would I, Mister. You took a reckless risk fighting Dagger alone. My brother was standing at my back two pistols, and our cousin was across the room with his musket across his lap."

John looked at the bullet hole through his shirt. "I take after my son, I guess. Maybe I was protected by Divine Providence like George Washington was."

"Godspeed," said the bearded man with the blunderbuss. They shook hands.

It was a long walk to town. My wars are over, John said to himself, but their war is just beginning. He thought of the suffering and grief to come. When he reached the house, it was dark and quiet. He washed his face in the large bowl, put disinfectant and a bandage from his travel kit onto the cut on his arm and slipped into bed.

193

Day 3-17:   Peter Drives toward Norfolk

The engine started with a roar and Peter noticed his foot was almost to the floor. Calm down, he said to himself. I have a feeling that this is where the trail leads and Annie told me to follow that feeling. He decided to take Highway 5 past New Hope to 156 South, cross the bridge, and follow the Colonial Trail toward Suffolk. He drove in silence and watched the woods and fields along the road.

After crossing the James, he headed east. When the highway curved south he veered left, drove east a few minutes, then crept north on a narrow dirt track to the river. He wanted a sense of the hills and inlets that would have been there in 1775. He parked and walked to the water. This is close to Norfolk, he thought. Maybe slaves passed by here long ago on their way to the British. He was glad to be in his own time and not in the past when armed men were skirmishing in these woods. It would have been dangerous around here back then.

Peter sat on a rock and tossed pebbles into the river. I would have been scared, running away and being put into battle, he thought. He wondered if his father had been scared when he was a young soldier. The woods were so profoundly silent he heard pebbles of varied sizes make different sounds as they hit the water. Throwing a few stones of unlike size high into the air, he listened to the notes. It sounded like the first four notes of a spiritual. "All night, all day, Angels watchin' over me," he sang to himself. He walked farther east then stopped again to listen.

The faint sound of singing drifted over the water. He followed a path along the shore around the next point and saw the glow of a campfire in the woods. He approached quietly. Through a veil of leafless branches, he saw a circle of African men seated around the fire. They sang in a major key with harmony and syncopation, similar to what he had heard at the Hush Harbor. Could he really have stepped back into the past? That was not possible. Then, just behind his head, he heard a metallic click.

"Hands up!" a voice barked. "Forward, march or get a new hole by your ear!"

"Don't shoot!" Peter cried. "I came to hear the singing." And I'm about to be shot if I don't think of something better to say, he thought as he neared the fire holding his hands in the air.

"Look who I found snoopin' in the woods," his captor gloated. "Likely a rebel tryin' to catch us back." The man shoved Peter forward so others could see his face.

"Good job, Aaron! You is a good guard."

"Stand him up against a tree. We need target practice," proposed one man.

The votes started coming in. "Yeah, shoot him!"

"Wit' a prisoner, the Redcoats see we ready for battle," the captor protested.

"Naw, we can do that wit' his body."

"Shoot him so we can sleep wit'out him gettin' away to tell where we is."

"You know what I think? No, you don't, so I'se gonna tell you. I think we ax this man what he doin' here and give him a chance to 'splain his self real good. I hopes for your sake you can 'splain yourself, young man," said a man across the circle.

"Are you William, the brick maker?" asked Peter hoarsely.

Before William could answer, Peter heard, "Hey, Mister Peter, what you doin' here?" from Augustus on the other side of the fire.

"Oh, Augustus! It's you! I'm glad you made it over the river."

"This here is Mister Peter. He helped me escape," Augustus explained. "Don't shoot him, he probably come here to help us. Good job findin' him, Aaron!"

Peter's captor lowered his musket. "Lord, don't forget me! I swear I wanna capture a slave owner to give him a taste of how he done to us."

"Come set by me, Mister Peter," Augustus called out. "Say good evenin' to the men of Governor Dunmore's Ethiopian Regiment. We made raids to take back black powder the rebels hid away. Soon we gonna be real soldiers. Like you said, we free now. We follow orders like any soldier do, but no massa owns us."

"That's right," echoed a number of voices around the fire.

"I'm happy to meet you, men. Thank you all for not shooting me."

Several men chuckled. They had scant experience of camaraderie with whites.

"How did you get here, Mister Peter?" asked Augustus.

"I came along the south shore of the James to see if the way was open to Norfolk in case I'm able to help anyone else get out of Williamsburg."

"Good thing you stopped 'fore you got there," William said. "The Governor sits on a ship 'cause Rebel militia is nearby. So don't send folk to Norfolk."

"That's true, Mister Peter," Augustus chimed in. "I met up wit' these men as I was comin' along the shore like you told me. You want a sip of corn mash?"

"No, thanks. I have to drive... I mean ride to Williamsburg. Do you have water?"

Peter gratefully took a cup of water. Around the circle, bright eyes watched the fire. Quick flashes of flame danced above the glowing coals. Brown faces glistened, reflecting orange, red, and yellow light. Logs popped — the showers of sparks gave a feel of celebration muted by foreboding that soon, with little training, they would be fighting for freedom and for their lives.

These newly freed men flashed grins of white teeth with gaps and broken corners. In the firelight they told tales of dancing on a Saturday night, occasional good meals snatched somehow, and willing women they had known. Any over thirty-five were old and even younger men were sun-baked and bone-sore. All had known gatherings in the woods and the risk of the lash or worse that could follow a late arrival home. Slaves were forbidden to carry a firearm unless hunting with permission on the master's land. A free black found with a gun off his own land risked being killed. But here, every man had a musket, powder, and shot at hand.

Augustus leaned close to Peter. "Have you seen Annie anywhere since I left?"

195

Before Peter could answer, Aaron sat heavily beside Augustus and took a swallow from a clay jar of corn mash. "I ain't on guard duty now. Mister, I ain't against you if you helped 'Gustus." He took a long drink. "'Gustus, you been good to me since we joined up. Folk say I'se angry all the time, but some folk been awful cruel to me. When I looks at you, Mister, I remembers them."

"I understand. I'm sorry about the way you good African men have been treated."

"I ain't no good man at all." Aaron took a long draught from the jar. "No-suh not a good man no mo'. And I ain't all African neither."

"Was you daddy white and ain't 'cepted you as his son like happened to me?" asked Augustus who was lighter skinned than the other men in the circle.

"No, he was a free man from British India. He was a real Dilli man."

"A Dilli man?" asked a surprised Peter.

"Yes. Folk from Delhi is Dilli men. Daddy traveled to a port and found work serving table for a British sea captain. After they got to 'Napolis he served in a big house near where the Potomac joins the Chesapeake. My mama was a tall African, so I was a tall boy. But mama was a slave, so by law I was born a slave even though Daddy was free. When Massa died, Daddy did not have money to buy me, so I got sold away as a field hand and never learned to serve in a big house like he done. Stuck out sweatin' in the hot sun..." His voice faded as he stared into the fire.

"A Dilli man," Peter said quietly. "I wonder..."

"Is Annie still talkin' to people about runnin'?" whispered Augustus to Peter.

"She tells people to keep ready but not to rush off."

"Well, I'se glad 'bout that 'cause some folk got to Norfolk and got catched."

Aaron took another swig and shook his head violently. He leaned against a log.

"I'll let people know Norfolk is not safe," whispered Peter, "

"Damn, how can they do that to a man!" shouted Aaron.

"What happened?" asked Augustus.

"I was thinkin' about it again. I ain't no man, and them yellow dogs done it."

Augustus put his left hand on his leather pouch with herbs Annie taught him to use to disinfect wounds or reduce pain. He put his right hand on Aaron's shoulder. "We all been done wrong. That be why we'se side by side to fight for freedom."

"I tried to run away. I didn't know what I was doin'. They catched me and... "

"You had the balls to try, Aaron. I was too scared to run."

"You say I had the balls to try. I ain't got them now!"

"You got balls, Aaron. You brave as a badger, big as a bear, and you be the strongest, fastest man around this fire. I wanna be next to you when we fight."

"Them yellow dogs cut me, Augustus. They cut me and laughed at me. I almost bled to death 'cept for a big woman healer that found me the next day. She put on a poultice, and sewed me up so I did not die. I ain't had balls for nine years!"

Augustus kept a hand on Aaron's shoulder. "They cut you?"

"It weren't my massa but the men who caught me runnin'."

"But, Aaron, them Burgesses passed a law that they can't castrate slaves no mo'."

"That law made in '69 but Slave hunters cut me before."

Aaron looked into the fire. "I never was wit' but one woman. That be why I was runnin' there when they catched me. There was a pretty girl washin' laundry in a fine house by the Capitol in Williamsburg. Massa brought me to load up supplies for building his new house and to drive the team. He needed me to help him get home since he was sometimes deep in the grog jar wit' other gentlemen.

"He went to visit a builder to ax how to do his roof right. At our quarters, the only time the roof don't leak is when it ain't rainin'. But Massa's house, he need to have it just so. They talked 'bout slate and cedar shingles, and whether squarin' beams wit' an adze be enough or do we need to plane them. They had a cup of rum and then more and they ax Massa to have bread and quail at the house."

Peter and Augustus grew very quiet as they listened.

"I was out back by the kitchen, talkin' wit' the cook and the washing girl, eatin' greens and potatoes. They was nice women and they had no men folk. I liked talkin' wit' them. It got to be time for the women to sleep 'cause they got up before the sun to start the fires but because I was there, they stayed up a little longer.

"The men sat outside the house so as not to wake the missus, so we heard them talkin' and drinkin'. They got louder and soon they wasn't fancy at all. One of them was such a fine gentleman he threw up over the fence.

"Massa said he should be movin' on. But the builder said, 'Joseph, you sleep here instead of in a crowded room at the King's Arms.'

"Massa Joseph said yes then he remembered me, and he said, 'Can Aaron sleep by the kitchen fire?' And the other Massa stopped and rubbed his head a minute.

"'Yes, we can take care of your boy,' he says. They came through the gate by the garden and me and the women stood up. The builder told Massa that his wife is gonna have a baby 'cause she started feelin' poorly in the mornin'. Then he said, 'Your boy can sleep in the loft. If he breeds wit' the laundry girl, we'll have a wet nurse here soon after the baby is born.'

"'I don't think he bred yet,' says Massa. 'I did not put him wit' anyone.'

"'Go on ahead inside you all,' the builder told us. Then they was laughin' and slappin' each other on the back as they went back into the house."

"You say there was a cook and a laundress. Where was the house?" asked Peter.

"I don't remember 'zackly. The Capitol was across the street."

Peter let out his breath slowly.

"Well, the cook says, 'She been wonderin' 'bout men for a while and she 'bout fifteen so you two go up into the loft and I'll sleep by the stove to warm my bones.'

"'What should we do?' the washing girl axed.

"'Do what I told you 'bout.' Then the cook went to the kitchen.

"So me and the girl went above stairs. Neither one of us knew what to do but Spirit moved us and I started to like her. Then I loved her like she was my wife.

"Next day, we was drivin' the cart back to Princess Anne County, by the sandy beaches not far from here. All the way home, I was thinkin' 'bout that girl and how close to her I felt. It was a deep feelin' like prayin' and I never felt like that before. I thought about jumpin' off the cart and runnin' back but I would not get far. So when we passed a fork, I looked back to see what it looked like goin' the other way.

"We got home in the evenin' and me and the stable boy unloaded the carts into sheds. Massa Joseph was tired and went into his house to sleep."

"I got to thinkin'. It was afternoon and Massa would not be callin' me until tomorrow. I could run all night and be far by mornin'. So when the cook gave me a biscuit and cob of corn, I wrapped them in a cloth. I took the papers Massa Joseph had in the wagon from buyin' them things and I took a few nails. I was goin' to say if someone ax me that Massa sent me back to get the right size nails."

"That was smart to have a story, Aaron," said Augustus. "If that was the first time you was wit' a woman, I can see why you had such a strong feelin' for her."

"Well, the story wasn't good enough, 'Gustus. I walked all night thinkin' of takin' that girl to Spanish Florida or west to join up wit' black Indians. Outside Williamsburg, men catched me and axed where was I goin' in such a hurry. I tol' them, 'To the store to buy more nails like this.' But they said, 'The store opens Monday and this is Sunday, so why you runnin'?

"They tied me to a tree and beat me and burned me 'til I cried I was runnin' to see a girl while I was waitin' for the store to open. Then one man said, 'Let's fix him so he don't go runnin' after no mo' girls.' I was tied and couldn't do nuthin' but beg and scream. They left me but a healer came by and cared for me. The men came back when she was off getting more herbs. They took me to my Massa and axed for a reward, which they got since they was carryin' muskets. I got ashamed to look after that girl 'cause I ain't no man no mo'." Aaron sobbed.

Augustus patted Aaron's back and kept his other hand on his poultice pouch. Staring into the fire, he began to pray on how to help. He chewed on his lower lip.

"You is a friend, 'Gustus. I been too ashamed to tell folk I ain't a man."

Augustus rubbed the herb pouch like a healing talisman. "Aaron, you is a strong man and a brave man. That washing girl in Williamsburg had a son the year after you was wit' her. Her name is Evie and that son named James. She named him James because his daddy live on the other side of the James River. She tell James his daddy pray for him every night."

198

"Evie! That was her name! That is what the cook called her when she say good night. I have a son? 'Gustus, do you know Evie? You know where she at?"

"I seen her at a Hush Harbor. She still live at that house by the Capitol and do the washin'. We both know Annie, the big woman who saved you. Annie teached me herbs for poultices so if any of these boys get shot, I can help stop the bleedin', ease the pain, and keep the wound from festerin'. More soldiers die from festerin' than from wounds. Annie taught me how to stop festerin' so don't you worry."

"I got a son? I will pray for that boy James every night. If we live through this fight, maybe I can do somethin' for my son. What's he like 'Gustus?"

"He's a big boy like you but a bit shy. He need a daddy to help him be brave."

"I met James, too, Aaron," said Peter. "You can be proud of your son."

"There be somethin' else I want to tell you, Aaron." Augustus confided. "Two years after she had James, Evie had a second boy."

"She done? Who is the daddy? Did they jump the broom together?"

"Naw. He was sent up the loft like you was, but he never paid Evie much mind. She call her second boy, Dilli. She been thinkin' about you, Aaron, all these years."

"She call him Dilli? I must have told her 'bout Daddy the free Dilli man. I can't be a man for they momma but maybe I can help them boys. Mister Peter, is that your name? You know my son, too? Good thing I ain't shot you. But damn! I still mean to take me a prisoner." Aaron flung the dregs of the corn mash into the fire. He lay back and closed his eyes.

The flash of Aaron's liquor in the fire reminded Augustus and Peter of Annie pitching rum into the fire at the Hush Harbor the night they met. "That was good, Augustus," whispered Peter. "Why didn't you tell him you are Dilli's father?"

"I thought 'bout Annie and the flash in the fire was a sign I done right. I don't got strong feelin's for Evie. She the only girl Aaron been wit' so I done that to help him. I ain't got no poultice for lost balls, Mister Peter, but maybe he can feel like the brave man he is. It feels good to help people. I feel strong. I ain't obliged to run home by dawn to avoid a whippin'. I am free."

"You did another kind of healing, Augustus. Now we should get some sleep."

"I want to help anybody who need it, so sleep be a good idea."

As most of the men around the fire had done already, Augustus nestled into the leaves and dozed off.

Peter lay back and looked at the stars, thinking about the beautiful woman two centuries older than he was. He was camped out with the fathers of her two children long before his grandparents were born. This must fit together somehow. He drifted off to sleep.

Day 4-1: Susan Breakfasts with the Better-Sorts

Susan woke to the sound of water pouring. Disoriented, she opened a curtain with a red rose design. An African woman was filling a washing bowl. Room service, she thought. As she dropped her head back to the pillow on her canopy bed, she thought, "God, what an intense dream! I hope John is all right."

Susan washed, dressed, and knocked on Jane's door to find her already up. "Good morning, Susan. I have never seen such a bed chamber."

Lucy Burwell came into the corridor, "Oh good! You are awake! I rise before the sun to be sure the cook starts breakfast. Sorry we have no extra housemaids to help with your ablutions and dressing."

"Lucy, that's fine," said Susan. "We're in the habit of dressing ourselves."

"Breakfast is almost ready. Most mornings we read the Bible with the children, but today is Sunday so we are going to Church. We will sit with Aunt Betty. Would you like to have a look at the kitchen?"

"Yes," said Susan. "We would love to."

As they descended the back stairs, Lucy said, "My husband insists on breakfast at eight. With coaxing and help from my daughters, meals are always on time."

They stepped into a busy kitchen. Pots of water for tea and coffee hung in a fireplace high enough to stand in. The cook, a large woman with a headscarf, directed the kitchen maids. "Effie, keep stirrin' and mind it don't scorch. *Claudie*! Don't hold that pan too close to the fire. Use the turner more. Mornin', Missus Burwell. Mornin', Ladies. The table laid wit' two more places for you."

"Good, Peggy."

Lucy explained, "Today breakfast is leftovers from last night. Ice cut from the ponds and stored in the icehouse is limited so we cannot store fresh food long. After breakfast, I go over the dinner plan and give the cook the expensive ingredients from a locked pantry. I supervise the house and gardens until dinner at 1:30. Let's step out of the kitchen so we can talk."

A girl scrambled downstairs and hugged Lucy's leg. "Good morning, Mother."

"Good morning! We leave for church after we eat so get dressed, my precious."

"Do your children go to school?" asked Susan.

"The children are schooled here, and my older daughters help me in order to learn how to run households by the time they marry. All children learn gardening, raising chickens, and managing servants. The boys learn about crops, animal husbandry, fishing with weirs, commerce, and the dealings of a large estate."

"Doest thou produce all your own food, Lucy Burwell?" Jane asked.

"We have vegetables fresh in summer and from the root cellar in winter, fruit from the orchards or in home-made compotes and jams, bread from corn and wheat; milk, butter, and cheese from our dairy. We have beef, pigs, and sheep, chickens, ducks, geese, doves, and game. From the river and the bay, we eat oysters, crabs, and fish, grilled or salted and dried. We get honey and wax from our bees and herbs from the garden. We go to town are to meet friends or visit someone ailing or to buy molasses, a tool from the smith, or some imported fabric.

"We do laundry every Friday, so everyone including bondsmen has fresh clothes on Sunday. Many of our bondsmen will ride with us today to church.

"The hour before dinner is busy in the hot kitchen. I keep a bowl of cold water near to freshen up before sitting down at the table in case I do not have time to hurry to my chamber to change. We often have guests. After the meal, the men stay at the table for brandy and a pipe. The women move to the salon for coffee."

Lucy sighed, "I try to find time in the afternoon to help my children with their studies or to be alone. I might read or talk with a visitor. Let us go into the gardens together for a few minutes before breakfast." The three women strolled through the garden past a flowering tree and Lucy became uncharacteristically quiet.

"Forgive me," Susan ventured, "but is something troubling you besides your uncle's passing?"

Lucy nodded but said nothing until they came upon the panoramic vista of the James River. "I love Kingsmill. I am grateful for all our blessings." She led them to a bench with an unobstructed view, nested in a crescent-shaped tapestry of Queen Anne's lace, and pink and yellow yarrow bordered with blue salvia, all still colorful in November.

"All this... is at risk of slipping away. Our debts are greater than the value of our land, buildings, and bondsmen combined. Last night the carriage took you by a plantation taken over by Scottish factors who owned the debt. There are many such disasters. My husband thrashes in his bed, worried a factor might ask full payment or that a poor crop will bankrupt us. If war comes this way, our home could be burned. If everything falls into ruin, what can I do for the children?

"You both show kindness that can only come from contentment and wisdom. I envy you." Lucy began to weep and Susan put her arm around her shoulder. In the distance, a three-masted ship glided toward a plantation upriver. "Sorry," Lucy said. "I criticize the hypocrisy of other families but we are caught in the same false facades. I know not what to do." They looked at the river until Lucy asked, "Is there anything you can tell me that might help?"

Jane said gently, "'Tis not the telling that can help thee. 'Tis thy knowing."

"What knowing, Jane?"

"Know thy life is lived in each moment and the Light within illuminates eternally. Some see it as light, some feel it as love in their heart, and some hear it in silence. It is all of those and much more. It is the Divine source of all that is."

"I have lost touch with my Faith." Lucy looked at the lingering mist near the shore. "I keep busy so there is no time to dwell on the travails in our lives. I feel an empty place within."

Susan spoke. "Lucy, do not fear that empty place — it is an opening. You have strength and the light within that Jane pointed to."

"You are saintly women."

"No," said Jane. "We are all pilgrims on a long journey. Life's hardships are neither punishment nor a sign of abandonment. They are part of the landscape we travel as we learn and grow."

Susan assured her, "I know what it is to have a husband thrashing in the night. If you can find grace within the empty place, you may calm him as well. You are blessed with a grand house full of laughing children. Let their joy lift you. Many people work hard in your kitchen and in the fields to support you and your family. Be grateful for their efforts as well. They are souls seeking happiness just as you are and everyone should be appreciated and rewarded for their contributions."

Jane added, "Good mingles with tribulations. Expect good and it will find thee. If thy future station is humble, thou can still enjoy thy family, and be grateful."

"Truth resonates in your words." They watched the ship sail out of view. "I have not so looked forward to singing hymns in years. You have given me back my appetite for life. Let us go in and you can meet the rest of the family."

Susan and Jane joined the Burwells at the table for Sunday breakfast. Steaming warm breads, smoked ham, and corn meal grits with a pat of bacon fat were added to the leftovers. Lucy gave her husband and children hugs as she walked around the table to her place. The Colonel led the family in a prayer and the meal began.

The children were delighted at Jane's way of talking. They found Susan's accent funny as well, especially when she told them a joke her students liked.

After breakfast, everyone bundled up and hurried out to two enclosed carriages and an open hay wagon, their teams of horses hitched and ready. The older children jostled to get seats in the second carriage with Jane and Susan. Colonel Burwell came back to the second carriage. "Ladies, your presence at Kingsmill has brought a salutary effect to my wife's heart. Lucy is in the carriage laughing with the children. You brought levity to our home." He made a respectful bow.

"It is an honor and pleasure to be welcomed in your home, Colonel. We will pray for your family as we move through these tumultuous times," said Susan.

"We are grateful for your prayers." The colonel returned to his carriage and they pulled down the lane. The wagon followed, crowded with fourteen adult slaves wrapped in the blankets Lucy provided, excited to be on their way to Williamsburg and hopeful of seeing friends or loved ones there. Bright-eyed children cuddled among them under the blankets.

When the horse-drawn convoy reached Bruton Parish Church, everyone clambered out into the bustle of the crowd. "Can you join us in our family pew, Susan?" Lucy asked.

"Thank you, Lucy, but I must check on my husband and children."

"I hope to see you again, Susan." Lucy ushered her children toward the church.

Susan turned to Jane and gave her a hug. "God be with you, Jane."

Jane was embarrassed by the hug but could not suppress a smile. "I thank thee, Susan. Thou hast truly brought me back to the Light."

"Jane, please keep the dress as a gift to remember the special times we had."

"Oh, Susan! It was wonderful to wear these clothes to Kingsmill and to touch the lives of the better-sorts including their suffering, but I cannot take thy clothes!"

"Jane, I insist. It makes me happy to think of you wearing it on special days. If you wear it at the Hospital once in a while you will cheer up the patients."

"I shall remember thee for all time."

When Lucy noticed Jane moving toward the church, she hurried back, took her arm, and prevailed on her to join her in the Randolph family pew.

Day 4-2:   Peter in the Smallpox Outbreak

Peter drifted to the surface of a fathomless sleep. He was covered by two frayed blankets beneath stark skeletons of winter trees in the moonlight. It took a moment to register where he was. Near his feet were the cold ashes of a dead fire, covered by a scattering of frosted leaves. His eyes widened. The Ethiopian Regiment was gone. He was alone in the woods by the wide James River. "How did the fire get cold so fast? If I drank corn mash last night, I would say I passed out like Rip Van Winkle, but I'm probably just totally out of my mind! All right—calm down. Crap! I've got to get back to Williamsburg."

He stood up and stretched. What year is this? He laughed aloud at his question. To the southeast, in the predawn sky, orange light glowed on drifting billows of black smoke. He wrapped the blankets around him and walked along a shore trail to get a closer look. Whatever it was, it would be big news.

Picking his way over rocks out to a promontory, Peter found a vantage point. Downriver a whole town was being consumed in a firestorm. No smoke rose from the charred ruins by the shore, which had been warehouses and homes. The rest of the town blazed fiercely as flames leapt above the rooftops and a steeple. He wondered what town it was. He moved a hundred yards closer to a flat rock above a beach and sat to stare at the conflagration.

When he stood up to hike back to where he hoped to find his car, he detected motion through the trees. Moving shadows resolved into two men lugging a blanket as a crude stretcher. In it, a third man swayed back and forth in time with the labored pace of his bearers struggling forward. Beyond them, Peter saw a house gutted by fire but other buildings seemed intact. He approached the men through the trees. "What happened to him?"

The exhausted men turned empty eyes toward him as they trudged forward, numb and perspiring, oblivious to the cold and to Peter's question. Peter moved to the back end of the blanket where the ashen man could scarcely walk, let alone carry, and took the bulky blanket from his hands. The man slumped to the ground.

"Where are we going?" asked Peter of the other ghost-like man.

"Yonder," came a mumbled reply, with a nod toward the stables. A man emerged through the haze from an open door, gesturing to lower their burden next to the fire. The blanket and the man in front were down in two thuds before Peter had fully lowered his end.

The man from the stables crouched next to the blanket, "He is dead." Only Peter heard him. This was the first corpse he had ever seen. "We must get water into them or they shall join their friend. If they got muscle aches and puking they is already sick wit' it. I will tell Annie and the others that we have another man dead, one staring at his feet by the fire, and a third fainted away in the pasture."

"Sick with what? Wait, Annie is here?"

"You know Annie, Mister?"

"Yes, I do. Can you take me to her?"

"People is dying wit' pox. Best get as far away as you can. Maybe it is too late."

"If you can go in and not get sick, I can, too."

"Many people who carried the sick, lie buried wit' them by those trees. I was inoculated in '68, got pustules, and felt sicker than a rotting hog, but I don't get the pox now, praise God."

"The pox, do you mean smallpox?"

The man took a pot of boiling water from the fire to rinse mugs he used to give water to the sick. "Yes, smallpox. Cow pox and chicken pox don't put hundreds of souls into the ground."

"Hundreds! You're telling me this is a smallpox epidemic?"

"That's what we got and little we can do, but give them water so they don't die of thirst and to keep the fever down. I wager them two will go soon and maybe you will follow."

"When I was very young, I was vaccinated for smallpox."

"Do you have the mark?" The man pointed to an ugly scar on his arm.

Without mentioning the eradication of smallpox, Peter rolled up his sleeve to reveal a pale circle on his upper arm. He was vaccinated as a toddler when his parents thought the family was going to be stationed overseas. Regular vaccinations had ended in the U.S. years before. He hoped his vaccination was effective against the smallpox of the Virginia Colony.

"We was forced to get inoculated," said the man. "People got sick and a few died. There was riots in Norfolk against inoculations, but now God help those people who did not get one! Annie is in the stable." The man turned and walked in and Peter followed right behind him.

A nauseating stench assaulted Peter's nostrils. A low fire failed to illuminate the space as smoke drifted vaguely toward a gash hacked in the roof. Straw on the floor had surrendered to a thin layer of soupy mud. Diarrhea-fouled blankets were piled to be burned. Moaning, snoring, and shouts from sick men in fitful dreams added a chorus of torment to the smoke-veiled images of suffering. In the shadows of the first stall, covered by a bloodstained blanket, lay another corpse, mouth and eyes gaping in a face disfigured by scabbed pustules.

Peter felt his stomach turn and warm saliva ran into his mouth. He dashed out the wide door and vomited. He looked at the billowing smoke in the distance and took a few deep breaths of fresher air. I've got to talk with Annie. He felt fear and aversion abate. Holding a blanket over his mouth and nose, he stepped with determination back into the stables.

Moving slowly past people laying two to a stall, Peter breathed through his mouth to reduce the smell. He almost tripped on another body. Living men lay next to those who died in the night. The dead would be carried outside and others would come to this rough clinic to take their place. He got to the back of the stable, and made his way past the stalls on the other side. He spotted the silhouette of a large woman sitting next to a cot. Annie nodded to him then turned to the man she was attending. Under a blanket, his face covered with the same violent rash and open or scab-covered sores as the dead men across the room, was Augustus.

"Augustus!" exclaimed Peter in a voice too loud. "What happened?"

"That you, Mister Peter?" Augustus rasped. "I got pox. Annie sendin' me over Jordan. Lord knows I'se glad to see you, but best you get out 'fore you get sick."

"I had what you call the inoculation, Augustus, so I won't get the pox."

"Good. I pray it ain't your time to die yet but we gonna meet again over yonder."

"You rest, 'Gustus, and say them prayers I taught you," said Annie leaning close.

"I say them Annie, but I got to tell Mister Peter somethin' afore I go."

"Annie, I have two blankets," offered Peter.

"They can use them. Set them over there. 'Gustus don't need them now." She nodded toward the cot and Peter squatted next to Augustus to hear the faint voice.

Augustus wheezed. "Mister Peter, a few weeks back you was sleepin' when Redcoats came in boats to fetch us. Aaron and me left blankets and leaves over you. We didn't want the soldiers to see you and think you was a deserter."

"A few weeks back?" Peter was astonished — but he focused on Augustus.

"We marched to Kemp's Landing on November 15 to fight the Princess Anne County Militia. They was in ambush but they fired too early. We fired our muskets like we was trained. Them Redcoats fired volleys fast like I ain't never seen."

Augustus pulled a breath. His voice was weak, "Most militia ran but their commander shouted 'Liberty or death!' tryin' to get them to fight. When he heard that voice, Aaron flew out like a spark off a pine log. He put the tip of his bayonet at the Adam's apple of the militia commander and shouted, 'Was that Liberty or Death you want, Mister Joseph Hutchings?' We could not believe our eyes. Aaron done captured his own massa.

"It looked like Aaron was gonna send a musket ball right through Joseph Hutching's throat, his hand was tremblin' so, but I hollered, 'Aaron, here is that prisoner you been prayin' hard to take.'"

Augustus' voice became a whisper. "I felt the whole world hangin' there on Aaron's trigger finger. He said, 'I'se a free man now Mister Joseph. I can barely hold off from shootin' you dead, but if just once you call me Mister Aaron, you can keep your life and someday get liberty again like I got mine now.'"

Augustus winced as he tried to take a deeper breath. "You tell him, Annie. I needs to breathe." Weak from smallpox, he was succumbing to pneumonia.

Annie looked at Peter. "'Gustus told me Massa Hutchings didn't answer quick since a wrong word would be his last. He slowly raised his hands and said, 'I am your prisoner, Mister Aaron. I always was sorry they cut you.' Aaron pulled back his bayonet and said, 'Thank you, Jesus.' Only 'Gustus and Massa Hutchings heard it. Hutchings was surely thankin' Jesus, too. Aaron told him to march in front over to them Redcoat officers."

Augustus nodded and pulled in another labored breath as Annie told the story.

"The British captain made Aaron a sergeant. He axed Aaron his family name and 'cause he never had one, he said 'Freeman.' The captain made a note in a book and said 'Sergeant Aaron Freeman, when the war ends you will get land in the Piedmont for your bravery and service to your King and country!'"

Augustus whispered, "Sergeant Aaron Freeman! I won't forget that day, Mister Peter, not for the rest of my life." He managed a smile. "That be easy 'cause the rest of my life ain't long. Annie, tell Mister Peter the other day I won't forget."

"You rest, 'Gustus," she said gently. "On December 9th, 'Gustus and Aaron met the Second Virginia Regiment at Great Bridge. There was more than two Virginians for each man on the British side. The British officers ordered a charge. This time the Regiment fired volleys from behind a barricade like Redcoats do. In minutes, they killed and wounded many.

"'Gustus tol' me Aaron charged out in front again and took a musket ball through his forehead. He fell while stormin' forward. 'Gustus dove to the ground beside him. I told Gustus hearin' goes last on a dying person so he spoke into Aaron's ear that he was a hero and goin' to heaven a free man. Droppin' down to help Aaron got 'Gustus out of the line of fire and prob'ly saved his life.

"The British signaled retreat and the Virginians shouted huzzahs to the Ethiopian Regiment 'cause they been brave. That ended Dunmore's fight for Virginia, and he sailed to New Jersey on his ship named *William*. He took a few men of the Ethiopian Regiment but left most behind. Because he was good at buildin' walls, they took William the brick maker. As the ship pulled away, he hollered, 'You know why this ship called *William*? 'Cause that's my name.'"

Augustus tried to laugh but coughing raked spasms of pain through his chest.

"Be at peace, 'Gustus," murmured Annie.

"I'se almost done," he whispered. "I was on my own then came fever, pukin', and these pox all over me. Now I'se ready to join Aaron and the others over yonder." Exhausted by the telling of the story, Augustus closed his eyes. "I join them as a free man," he rasped. "Help Evie and her boys."

"I will. You can make it, 'Gustus." Tears welled in Peter's eyes.

A look from Annie told him this was not so. "Of eight hundred in the Ethiopian Regiment, five hundred is dead or dying from wounds or pox," she said.

Peter put a hand on Augustus's shoulder. "Mister Augustus, when you get over Jordan, hold a spot for the only white boy you know who can run as fast as you."

Augustus smiled faintly and whispered, "Almost as fast, Mister Peter. I'se bound to get to Glory first." No one spoke for a few minutes. Then, with Annie beside him and Peter's hand on his shoulder, Augustus, planter of corn and tobacco, healer, father of Dilli, soldier, and free man, slowly exhaled for the last time.

"Annie, I have never..." He could not finish.

"Death be hard even when you 'round it as much as me. 'Gustus on his way home now. You would have come in even if you ain't been 'noculated, and it was good you was here, but I saw you puke beyond that door. You was prob'ly riddin' yourself of fear but we must go to the river to wash and pray. Half the folk here will die. Some will go blind."

"Why don't you get sick?"

"Ain't you seen the marks on my face? I got cow pox travelin' wit' the Fulani cattle herds. I tol' you we is leopard ladies. We don't get smallpox. You and I will surely die, Peter, but it ain't gonna be from pox. Now, let's get down to the river."

Annie carried a pot of hot water to a rock jutting into the river. She pulled off her dress and a padded petticoat and stepped into the shallow cold water. Peter noticed with surprise that the petticoat was made to make her look heavier than she really was. She washed her face, and body with a chip of soap and a rag she rinsed in the hot water. "Now it be your turn. We don't want to carry pox to Williamsburg." She waded back onto the rocks. Peter had never seen such large breasts. He looked away after Annie handed him the soap and the rag. With her generous girth, he had thought her to be older. He guessed now she was only in her thirties.

"Don't be so shy, Mister Peter. The Lord made us all about the same. Maybe He gave me a big bosom 'cause I got to comfort many folk. And yes, I tries to look too old and too fat to be 'tractin' attention I don't want to be 'tractin'. It ain't safe for a woman travelin' alone, so I make myself look like a granny. Most men don't see fat grandmas as beautiful, do they?"

"You're plenty beautiful, Annie. Get dressed or you'll attract all kinds of attention."

"Or at least 'tract a chill."

Peter followed Annie's example, stripped, and stepped into the bracing river. "What's that huge fire over there, Annie? I've never seen anything like that."

"Nobody here never seen nothin' like that. That used to be Norfolk. The British burned buildings along the shore so the militia could not fire on British ships even though Norfolk was a Loyalist town. The patriots set the rest of the town ablaze New Year's Day. So the two sides fightin' for what they believe is right, done destroyed the whole town."

"Norfolk is destroyed and it's New Year's Day, 1776?" asked Peter, shocked.

"Yesterday was New Year's Day. Since Norfolk was where African folks was runnin', they be in a bad way. Them that don't have smallpox are runnin' homeless in the cold of winter or gettin' caught back into slavery. Many is hungry and desperate. Some is goin' back to they own massa sayin' they is sorry 'bout runnin', beggin' to be taken back."

"Didn't any get away?" Peter came out of the water and pulled on his clothes.

"Governor Dunmore took 'bout three hundred African folk on ships to New Jersey. Others is findin' their way along the shore or into the forest, but it be hard. I must go to Williamsburg to warn people not to run here. There may be other chances someday. It will take me days to get there since I got no boat for safe passage over. First, let us pray."

Annie took Peter's hand and they looked across the water. He prayed to help people at this hard time. Annie prayed to get to Williamsburg quickly. "Amen!"

"I am not sure this will work, Annie, but I might know a way for us to be in Williamsburg this morning. 'Not sure' doesn't say it right. I am totally confused and have no idea how I slept for six weeks from November to January without freezing to death or dying of starvation."

"You ain't slept six weeks. You slid through again. I hope to learn how to do it."

"Slid through?"

"You done it like you slid here in the first place, Mister Peter. You let go of where you was and slid through a gate in the fence of time."

"Do you think we can do it again? I want to help you warn the people not to run toward Norfolk," he replied, hoping it was not too late for Evie and the boys.

"I'se worried about many folk. For now, Evie, James, and Dilli are fine."

"Annie, you want to learn how I slid through as you call it, but I want to know how you know what I'm thinking."

Annie looked at him and tilted her head to the left. "I can't answer wit' words, but you don't hear much wit'out words yet. A few words might point you on the way, so listen careful. What we feel and what we think pours out from us even if we can't see it. It be like heat from a fire. You can't see heat but you feel it. I listen careful to what people says to feel what they mean. After a while, I began to feel what people mean that they ain't sayin'. Do them words make sense to you?"

"I get it about feeling heat from a fire even though you don't see it. Feeling what people mean when they talk? I know what that is. Feeling what they're not saying sounds possible. It's like radio. We can't see the waves but if we tune in we hear the voice or the music."

"Radior?"

"Sorry. If we are lucky maybe I can show you."

Peter led Annie west along the shore. They passed the site of the Ethiopian Regiment's campfire and the woods beyond. "I hope this works, Annie. Give me your hand and close your eyes. Then we'll walk over that hill ahead."

"If you tryin' what I think, you better know it will happen. Hope ain't enough."

"I know it'll happen if you close your eyes, hold my hand, and listen to my voice."

"Good, Mister Peter. Don't wonder how you know, just know it, and let's go. I'll stay right wit' you." Annie closed her eyes and they walked slowly through the woods over the hill. Peter told her where to place her feet, advice she didn't seem
210

to need even with her eyes closed. She listened to his voice and heard him catch his breath when he saw his father's car.

"What you see, Mister Peter?"

"Don't open your eyes yet. Come put your hand right—here."

"I feel cold metal, Mister Peter."

Peter pressed his lips together, stared at the car, and held tight to Annie's hand. "Open your eyes, Annie. Tell me what you see, and please don't disappear."

Annie laughed. "I see a tall worried man, quite a fine lookin' white man, holding my hand next to a... shiny metal carriage wit' a curved glass window."

"Welcome to my time, Annie, where you should just call me Peter." He opened the passenger side door and held it open for Annie. "We say, 'hop in'."

"Ain't we gonna need four horses to pull this carriage?"

"A hundred years ago this was called a horseless carriage. Now it's shortened to 'car.' I never thought I'd say this but wait 'till you see what this baby can do!"

Annie sat in the car and Peter got in behind the wheel, helped Annie close her seat belt, told her there was about to be a noise, and started the engine.

"What that growlin' sound?"

"It's an engine that has the power of many horses. It pulls this wagon well. Ready?"

"You do what you got to do to get us to Williamsburg."

Peter slowly turned around and crept through the woods along the rutted track.

"This moves quick for a horseless carriage."

At the highway, Peter said to Annie, "This will be faster than you're used to." Looking to be sure no one was approaching, he pulled onto the highway and edged up to thirty miles an hour. The heater began to warm them.

"Oh, my! This is fast! And the tar road is so smooth!" cried Annie.

"We can get there sooner if you can handle going faster."

"If you can, I can. I trust you Peter."

Peter edged up to fifty-five.

"My Lord! Someone comin' right down the road at us!" Annie heard the whoosh of air and the Doppler-effect eee-yuhh change of pitch as the oncoming car sped by. "We was almost kilt!" she patted her chest with her right hand.

"Don't worry. Everyone stays on his own side of the road most of the time."

"Somethin' happened in this carriage, I can feel it." She closed her eyes and took a breath, "A few days back the road was wet, and you all was spinnin' 'round."

"That's true, Annie! On our way to Williamsburg, a car cut in front and we slid 'round and 'round. We thought we would die, but the two cars never touched."

"Let me be quiet for a moment, Peter. I need to sit wit' this."

Peter crossed the James River, and turned east to Williamsburg. There was no great pall of smoke on the south shore of the James. Norfolk had been rebuilt over two centuries ago, its destruction not even a memory for most Virginians.

"That be how you slid through, Peter. When a hoop spinnin', ain't no tellin' where it gonna stop. When this carriage spun, your family could be hurt or die. So, you let go. Holdin' tight be a painful way to live and a painful way to die. But you stopped wit' nobody hurt. You was ready to fly away home but still here. That be a good way to live every day."

"You said maybe I came because somebody prayed for help. Was that 'Gustus?"

"'Gustus was happy to have you as a friend, but it wasn't him. Don't keep guessin' 'cause I ain't tellin' nobody else's prayers. You can hear them yourself."

"That's fair." Peter turned on the radio to Sunday morning gospel music.

Annie looked around. "Who be singin'? You got angels in your time?"

"That's a radio, Annie. It's a machine that picks up invisible waves from the air and makes them into the sounds they were in the first place. It can tune to different stations sending out waves at once. You listen to whichever one you choose."

Annie nodded her head. "Waves. Good word. Everyone sendin' out waves. In a crowded room, there be people you would rather stand close to than others. That come from what thoughts they thinkin', what they feelin', and how those comin' out as what you call waves."

"Can you feel those waves?"

"Everybody feel them, but most times people don't notice they do."

Very soon, from Annie's point of view, Peter pulled into a giant parking lot by the Colonial Williamsburg Visitor Center. Annie was amazed at the horseless carriages and their bright colors reflecting electric street lamps. "This land used to be... oh, never mind! Everything changes." They walked over the Bridge to the Past, but as they walked past Great Hopes Plantation, where visitors got a taste of rural life, Peter saw they were in a restored Williamsburg full of shops and historic buildings that would open, in two hours, in the twenty-first century.

"This changed a lot." Annie looked around. "Where do slaves and servants live?"

"In my time we don't have slaves in shacks and shanties and few people have servants in their homes or gardens anymore. Annie, we have a problem."

"What problem? You ain't got no slaves or servants?"

"No, Annie, ending slavery was a good thing. You and I have a problem. We are in my time even though we crossed that bridge. I don't know how to take us back."

"You the best slider I ever saw, but seems like you had to almost get killed befo' you slid through," Annie teased. "Come wit' me, I got an idea."

They walked to the cabinetmaker's shop and the pasture where Peter first met Annie. "I never slid over like you done but I come here and sit quiet. Some days I see people in strange clothing walk by and I hear what they sayin'. They talk like
212

Williamsburg was a long time ago. Almost nobody sees me 'cept once in a while someone dressed like people in my time looks at me and keeps on goin'. Then half a year ago, a young white man in strange clothing walked over and asked me if I was preparin' food. That never happened befo' so I knew I should talk wit' him."

"Half a year ago for you. For me it was three days."

"Didn't I say you been slidin' all over? Now sit here, hold my hand, and close your eyes like you done wit' me. This be a special place for me. Imagine you and me is back where you want to be and where I belong." Peter sat on the grass, took her hand, closed his eyes, listened to the hum of a distant truck engine, and relaxed. The engine faded away. Peter was startled by the shrill cry of a jay nearby.

Annie squeezed his hand. "Here we is, Mister Slider, right where you left off. I ain't gonna forget that car ride. I got to hurry off. I have many things to do."

"When are we? I mean when is this? You know what I mean."

Annie scanned the sky. "It be dawn the day after you rode your car to Norfolk."

"We are back in November, 1775?"

Annie stood up. "That's a fact. But you best hurry because for you, it will be much later when you wake up. We gonna meet again in a few months. There be many people I got to warn not to run away. Can you run and tell Evie that for now it be best for her to stay where she is?"

"Yes, I will." Peter gave her a hug. "Meeting you changed my life, Annie."

"I feel the same but if you hug me 'round here, we gonna get thrown in gaol."

Peter jogged to the Powell House to deliver the news. The house was dark so he entered the yard quietly and climbed to the loft where Evie slept next to her sons. "Evie," he whispered. She did not stir. "Evie!" He reached into the dark and felt a small foot under a blanket.

Dilli sat up with a start. "Mister Peter! Have you come to run away with us?"

Evie sat up. "What you say, Dilli?"

"Mister Peter is here to take us to freedom. I gonna put my good shirt in a sack."

Peter climbed the last rungs into the loft. James sat up. "I'se ready, too, Mama."

The impact of what Peter had witnessed during the night hit him again. "I just got back from near Norfolk."

"What happened?"

"War is coming to Norfolk and the town will burn to the ground, Evie. Dunmore and his soldiers will leave on a ship. Right now, there is nowhere to run."

"Did you see 'Gustus, Mister Peter?" asked Dilli. "Did he get his self free?"

Peter looked into Dilli's bright inquisitive eyes. "Yes, Dilli, he did. We can all be very proud of him. He became a brave soldier. And so did Aaron."

Evie twitched at the shock of hearing the name. "You saw Aaron?"

"Yes, Evie. Aaron became a soldier, too. He led a charge and took his own massa prisoner on the battlefield. An officer immediately promoted him to sergeant."

"Aaron..." Evie put her hand on James' shoulder. "He tol' you?"

"Yes, Evie, he told me. Years ago, he was caught trying to get back to you. Slave hunters looking for bounty hurt him badly. He never got another chance to come back, but he never forgot you. You can be proud of him, too. He was happy to hear you and the boys are well. I need to tell you that life is very dangerous for Aaron and 'Gustus now. Only three hundred runaways were... uh will be taken on the ships when Governor Dunmore leaves. One of them is William the brick maker. It looks hard for the others. There is fighting and smallpox."

A moment of silence passed before Evie asked, "What should we do?"

You and the boys stay here—maybe for a long time. Pray for those who ran. They are on a hard road. Many are finding their way back to be slaves again."

"But, Mister Peter, Annie and you said we should be free. I told the boys."

"Annie and I came back together from Norfolk. She is warning people this is not a good time to run. The hoop can fall in many ways. It landed in Norfolk in a way that shows us you should stay. You and the boys are safe here. Soon I will have to travel far and I don't know if I can come back. Boys, mind what your mama says."

"Peter, this be very hard. I feel..." Peter waited but Evie found no more words.

Peter took them all in a hug. "Keep your eyes open. The hoop rolls every day and another chance will come. You can be ready then."

"Thank you, Mister Peter," said Dilli.

"Mister Peter," Evie said, "you is family to us."

"You're a good family to be part of." Peter climbed down the ladder and walked home. Exhausted, he quietly entered without waking his family and slipped into bed. In seconds, he dropped into a deep sleep.

Day 4-3:   John and Susan Sleep In

John opened his eyes. "Good morning, Mrs. Sinclair."

"Sorry I woke you. I was sneaking into bed for a nap." She kissed his cheek.

"I've warmed it up for you. I looked in on Megan when I got back last night. I was worried about her, but she was there, fast asleep. Peter wasn't home yet."

She got undressed. "They're both asleep. He must have come back after you."

"Good. How was your visit to the better-highfalutin-sorts?"

"They are good people, John, living with privilege and with difficulties at the same time. They have a house full of great kids."

"Good people own slaves? Who kidnapped the civil rights activist I married?"

"She still believes all women and men are created equal. She is learning the only way to move ahead is to start from where you are. Interesting you mention dreams. I had a vivid dream about you in a fight in a tavern."

"That's amazing!" He stretched, feeling the sting of the cut on his arm as he sat up. "There was a fight in a tavern last night."

"What happened? Are you all right?"

"I'm fine. Uncle Sam trained me for that contingency, so no one was badly hurt. A guy with a knife and that puffed-up dance instructor we saw at the Palace were preying on buckskins from the hills. They won't be doing much of that anymore."

"Did the guy with the knife hurt you? Did you hurt them?"

"Nah, his knife wasn't loaded. They were not hurt seriously. You wish it were a dream, don't you? But, there is the small matter of a cut on my arm."

"You've always been my hero, John." Susan gave him another kiss. "Let's not wake up the kids yet." She slipped naked into bed.

John and Susan made love for the first time since coming to Williamsburg. She felt a communion uncommon even in the exciting sex of their early days together. Something was shifting. An hour later, John woke and gave Susan a gentle kiss on the forehead.

"Mmm," she murmured.

John got out of bed and headed to the outhouse in his robe. On the way back, he saw Peter and Megan still asleep. "It's warm out there—more like when we arrived. But we aren't back in our time, still no indoor plumbing," he told Susan.

"So it is hot in here. I thought it was just me," she said.

"Both—hot in here and you are definitely hot. I'm the luckiest man in this bed."

"Oh you! John, that was beautiful and tender. Such a connection!"

"Thank you, Mrs. Sinclair. They're both still sound asleep." He ran his fingertips lightly on the skin of her shoulder and along her clavicle. "There's no hurry."

"Mmm, no hurry."

Day 4-4:   Plain Truth and Common Sense

"Good morning, Megan."

Megan opened her eyes to see her father sitting on the side of her bed.

"Good morning, Dad. Sorry I was so crabby."

"Megan. I apologize to you, too. You were right on the taxes. They were repealed long before the revolutionary war broke out. You were right and I was stubborn."

"It takes time to get something new. I was in a hurry to show you my work."

"You did well. I'm proud of you, Megan. How was your time with the Indians?"

"Thanks, Dad. The Sweat Lodge was awesome. I felt our ancestors sitting around a fire. I felt the Earth deep under me – glowing hot rocks and molten magma. I felt the mountains and oceans and all of us moving together in space."

"That's extraordinary, Megan. Mom thought we could start out together this morning. But if you'd rather be on your own..."

"No, I would really like to do something with you guys this morning, seriously."

"Great. She's making breakfast. I'll go wake Peter. By the way, it's spring again."

The Sinclairs ate in the garden. "Let's pack so we're ready to go," John proposed.

"Are you sure we can just walk out of here and find the car?"

"I drove almost to Norfolk last night, Megan, mostly on asphalt highways."

"But Pete, I rode an hour on wagon trails and stayed in the past."

"We'll cross the bridge to where I left the car this morning."

"This morning? Did you stay out all night?"

"Almost all night, Mom. I camped with a platoon of freed slaves near Norfolk."

"Pete, you don't get to do that every weekend! Can I put it into my paper?"

"You can, Meg, but it's not a happy story."

They packed up and Susan said, "I'd like to start at Market Square."

"I'll find you there after I take the bags to the car," Peter offered. He left carrying the bags as the others walked toward the market.

"Sir," John asked a passerby walking by, "can you tell me the date?"

"Why, yes. 'Tis May 15, 1776."

"The Declaration of Independence is only seven weeks away," John calculated. "Last fall, few were openly in favor of independence. What changed?"

"Don't know, Dad. I'll meet you guys at Market Square in a few minutes." She hurried ahead and disappeared down a walk to the left into the blacksmith shop.

Mark noticed her come in. "Megan! It has been months! I was worried."

"I'm so sorry, Mark. My family left suddenly and we just got back this morning. There was no time to get a message to you. I wanted to thank you for taking me to the Spirit Lodge. I've been concerned about you too, Mark. Is everything all right?"

"I can't talk now. We are rushing to finish an order Mister Anderson got from the Virginia Militia. We shan't stop for lunch today, but I might be able to step out in the afternoon. Can you come by again?"

"I'll come back. We have to leave again but I won't go without saying goodbye."

"You are going again? It was hard when you vanished. We must talk."

"I'll be back before I vanish," Megan promised.

By the market, a man holding a pamphlet in each hand paced on a sturdy table. Pamphlets were stacked precariously at the end of the table, where a helper strove to keep the speaker from kicking them over. "We hear more talk of independence than people dared utter before. The pamphlet in my right hand is a reason for that. In January, Robert Bell in Philadelphia, published *Common Sense* by Thomas Paine, an Englishman recently arrived in the colonies. Paine says of the power of kings:

'How came the king by power which the people are afraid to trust, and always obliged to check? Such power could not be the gift of a wise people, neither can power which needs checking, be from God.'

"Paine's views would have been treasonous a year ago:

'To the evil of monarchy we have added that of hereditary succession... an insult and imposition on posterity. For all men being originally equals, no one by birth could have a right to set up his own family in perpetual preference to all others, and though himself might deserve some degree of honors... his descendants might be unworthy to inherit them. One of the strongest natural proofs of the folly of hereditary right in kings is that nature disapproves it, otherwise she would not so frequently turn it into ridicule by giving mankind an ass for a lion.'

"This pamphlet is shaking the ground from Florida to Nova Scotia. My assistant will be happy to make the transaction."

Peter spotted his father in the crowd, and pressed through to join his family. He'd gone to look for Evie first. "Evie gone to market," Rosie had told him. He turned his attention to the speaker.

"In March, my employer also published *Plain Truth*, a response to *Common Sense* by Candidus, who is a successful Maryland planter taking a view loyal to the crown:

'If indignant at the doctrine contained in the pamphlet, entitled 'Common Sense' I have expressed myself... with some ardor; I entreat the reader to impute my indignation, to honest zeal against the author's insidious tenets... I love my country.'

"Patriots and Loyalists both love their country. Candidus also says:

'Demagogues, to seduce the people into their criminal designs, ever hold up democracy to them... examine the republics of Greece and Rome... No government is so subject to civil wars and commotions, as that of the democratical form...'

"This pamphlet by Candidus can be purchased here."

"Are you here to gather shillings or do you take a stand?" shouted an onlooker.

"Well, let me read an excerpt I personally like from Tom Paine:

> '*Small islands not capable of protecting themselves, are proper objects for kingdoms to take under their care; but there is something absurd, in supposing a continent to be perpetually governed by an island...*'

"Huzzah!" shouted several men.

"As I travel south, another man goes north. He heard John Adams call *Common Sense* a poor, ignorant, malicious, short-sighted, crapulous mass.'"

"Why? We love Tom Paine's words!"

"Because Paine rightly challenges the misapplied power of the Crown but envisions a society in which each follows his own fancy without governance. Our leaders benefit from Paine's arguments for independence. I expect they shall soon declare independence so France, Spain, and the Netherlands can support them without all-out war against Britain. Some of us are loyal to the crown and some support independence. However, most care little about what happens in London and Philadelphia. I pray for reconciliation. Nevertheless, as Paine says:

> '... *instead of gazing at each other with suspicious or doubtful curiosity, let each of us, hold out to his neighbor the hearty hand of friendship... of a good citizen,... and a virtuous supporter of the RIGHTS of MANKIND and of the FREE AND INDEPENDENT STATES OF AMERICA.*'"

"Huzzah!"

"Many are still loyal to the Crown. Were we not all loyal a short time ago? Buy pamphlets to reason with your neighbors rather than tar and feather them."

A few men moved forward coins in hand.

"We should buy fifty of each to sell to museums when we get home," Peter advised. "If we gather documents signed by Founding Fathers we could set up the Sinclair Institute for American Studies and have money left for nice houses and cars."

"That's not what we came here for," said Megan. "If we made the story of this weekend into a movie, the script writer would not let us get rich carrying anything home with us."

"I was kidding. What do you think we came here for?" Peter asked. "Annie told me we may be here in answer to someone's prayers."

"Can we do that without interfering?" John asked. "I hope I did not mess up history when I got into the fight to save a guy from getting hurt at the tavern."

"I didn't know you could fight!" Megan said. "Maybe that's what happened all along and no one in our time knows you had anything to do with it. Can I interview you about it?"

"Sure, but you just gave me an idea, Megan. Some mysteries happened in the Revolution. We might be able to do something to help. I'll tell you more at lunch."

"I want to say goodbye to some friends," said Peter. "Where should we meet?"

Susan had an idea. "Let's have lunch at the Brick House Tavern. It does not operate as a tavern in our time and this will be our chance to try eating there."

Day 4-5: John in the St. George Tucker House Garden

John was troubled as he settled into an armchair in the St. George Tucker House with a mug of black coffee. How did the colonies, with many disputes among them, survive against the strongest military power on Earth? Would independence have come without war as it did later in the case of Canada, Australia and many other British colonies? He was surprised by Frances standing near him. "Oh, hello, Frances. I thought you didn't work mornings."

She had a serious expression. "I do not work here John. I dwell here."

"Did I see you in the tavern when I fought with Roger?"

"Did you see me? That depends. You have a vivid imagination. When we focus our imagination in a chosen direction, we can experience directly through the mind, skipping the physical senses. Imagination is not just for fantasy."

"You were there, but then you were gone..."

"John, sorry to interrupt, but there is someone who cannot come into the house, shall I say, at this time. Please come out to meet him." She glided into the hall.

John put back the book and through a back window saw Frances outside. He followed her along a path between tall hedges to a clearing not visible from the street. Bruce Wallace waited on a bench and stood to clasp John's hand. "Damn good to see you, Johnny! Sit down here where my old ears can hear you. Frances told me she could find someone to help. I dinna know it would be you."

"How can you be acquainted when you are...?" stammered Frances. "Curious!"

"Johnny and I are old soldiers," said Bruce. "We met properly over a glass of ale. John, Fannie Bland Randolph is the widow of a cousin of Peyton Randolph and manages two large plantations while raising three children. St. George Tucker seems to have an eye for her."

Frances looked embarrassed but held a finger to her lips. John accepted her unspoken request not to mention the time in which they met. "Frances, what's happening here is unknown to most people. Indentured servants are sent to clear Indian land and people are entering a war without knowing why. I fought in wars people did not support or even know about. What were we doing there? I did not think about it before I flew—uh sailed over and did what I believed was my duty. When you said we're clever as fence posts you gave too much credit."

"Once we notice what is going on, we get smarter, John. The history of humanity is a story of exploring and slowly waking up. You did your duty to your country and learned much and built character while you served. So did you, Bruce."

"Aye, but I lost friends, was wounded myself, and killed men who were probably good lads aside from the fact that someone ordered them to shoot at me."

"Be thankful, gentlemen. Peace always comes. Divinity and Peace underlie all."

"John, I heard you met Dagger and Dancer a few months ago. Two militiamen I know said your style of fighting was astonishing. Where did you learn it?"

"I gave a class on hand-to-hand combat at a tavern. I trained in techniques used in China and the islands you call 'the Japans.' They can fight without weapons."

"Methinks there is more to your story than what you tell."

"Some stories are best not told in their entirety, Bruce." John saw Frances smile.

"John, I dinna ken how ye did that at the Walking Stick nor have I heard of the wars you fought, but I believe we share distaste for what we once did so well."

"Concern about the loss of life in war brought me here today, Bruce."

"People have gone mad. Reasons for a quarrel last year are now reason enough to kill a man. A friend of mine was hanged for refusing to take the test."

"Take the test?"

"They force men to swear an oath to support the Congress against Britain. My friend stood with his neighbors against the Stamp Act, but chose to be loyal to the Crown that last year had the loyalty of the crowd that hanged him.

"Where Loyalists are stronger, they attack Patriots, burning farms. Mayhem is spreading. There are raids on the Loyalist Floridas and 'tis rumored Congress invited Spain to take the Floridas back, to deprive the King of bases to the South. This after all we did to win those colonies from Spain! A Virginia planter named Charles Lynch runs a mock trial of loyalists. They are whipped and their property seized but none has been hanged yet. People call his mockery of justice 'getting lynched.' I do not wish to shoot a hole in a man's head because of what he might be thinking inside it. If I kill him, how could he be persuaded to change his mind?"

"What will you do, Bruce?"

"John, arguments against the Intolerable Acts are sound but people's choices are muddled. New Englanders do most of the fighting, but their kin in Nova Scotia petitioned King George to allow them to stay out of the war. They avoid the strife and get rich on trade and shipbuilding. In Georgia and the Carolinas, loyal settlers are fighting against rich revolutionary landowners who oppressed them for years.

"The French in Quebec sided with their old enemies the Redcoats. Congress sent an army there under General Montgomery but he was killed. His second in command, Benedict Arnold, was wounded taking Quebec. Arnold asked for support but Congress failed to send it and the campaign was abandoned for lack of supplies. Arnold seethed at the Congress and recently he was passed over for a promotion. He is proud and now bitter. Who knows what he shall do next?

"No one from the Caribbean went to the Continental Congress, except Henry Tucker who went to trade gun powder. His son St. George rolled barrels of powder onto boats on a cloudy night. Like New Englanders, they profit from smuggling."

Frances shuffled noticeably.

Bruce went on, "More British soldiers fell taking Breed's Hill and Bunker Hill than in any battle since. Even so, Washington complains about the discipline of the men who dealt that blow before he took command. Congress has trouble raising an army. I can't blame men for not making war on their countrymen.

"In March, Congress voted letters of marque for privateers, authorizing piracy against British ships. The Royal Navy will send our ships to the bottom.

"I thought I was done with war; done with time slowing amidst the havoc, done with my heart racing, except in the company of a willing lass, pardon me, Fanny. I am too old to rush up a hill as musket balls whistle past my ear. Friends have joined both sides. We are fools to kill each other over these arguments."

"Time slowing down—I remember that feeling," said John. "Maybe the painful experience of bad decisions will teach us to stop making such foolish choices."

"How much pain does it take?" Bruce asked. "New fools aplenty are born every morning. They get a spank to start them breathing, but it seldom cures the foolishness. The idea of democracy that New England Sons of Freedom shout about is combining with the Virginia gentry's wish to form a nation. Since Thomas Paine made the notion of independence popular, that combination makes sense to me. We canna' win this without help of other countries, but none can take the daring leap to support us unless Congress declares us independent. The Virginians and Bostonians ripen the others. I think it will come to fruition soon.

"There was a vote for leader of the 1st Virginia Regiment. Patrick Henry, with little military experience, narrowly defeated Hugh Mercer. They chose the maker of fiery speeches over the officer and doctor forged in the fires of battle! Someone called Mercer a 'North Briton' because he is a Scot like me."

"Don't be too harsh on Patrick Henry, Bruce, even though Mercer is a better military commander. We need political men if we are to steer through to success."

"Fortunately, Mercer was later given command of the 3rd Virginia Regiment. The British also have trouble fielding an army. The King hired regiments of soldiers conscripted by his German cousins. Those Hessians are a quarter of the invading troops. The Continentals worry about a German colonel named Johann Rall who takes no prisoners. King George asked Catherine the Great of Russia for twenty thousand troops, but she turned him down, God bless her!"

"What drives this, Bruce? How big is the land issue?"

"I shall show you something important. My wife's sister is the widow of a soldier maimed in the French and Indian War who sold his veteran's land grant to one William Crawford. She cooks in a house near Mount Vernon. One evening, a guest left his coat on the chair when he went to bed. She searched the pockets to learn the owner so she could return it. In a leather sheath, she found a letter from George Washington to William Crawford. Her husband died believing the grant to be of no value since no one could settle west of the Proclamation Line. She knows how to read so she made a copy of the letter and sent it to me. It is dated September 21, 1767. Would you like to read what she copied, John?"

"I would, Bruce. I heard of William Crawford from a member of his family right there in the St. George Tucker house." John took the letter and began to read:

"I can never look upon the Proclamation in any other light (this I say between ourselves) than as a temporary expedient to quiet the minds of the Indians. It must fall, of course, in

a few years, when those Indians consent to our occupying those lands… If you will be at the trouble of seeking out the lands, I will take upon me the part of securing them, as soon as there is a possibility of doing it and will be at all the cost and charges surveying and patenting the same. My plan is to secure a good deal of land."

"It goes on…

'… this can be carried on by silent management… and carried out by you under the guise of hunting game, which you may do at the same time you are in pursuit of land. When this is fully discovered advise me of it, and if there appears a possibility of succeeding, I will have the land surveyed to keep others off and leave the rest to time and my own assiduity."

"This deal to usurp land from the Indians might be secret forever, Bruce. The investors in land are willing to have a war in pursuit of their personal interests."

"There are many investors, John, on both sides of the ocean. What they are doing is against the law but that doesn'a bother them a whit."

"You two can think of something," Frances offered. "You both know war and saw peace come in the end. Can you imagine bringing peace into this?"

"It sounds like a riddle, Fannie." Bruce scratched his beard. "If I can help, I will."

John heard Frances use the word 'imagine' and knew it was not an accident.

"Bruce," said Frances, "you know many leaders in Virginia. You knew Governor Dunmore before he ran off, and served him well."

"Aye, Fannie, but we are at war. Many are dead already and no one is winning."

"John, you have knowledge that can be useful. I pray you can save lives."

John was studying Frances and thinking fast. "I think I know why I came. Bruce, can you meet me here later? There are others I want to bring into this conversation. I think… no, I know there are things we can do together to save many lives."

"I must work in the afternoon, John, but I can be here at four."

"Frances, will you be able to join us?"

"I have waited for this day a very long time. I shall be here."

Bruce took his leave and left between the hedgerows.

"Frances…"

"I know you have questions about me, John, but if I tell you now, it could be disturbing. I promise I will tell you soon, after the work has begun."

"Am I crazy, Frances? Am I imagining you?"

"No and yes and 'tis not what you think. You will find a way, just as you once did to save your men in battle." Frances curtsied and disappeared around a hedge.

If we pull this off we will make history, John thought. Then he realized, we helped make the history we have, and no one knows!"

Day 4-6:   Megan at the Gaol

Megan left her parents and ran most of the way to the blacksmith shop.

"This is a rehearsal, Mark. I'm practicing not vanishing."

"I won't be free until four o'clock, Megan, but I will quickly say that Standing Elk just came by to give me the news that Bartholomew is being held in the gaol."

"Oh, no! Did he do something wrong?"

"A planter who failed to cheat him spread rumors that Bart is a Loyalist. When the county militia accosted him in the market, Bart told them he had earned his freedom and was true to Virginia. When he refused to take the test, they threw him into gaol. Maggie is in town today trying to get him out. Can you help her?"

"I will run right over and see if I can find her. I'll be back at four."

"God speed!

Megan was out of breath when she ran up to Maggie outside the gaol holding a basket of food, a clay jug of water, and a blanket for Bartholomew. "Oh, Maggie, I'm glad I found you," she panted. "We have to get Bartholomew out."

"Megan Sinclair, whom I have not seen for months, arrives right on time. Bless you! How do you propose getting him out when his bullheadedness put him in?"

"Why wouldn't Bartholomew take the test, Maggie?"

"Oh you heard. He refused because he is a stubborn old fool. He worked hard for years to finish his indenture and be free. He says he will not be cowed by young firebrands who have not thought through what they are on about."

"Is he a Loyalist?"

"Heaven's no. He is neither a Tory nor a Revolutionary. He is a planter and an egg man who has beehives to tend. He does not want to be forced into a fight. He hopes that facing resistance and lack of fighters, Congress and the Crown will have to negotiate. He has friends on both sides but most just seek to live in peace."

"Why do some choose the Loyalist side?"

"Some feel Britain is their home country. Others think Britain will win and want to be on the winning side. Families given royal land grants think their claims safer if we stay loyal to Britain. Still others fear losing positions or pensions given by the Crown. Some wealthy Loyalists fear Levelers like us may end their privileges and take their property. There are about twenty-five loyal colonies and thirteen in rebellion. Most colonies are loyal.

"What about the Indians? I'm angry Virginia leaders want to take their land."

"'Tis unfair to the native nations. That is one reason Bartie refused to take the test. Another is slavery. Patriots push for freedom but have no intent to end the abomination of slavery. The British are freeing slaves but help few and leave the rest destitute without a way to escape. 'Tis not easy to see righteousness on either side."

The gaoler's wife arrived to let Maggie in. "My niece is coming in too," Maggie announced as she walked through the heavy gate and Megan followed.

They found Bartholomew seated on the floor of a dark cell shared with three other prisoners. None was considered dangerous, so none were chained to the wall. "Hello, Maggie. Oh, 'tis the long-lost Megan. How are you, Ladies?"

"Bartie, I brought you food, clean water from your own well, a change of clothes, and a blanket. It smells in here. I should have carried a wash tub as well."

"Thank you, Maggie. What brings you to my castle, Megan?"

"We're going to get you out of here today, Bart."

"Will you break the wall so I can die running like an old fox before the hounds?"

"You can walk out of here as soon as you choose, Bart. If Congress breaks with Britain, and they probably will, you and Maggie will help people renew their land, raise crops, and feed their families. If the Redcoats march in, and they probably will, you and Maggie will still help people renew their land, raise crops, and feed their families. This war is hurting many people while you, by your own choice, sit in this dark, stinky place. Maggie struggles without complaining. You are not helping at all except by creating manure for compost with these other gentlemen."

"Did you put her up to this, Maggie?"

"I swear I did not have the foggiest idea Megan would be here or speak so strongly. Megan, hush. Can't you see that Bartie enjoys being caged up in here?"

"Bart, take the test," persisted Megan. "You're loyal to Virginia, so it's not a lie. We can leave this basket for your friends here. You are old enough so no one will drag you off to war. You feed and encourage people. They need what you offer."

Bart needed only a few seconds to think. "You are right. Maggie, please tell Peter Pelham the gaoler, that I am ready to end my protest and take the test."

"Well, that was not hard," said Maggie.

Another prisoner said, "Tell the gaoler, I will take the test too."

"You stole a pig. You ain't no Loyalist!" chided a third man.

"I swear to steal a Loyalist pig to repay the Patriot I stole from, if I can go home."

"But you ain't got a home."

"True enough. Give me a moment to prepare my plea. All right, I shall take the test if they pardon my crime and give me a house to go home to."

Hoarse laughter broke out in the cell, rare levity in their dank, gloomy world.

Maggie and Megan went to the Capitol to register Bartholomew's change of heart. The Secretary knew Bartholomew; he had hired him to haul away ashes.

"That stubborn old oak tree is in gaol for standing up to young poplars?" asked the Secretary. "Let's give him the test right now before Lynch gets a coat of tar on him. Bartie should stop lazing in a cell and get back to work like the rest of us."

Bartholomew swore his loyalty to Congress in the courtyard. After washing and putting on the clothes Maggie brought, he was out of gaol in time for lunch.

Day 4-7: Lunch at the Brick House Tavern

Peter almost ran into Evie as she stepped out of a shop behind Missus Powell. She was surprised but shook her head. She could not speak when her owner was three steps ahead. He touched his chest then gestured in the direction of the Powell House. He would drop by later. She understood and hurried off with the packages.

Entering the noisy Brick House Tavern, Peter spotted his family on benches at a long table and squeezed in beside his mother. The pot on the table was coated with carbon and half full of chunks of venison, onions, and potatoes cooked in broth with bacon fat and salt. A basket of hand-torn bread sat next to the pot. "Welcome to the land of 'Be happy with what you get'," said Megan as Susan ladled stew.

John leaned forward so his family could hear. "I think we are here to help."

"Dad, you were the first to say we should not change history."

"That's true, Megan, but your research has given me ideas."

"What can we do about it?"

"We can tap the rolling hoop to steer it, but not get in front or try to lift it."

"You told me about the hoop, Peter, and that's right. Megan, I followed your example and made notes. Amidst the hubbub here, I can tell you without being overheard. The Declaration of Independence that hardly anyone reads lists 'a long train of abuses and usurpations' and 'establishment of an absolute Tyranny over these States'. Taxes are one example, but Megan pointed out, those were repealed."

John paused until an outburst at the next table quieted down. "The Declaration says the King refused to assent to laws passed here, dissolved legislatures to deprive people of local leadership, limited immigration, blocked appropriations of new lands, and made judges dependent on him for positions and salaries. He sent appointees to oversee the people and kept standing armies here, making the military superior to civil authority. He blocked trade, imposed taxes, and transported citizens to England for trial far from their peers. It says the King abolished English law in a neighboring colony but neglects to name Catholic Quebec. He established appointed rather than elected government there, and enlarged its boundaries to enclose the English colonies on the west. The drafters of the Declaration feared Quebec was an experiment for absolute rule in all colonies."

"Wow, Dad! You did tons of research." Megan was impressed.

"I had to memorize the Declaration in high school. I never paid attention to what it said. Once the fighting started, the King 'plundered our seas, ravaged our coasts, burnt our towns, and destroyed the lives of our people.' He sent armies of foreign mercenaries, took citizens captive on the high seas to bear arms against their country, encouraged Loyalists to start insurrections, and invited Indian attacks."

"There are things it doesn't say," added Peter. "Jefferson had a clause about slavery in the draft of the Declaration. I wrote it down: *'He has waged cruel war against human nature itself, violating its most sacred rights of life & liberty in the persons of a distant people who never offended him, captivating & carrying them into slavery in another hemisphere,*

225

or to incur miserable death in their transportation thither.' It was deleted from the final draft at the insistence of slave owners."

"That's true, Peter. The colonies will survive against the strongest military power on Earth combined with Loyalist militias almost as big as Patriot forces. How will they do that? Next question—why were British casualties never again as high as at Boston at the beginning of the war? Why do official records of the Defense Department show American battle deaths in the Revolution to be relatively low?"

Megan jumped in. "How did the local Indians survive when the Revolutionary War became the biggest war on the Indians before or since?"

"Good question, Megan. Here's another," John continued. "Many German troops were shipped to quell the Revolution. One leader, Colonel Johann Rall, took no prisoners. He was killed at Trenton. Washington, however, authorized land and freedom to German prisoners who changed sides. How did he think of that? Conditions for prisoners on both sides were grim. Ten thousand Americans died on British prison ships anchored off Brooklyn. Even knowing that, the Americans placed many Redcoat prisoners to work on farms, and many stayed after the war, married, and never returned to England. Who planted that idea?"

"And how did thousands of slaves get free during the Revolution?" added Peter.

"That was news to me. And Peter, our first day here we learned Patrick Ferguson invented a breech-loading rifle that had superior range, accuracy, and speed. At Brandywine, Ferguson was wounded and the rifles disappeared. Where did they go? It is still a mystery. We do not know how Washington kept out of the way of stronger British forces, choosing to fight when surprise and circumstance gave him an edge. Did he have intelligence of British movements?

"My friend Bruce Wallace and I meet at four o'clock today behind the St. George Tucker House to save lives. Do you guys have friends who could join us?"

"At the Sweat Lodge, my friend Standing Elk prayed for a warrior on the path of peace. I think you are the man he is looking for. May I bring him to the meeting?"

"Perfect, Megan. I would like each of you to suggest folks you trust. Use your head, your heart, and your gut on this. It may be an unlikely cast of characters, but if they trust you, they may trust each other. We have only one shot at this—we leave today at six so we have to get the people together at four in that garden."

The Sinclairs ate without adding to the din for a few minutes. Then Peter said, "Annie, the wise woman I met has insight. Something tells me I'll find her."

"Bring people you would trust with your life. The lives of some of our friends here will depend on their being able to trust each other," said John.

Megan had been thinking. "I can invite Mark the blacksmith, and Bartholomew and his wife, Maggie. Bart went to gaol rather than take a side in this fighting."

"I know people, too," said Susan. "I'll head over to the hospital after lunch. Jane Harding is ready to do this work and there might be others there who can help."

"All right, gang. See you in the garden!"

Day 4-8:   Peter Gives a Ride to Jamestown

Peter turned around outside the Brick House Tavern. "Dad, I'm proud of you."

John gave Peter a hug and said, "I'm proud of you too, son. Be safe."

Peter jogged straight to the Powell House. A wagon sat in the lane and a white draft horse harnessed but without a bit, grazed on long grass along the fence. Inside the gate, Annie sat on the bench talking with Evie and she beckoned to him to enter. Neither woman looked surprised to see him.

"Annie told me you was back. We got to decide so I'se glad you here."

"What do you have to decide?"

"We heard a Loyalist ship done anchored off Jamestown and a boat come ashore this mornin'," said Annie. "We talkin' 'bout gettin' on a ship to Maryland or up to Long Island. From there, a ship might go to England where there ain't no slaves."

Peter looked from Annie to Evie. "What do you think, Evie? Is it time to go?"

"The Powells ain't home so I could run, but I don't see where the road leads."

"What do you think, Annie?"

"A ship been in my mind for a week. It was off in the distance so I figured it was in the future. When I heard 'bout a ship I came over to think on it wit' Evie. It could be that the distance mean it be a small chance, but I don't feel danger either."

"How long does it take to get to the river near Jamestown by horse and cart?"

"It be four miles so about forty-five minutes."

"Annie, who owns that horse and cart in the lane? Maybe he'd rent it to me for a couple of hours and I could take Evie and the boys to Jamestown. If the ship is sailing to New York or Loyalist New Jersey, I could pay their passage."

"How 'bout me and the boys go home with you, Mister Peter?"

"In Northern Virginia there are many slaves—not a good place for you guys."

"If Evie decide to go, the owner of that horse and cart is ready to take her to the ship. The owner ain't visitin' the Powells. She be sittin' on the bench visitin' Evie."

"You have a horse and cart now?"

"It make it easier to move around. Since we saw each other I made some purchases to help get the work done and help more people."

"If you lend me the cart, I could take Evie to Jamestown to check it out. I can write something that gives me a reason to be going there with three slaves."

"How 'bout a bill of sale?" asked Annie.

"I can't make an official bill of sale, Annie. My father is meeting people at four o'clock in the garden of the Tucker House. I was looking for you to invite you and I found you here. My dad wants a group of people who trust each other to work together. He fought in wars, lost friends, and he lives with the knowledge he killed people. He wants people to help during the war so fewer people are hurt."

"You found me right where I is, again. I want be at that meetin' wit' your father. I can bring other folk that can help. Now 'bout that bill of sale. How do this one look?" Annie pulled a sheet from her bag and handed it to Peter.

It had "Bill of Sale" printed at the top, an official-looking border, and names, dates, and prices neatly written in on printed lines. It showed Evie, James, and Dilli were purchased by Annie a month before. Peter was shocked, "Did you buy Evie and the boys? What are they still doing here?"

"I never bought them. I got a paper an hour ago that says I did. I can say I'se sending Evie and the boys to help my half sister in Rhode Island. She be white. We had the same white daddy and I had a African mama."

"You got a white sister, Annie?" asked an incredulous Evie.

"I ain't got no sister at all. What I got is a story to get you on the ship."

"I have another story," said Peter. "Annie, you're white and I'm your husband. I'll take the slaves you bought last month to put on a ship to work at your sister's house. You can easily pass for white if you're not sitting in the wagon next to me."

"But Annie, you ain't white and you ain't married to Peter is you?"

"No I ain't but if I ain't on the wagon, no one can see what color I is. Peter is smart. He look white. That helps his story. Now Evie, is you going or ain't you?"

"I'se gonna get the boys and we goin'." Evie hurried to the kitchen.

Annie walked to the wagon and patted the horse. "On a short trip he can go a bit faster, but don't rush him on the way home."

"Will this work, Annie? I have money to pay the boat captain if we find him."

"I'se gonna tell you if it work or not when you get back. Don't dawdle down there. This meetin' at the Tucker House be important."

"What did you mean when you said I look white?"

"What color you think you look?"

"White."

"That be what I meant."

The boys scurried back carrying their belongings in sacks. They climbed into the wagon as Peter helped Evie onto the front bench. Annie handed him the reins.

"Lie down in the back, boys, and don't make noise," said Evie.

Peter pulled on the left rein and turned the horse back to Waller Street. Avoiding crowded streets, he found his way west to the Jamestown Road. Dilli lay on his back looking up. "Mama! James! Mister Peter! Look up at those clouds and that big blue sky! Each tree look different as we go by. Being free feels good, don't it, Mister Peter? I'se gonna draw that beautiful freedom sky through the trees."

"It does look beautiful, Dilli. I'd like you to show me that drawing someday. You boys enjoy the ride. If anyone stops us, follow what I say to them."

Dilli found a stick in the wagon. Tossing it into the air, he watched it turn end over end. He stood and caught it as fell back to him. "Free!" he shouted.

"Hush, Dilli," said Evie. "Sit back down and stay quiet so you don't get us kilt."

They rode past the College of William and Mary, small farms with livestock grazing behind zigzag fences, and woods. They passed The Walking Stick Tavern at a crossroads. Peter was tempted to look for the blade his father had embedded in the beam but it was already late to find the Loyalist ship, so he kept moving. He went over in his mind what to say in the unlikely event that someone stopped them.

As they rounded a curve, ten militia men rode up from the opposite direction. "Halt!" ordered the leader. Peter recognized Hugh Mercer from the encounter with his carriage in front of their house. He had not rehearsed this possibility.

"Where are you going and why are you going there?" demanded Mercer.

"Mister Mercer! Good day, Sir. I appreciated your kindness in Williamsburg a few months back when I absentmindedly stepped in front of your horses."

"He is Colonel Mercer, not Mister Mercer," declared a lieutenant. "He commands the 3rd Virginia Regiment in the North under General Washington."

"Sorry, Colonel Mercer. It is an honor to meet you again, sir."

"I remember you. Ye had on peculiar attire and your thoughts seemed miles or years away. What brings ye on this journey? What do ye have in the wagon?"

"I'm on my way to Jamestown, Colonel. Sit up and say hello to Colonel Mercer, boys." Dilli and James sat up in the wagon and waved.

"Evie, these are good men, Patriots. Say hello to them."

"Hello, Sirs," Evie said weakly.

"We were just in Jamestown," Mercer said. "A Loyalist ship put a boat ashore, and we rode down to see what they were up to. The ship left after briefly sitting at anchor. Our search of the area turned up nothing amiss. They may have spirited Loyalists away to Southern Maryland or they may have put an agent ashore."

"Thanks for warning us, Colonel. Bruce Wallace told my father how you helped him when he was wounded and got safely away on ships from the Hebrides."

"Bruce Wallace? Do you know where he is?"

"He is still at the wheelwright shop. Have you not crossed paths with him?"

"Not for some months. I could use his help in the 3rd Virginia Regiment."

"Is it dangerous for us to go on to Jamestown today?"

"We don't know," replied Mercer, "perhaps they put men ashore."

"Thank you for alerting us, Colonel Mercer. My business in Jamestown can wait for another day. I will turn around and go back to Williamsburg."

"That might be prudent, lad. Forgive me, but I don't recall your name."

"Peter Sinclair, Colonel."

"Peter Sinclair, if you see Sergeant Wallace before I find him, please let him know I am staying at the home of Doctor John Galt, the apothecary, for three more days. I would very much like to see Wallace before I return north to my regiment."

"I will do that, Colonel Mercer."

Hugh Mercer signaled the men and they rode off toward Williamsburg.

Peter turned the wagon around. "Evie, you and the boys did very well."

"We ain't goin' to be free today, Mister Peter?" asked Dilli.

"You are free right now, boys. We tried it out to see how you like it. Those men told us the ship left already, so this is as far as we go today. We can do this again someday when circumstances are right. Meanwhile, don't speak of this to anyone. Running has to be a secret. Do you understand, boys?"

"Yes, Mister Peter. Mama showed us how a hoop roll and how it fall. It gonna roll again and I know we gonna find a road to freedom," said Dilly.

"I got a fright when he axed where you was goin'. Oh! Riders is comin' back!"

"Don't look afraid, Evie. Just sit here and be calm," Peter instructed.

Peter watched two men approach and saw they were Indians. He waved a greeting, which they returned. "Good afternoon," said the elder of the two as they got to the wagon.

Peter pulled up on the reins. "Good afternoon."

"I am Standing Elk and this is my nephew, Thomas. You look familiar."

"I'm Peter Sinclair. We haven't met but I heard your name from my sister."

"Your sister is Megan Sinclair. You look alike."

"This is Evie and her sons James and Dilli."

"Is you real Indians?" asked Dilli.

Standing Elk smiled. "Yes, young man, we are real Indians."

"I heard you know how to live free in the forest," said Dilli.

"We know how, but we live a different life now than how our grandfathers did."

"You is still free?"

"Yes, we have difficulties but we are free. Free is a good way to live."

"We gonna be free someday, too!" James spoke up, surprising his mother.

"Hush, James!"

"Your sons are good boys." Standing Elk and Thomas nudged their horses.

"Good to meet you," Peter called out. "I'll tell Megan we met."

"I gets so 'fraid when men rides up to us. We could get catched."

"Evie, Hugh Mercer helped us and Standing Elk said Dilli and James are good boys. It doesn't help to give in to fear."

"I gonna try, Mister Peter. Least we gonna get home before the Powells. I feel good we tried. It be scary but it ain't so scary like I feared."

"You and the boys have been free for almost an hour, Evie."

"I suppose we is."

Peter looked far ahead to a rider approaching at full gallop and he steered the cart along the edge of the road. The rider was a woman. As the horse thundered by, he recognized Megan leaning forward in the saddle. "Hey!" he shouted.

"Hi, Pete!" Megan called out as she hurtled past and out of hailing distance.

"Wow! That was my sister."

"She look like a fearless woman," Evie said.

"I think of her as my little sister but, seeing her ride, I guess she *is* fearless."

"Where she ridin' so fast?"

"It might have to do with a meeting later." Peter signaled the horse to speed up.

As they pulled into the lane, Annie greeted them. Robert and Claudius stood near her. Evie shooed the boys to the kitchen, said a quick goodbye to Peter and Annie, and hurried inside to finish the laundry.

Peter watched her go, wondering if he would ever see her again. "Annie, the ship left already, so we did not get it done. We ran into Colonel Mercer and the militia. Imagine if they had caught us trying to get Evie and the boys onto that ship!"

"I don't want to imagine it, Peter. Why use my mind to help that happen? I gonna imagine Evie and the boys bein' free someday. How did you stay out of trouble wit' the militia?"

"I hid nothing and I talked about something else."

"That be why I don't imagin' Evie bein' catched. Keep your mind on what you want to happen. Watch for problems but imagine solvin' them not fearin' them. We find a path through the tangle or live to try again like you helped Evie do."

"How did I help? They did not get far."

"Evie took a bold step for the first time in her life. Until now, if a chariot from heaven came by to carry them all the way to England, she'd be too scared to climb in. When she thinks on today and prays on it, courage gonna grow inside her like them boys did. Someday that idea gonna be born."

"Someday may be a long time."

"They safe where they is. Around the time them boys might be sold off, she may have a chance to move again. I pray she gonna be ready. Now, Peter, let me introduce you to some other folks."

They walked to the shade tree where Robert and Claudius were waiting. "How are you doing? I'm Peter." He remembered them from the Hush Harbor.

"We'se doin' good, Mister Peter. I am Robert and this here is Claudius. Last January, before tobacco plantin', Annie axed if we was willin' to take two whippin's to be free. We said we could never be free. She said, 'Time's a wastin' and there be much to do. What if I buy you from yo massa and you work wit' me?'

"We could scarcely believe it," Claudius told Peter. "We said we would take ten whippin's to get out of the fields and work for her. She said, 'Workin' for me could be the most dangerous, hardest work you done, but you could do good for people.' Then she axed again if we was willin' to take two whippin's."

"We told her yes, we was willin', but why two whippin's? She said she had money enough to buy one field hand but Annie wanted to buy us both. She said we gonna have to stop bein' good field hands and be failin' field hands so we be sold cheap. Failin' field hands gonna get a whippin'."

Robert said, "We told Annie yes and when hoein' time came, Claudius and me pretended we was old and lame and not fast and strong like before. Poor Mister Jack, the overseer! He shouted and shoved us, but for days, he did not whip us. He did not want to report to Massa that he could not get the slaves to work 'cause that look bad for him, too. Finally, he whipped us but he gettin' older, too. You know what? I think he did not like to hurt us, so he ain't kept it up long."

"That be true," Claudius said. "Robert and me prayed out loud and begged and the whippin' stopped quick enough. The next day we worked faster for about two hours like we was scared of gettin' whipped again and then Robert pretended to be gettin' cramps in his legs. I fell over twice. Mister Jack reported us to Massa Carter, but another week went by before he gave Robert and me the next whippin'. I heard him say, 'They can't help gettin' old.' I think he feelin' old, too."

Robert continued, "We got word to Annie that we been whipped twice, and she come by the quarter to buy field hands. It were for workin' in her garden she said. Massa and Mister Jack was happy to get rid of us for the price of one good slave. In less than an hour Massa had a handful of ready money he needed so bad, and we was in the wagon wit' Annie holding a real bill of sale for the both of us."

Annie was obviously enjoying the story the way Robert and Claudius told it. "It be all right to tell Mister Peter what I got you workin' at boys."

"Annie taught me how to make a poultice for Claudius's whipped back, and she taught him to do the same for me. She been teachin' us healin' for three months."

"Tell him all of it," said Annie. "He be our friend."

"After she bought us, Annie teached Claudius how to remember the long stories of a griot. She finished teachin' me letters so I could read the Bible. Annie and Sal showed me how to read words I never knowed how to say. Claudius and me got good at what we did then she told us the rest of her idea.

"She rents me out to the print shop. I set type for the *Virginia Gazette*. I sleep in a shed next to the print shop, and by livin' in town, I get to know slaves and servants here. The rent Annie get for me workin' helps all three of us and some other folk to get along," Robert explained proudly.

"Mister Peter, wit' Robert workin' at the print shop, Annie took me wit' her to tell stories at Hush Harbors and to listen to folk the way she do wit' us. I is learnin' to comfort and help folk when I can. I can also take messages across the county and

I can do a Hush Harbor by myself now, so it be like Annie workin' in two places at once. I take the wagon and go slow in daylight so I don't look like a runaway."

"Claudius and me listen to news we hear from print shop customers, slaves, and runaways at Hush Harbors. We talk over wit' Annie what we hear. Sometimes we help a person get to New Jersey or out to the Indians. We already helped folk."

"Have you helped people by printing false documents, Robert?"

"You real smart, Mister Peter!" Robert laughed. "I won't say where those manumissions and bills of sale is comin' from but I can say I is gettin' pretty good at settin' type 'specially when I is working alone late at night as a favor for the printer when we is busy. He gives me a coin to do that so he can sleep."

"In case I get stopped, Robert made me a paper to show what I is supposed to be doin' like you done for 'Gustus when he ran to Norfolk," Claudius said.

"You men are amazing!" said Peter. "Please be careful."

"We is. Jesus helps me and the ancestors helps Claudius. We help other folks."

"It feels good to hear it. I'm sure you can help at this meeting. Let's go together."

"Let's ride in my wagon."

Claudius and Robert rode in the back and Peter sat next to Annie up on the bench. "Where did you get the idea to buy them, Annie?"

"I was sad when 'Gustus died. I wanted to teach healin' to someone else. William was gone and Sal be busy at the hospital. These two is rooted in spirit and was learnin' from what life was givin' 'stead of givin' up. That be why I picked them."

Annie lowered her voice so only Peter could hear. "You heard them say when I axed if they was ready to be free they was sure it could never happen. They was born slaves and did not know how to imagine bein' free. People need help and those two need to get on with helpin' so I gave them the first step to be slaves for me. Las' month I tol' them I put their manumission into my will so they gonna get used to the idea of bein' free someday. I will set them free soon as they be ready. Maybe I gonna sell them to theyselves so they can be part of gettin' free. I can use the money to buy more folks into freedom."

"I see the path you are inviting them to follow, Annie. It should work."

"I hope they can pass somethin' on to them who come after. I know Sal can, but I don't think he be stayin' here forever. He got business in another place."

"Sal's story and the baby named Sally, who lives in a good home, stayed with me since the Hush Harbor that night. I still get tears in my eyes when I think about it."

"God touches Sal and he touches whoever can receive it from him. Haw! Haw, Promise!"

"Pardon me?"

Annie laughed. "I'se tellin' Promise, my horse, to go left to the St. George Tucker House."

Day 4-9:   Susan's Helpers from the Hospital

Susan pulled the bell cord by the door of the Public Hospital. The bolt slid and the door opened to reveal Jane Harding in a green middle-sorts dress. No longer wan, she looked vital and happy. "Susan! I have not seen thee for months!"

"I'm happy to find you, Jane. Is there a place we can talk a minute?"

"I have a nook by the kitchen. We can chat there over tea if thou hast the time."

"That would be nice, Jane." In an alcove next to the kitchen, Susan took a seat by a bird's eye maple table. Jane reappeared carrying a teapot and two cups on a tray. "We should let it steep. It pleases me to offer thee hospitality, and tell you my appreciation for what thou hast done for me."

"I'm happy to have been able to help, Jane."

"Susan, I have good news. Doctor de Sequeyra noticed changes in me after you and I sat in silence and had that fine visit to Kingsmill. I enter silence each day and my mind and emotions have calmed. Recently the doctor asked me to be the matron of the female patients. I have my own room and I receive pay for my work. The doctor says he appreciates the service I did even though I was suffering.

"I seek to help people. I invite patients soon to be released to have tea. A bit of normal life is good for them. We talk about the homes they will return to, and try to calm their fears about the future or ease their pain about the past. I take patients for walks in gardens. Those whose minds are being cured help me at the market."

"That is wonderful, Jane. The doctor made an excellent selection for matron."

Jane poured the tea and Susan took a sip. "Ah, delicious! I have something to tell you. My husband John will gather a few people in the garden of the St. George Tucker House today at four o'clock. Although we can't stop the war, he hopes people can work together to reduce the loss of life. You should be at this meeting."

"Susan, I lived in fear of war most of my life. Now my fear has receded and I look for ways to help others. I have spoken about this to Doctor de Sequeyra. Oh, here he comes now." Jane stood up.

"Hello, Doctor. Do you remember Susan Sinclair, the woman who took me out for that wonderful walk in the garden and the trip to Kingsmill?

"Yes, of course. Missus Sinclair, you contributed to a miracle. Welcome back to the Public Hospital. You can see that Jane and Sal have done much to make this a better place. Did Jane mention I purchased Sal from his owner? Previously I rented his service. He saves his wages to pay back the cost to buy him so our secret is that he is indentured rather than a slave. Jane paid for a month of the time he owes as a birthday gift so I did the same and will do that each year until he is free."

Susan had not decided about inviting the doctor, but she explored the possibility. "Doctor, my family is concerned that as war is spreading, the suffering will be great and losses heavy. My husband was a soldier and he is seeking ways that people could work together to save lives."

"Missus Sinclair, I am still an outsider here, being a Jew from Holland. I perceive, after the effect you had on Jane, that we may have some common concerns."

"I think we do, Doctor de Sequeyra."

"I have observed at my office in town that many physical ailments begin when people are unhappy, confused, angry, or fearful. They may struggle as if their life is at stake even over status in the community, or money, or other non life-threatening conditions. I witness in individuals, families, and even communities, the same delusions or failure to notice reality that we see here in the hospital. My professional diagnosis is that most of us are as crazy as crows in a windstorm. We dive and spin in the air if we are not fulfilling a fantasy of what we think life should be. Rather than be grateful and celebrate what we have, we pine for what we do not have, or worry about what we might lose.

"I see the failure of the Parliament, and Continental Congress to resolve their claims on jurisdiction and power and conclude that a county court could resolve such a dispute among plantations. Unfortunately, kings and congresses heed no higher authority, nor do men who dedicate their lives to amassing money and power, willingly surrender their ambitions to such arbitration. We witness lunacy at the level of nations. It is not mad to pursue an ambition. What is insane is the manipulation and violence men use to have their way. They sacrifice the lives of others and lie about the reasons for sacrifice. They risk their own sons as officers to demonstrate their commitment. Sons who return alive are deemed qualified to lead estates or nations because they succeeded in leading men in killing others."

"What would you do, Doctor de Sequeyra?" asked Susan.

Doctor de Sequeyra sighed. "Ending war will take a long time. I have one small idea. More soldiers die of infections after being wounded, or from disease in unhealthy camps, than die directly in battle. If every militia unit had men trained to reduce festering of wounds and to support healthy camps, more men might survive the madness. Some might tell the truth to the next generation of how mentally sick it is to send young men to fight each other to the death. Do you consider it unpatriotic for me to speak this way, Missus Sinclair?"

"No, Doctor. I would say you love your country and have compassion for young people and parents of all countries. I want to invite you to a meeting at four o'clock beside the St. George Tucker House with others who seek to reduce the carnage."

"There will be a meeting of souls who care about this? I shall be there, Madam."

"I should be off. We leave on a long journey after the meeting. Thank you for the tea, Jane. I'm happy you found such a wonderful way to make a contribution."

"Let us walk you to the door, Susan," said Jane. On their way down the corridor, they were passed by a patient walking the other way repeating, "*Gloria in excelsis Deo, Gloria in excelsis Deo, Gloria in excelsis Deo...*"

"He changed his prayer." The doctor smiled. "This may be a step in the right direction."

Day 4-10:   Megan Gathers Her Friends

Megan hurried to the blacksmith shop from the Brick House Tavern. She was told Mark would return in an hour.

She walked through town, hoping to run into Standing Elk, and toward the market where Bartholomew and Maggie were selling their wares.

"Bart, it's nice to see you back at work so soon. My dad is having a meeting by the St. George Tucker House. He asked me to invite people who can keep a secret and want to save lives and reduce the damage of the war. You were willing to sit in a stinky cell to try to slow the race toward war. Are you willing to join others even if it's dangerous?"

"I am willing to hear what the plan is, Megan. If we have a chance to save lives, we must give it a go."

"Have you talked to Standing Elk about this?" asked Maggie.

"I've been looking for him all over!"

"He left minutes ago, riding to the Jamestown road with his nephew Thomas," said Bartholomew. "They had to stop at a farrier at the crossroads beyond William and Mary, so they will not have gone too far yet. If you like, you can borrow the Earl of Loxley to catch up with them."

"The Earl of Loxley?"

"He is a fast horse. Bartie, do you think she can handle him?" asked Maggie, concerned for Megan.

"Oh, the Earl of Loxley is your horse?"

"Yes. He pulls both cart and plow nicely but he loves to race the wind on an open road." Bartholomew glowed with pride. "You rode with Mark. Can you ride yourself?"

"I took riding lessons for two summers."

"Riding lessons? You are fit to be a cavalry officer in the Continental Army. To catch Standing Elk, you must leave now to reach him before he turns off the Jamestown Road and heads west. There's no tellin' which track he might take."

"I'll do it!"

Bartholomew unharnessed the Earl of Loxley from the cart, tossed a saddle over his back, and attached the stirrups. "There you are, Robin, a good run with Megan will do you good."

"Robin? I thought you said his name was the Earl of Loxley."

"Robin Hood was the Earl of Loxley and a supporter of the people, like you and your family, Megan. He is a spirited horse. Better to ride him astride."

There was enough material in the fabric of her dress for Megan to put her left foot into the stirrup and swing her right leg over the horse. "Thank you for this. See you at the St. George Tucker House at four o'clock."

236

"I hope we see you here before that with the Earl. We cannot pull the wagon without him.

"Darn! I wanted to keep him, OK, I'll be back." She gently guided the horse out of the market.

"OK?" Bartholomew looked at Maggie, puzzled.

"I heard her say it before. I think it means 'yes' or 'doing well' or 'that will be satisfactory, thank you.'"

"Young people today have their own language, don't they?"

Megan brought the Earl of Loxley to a trot and posted in the stirrups to avoid the bump, bump of her backside against the saddle. Reaching the Jamestown Road, she nudged the horse to a canter. There were no horses tethered at the farriers, so she knew Standing Elk and Thomas had already moved on.

She looked ahead on a long, straight stretch and saw no one else on the road. "All right, Robin Hood, Bartie says you're a fast horse who longs to race the wind. Let's see if you can race against time."

She made a clucking sound with the side of her tongue and cheeks through closed teeth, gave a subtle squeeze of her knees against the horse's sides, and a mild swish of the loose ends of the reins against the Earl of Loxley's right side. That was all the encouragement he needed to change his rhythm and lean into a full gallop.

Megan had never ridden so fast. She stood in the stirrups, knees pressing the flanks and entwined the fingers of her left hand in the Earl's mane. Her hair streamed behind her in the wind and a smile spread on her face. The smile widened when she recalled a slapstick cartoon image of a rider knocked off a horse by a low hanging branch, and she bent low, intently scanning the road ahead.

In the distance, a cart approached and without guidance, the Earl kept to the right. There was no sign of two riders and Megan looked west down each lane and track hoping for a glimpse of Standing Elk. As she passed the cart, someone shouted "Hey!" and she glanced left to see Peter at the reins with an African woman beside him.

She shouted, "Hi, Pete!" as she hurtled by.

The Earl of Loxley slowed to a cantor to round the next bend. Megan spotted two riders and pulled back slightly on the reins. The younger rider turned to see who was approaching and said something to Standing Elk who looked back as well.

Megan slowed to a trot as she rode up. "Hello Standing Elk, Thomas. I'm glad I found you."

"We just passed your brother, mentioned your name, and here you are," said Standing Elk.

"I hope you're not disappointed."

"What brings you down this road at such a pace? And how did you get away with stealing Bartie's horse?"

"He lent me the Earl of Loxley to ride after you.

"Standing Elk, at the Spirit Lodge, you said we should pray to find warriors who rise beyond fear and hate and can lead on the path of peace instead of the warpath. I prayed and realized I know such a man. He is my father."

"Megan, it is no surprise to me that a woman like you should have wise parents. Is he a warrior?"

"Yes. When he was a little older than I am now he fought in forests, deserts, and mountains far away. He managed to save the lives of many of his men. A while ago he stopped a fight in a tavern called the Walking Stick to save a man from getting injured."

"The man in the Walking Stick was your father? That tavern is on this road and that fight is a legend throughout the Tidewater. That was your father? He was a hurricane that did not harm. No man there had ever seen such a thing. He changed many men. I have prayed that I might meet him some day. What is his name?"

"His name is John Sinclair. I rode here to find you. If you come with me to Williamsburg, you can meet my father and others who choose to walk the path of peace. My father is having a meeting in the gardens of the St. George Tucker House at four o'clock."

Standing Elk was silent as if in prayer.

He turned to his nephew. "Thomas, I felt the Spirit Lodge today would be deep. Now we learn a sacred secret gathering will take place at the same time as the Lodge. This is a sign.

"Today, you will lead the Lodge and choose someone to be your fire-keeper. You will know who to choose when you see him. He may have been a fire-keeper before or perhaps not. If not, teach him the main points, help him to build the fire, select the grandfather stones, set the altar, and give him clear instructions. You are prepared to lead, and I am pleased.

"I will go to the gathering. Tell the people that I had to meet someone and that I send my blessing to everyone. Do not speak of the meeting. I will share what I learn with you when I return. Thomas, you are ready."

"Uncle, this is important. I feel it. Thank you for the trust you have in me. I shall walk the road I learned from you." Thomas nudged his horse and turned off the Jamestown rode down a wagon track.

"I'm glad I met you, Standing Elk. It is an honor," said Megan. "Now we have to go. Let's ride beside each other. I have many questions I want to ask."

Day 4-11:   Hidden History in the Garden

John sat behind the hedges, savoring the scents of cedar and yew. His posture was erect, hands clasped and resting in his lap, mind calm. He listened to the rustle of wind in the tall trees. He mentally listed what to cover when people arrived.

With a crunch on the path, Bruce rounded a hedgerow carrying chairs from the Tucker House, which he arranged, saluted John, and sat near him without a word.

More footsteps sounded and Peter entered accompanied by three African Americans, two strong men in their late thirties, hair graying but eyes bright, and a large woman moving with a confident and kindly presence. "This is Annie and these are her helpers, Robert and Claudius. Folks, this is my father, John Sinclair."

John stood. "Welcome and thank you for coming. This is Bruce Wallace."

"You be plantin' precious seeds of peace, Mister John." Annie took John's hand. "The seeds you sowin' will save lives. We is happy to help this garden grow."

"Peter told me about you, Annie. Clear seeing will be needed in the days ahead."

Annie and her helpers sat together. Moments later, Susan arrived with Jane Harding, Doctor de Sequeyra, and Samuel Abdul Latif. Susan took a spot by John.

There was no awkwardness in the silence as they waited. John thought about one person he had hoped to invite but had not found. Horses stopped beyond the hedges and Megan entered with Standing Elk. Mark, Bartholomew, and Maggie walked in followed by Frances who sat next to Jane. When all were seated, they formed a square of four people on each side.

John looked slowly around the square. "Greetings, friends, my name is John Sinclair. I live near the Potomac River. Frances, thank you for inviting us to this garden, a tranquil contrast to the turmoil of these times. We are here to find ways to save lives. Some of you know each other well and some have never met. Either I know you or my wife Susan, daughter Megan, or son Peter told me they would trust you with their lives. Their judgment is good enough for me. We ask you to trust each other, and to be worthy of that trust. We have all gathered here to work together to save lives. Does anyone wish to speak?"

Frances raised a hand and John nodded. "My father's ancestors included Pocahontas, who was of the Algonquin tribes as you are, Standing Elk. My mother's line includes a black slave in Jamestown who completed servitude and was freed. He married a white widow, which was permitted then. Their son's wife was a white servant whose freedom he purchased through his labors. Their grandchildren were pale as I am. All of you, red, black, and white, are my family."

"Thank you, Frances. Does anyone else wish to speak?"

"I would like to pray," said Standing Elk, stepping to the centre. "Creator, we thank you for this gathering. Help us to be patient and generous, and please make clear the paths to walk on this journey together. Miigwech, Creator, for bringing together people of courage, skill, and energy to walk together on the path of peace." He turned to John. "Thank you for inviting us to this place, John Sinclair.

My people will do everything we can to reduce the suffering of war and to live in peace with all our neighbors."

"Thank you, Standing Elk."

"I have a question for thee," said Jane. "Thou sayest we are here to work to save lives. Will the war against Britain continue? Can something be done to stop it?"

"I expect this war will go on for years," John answered. "Blood has been shed already. Like all wars, it will end and enemies will become friends. Meanwhile, we have ideas about how to reduce the harm of this war. First, we can reduce losses in battle by averting large direct confrontations. Casualties on both sides at Concord and Breed's Hill were heavy. If we warn General Washington when massed troops are coming, he could move out of the way to save lives on both sides. Bruce, can you get close to the British command?"

"To tell it true, though it pains me to see war come, I agree more with Congress."

"Bruce, you would let the command of the continental forces know you support them. You would become a vital contributor to their cause by informing them of major British movements. The task is dangerous,"

"I suppose I could do that until the British hang me, but how can I build trust with the Continental Army? They will think I am on the British side."

"I know how you can connect with the Continental Army, Bruce," said Peter. "I met Colonel Hugh Mercer today. He asked me to tell you he is staying at the home of Dr. Galt, the apothecary, and he can use your help in the 3rd Virginia Regiment."

"Bruce, it's being served to you on a platter," said John. "You can visit Colonel Mercer here. His 3rd Regiment is in the North with General Washington. He can introduce you to Washington and you can offer directly to be an agent. Then meet the British command and remind them of your service in the last war and of your connections to Dunmore and Oglethorpe. Once you give the British Generals information and they see you were right, though they arrive after Washington has left, you'll have credibility with them while helping the Continental Army."

"I could give that a try, John." Bruce decided.

"Keeping George Washington alive is worth a try, Bruce, and reducing casualties on both sides will be a great service. Do you have friends who speak German?"

Suddenly the sound of footsteps on gravel brought everyone to an anticipative silence. Into the opening stepped James Walker the Episcopal priest and Master of the Masonic Lodge. "Oh," he said surprised, "sorry to interrupt." He turned to go.

"Reverend Walker," said John, "I was hoping to invite you to this meeting."

"Hello, John. Oh, and Susan. Frances, you're here? I come to this sheltered place to imagine life in..." It slowly dawned on Reverend Walker what he was seeing.

"Welcome, Reverend," said Frances. "I am happy you could join us today."

"This is astonishing. If you don't mind, John, I feel a need to sit down."

"Please take this spot and I will stand," John offered.

John asked again, "Bruce, do you know any German speakers?"

"*Ich kann gut Deutsch sprechen.*"

John looked around to see who had spoken.

Jane held up her hand. "*Ich arbeitete für vier Jahre als Küchenmädchen bei einer deutschen Familie in Pennsylvania...* Sorry. I worked four years as a kitchen maid, living with a German family in Pennsylvania after my family was killed. They were kind and I learned their language."

"Jane, that's extraordinary! Bruce can introduce you to General Washington. You could offer to circulate among German prisoners and, if you are willing to take the risk, among the German conscripts in British service. You could tell them they could end their serfdom and get free land here by joining the Continental Army as free men. Washington will like the idea. Otherwise, since Colonel Rall is taking no prisoners, the Americans could decide to give no quarter either."

"Thou hast a good idea, but I am busy at the hospital as the doctor can attest."

"Jane Harding," said the doctor, "if you can persuade General Washington of the merits of this idea, you will reduce the greater madness in the world and will put into service what you learned as a result of the tragedy in your family."

"If thou thinkest it worthwhile, Doctor, I am willing to do it."

"You have my complete support. I shall continue to pay your monthly stipend so you may concentrate on the work rather than worry about sustaining yourself."

"That is generous, Doctor," said John. "Now, we need someone close to the command of the Continental Army to deliver information coming from Bruce and other sources directly to General Washington. Mark, you could travel with Washington, ostensibly to repair swords and bayonets. Runners could bring news and warnings to you without observers knowing the true purpose of their visit."

"I would like to reduce the loss of life, Mister Sinclair. However, as Mister Wallace agrees more with Congress, I lean to the Loyalist side. The large landowners are taking land from native people and have no interest in freeing slaves or servants. It seems they fight for personal gain. Besides, I am in bondage at the blacksmith shop."

"Thank you for your honesty, Mark. With Bruce near the British command, it would be perfect to have you with your Loyalist leanings in the service of General Washington. You will both work to reduce loss of life on all sides. You can hasten the end of servitude and slavery for volunteers on the Continental side. The army is short of men and will see the benefit of granting freedom to volunteers."

"Mark," said Standing Elk, "slaves and servants are here together and my people will support it. You can keep the freedom of all people in mind."

"The thought of speaking to the commander of the Continental Army frightens me. But good idea or not, I do not have freedom to leave the forge."

Standing Elk studied Mark. "I can contribute money toward your freedom."

241

"I can contribute," said John. "We'll give the money to Bruce to buy your freedom. When he tells Anderson that you'll work for Washington and will be able to direct business to his armory, Anderson's answer will be an enthusiastic yes."

Standing Elk handed a leather pouch to Bruce. "Mark, you are my friend."

"I will contribute to your freedom," said Megan. "Servitude is not fair."

Bartholomew spoke up. "Maggie and I can offer coins to unbind you, Mark."

Whispers came from the bench where the slaves sat and Robert stood up. "Claudius and Sal and me been saving coins for our freedom. We will give some to you, Mister Mark, so you gonna be free to do this. This be a day to remember. Since we is bound for freedom, if we is slaves a bit longer, it don't matter."

"This indeed be a day to remember." Annie stood as Robert sat down. "'Bound for freedom' you said? Robert and Claudius, I is very proud of you. We will get your manumission now. You can carry papers saying you is slaves to keep you safe as you travel, but now you know that you is free just as God has always known it. Mark Smith, I gonna put in money to help you do this work."

Doctor de Sequeyra stood. "I shall donate. My people were Pharaoh's slaves and miracles set them free. Mark, this meeting is your miracle. And yours, Sal. I shall sign your manumission now. You are free to work on this however you choose."

Mark wiped his eyes. "I have never known such kindness. I should introduce myself honestly. This is not easy... My name is Edmond Brown. The words 'his mark' were next to the place to make an X on the indenture paper. I copied the letters M, A, R, and K, and ever since I use the name Mark because I can write it and because I feel less trapped in bondage having a contract that is not in my name." He looked around at the faces staring at him as if for the first time.

"Edmond Brown, do you accept freedom through the generosity of these friends and will you meet General Washington?"

"Mister Sinclair, I gratefully accept. Your confidence gives me faith in myself."

"And Edmond..."

"Yes, Mister Sinclair?"

"I suggest you continue using the name Mark. It will help you remember that you have a special mission to help those in bondage."

"Yes, Sir. I shall be Mark Smith as long as it is helpful."

"Now," said John, "as Bruce Wallace moves with the British and Mark Smith is in service to Washington, they will need messengers to carry information between them. Look around this group. We have native people who can move freely, slaves who can travel for their owner, vendors of vegetables, and a travelling preacher woman. There is strength in your differences. Do not mention people in this group to anyone. Others can work with you without knowing anyone beyond the people they directly contact. Standing Elk, you have experience and wisdom to lead the work. You can find Indians on both sides throughout the colonies to recruit that you judge safe and helpful. Annie and her friends can work with you."

"I am honored by your faith in me, as we meet for the first time."

"Standing Elk, though few will ever know it because you will work in secret, you will contribute to all the peoples of this land."

"I have something to offer," said Doctor de Sequeyra. "Most who perish in war die of infection rather than wounds. I can teach methods that would save lives."

"I can share what I know about stoppin' infection, and other physic, Doctor," said Annie. "I been teachin' Claudius and Robert and they teach others."

Standing Elk nodded. "My people know leaves and barks that stop infection, slow bleeding, and ease pain. We taught those cures to Annie and she added to our knowledge with what she learned from African healers and colonial doctors."

The doctor spoke. "I can offer the Public Hospital as an indoor meeting place. People come to the hospital to deliver food or visit family without townsfolk taking notice. Superstitious souls avoid even looking at the hospital out of fear."

"That is a good idea, Doctor," said John.

Frances added, "These hedges offer shelter from curious eyes and you are welcome to use this garden as a place to meet as well."

"Thank you, Frances. The path will become clearer as you move along it. My family and I are going away today, so I leave this work to Bruce, Standing Elk, the Doctor, and Annie to lead. Whenever Annie has an idea, I suggest you all listen."

"Thank you, Mister Sinclair. I want to let folks know that we can get printed bills of sale, military orders, manumission, and whatever folks need to help them move freely. I would rather not say 'zackly how we be able to do that."

"Annie, the papers will be helpful. Thank you all for coming to this meeting. May God smile upon your undertakings. Bruce, may I have a word?"

Peter stood by Annie. "I will pray for the success of this work, Annie."

"We all got to do the best we can. We pray the leaders wake up and them who profit from war find more helpful ways to get rich. You helped more folk here than you know, Peter. We gonna meet again."

"Annie, knowing you has changed me. I'll remember you all my life."

Next to a hedge, John spoke to Bruce. "I learned that a Patrick Ferguson in Britain is designing a breech-loading rifle, accurate at 200 yards. It fires six rounds a minute standing or four advancing, and doesn't misfire in the rain."

"My God, Man! If that rifle works, the Continentals have no chance!"

"Precisely, Bruce. So an important, secret part of your work is to find and steal or destroy those rifles — whatever you need to do to remove them from the field."

"That doesna' sound like an easy task, John."

"It won't be easy, but you'll be close to the British generals, so you'll know when Ferguson arrives. The road ahead will be difficult enough without a superior weapon ranged against the Patriots. You will think of something. Oh, another thing—American marksmen are shooting British officers but see if you can persuade Ferguson not to shoot American officers."

"Is that all you need? If you like I could fly to Heaven and ask Saint George the Dragon Slayer and the Archangel Michael to help us."

"Saint George is patron saint of England, so chances of his joining you are slim. Ask Saint Andrew, patron saint of Scotland, and keep your head down when it gets noisy. Your position is too critical to sacrifice yourself in a heroic gesture."

"'Tis too late for me to die young, John, and the temptation to be a hero, like so many of life's temptations, is slowly fading."

Reverend Walker approached them. "Thank you for including me in the circle, John. I won't forget this experience and in church and the Masonic Temple, I will pray for success of the plan."

"I am a Mason, too," said Bruce, taking Reverend Walker's elbow in his left hand and giving him a firm handshake with the right. "Where is your Lodge?"

Reverend Walker hesitated, not knowing what to say. "I... came far to be at the meeting and my Lodge is not easy to reach from here."

"Perhaps Reverend Walker can meet you again in these hedges, Bruce. I'm sure if he can find a way to help through the Church or through the Masons, he will."

"Yes, I will do what I can to help," said the Reverend. "Goodbye for now."

John put a hand on Bruce's shoulder. "I'm not usually a praying man, but I'll pray for you and the success of this mission."

"Thank you, John."

Megan followed Mark out of the hedges. "Edmond Brown!" He turned around.

"Yes, Megan? I am sorry I did not tell you my real name."

"You did what you had to. I'm proud of you." She kissed his cheek.

"Can you come with me to the North, Megan?"

"Mark, I'll always remember you but I can't go with you. I know you will find a wonderful woman."

"I shall never find a woman like you. Now I have reason to wear those fine clothes you bought me, and I will think of you when I do."

Only Frances and John remained in the garden. "Frances, can you tell me now how you are able to appear in my time when you live in the eighteenth century?"

"I can tell you, John, but you might find it hard to believe or disturbing."

"This whole experience is hard to believe, Frances."

"In 1778, I married St. George Tucker after he returned from Bermuda. I became distraught when I learned my new husband and his father supplied gunpowder to the Continental Army. I swore to Heaven I would find a way to reduce the suffering of the war however long it took. St. George and I had five children in addition to the three I already had. The war ended and we settled into our life. He spent time in Richmond conducting his law business, which left me time to pray to

244

atone for people killed in the war. About ten years after St. George and I married, I died, as all of us eventually do."

"But..."

"This may not be easy to believe but, after my years of prayer to do something about the violence, I lingered here at this house, where my husband moved, and where my children grew up after my death. I have long watched for a way to reduce the damage of the gunpowder."

"Why did you decide to work with me?"

"It is unusual that a person can see me or hear what I say, because, of course, I am not saying anything, just thinking it. You saw me and heard me so I knew I should talk with you. Today in the garden is the first time I have been heard by so many. It is the fulfillment of my long-held prayer."

"That is amazing, Frances. ·You're telling me that you are a ghost? If I had not experienced so many strange things in the past few days, I would not believe it."

"Those who are alive would call me a ghost. I am a soul that has lingered for a purpose, longer than my body was able to live. I have two small gifts to give you John to help you believe what I have told you. First, two men contacted me this morning and asked me to tell you they are well. They expressed their gratitude, 'For back then, and for now,' they said. Their names are Danny and Sargon — does that second name make sense to you? They were soldiers. Danny was younger than your son and Sargon a few years older."

John was stunned.

"The second gift is that I want to leave you no doubt that there are things that are real beyond what most people know. It is finally time for me to move on. Goodbye, John. I deeply thank you for who you are and for what you have done for so many." Frances curtsied, turned, and glided straight into the tall hedge, disappearing without rustling a single branch.

John stared at the hedge where Frances vanished. A breeze rustled tree branches high above. He looked up. "Go ahead, laugh, Danny and Sargon. You put her up to that trick."

On the street, Susan waved goodbye to Jane, Doctor de Sequeyra, and Samuel Abdul Latif. John joined her, Peter, and Megan and they set out toward the bridge.

Day 4-12:   Virginia Declares Independence

As the Sinclairs walked together up North England Street suddenly shouting and cheering came from several directions followed by the pealing of bells from the Capitol, the Palace, and Bruton Parish Church. "What's going on?" asked Susan.

"There's a crowd by the Palace," said John. "Let's see what it's about."

A man placed a chair by the Palace gates and stood on it waving his black tricorn hat in the air. He shouted out, "Hear ye, hear ye! History is made in Williamsburg! Today, May 15, 1776, the Virginia Convention, meeting at the Capitol has resolved to instruct its delegates to the Continental Congress to declare:

'That these United Colonies are, and of right ought to be, free and independent States, that they are absolved from all allegiance to the British Crown, and that all political connection between them and the State of Great Britain is, and ought to be, totally dissolved.'

"They have asked Richard Henry Lee to propose the resolution at the Congress in June. Three cheers for Independence and the Continental Congress!"

The crowd cheered. Celebration began as more people came out of their homes and patrons spilled out of taverns into the streets.

John stroked his chin. "It's rolling and we're here at the beginning. Now it's time to go home." They threaded their way through the crowd, crossed the bridge in silence, and walked to the car waiting for them in their own time.

Day 5-1:   Return to Williamsburg

Megan burst through the front door. "I got an A on my history paper! My teacher says I can get college credit if I write more about how I did the research!"

"That's great, Megan!" said Susan. "Dinner's ready—homemade lasagna."

As Megan took her spot at the table, John said, "Megan. Did I just hear you got an A on your paper? Excellent! When you add the research, will you say we went back in time?"

"I want to. I can write it as a story. Can we go back to Williamsburg this summer to check a few things out, or should I do it using books and the web?"

"I found a program at Colonial Williamsburg the last weekend in June called 'Under the Red Coat,'" said Susan. "It's a reenactment of the British occupation in June of 1781. Peter will be back for the summer and he'd probably want to come."

"The British occupied Williamsburg in 1781? What do you think happened to all the people we met, Dad?"

"I don't know. When we got home, I looked online for folks we met. Doctor John de Sequeyra really ran the mental hospital and Frances Tucker was a real person. Patrick Ferguson invented breech-loading rifles that disappeared after the battle at Brandywine and a militia leader named Joseph Hutchings was captured by his own slave. I couldn't find Bruce, Standing Elk, Jane, or Peter's friend Annie."

"I wonder how they made out," said Megan. "Dad, if we slid to the past because our car spun, does something intense need to happen for us to go back again?"

"Good question," Susan said. We can try. Peter's summer job has him working Saturdays, but I will book a room for that Saturday night. We can get an early start Sunday to check out the British occupation and look for our friends."

247

5-2: June 1781 The British Occupation

The server returned to the table. "Here are the granola pancakes and the poached eggs with ham. I see you two already got to the buffet.

John asked for a fill-up on coffee.

"Coming right up!"

"When we walk into the Historic District, British soldiers will be camped in town," Peter reminded his family. "If we find a way to 1781, our friends will be five years older. Some may be dead and some may have left."

"It's not likely we can go back in time again," said John. "But it wasn't likely that would happen last month either, so who knows?"

"I just looked up where George Washington was in June, 1781." Megan looked at her phone. "He was in Peekskill, New York, until July 2 then he moved to Dobbs Ferry. He didn't get here until September."

"So Mark Smith or Edmond Brown may not be here either," Peter remarked.

Megan shot him a look to be quiet.

After breakfast, the Sinclairs walked through town together. In an open space near the Magazine was a large camp of reenactors in British uniforms and civilian dress. The air had the scent of sweet acidic smoke from a hardwood fire. A barefoot English woman had set a large cut of beef to roast in a reflector oven made at a forge in Williamsburg.

"What are you making?" asked Susan.

"Well, Love, we're cooking for a hundred men. Some like their beef salty and some do not. Some like potatoes with garlic and some do not. I keep salt set by for those who want more. I shall use a honey and pepper baste on that roast to make it tasty. I enjoy doing colonial era cooking each year. I don't need to pretend to be English because I am English, but I like pretending we are in the past."

"Being here is like a journey to the past isn't it?" Susan said.

"Indeed, it is. We are here for the weekend, and then back to our time we go."

A faint melody from a British soldier practicing a fife could be heard above the bustle. Redcoats polished their brass buttons and buckles, oiled bayonets and muskets, or made cartridges with powder and papier-maché musket balls. Several stood in clusters, talking with passersby. A trio of young men practiced marching and wheeling together to be crisp for the drill later in the day. John scanned the area for familiar faces but saw none.

The Sinclairs walked beyond the north side of the square. "Hey!" said Megan, "I remember that zigzag rail fence; they call it a worm fence. It has no nails or fasteners except that rail wedged at an angle at each corner. I sat reading near here when Standing Elk came by and showed some plants. Come on! I'll show you!"

Megan led her family to the spot by the board fence where Standing Elk had opened her eyes to nature. "Maybe if we sit here quietly, he'll come walking by."
248

"It feels like we're next to a fence separating us from the past," Peter said.

Megan described the plants and trees she learned from her Indian friend. "When we were here last month it was November in this garden. Isn't that weird?" They sat quietly, lulled by the buzzing of diligent bees and soft whisperings of leaves high in the canopy. An unseen blue jay called from the upper branches.

They felt the warmth of the sun in a mottled pattern as it shone through the leaves. "I remember that grove of trees, guys. But we're still in our own time."

"Let's go to other spots where we have a clear memory of being in the past. We may find a way through," suggested Peter.

Susan brightened. "Let's try that."

Peter led them to the stream behind the printing office where he and Evie met Annie at the bridge. In that little park known as Ginny's Bottom, lilies grew near the water gurgling from a culvert. Some trees were wound with honeysuckle vines. The Sinclairs stood on the bridge, watched, and listened. Frond-like branches of ash trees swayed gently. Out of sight a large frog rumbled.

Peter noticed a small apple orchard he had not seen when he was in the garden with Evie. All my attention was on her at this bridge, he thought wistfully. I wish I could have helped them get to freedom. I wonder what happened to her sons. He turned around half expecting Annie would come down a path.

"Let's visit other spots," said Susan. "What about where you first saw Annie?"

They left the garden and walked to the pasture where Peter had seen Annie preparing food. They sat in a row along the fence. Several minutes passed without conversation. They were calmed and lifted by the sounds of nature.

"It's amazing how much life you can hear going on when you stop and listen," said Megan. "Don't you think we mainly live in our heads?"

"What do you mean?"

"When I sat next to Standing Elk and Mark behind the blacksmith shop and in the Sweat Lodge, I had a sense of how huge it all is and how connected we are. I looked into the deep black spaces between the stars. When I look at stars, I'm looking at something—either the stars or the patterns people see in constellations like the Big Dipper and Orion. But when I looked into the space between the stars, I had a sense I never felt before. Space is everywhere, way out there, around us, and inside us, too. It's hard to find the words because the feeling had no words."

"You're doing a good job saying it," Susan said. "I felt like that when I sat in silence with Jane Harding in a garden near the Public Hospital, and again at the Kingsmill Plantation. Looking at a flower or at a ship sailing by the far shore of the river felt timeless, like looking at the Infinite—no, more like being in the Infinite."

"That's good, Mom. I might mention that in my paper. I had trouble finding a way to say this the first time, so I gave up."

"I feel very relaxed," said John. "This might be like when we let go in the spinning car. 'Timeless,' you said, Honey. It does feel timeless. When we aren't thinking about the past or the future, we can be in this moment in the stream of moments. By being fully present now, maybe we can touch something bigger."

Peter closed his eyes and imagined Annie smiling. A warm feeling of well-being flowed through him, and he joined her in a wide smile. He opened his eyes. He did not see Annie but in that instant, it made no difference.

"What are you smiling about, Pete?"

"I'm happy to be here again. Let's check out some other places."

Passing the old gaol, Megan remembered coaxing Bartholomew out of the dark cell. Peter recalled learning from the gaoler's wife that there was no Underground Railroad yet.

They reached the Benjamin Powell House. "I'll see if anyone is out back." Peter dashed down the lane but a woman at the gate was directing visitors out. No one was behind her in the garden.

Peter rejoined the others and asked if they would be willing to go through the house again. "This is where the time change began for me."

"Sure, let's go in, Pete." Then Megan whispered to Peter as they followed their parents to the front of the property, "I'd like to meet your friend."

"She was not my..."

"I know... it was the same for me."

After a short wait, they joined a group of other visitors. The hallway, living room, and front bedroom looked the same but there were no reenactors in the rooms.

"Is the Powell family not in today?" Susan asked a woman in period costume.

"No, but a maid is in the dining room explaining foods of a midday dinner."

The woman in the dining room welcomed them. She explained how food prepared in the Powell House kitchen was now set out ready for a Sunday feast. "The Powell family would have such a large dinner on their return from church."

"It looks as if they will be home any time," said Susan.

Peter asked, "I was wondering about an African woman named Evie who was a laundress here last time we came. Does she still work here?"

"I have been here for two years and we have not had a reenactor by that name. Perhaps there was once a slave named Evie in this house. Were you here back then?" she laughed.

"I guess I was!" Peter laughed along with the woman — if she only knew. He was disappointed to see no sign of Evie and her sons other than in his memories.

They meandered to spots they remembered and others new to them, talking with reenactors and asking about the people they knew. Progress had been made on the Public Armoury at the blacksmith shop and Megan went inside to ask a smith there about Mark Smith or Edmond Brown who worked at the forge long ago.

"Never heard of either one of them."

"How about an Indian named Standing Elk who used to buy iron goods here?"

"Sorry, I've never seen an Indian customer."

"Thanks anyway." Megan followed her family to the bench near the Public Hospital where Susan had sat with Jane. "Look, Mom! It's an art museum now."

"It's good to see beauty at this place which housed many tormented souls. Part of it is a display of the old mental hospital. Let's sit out here for a while." The Sinclairs sat in stillness, as Susan and Jane had done long ago. A squirrel abruptly peered at them from behind a tree and as quickly scampered out of sight. "He looks like the same squirrel we watched last month."

"It was way over two hundred years ago, Mom. That's a distant descendant."

"You're my descendant, but not distant, Megan." Susan gave her daughter a hug.

"Not distant at all." John put a hand on Megan's shoulder.

"Having you two is the best thing that ever happened to us. Guys, I feel the memory of Jane Harding as we sit here. When I close my eyes, she seems near."

"It's strange being in these places, Mom," said Megan. "Sometimes I think there's no way we can get back to that other time. But that's just an idea going through my mind and I let it go. When my mind is quiet like the space between the stars, the past seems very close, but how do we get there? What do you think, Dad?"

"I get what you're saying. We didn't do anything to slip back in time. We just woke up in the morning, walked around a corner, or ran into someone, and there we were. So maybe it won't be our doing if we get back again."

"That's good, Dad. It wasn't our doing. Annie said we 'let go' when the car was spinning and slid back into her time. She was able to walk with me into ours. But she said maybe we slid back because someone was calling for us."

"Right! Frances Tucker said she had been praying for a long time, and at the end of the meeting in the garden I learned how long."

"Jane sought a way to move beyond the violent loss of her family," said Susan.

"Standing Elk said he was praying for a warrior who could lead on the path of peace, and that turned out to be you, Dad."

"Right," said Peter. "So maybe we were called back and we did nothing in our time to make it happen other than 'let go.' Maybe no one is calling us now."

To avoid the crowds around the Redcoats' camp they walked north. John ducked into the wheelwright's shop to find it exactly as he remembered, with iron tools hanging on a white wall and partially finished wheels leaning against a workbench. A young man fitted hardwood spokes into holes he chiseled in the wooden hub. John said, "I'm looking for a wheelwright named Bruce Wallace."

"I've worked here four years and don't know him. He must have worked here quite a few years ago. I hope you find your friend."

John thanked the young wright and joined Peter looking over a fence at colorful chickens in a yard. "Did he know Bruce?" Peter asked.

"No. Bruce retired 230 years ago — they didn't overlap. Where are the girls?"

"They stopped in to see the basket maker. Here they come now."

"Hi guys! Megan and I just learned something. Let's sit in the shade on Palace Green." Admiring the view of the Governor's Palace, they sat on a bench and Susan told them what she and Megan saw in the basket maker's workshop. "When I think of baskets, I think of thin materials like grasses or vines. But here they wove baskets from six-foot long white oak logs a foot in diameter."

Peter was puzzled. "They might be a bit hard to weave."

"That's what we thought," said Megan, "but they split the logs into long shafts and peeled off strips. They soak the strips and weave them into a strong basket."

"What did you learn from that?"

"They take something solid, and slice it down into thin strips that bend," said Susan. "When woven together, it's strong. Something we thought impossible, like weaving a basket from a log, can be done by seeing the form differently."

"Something impossible like travelling back in time?" asked Peter.

"Right! Everyone knows it's impossible to weave a log into a basket or to go back in time. But when the log is transformed, something unexpected can happen. I think there is a way we can do this."

"So do I," said Megan, "but that doesn't mean I know how, because I sure don't."

"Me neither," said Peter, "and I went back and forth a couple of times when we were here last month. So, how do we transform ourselves?"

"Last time, for a while we worried about being stuck in the past. Now, here we are feeling stuck in our own time," said Susan. "There could be a key in that."

John had a thought. "There's a place that never failed to shift time for me."

"Why didn't you say so, John?" asked Susan.

John led them to the St. George Tucker House where he signed in and took them to a comfortable parlor. They got a cold drink and relaxed in the stuffed chairs."

"So is this where you always had a time shift, Dad?" asked Megan.

"Yes and its working this time. Look around. When we were here last, every time I came in here I jumped right back into our time. And see, here we are again!"

Peter and Megan began to laugh. Looking at them, Susan broke out laughing. It was infectious and John could not keep a straight face. "What a relief to be back in our own time." Peter stifled his laughter then he and Megan erupted again.

"That's funny," Susan said, wiping her eyes. "A magic place that puts you right back in your own century without any effort at all! Just click the heels of the ruby slippers and we're back in Kansas again. There's no place like home!"

"Well," said her father taking a breath, "there's another thing I didn't tell you because I didn't want you to think I was completely crazy."

"We remember wandering around here in the eighteenth century," Peter smiled. "Most people would say we're all crazy, so your story is safe with us."

"When we were sitting beside this house among the hedges it appeared that just the four of us and Reverend Walker crossed from one time to another."

"That's true. What are you saying, Honey?"

"Six of us travelled in time. I first met Frances Tucker here in our time. She explained many things to me and I thought she was a docent. Then on our last day she led me out to the garden to talk with Bruce Wallace in May of 1776."

"So she slipped across time like we did? Do you think she's here now?"

"She moved in the other direction like Annie did with Peter. She was the widow of St. George Tucker; she moved to this house... after she died."

"She died? Then how..."

"I didn't know it at the time, but she was a ghost. I wouldn't have believed it except that when the meeting was over I stayed behind to say goodbye. She wanted me to know what she was, so she faded away as she glided into a hedge."

"Like going into the corn field in that movie?" Megan asked.

"Exactly like that!" They got quiet, wondering whether Frances would appear.

John closed his eyes and leaned back in the chair. He pictured Frances and recalled that he never saw her take a book from the shelf or move anything. She seemed to glide when she left the room. He thought at the time that she moved with the elegance of nobility. In contrast, he and his family had bodily experiences of the past. They had moved things and eaten the food. He had been in his first fight in twenty years. He recalled what Frances said about that fight...

"Did it really happen? You imagined it really happening."

"But you were there, too," he said to her.

"The imagination is not just for fantasy," she replied. "When we focus the imagination in a chosen direction, we can experience directly through the mind, skipping the physical senses."

John sat with that a moment before opening his eyes. "Listen, gang. We have identified several pieces of what it took for us to move through time. First, we completely let go, not by choice but through instinct when it seemed we were about to die. Then we used our imaginations to make the experiences more real. Next, we became more open—we could say more porous. I was unwilling to accept it, so naturally I was last to experience a shift. Finally, someone in the past was praying for or expecting someone—and in our open state, we responded to the call and experienced the past."

"Do you think we can do that again?" asked Peter.

"It was not anything we did. It was what we were willing to experience. I have an idea that there are two kinds of 'willing'—opposite meanings in the same word. When we are 'willing something to happen,' we are focused, working at it, determined to make it happen. But when we are 'willing *for* something to happen', we accept what happens and our acceptance shapes what happens like a mold shapes plaster. We allow it and welcome it like letting it flow into a valley rather than applying effort to force it up hill. I think we need both approaches in life."

"Sounds like masculine and feminine approaches, Honey. Are you saying there is nothing we can do to get back in time again?"

"It doesn't seem to be about 'doing', Susan. But if we let go, use our imaginations, become open and listen for the call, it will either happen or it won't."

"That definitive, huh? It will either happen or it won't?" asked Peter.

"And like last time, we won't know until it happens," said Megan.

Susan made a slow wave of her hand. "It could start subtly, like when I smelled tobacco in the meeting of the Burgesses, or suddenly and dramatically like when we woke up and our bathroom had been replaced by a stone hearth."

"Maybe all we'll get is a hint this time and not a full-on experience," said John.

"Speaking of a bathroom and kitchen, I could use both in that order," Megan said. "We travelled through time all morning and got to lunch time, Dad."

"Looks like we did. We can use the bathrooms here."

Susan had an idea. "The finest dining here is at the Williamsburg Inn which wasn't built in 1775. Since we're stuck in our time we might as well enjoy it."

"Great idea, Mom. Let's go."

"One more thing," said John. "Last month, every time I walked out of this house, I stepped into the past on the very same day I left it."

"It's worth a try."

They slowly opened the front door and stepped out of the St. George Tucker House. The aroma of wood smoke was in the air and the large open space across the street was filled with bivouacked British soldiers and camp followers.

"You see? It worked again," said John as he opened the gate at the end of the walk. "We went straight to the day we were in when we walked into the house."

"But this time we came in from our time," said Megan, then she got it and laughed. "Like you said, it works every time."

They wandered south to the Williamsburg Inn. The Regency Room was open only for dinner but the Terrace Room would begin serving lunch in ten minutes.

"I'm happy we came back," said Peter as they waited, "but I wish we could connect with our friends to learn if they made it through. They've been dead since long before our grandparents were born. It would be nice to know how it turned out for them. I hope they lived long and happy lives."

"We know the big outcomes, like thirteen of the British colonies in North America won a war of independence," said John. "We know George Washington managed to evade the large concentrations of British troops through the entire war and the breech-loading rifles are still missing. But we don't know how our friends fared during the many years of fighting the Revolution."

Day 5-3:   Lunch at the Williamsburg Inn

"Sinclair, table for four," called the Maitre d'. She led them to a table by a window. John pulled out a seat for Megan, giving her the best view.

Megan broke open a roll. "It is better around here now than it was in the eighteenth century. We have indoor plumbing and we ended slavery and indentured servitude, but many people still don't earn a living wage. We are still depleting our soil, fresh water, forests, and fisheries just as our ancestors did. After more than two centuries of democracy, we don't yet have fair elections without manipulation by those with money."

"Have you become a revolutionary, Megan?" asked John.

"I was leaning Loyalist until I learned their leaders were no more helpful to Indians, slaves, and settlers than many revolutionary plantation owners were. It bugs me that so long after the Revolution, most Americans don't know how big a role land profits played at the time."

"When people forever crave to increase their personal wealth, they can be willfully blind to the impact of their actions on others and on nature," said Susan.

"Our worth is not determined by our wealth," said Megan. "Needy people don't feel what they have is abundant or even sufficient, however much they have."

"Money in politics, corporate lobbying, and public relations often aims to increase the assets of those who are already rich. We need to increase honest and open democracy in our country," said Peter.

"Do you think public funding of elections would help, John? What about regulating truth in advertizing or sources of lobbying money?" Susan asked.

"It could help if we the people of the United States, pay attention to what is going on, learn how it affects us and the nation, and then decide what balance we want between personal freedom and prosperity on one hand and equity and the well being of the whole community on the other," said John.

The waiter placed a hearty soup and a salad in front of John and another server placed grilled salmon in front of Susan. Peter and Megan both had the crab cakes.

By the time they finished eating, the Terrace Room had diners at every table. Megan looked around. "Do you notice that we are the only ones in eighteenth century outfits? Even the wait staff is in modern dress."

"Strange—I feel out of place, as if I walked in from colonial times," Peter added.

"It's subtle, but I feel it, too," said John. "Check, please!"

Under an arch at the entrance of the Williamsburg Inn, Susan suggested, "I think we should go off on our own and find what we can about our friends in 1781. Where should we meet—and when?"

"In this case, 'when' is a funny question," said John. "Redcoats will be marching on the square today at 5. Let's meet near the gate of the Governor's Palace after the drill. It will be a short walk over the bridge to the car."

Day 5-4:   Susan in the Light

Susan sat near the Public Hospital, on the same bench where she was with Jane long ago. She relaxed, took a long breath, and imagined Jane beside her. A rustling noise brought her right back and there was the squirrel again. She laughed. It was a happy distraction.

She slipped into silence, open and lightly scanning for subtle impressions. She heard or sensed, "Susan, I sense thy nearness. It gives me comfort."

I hear you, dear Jane, thought Susan. She felt a sparkle like laughter and heard Jane's voice, "That squirrel is such a happy distraction."

Susan looked at the squirrel, surprised. Yes, she is. How are you Jane?

"Well, thanks to thee. John and I talk about what we learn from Annie."

John? Susan felt a sudden blush and knew the feeling was coming from Jane.

"Doctor John de Sequeyra," said Jane. "Neither of us is lonely any longer."

Jane, that is wonderful! No need to feel embarrassed — I felt you blush.

"We are close as sisters."

Jane, in the light, we *are* sisters. What has Annie taught you?

"I see the Paxton Boys who massacred us acted on fear and rage from their own wounds. I am learning how the circle turns. How art thou?"

Feeling as if I am finding something I have looked for a long time. Did you meet George Washington?

"I met the General. I wore the beautiful dress thou gave me. He encouraged me to circulate among German prisoners and later in the Hessian's camps. When I was successful, we asked other German speakers to do the same. Hundreds chose to change sides for the promise of getting a homestead in this country. It worked so well we made the same offer to captured Redcoats."

You are a courageous woman, Jane.

"'Tis getting late. John has invited me to a reception tomorrow in Richmond. It will be the first time we present ourselves in public as a couple."

I am very happy for you both. I will reach out to you when I sit in silence. It may not always work so well. I am sitting on the bench where we sat together.

"I am on the same bench. I hear you, Susan, but when I open my eyes to look to the place where thou sat five years ago, I see thee not."

I am speaking from a time not yet come to you. Perhaps it will not happen again.

"I fervently pray it does."

I do as well. Goodbye Jane.

"Fare thee well, Sister Susan."

The squirrel raced to a shrub behind the bench. Susan smiled and closed her eyes to slip back into the silence to listen for guidance for her life journey.

5-5:   Annie, Evie and Her Boys

Peter closed his eyes and thought of Annie. What had she said when he went out looking for her one evening and found her sitting by the road?

"We found each other by me feeling where you was comin' from and you feelin' where I was waitin'."

"I didn't notice I was feeling where you were waiting," he had admitted.

"Then you wasn't paying attention to what you was feeling."

This time, Peter did notice a subtle feeling. He cleared his mind and an image of a quiet shady spot near a zigzag worm fence came to him. He walked slowly past Christiana Campbell's Tavern looking between the houses as he went. "I have a vague sense that something is present but hidden," he said to himself. "I'm looking and someone is waiting."

He paused and turned up a lane between the tavern and the Powell House. A street sign said Lafayette Street, but this lane was a long curved driveway to a parking lot. A busy parkway called Lafayette Street bordered the Historic District just beyond these pastures. This shady lane was a remembrance, an echo of an ancient street. He stopped to look over the fence into the garden of the Powell House where he had gasped at seeing Evie in May 1775. A few visitors wandered in the garden.

"Not here, but near." He walked past a garden shed. On his left, a solid white board fence penned a few sheep behind the Powell House garden. By the curve in the lane, an aged worm fence stretched off under the trees. Between him and the pasture was an unpainted gate. Looking around to be sure he was unseen, Peter opened the gate and stepped through, closing it behind him. A faint shift occurred in the tension that pulled him forward.

He turned toward the worm fence and closed his eyes. "Over the fence," he heard. He ran to the fence at an angle, placed one foot halfway up the sloping rail wedged between the ground and an end post, and vaulted into the next pasture. The murmur of female voices blended into the hum of other sounds — the insects, the birds. He climbed the steps of a style over the next fence and stood at the top.

Laughter came from behind an ancient tree. "I ain't laughin' at you. I'se laughin' at how many ways Mister Peter is goin' through and over fences to get here."

"Mister Peter is coming?"

"Annie? Evie?" Peter came around the large oak and they stood to greet him. Evie hugged him and Annie put her big arms around both of them.

"Right on time, Mister Peter," Annie said.

"I'm so happy to see you ladies again."

"You see, Annie. He calls us Ladies. I is poor African folk, not even free, and he calls us Ladies like we was better-sorts women." Evie turned to Peter. "Oh, Mister Peter, where have you been so long?"

"Evie, I had to come a long way to be here this afternoon."

"That's true enough, Mister Peter. You walked around town all day to get here."

"You could feel me coming, couldn't you, Annie?"

"I knew you would be gone a long time, Mister Peter, but I knew you was comin' back. And today I felt you when I sat behind the fence near the Brickyard."

"You were *behind* the fence? You smiled at me."

"And you smiled right back. You felt me, didn't you? It was about mid-morning. Now go ahead and tell Evie what you came so far to tell her."

Peter took Evie's hand, "I'm very glad to see you, Evie, and relieved to know you are well. How are James and Dilli?"

"The war been hard. Sometimes we ain't had much to eat. Massa Powell was rentin' the boys out to work. I worry he be ready to sell them away but when the British was comin' here, the Powells is gone to Richmond. Maybe the Redcoats or militias gonna grab my boys to be soldiers. I told them they daddies was brave and fought for freedom but now they is ready to fight for our freedom, too. But I tell them those English left African soldiers behind when they sailed away. If you fight, you is goin' to hurt people and be hurt.

"I want my boys to grow up free," Evie continued, "but the only home I knows and the only folks I knows is right here in the British Colony of Virginia."

"It won't be British much longer." Peter stopped himself but Annie noticed.

"My boys heard Redcoats is working on a dock at Yorktown and feedin' folk who help build it. They want to get work there then take a ship to England."

"Evie, they should not go to Yorktown. A ship is a good idea, but there may be too much fighting there. The French navy may be coming that way..."

Annie interrupted. "Evie, bring our two watchmen to say hello to Mister Peter,"

"The watchmen? Oh, yes! I will fetch them."

As Evie walked away, Annie said in a low voice, "Mister Peter, I have a bad feelin' about Yorktown too, and there be things I want to tell you quick. The folk who met your family in the hedges all doin' good. Mark Smith warned Governor Jefferson before General Benedict Arnold attacked Richmond early this year. Jefferson got away. After Arnold went north, Bruce Wallace learned the British is makin' the port at Yorktown bigger cause troops comin' from New York. Now why Yorktown be a bad idea for Evie and the boys?"

"Annie, I'll tell you straight out. Hundreds of Africans in Yorktown working for the British forces will be trapped. The British, short of supplies, will drive the Africans outside the stockade where most will be slaughtered by American and French artillery or die from hunger. It will be a greater horror than what we saw at Norfolk. New York may be a place to go because a few thousand Africans will sail from there to England but at the end there will be panic to get on ships and many will be left behind. The best chance is to get all the way to Halifax in Nova Scotia, or England. If they can't get there, they should go to towns in New England, far north of New York City. The future looks grim for Africans in the South."

"I feel great pain comin', Mister Peter. The British pretend to help, but win or lose they forget about Africans. You say Halifax? Oh, here they come."

Evie rounded the corner of the fence with two young men. Peter thought the 'watchmen' would be Robert and Claudius, but these men were too young and thin. One walked with an irregular step partially overcoming a bad limp he had since childhood. Peter hugged them. "James! Dilli! You guys got so big!"

"James fourteen now, Mister Peter, and I'se comin' to twelve. I knew you would come back some day." Dilli was bright and animated.

Peter turned to Evie. "Five years."

"Yes, Mister Peter, they is almost men now."

Annie said, "Sit down here everyone. Mister Peter come wit' things to say."

"Well," Peter began, "I heard you boys are ready to go to freedom like we tried five years ago when we went to Jamestown in the wagon. Is that right?"

"Yes, Mister Peter. I still got the drawing I made of the freedom sky we saw through the green leaves from Annie's wagon. It be on the wall in the loft above the kitchen."

"Mister Peter. We's ready to go." James was less shy than he had been at eight.

"It's a good idea. But like last time, you have to be awake to notice which way the hoop is rolling. Many folks are going to Yorktown but the wind may blow British ships or French ships into the Chesapeake. There could be a raging battle and you would not want to be standing there in your bare feet."

"Where you gonna take us if Yorktown be dangerous, Mister Peter?" asked Dilli.

Peter hesitated and Annie stepped in. "Mister Peter ain't goin' this time, Dilli. If you decide to go, my wagon sittin' in the lane wit' someone ready to drive the horses. Someone else goin' who can get on a ship wit' you and help you. Then he goin' much farther on, a very long way. Now we need to hear Mister Peter say what he think 'bout where the best place to go is."

"Well, you could cross the Bay to Maryland and look for ships unloading at the docks of loyal plantations. Do you have money for your passage somewhere to the North?"

"No, we don't," said Evie.

"We will put money in your hand if you get on the wagon, child," said Annie.

"Annie! You don't need to..."

"Hush. Mister Peter been studyin' since we seen him last. He know what to do."

"Do you have papers that explain who you are and where you're going that will work whether the Continentals or the British stop you?" Peter asked.

"We ain't got no papers."

Annie spoke again, "If you get in that wagon, I'se gonna give you these here three perfect passes on fine linen paper makin' you all look important, which you all is. One pass is to show the British. One is for the American militias, and one is for when you don't know who you talkin' to."

"Evie and boys, I have a feeling this is a big day for you. I told Annie that New York or New Jersey could be good places to go for a while. Better would be Nova Scotia, over the river into Quebec, or across the ocean to England. There are no slaves in England, and I have a hunch there will be none in the northern colonies soon. Whatever happens, do not get on a ship sailing to the Caribbean — no ship to Jamaica, Barbados, or other island colony. It doesn't matter if the ship captain is English, American, or Dutch. They will sell you back into slavery in the sugar cane fields where life is short and much worse than the lives you have now. Do not go south to the Floridas even though the Spanish fleet has taken them back."

"Why not, Mister Peter?" asked James.

"Because when the Americans win, I mean if the Americans defeat the British, they will get Florida back from Spain and could recapture runaways."

Evie and the boys looked alarmed. "Besides, in Florida they don't have the same freedom trees you saw from the wagon. I think you should go where you can see those trees, don't you?" The mood brightened noticeably.

"Even after you get away, be careful. The Northern colonies, should they make slavery illegal in a few years, might still agree to return runaways to their owners. Farther north is better. Nova Scotia is safe and not as cold as Quebec."

Annie was sitting pensively. "I know a man named David George. He preaches down in Charles Town, which like here has British troops all over."

"Charleston, South Carolina?"

"It be called Charles Town these days, Peter. Now let me finish. Things gonna be 'zackly the way they gonna be."

"But we can do something about it, can't we?" asked Peter.

"You can't not do somethin'! We is all part of the *it* you talkin' about. What you do today is part of what gonna make it be like it will be tomorrow."

Suddenly that became clear for Peter.

"Now David George run away and been caught so many times he got good at both!" Annie laughed. "He is free again and plannin' to stay free by sailin' to Halifax later this year. Evie, if you get there seek out David George. There will be enough of your folk you won't feel alone."

"Will you be goin', Annie?"

Annie sighed. "Many folk 'round here troubled and weary wit' hurts and lacks. So I gonna wander these parts as long as the Lord let me do what I can to help the captive peoples and bring comfort."

"Mister Peter, will we see you when we go?" asked Dilli. "You live up North."

"I'd love to see you again, Dilli. I will think about you guys for the rest of my life. I live far from where you guys are going so we will say goodbye when you get on the wagon. At least, I hope you get on the wagon."

"We is goin', ain't we Mama? I can run to pee and get my things," said Dilli.

"Evie, watching you leave will make me sad, but knowing you and the boys can find a new life in freedom fills me with a deep happiness."

"This happenin' so fast I'se dizzy," said Evie. "Does we have to choose now?"

"The wagon is sittin' in the lane right now," said Annie. "So you got to decide. When the wagon leaves, it will be gone and another chance may be a long time comin'. Mister Peter come here to help you get on the road to freedom."

"That's right, Evie."

"Come on, Mama, it be time for Dilli and me to grow up to be free men."

"You right, James, of course you right. Oh, sweet Jesus! I pray we gonna make it. Fetch your things, boys. Put them in a pillowcase and get in the wagon. Remember your picture of the freedom sky, Dilli." The boys ran to get their few belongings.

"Just like when we went down that road to Jamestown, Evie, the moment you make that choice, you're already free," said Peter.

"I feel scared, but I'se ready. I got to get my clothes." Evie hurried inside.

The conversation was short and the decision sudden after years of waiting. Peter would never see Evie or her boys again. He felt sadness but profound satisfaction to be part of something that would change the lives of a family forever.

Annie leaned on the fence smiling at him. "It ain't easy havin' love for people in your heart. Sometimes what feels like a broken heart is a heart breakin' open. There be so much space in an open heart it can feel empty. But light shine through that open space, Peter. It ain't empty. Wherever you go, light shine on you and through you when you let it. You won't never lose that, Peter. Let's go to the wagon."

"Annie, you opened up something deep that I never thought about before. I would like a deeper faith in Spirit, but many people who say they are religious in my time are intolerant, narrow, or opinionated. Those folks are not filled with love and don't have light shining from them like you do."

"It wasn't me who opened you, Peter. It was you openin' to the movin' Spirit, or the Light, or the Lord, whatever name you use. I know many folk who speak about heaven don't yet know where it is or what it feel like. But holdin' so tight to they religion help them be less afraid, and bit by bit, light will dawn in they hearts. You do more good by helpin' them than by fightin' them. They fight each other about which religion be true and they don't look around to see the real, right now, right here, love and light their religions reflectin' like a mirror.

"From Creation to Revelations and all the parables in between, the stories ain't 'bout something beautiful that happened five thousand or two thousand years ago, or some glorious time that ain't come yet. You is beginnin' to inkle that all them stories be 'bout what always is and always was and always will be, everywhere and every when. The wheel wit'in the wheel and the fire wit'in the fire never stopped after Ezekiel saw them. They turnin' and burnin' right now. It takes time to open our eyes, ears, and heart to see and hear and feel. You know more about this than most folks, Peter. You will keep on travelin' on your journey."

They walked in silence as Peter let the essence of Annie's message find a home in him. He would practice its embodiment until the end of his days.

"You been gone five years and you still the same age. How much time done passed in your time between when you left and when you came back?"

"Five weeks."

"You done lived five weeks and we done lived five years. I gots to learn more about time. Maybe I can visit you in your time again someday, Peter."

"You will be most welcome, Annie. Meanwhile we can feel each other in the space between the sun and its warmth on our faces."

"We will." Annie gave Peter a kindhearted smile.

They approached the wagon and there was Robert holding the reins. "Hello, Mister Peter. I'se happy to see you. Look who we got here."

Samuel Abdul Latif climbed out of the wagon and put a hand over his heart. "Thank you for being here to wish us well on our journey, Mister Peter. I pray that by the help of God your family will be blessed for all time."

"Thank you. It warms my heart to see you, Sal. Are you going north?"

"Doctor de Sequeyra gave me my freedom five years ago and last week surprised me with money to help me on this journey. Annie taught me to remember who I am and who we all are. Today I set out on a road that I pray will take me north to a place where I can help this wonderful family and others place roots in freedom. Then, in God's time, I will find my way to England to help former slaves seeking refuge there. In a few years, if it is God's will, I shall sail to the British territory on the Gambia River and travel into the interior all the way to Timbuktu. I am beginning my long journey home, Mister Peter."

"This takes courage, Sal, and a big heart to help so many along the way. I will think of you often. *In sha'Allah,* you will tell stories of your time here to young people in Africa. We need bridges among peoples of this world — bridges like you."

Samuel Abdul Latif smiled. "I will tell them about Annie and Doctor de Sequeyra, about Robert and Claudius, about the memory of Augustus and Aaron, and about you and your family, Peter Sinclair. Thank you for helping us all."

A sudden commotion erupted as Dilli and James came bumping through the side gate with Evie close behind, each carrying a pillowcase filled with their meager belongings. Evie carried a bag of food Rosie the old cook had hurriedly packed for them. Rosie limped out leaning on her walking stick to watch them leave. She had tears in her eyes, tears of empathetic joy that Evie and the boys she had known their whole lives were leaving to seek a freedom she herself would never know.

The boys climbed into the wagon with a hand from Sal.

Dilli reached out with a piece of paper in his hand. "Here, Mister Peter. It's a present for you." Peter turned the paper over and saw a drawing of white clouds against a light blue sky seen through a lace pattern of branches, spring-green leaves sprouting everywhere. The Powell girls had seen the pencil sketch and shared their watercolors so Dilli could finish it. They had showed him how to print the words "Freedom Sky," at the top of the drawing.

"This is beautiful, Dilli. Don't you want to take it along with you?"

"We gonna see the freedom sky for ourselves. I can make another picture like it when we get there. I want you to have this one, so we have the same picture and think of each other."

"Thank you, Dilli. I am moved by this gift. You are going to be free and will make another picture."

Annie handed the passes to Evie who put them in the pillowcase and placed her things in the wagon next to the boys. She looked at Peter.

"Come with me, Evie." He led her through the gate to the porch where they first spoke.

"Peter..." Evie looked into his eyes. "There will be thanks driftin' to you through the mist from wherever we end up, for the courage you gave me to take this step." She took his hand. "And prayers will shine upon you from my spot in Heaven when I is gone, for how you helped me find a path to freedom inside my soul. When me and the boys is on that ship, I gonna look for that water dipper in the sky and the North Star you told me about. The boys gonna teach their grandchildren about the pointer stars like your grandfather taught you."

Peter nodded. He took her hand in both his hands and pressed. They both would remember that moment, Peter more than he could now imagine. Evie held the steady gaze he saw on the porch long ago. "It still feels like you is family."

Evie returned to the wagon "All righty, boys, let's say goodbye and get movin' before Robert leaves us here pickin' vegetables. We gonna get our own garden."

"Don't stop at New York or New Jersey for longer than you must," said Peter

"I got to learn to read," said Evie. "The things you learn in them books spins my head around to face another way. God be with you, Peter."

"May you and your family be blessed, Evie," Peter said.

Peter, Annie, and Rosie watched Robert urge the horses out of the lane onto the street as Evie, Dilli, James, and Samuel Abdul Latif waved goodbye. Dilli, laughing brightly, threw a smooth stick into the air, which turned end-over-end as it arched up and back down to where Peter stood.

He caught it and in that instant Peter was standing alone in the lane as the sound of Dilli's enchanting laughter faded away into antiquity. Annie, Rosie, and the wagon were suddenly gone. He drew a long breath, carefully wrapped the picture of the Freedom Sky around the stick, and walked through the Historic District to meet his family.

5-6:   John Meets the Redcoats

John watched his family walk together to Francis Street where they hugged. Susan went to the left toward the Public Hospital, Peter headed east on Francis Street, and Megan walked straight to Duke of Gloucester Street. I'm a lucky man, he thought. I hope they find what they're looking for. Now, where do I find Bruce?

He decided to walk to the Capitol where he first saw Bruce Wallace leaning on a post. He found a small military encampment manned by Redcoat reenactors. They had just finished a demonstration of loading a Brown Bess musket.

"Good morning. How goes the war?" John asked.

"The war is going well, if any war could be said to be going well," the older reenactor said. Philadelphia was seized and the Continental Congress fled to Baltimore to hold its meetings. Williamsburg, Charles Town, Savanna, and New York are in British hands. General Benedict Arnold ended his treason against the Crown. He sacked Richmond, the new capital of Virginia, back in January. Governor Jefferson unfortunately escaped capture."

The younger Redcoat intervened. "I am uncomfortable when we burn a town, ruining innocent lives. Cornwallis is cleaning up the South but Clinton fattens his fanny sitting in New York and has not finished Washington up the Hudson nor engaged the Comte de Rochambeau's French troops in Rhode Island. Many in Parliament did not want to send troops and some generals offered command of this campaign declined. Some commanders here perform poorly. Clinton is not the first to enjoy soirées in the towns as rebels hold the countryside."

The older Redcoat got excited. "Finally, the rebels are hungry to end this nonsense, and we shall all go home soon."

The younger man had another idea. "We have been promised land for our service to His Majesty. If many stay, there will be less chance of future rebellion."

"You guys know your history," said John. "Stay safe through the war."

John strolled past the post where Bruce was standing the first time they met by the Capitol and approached Shields Tavern where they had a long talk. He heard singing inside. The melody was unmistakably the *Star Spangled Banner*. He swung open the door and entered the tavern, dark, smoky, and full of off-duty Redcoats, jackets hanging over the backs of their chairs. Why were they singing *The Star Spangled Banner*, not written until the War of 1812? He listened to the words.

> *To Anacreon in Heaven, where he sat in full glee,*
> *A few Sons of Harmony sent a petition*
> *that he their Inspirer and Patron would be,*
> *When this answer arrived from the Jolly Old Grecian:*
> *"Voice, Fiddle, and Flute, No longer be mute,*
> *I'll lend you my name and inspire you to boot,*
> *and besides I'll instruct you like me, to entwine,*
> *The Myrtle of Venus with Bacchus's Vine!"*

When the song ended, a sergeant stood and raised his glass, "God Save the King!" The whole assemblage was on its feet shouting the toast.

A soldier grabbed John's elbow and said, "Don't gape as if you were gazing at ghosts, man. If you have no better offer, please join me."

"Thank you," responded John. "May I buy us both a beer?"

"I took you for a gentleman. This confirms it."

"What song were the men singing?"

"Have you not heard it before? *Anacreon in Heaven* is a popular drinking song published in London three years ago. The tune is complicated and most people have trouble singing it."

John smiled. Most people still had trouble singing the melody of that old English drinking song when they sang the American national anthem. "To your health and long life!" he said and they clinked glasses.

"Now there is a toast I can join without smirking," said the soldier.

"How would you say the war is going?"

"Sir, I can say His Majesty's forces are winning in spite of bad leadership."

"Why are you willing to share that thought with a perfect stranger?"

"I agree you may be strange but I doubt you are perfect."

"Are you committed to this fight?"

"What are we fighting for? The revolutionaries here speak of rights most Englishmen do not have. The English gentry seized the Scottish highlands and enclosed the common land for their private use, driving tens of thousands into exile or poverty in the growing cities where they must sell their labor cheaply to survive. The success of this expulsion is leading the great and greedy families of England to enclose and make private millions of acres in England as well. This will drive many more to flee here or to other colonies in the new worlds.

"That disease of many people, to covet ever more land and wealth for their private benefit, infects leaders on this continent as well. I do not say powerful people are more avaricious than a chimney sweep or fishmonger. They are just more cunning at grabbing what they are greedy for. The big landowners here plan to seize vast lands from the Indians. Those men abhor the ideas of the levelers as much as the King does. John Adams does not like what he calls the 'notions of Southern gentlemen' and their reluctance to agree on a republican form of government. Some woodenheads even proposed Washington become king. They don't know a better way."

The soldier lowered his voice. "Perhaps I should fight for the people against both the self-declared aristocracies of the colonies and the German potentate of Britain and the land-stealing so-called nobility at home."

"Perhaps," said John, "although I expect the manipulation of ordinary people who are uninformed about the maintenance of power and wealth will continue for generations to come."

"I agree, Sir. Fog is created by leaders to obscure their true motives and benefits, and the people's indolence prolongs their ignorance. Now that we find ourselves in agreement, I am waiting for you to say what brings you to a smoky tavern on a sunny day."

"I'm looking for Bruce Wallace, a Scottish wheelwright. Do you know him?"

"Aha! It *is* you. Bruce Wallace said if I met a man named John wearing unusual apparel mingled with normal garb, I could trust him. Wallace is no longer a wheelwright but an aide to General Lord Charles Cornwallis! I am a messenger on the General's staff. I tipped many a glass with Wallace after I saved his life at the Battle of Cowpens."

John was surprised but said, "My name is not John. It's Roger."

The soldier almost choked on his beer. "That is funny, Sir. Wallace told me that you are the man who subdued Roger and his dagger in a tavern on the Jamestown Road. I had a few pints with Wallace there one night and he showed me the blade embedded in the beam. He said Roger was shot dead soon after by a one-eyed man he harmed the year before."

"I'll be damned. Do you know where Wallace is now?"

"Cornwallis sent him to negotiate peace with Lafayette who is harassing the British near Richmond. That negotiation was unsuccessful of course. From there he went north to inform Washington. You and I just met," said the soldier, "and we've already said enough to be court-martialed."

"We'll swear we were drinking to the health of the King and Lord Cornwallis."

"Yes, and it would be an irrefutable truth with forty witnesses." The Redcoat stood and raised his glass. "To the health of the King and Lord Cornwallis!" The men in the room stood and echoed the toast.

"Sheep," the soldier murmured. "Most likely Wallace shall be back in a day or two. Where shall I tell him to find you?"

"I'll be leaving later today. In case I miss him, I have a message that may benefit you as well. Neither of you should go to Yorktown. If your regiment moves there, get sick, or take a long walk and change your coat along the way."

"Understood."

"Good," said John. "I must try to find Wallace. Keep your head attached."

"Thank you, and may they always miss when they shoot at you."

John stepped out of the tavern and walked to Palace Green. He was concerned the timing was off and he might not find Bruce Wallace even though he had found his way into the past.

5-7: Megan Sends a Signal

Megan had an idea. If I sit in the lane next to Mark's hut where we looked up at the trees that evening, maybe I can connect with Mark or Standing Elk. She crossed the yard and slipped through the back gate. The weight of the cannonball on a chain pulled the gate closed behind her. No dogs barked and no brood sow grunted. Instead, a squirrel chirruped a warning of her approach.

The layout was different from what she remembered. The huts were gone as was the large hedge, replaced by a fence that shielded a private driveway from view. Megan paced off to where she remembered Mark's lean-to had been and looked around for something to sit on. The nearest place was a wide stump. She sat and repeated to herself the steps her father had talked about. Relax and let go; use my imagination; be open, and listen for someone calling me.

She listened to the sound of her breath and the gentle wind in the trees. She remembered the paths of fireflies and visualized them again. The paths had been invisible in the dark except for the momentary points of light, but as a pattern emerged she saw that the fireflies' motion was not random like dust particles in a sunbeam. They approached and related to each other along those invisible paths.

Who is approaching me? Megan wondered. How do I flash a light so my invisible path can be known to another? What is the signal?

She sat in silence. Her thoughts calmed as she gradually became aware of the open space in her mind through which thoughts come and fade away. "The space between the firefly flashes, the space between the leaves, the space between the stars, the space between my thoughts..." Megan was calm and attentive.

She looked up to the pattern in the branches above her. It had changed in 230 years. Mark's lean-to had been over there against a fence. We were sitting twenty feet from here, looking up this way at...

Suddenly a thought flashed like a flare bursting in her mind. Right here was the tree with the fireflies! I'm sitting on it! She noticed sawdust around the stump of the tree. It had been cut down recently. It grew for over two centuries to become so big around. This is part of the pattern; another twinkle on the path of time we saw that night, thought Megan.

Dragonflies hovered and cruised across the open spaces. They had seemed mystical to Megan since she was a child. She was grateful when she learned they could eat their weight in mosquitoes in an hour. They have cruised here for two hundred million years, a million years for each year we went back in time.

She closed her eyes to scan the sounds. What did a dragonfly sound like? She heard whispering leaves, a hymn from bees on pilgrims' rounds to flowers behind her, the high-pitched whine of a mosquito near her ear. She was about to brush the mosquito away but hesitated. The whine was cut short by a buzz of whirring wings and a whoosh. Her exhalations of carbon dioxide had attracted the mosquito and a great blue skimmer dragonfly swooped past her head to swallow the mosquito on the wing. This is the pattern too, mosquitoes, dragonflies—all of us. Standing Elk said we turn and turn into what we are becoming.

Megan listened to the soundscape again—the breeze rising and falling away, her breathing in and out, the call of a blue jay in a nearby tree, hooves on a hard packed road, the distant responding cry of a second blue jay, the crunch of footfalls on a path, the scolding of a squirrel to warn others of an approach. Someone is coming, Megan thought. I'll close my eyes and let the person pass. A moment later a thought entered her mind as the quiet footfalls drew closer. "Could it be? I know the sound of those steps!"

The footfalls drew close and stopped. "Hello, Standing Elk," Megan said without opening her eyes.

"Hello, Megan. I was riding on Francis Street when I felt a flash of light. I asked Creator what it was and a line of dragonflies flew past me down this path. I hitched my horse to a post and walked in slowly, feeling the sacred. Where are the huts and Mark's old lean-to?"

"I've been waiting for you, Standing Elk." Megan opened her eyes. "I was also surprised to see the huts gone. I want to know how your people are and what happened to Mark."

Standing Elk drew a long breath and exhaled. "It is hard to tell you how much joy I feel to see you, so I won't try. Miigwech, Megan, I am grateful."

"I was praying we would connect."

"Megan, Mark has enjoyed five years of freedom and saved many lives including that of General Washington. If he survives the war, he will receive more land for his services than he ever imagined owning. He told me he will share land with my people. Every woman and man can learn from Mark's generosity. My peoples, the Pamunkey and the Mattaponi, are surviving through this terrible war and we are seen as friendly by all sides. We heal their wounded and sick. We help them gather and hunt when we find them hungry. Sadly, war has devastated larger tribes to the north and west. Many entered the war on the American or British sides in the hope of benefit. The costs have been high and the benefits few. Fighting is not the way to prosper. The path of victory is the path of peace."

"It's not easy to point that out in a way warriors or nations can see or hear, is it?"

"You are wise for your age, Megan."

"Only when I calm down and pay attention, Standing Elk."

"Practice that each day and you shall be a wise old crone some day."

"Thank you, I think. Is Mark still at the forge for George Washington's army?"

"No longer. The messages he brought to Washington made him a valuable aide-de-camp to the general. When the Marquis de Lafayette came south to defend Richmond, Washington sent Mark to keep Lafayette informed."

"Mark is nearby? In Richmond?"

"Not far but a hard journey. This area is thick with Redcoats, and Richmond is back in American hands again. The lands between are filled with raiding parties and sharpshooters seeking to damage the other side. They are nervous and do not ask questions before firing."

"Is Mark safe?"

"He is not in combat, but we would not want the British to catch him as an agent. So far, that has not happened to any of us." Megan was about to ask another question when a low hum could be heard far away but getting louder. They paused and looked up. "What is that sound?" asked Standing Elk.

"It's just a plane flying over." Megan froze. Standing Elk had walked down the path into her time responding to her call rather than the other way around.

They looked up as the sound got louder and watched the twin engine Piper Seminole move slowly, high above the trees. "Is that a wagon that flies? Who has such a thing?"

Megan decided to tell him. "They are all over the world, Standing Elk, flying carriages called airplanes. Some little ones are named after Indian tribes like the Seneca and the Cherokee. Big ones have numbers like 747 and carry more people than a sailing ship. I flew on one of those all the way to London in seven hours."

Standing Elk sat on the ground next to Megan listening to the sound of the plane fading away in the distance. "Can you tell me what is happening, Megan? This is big medicine I am feeling."

"When you felt me calling you, you hitched your horse and walked down a sacred path into your future. The big medicine is yours. You have a clear mind."

"Is this something you know how to do, Megan, to walk into this future?"

"No, I have never walked into the future. I live in this time. When we met five years ago, I had slipped into your time, which is in my past. I would not tell this to everyone, Standing Elk, but I know if I can handle it, so can you."

"How can this be?"

"I don't know, Standing Elk, but it is good that you and I found a way to be connected across time. Look around. Mark's hut was right over there, and this stump you are sitting next to getting sawdust on your deerskin pants is the exact tree where we watched the patterns of the fireflies. It grew for over two hundred years to become a giant, and judging from the fresh sawdust and dry bubbles of sap on the outer rings of the stump, it was cut down in the last few weeks. And look up. The dragonflies that led you here are sailing through the air as they have since long before they came into the dreams of our ancestors." Megan pointed.

Standing Elk looked around at the trees, at the giant stump, at the fence, at the open lawn where the huts and lean-tos stood chockablock against each other when he rode by this very morning, and he looked at Megan for a long time. She looked back smiling and watched his eyes change slowly from confusion to recognition to sparkling mischief.

269

"You are not older," he said slowly. "It is five years since you left, and you have not aged."

"I am five weeks older," she said. "And this is 1781, five years after when we first met."

"But it is not 1781 here with you. More than two centuries have passed, judging by the girth of this stump. Megan, you are the most youthful wise old crone I have ever seen!"

They laughed.

"Can you answer some questions, Megan?"

"Yes, I may be able to do that. Britain and America have been at peace for a long time and are good friends and allies. Neither country has fought a war against the French nor Spanish since long before my grandparents were born. The Pamunkey and Mattaponi peoples still live nearby, and my family is well and happy."

They looked at each other and laughed again.

"Am I stuck with you forever, Megan?"

"Well," said Megan, "we'll be blessed with memories of each other for the rest of our lives. If my experience is any guide, when you walk out that path you will find your horse waiting for you by the fence in June of 1781. I have some questions."

"My family is well. I have three grandchildren now. I was on my way to find Bruce Wallace. We expect he is carrying important news. Mark may try to get through the British pickets to meet him as well. Finally, my horse's name is Powerful Spirit. I named her after you, Megan."

Megan smiled.

"Megan, I will sit and pray about the wonder of this in many Spirit Lodges. My duty is calling me and I must go quickly to find Bruce as soon as he arrives. These are difficult times and we hope the news he carries is good. Can we meet tomorrow for a long talk?"

"I must go home with my family today, so I doubt we will see each other again. Now you know my time is in your future. You can tell your people to take heart. They will endure."

"I know you have knowledge, and I am encouraged by your words."

They both stood and Megan hugged him. "Goodbye, Grandfather."

"Goodbye, granddaughter. Please give my thanks to your family."

Megan watched Standing Elk walk out of the clearing along the path. When he was out of sight, she looked up at the dragonflies and closed her eyes again. She listened to the insect drones and chirps, to the sound of Powerful Spirit's hooves fading away on the dirt road, and to the spaces between the sounds.

5-8:   The British Grenadiers March

The drums began crisply as people gathered to watch the drill. "Prrr-ratz, Prrr-ratz, Prrr-rat-tata-tatz." The regimental sergeant major's shouted order was clear above the drums: "Quick, march!" Rank after rank of Redcoats stepped forward in unison marching from the Powder Magazine toward the Governor's Palace. To a man, the regiment displayed practiced discipline, determination, and confidence.

The fifes began the stirring melody of *The British Grenadiers March*. The familiar, stirring tune was written long before the British marched to victory in the Seven Years' War. It was played on parade to impress citizens and inspire young men to enlist. More, it served in battle to support discipline and focus as blocks of infantry advanced under fire, returning fire only when ordered.

Peter stood on a slight rise and scanned for his family in the crowd. He spotted his father on the other side of Palace Green. He waved, but John did not respond.

John studied the tight formation. He imagined the ranks marching toward lines of infantry ranged against them. The soldiers would follow the rhythm of the drums and fifes, maintaining formation and pace in the midst of chaos. Volleys of musket and cannon fire would cut down soldiers dead or screaming. As they fell, men in the next rank would step over them and run forward into the empty spots, replaced in their rank by men behind them. Casualties would be high against a well-trained foe, but the British infantry remained disciplined and deadly.

John looked up and down the crowd but did not see Bruce Wallace. Three senior officers in elegant uniforms and powdered wigs stepped onto the small balcony of the Palace to review the infantry as they reached the gates. The one in the centre was General Cornwallis, but John did not recognize the others.

Peter got the impression his father across Palace Green was experiencing the past. He saw his mother wave from near the Palace gates. That left only Megan unaccounted for. He returned his gaze to the Redcoats.

As the first rank reached the gate of the Palace, the sergeant major shouted, "Regiment, halt!" With one last repeat of the drum pattern, the Redcoats stood at attention in straight ranks and perfect files with no need to dress the lines. They were part of the world's best professional army in 1781.

Lord Cornwallis stepped to the railing. "The long war to subdue the rebellion shall soon end. Your discipline and vigor will bring that long-awaited outcome. On behalf of the King, thank you for your contributions to return these colonies to their rightful place in the British Empire. There have been skirmishes nearby and enemy agents may try to infiltrate to gather intelligence on our numbers, positions, and plans. They seek to spread disaffection among the citizenry. Therefore, for your protection, and to ensure the success of our arms, I declare Williamsburg to be under martial law. All residents must secure themselves in their homes by the setting of the sun every day until this order is rescinded or be arrested by His Majesty's forces. It will soon rain, so please hasten home to be warm and dry."

There was a ripple of concern through the crowd and silence among the soldiers, who wondered whether this indicated the arrival of a serious military threat. Cornwallis sensed the mood. "I assure you that this temporary measure is taken for your protection. Our pickets effectively repel attempts to cross our lines. Tell your friends of the precision of British forces you witnessed on parade and advise them not to fear the rebels. Colonel, instruct the sergeant major to put the infantry at ease. I ask the citizens to disperse now. In a few minutes our soldiers shall escort any people remaining on the streets back to their homes."

"We've got to get out of here," thought Peter as he made his way to the Palace.

John moved to the southern end of Palace Green as a misty drizzle began. Moving into the haze from the British cooking fires, he spotted Bruce Wallace by a white picket fence. He had watched the Redcoats drill from a distance.

"I heard from Standing Elk that your family returned," Bruce said. "Over these five years as things you talked about came to pass, I wondered how you knew."

"We never know, but I studied the situation and made some good guesses. Most of what I said probably faded from your memory because it was wrong."

"You are not a good liar, but ach, it's good to see you, John."

"Good to see you too, Bruce, but you look a little worn."

"You are looking at a tired old spy, John. Your idea worked. I do not have to kill old friends or strangers whose only crime was to make a different choice than mine. The brave group you convened in the hedges and good-hearted souls we recruited along the way help the Continental Army and militias stay out of trouble or win if trouble is unavoidable. Reverend Walker, the Freemason, has been helpful with information he says comes through the Church and the Lodges. Like you, he has an uncanny knack for making good guesses about what will happen."

John smiled. "And the Reverend once thought there were no grand mysteries in the Masonic Order. How is the campaign going?"

"At moments we made a big impact. I met Captain Patrick Ferguson. You were right about his invention of a breech-loading rifle. At Brandywine Creek, I told Ferguson that British generals frown on sniping Continental officers because it encourages them to shoot ours. That chat saved the lives of Washington and Lafayette. Later that day the Americans were chased back but Ferguson was badly wounded. I assigned myself the task of gathering up the rifles for safekeeping."

"Good work, Sir. Where are they being stored so carefully?"

"Well, if you promise not to tell anyone," Bruce smiled. "They are safely under the Thousand Acre Swamp in Delaware. I was up all night getting there in a wagon and out in a rowboat throughout the next morning. I worked alone. If someone finds them, I doubt the years under water helped them much."

"Well done, Bruce!"

"Remember Flora McDonald, who helped Bonnie Prince Charlie escape the English over the sea to Skye? She sided with the Crown in North Carolina. Can

272

you imagine? The English imprisoned her after Culloden but she took their side out of anger against the large land holders who kept the frontier people down."

Bruce sighed. "Hugh Mercer fell during Washington's victory at Princeton in '77. He was on the ground wounded. Redcoats demanded his surrender but he kept slashing his sword, so they bayoneted him. As he lay in bed dying of wounds, Mercer swore he swung his sword and the British followed the rules of war to stop him. He died with honor and prevented more brutality against British prisoners." He paused at the memory of the friend who saved his life after Culloden.

"I found George Washington by the Hudson last week and urged him to secretly march south. He was not happy when I told him the warship *H.M.S. Savage* sailed up the Potomac, burned plantations, and pressed his manager at Mount Vernon to provide supplies or see his plantation in ruins. Seventeen of Washington's slaves ran off with the British. The economy of the colonies has been devastated. When I compare the well-fed Redcoats around here to our hungry militiamen, I see we are losing this war. Our men return to their farms when their enlistment is up or desert to wander home in hope of finding someone or something there after the Redcoats marched through.

"We heard the French Navy would sail here to turn it around, but if they are coming they are as invisible as fairies. I was encouraged when Washington said he might reach Virginia by autumn, but I since learned from New York that General Clinton has committed to sail down here with a larger force than Cornwallis has. Together they could finish Lafayette's raids, occupy Richmond permanently, and defeat Washington. The American cause may be lost, John."

John listened and studied Bruce. "It may not be as bad as you think."

"I have not given up but there are so many towns in British and Loyalist hands, the future for independence does not look bright. Tell me what you know, John."

"I told you, none of us know anything for sure."

"Aye, but can you make one of your extraordinary guesses again?"

"Well, I would guess a tough old warrior like you might be paying attention to the work on a deep water port at Yorktown."

"Not a hard guess for a grizzled old fighter," replied Bruce.

"Well, Bruce, wouldn't the victorious army under Cornwallis be better off by the water where they could greet Clinton and get resupplied or redeployed?"

"They won't leave before defeating Lafayette, whose men harry the British. Cornwallis received orders to build a deepwater port at Yorktown for the British fleet, but work is proceeding very slowly. It might be better for the British, but how would it be convenient for anyone else?"

"How would Yorktown be convenient for anyone else?" John wondered how much to reveal. "The port and fortifications would be within range of ships' guns." He began to hum a tune and he softly sang: *"Frère Jacques, frère Jacques, Dormez-vous? Dormez-vous?"*

"I have heard that tune. The French volunteers sing it over a flagon. Oh! I am slow in my dotage, John. Is it the French army or the French fleet? Both? When?"

"Bruce, I suggest you encourage Cornwallis to move to Yorktown, the sooner the better. So much history happened in Williamsburg before the Virginia capital moved to Richmond, that someday people might visit here and imagine what it was like long ago. It would be a shame if the town were destroyed in a bombardment. Speaking of which, can you do me a favor?"

"Certainly, what can I do?"

"Find a reason to be far away from Yorktown by the end of summer. Find a task here in Williamsburg such as welcoming General Washington if he should come."

"Understood, John. Thank you."

"Well, Bruce. My family is wandering around somewhere, and I don't want them arrested by the Redcoats because I hummed a French tune to a double agent, do I?"

"No, I would surmise you don't."

"Stay alive, Bruce!" John extended his hand.

"I expect I'll be alive a while longer, especially if I hear soldiers singing that tune," Bruce hugged him. "John why do I feel I shall never see you again?"

"I'm sorry to say it's probably true, Bruce. I will remember you and I pray you and your family thrive."

"I will pray the same for you, John."

John began to walk to where he hoped to find his family two centuries later.

"I have a question for you, John," Bruce called out. "You don't just come from another place, do you?"

John turned and looked at Bruce through the mist.

"You come from a future time, don't you? How are you able to do that?"

"I've been told I have a vivid imagination."

"If it is your imagination, how can I see you?"

"You must have a vivid imagination, too." John turned to go.

"One more question, John. I promise; the last one."

"All right, Bruce. One more question for *auld lang syne*."

"When you fought those wars in the jungles, deserts, and Asian mountains wherever it was you were, what nation were you fighting for?"

John looked back at Bruce Wallace. How much harm can it do? He needs a little encouragement. "I fought for the United States of America."

"I'll be damned. Thank you, John. I shall get Cornwallis to Yorktown."

John turned and walked purposefully up Palace Green. Bruce watched him disappear into the mist.

When John got close to the Palace, the rest of his family was watching for him. He waved and Peter saw him and excitedly waved back.

274

A Redcoat approached Susan and the kids. "You had best be moving along home quickly. It is safer and drier inside your homes."

John approached and called out in a commanding voice, "Thank you, Corporal. That is my family and I will personally escort them safely home."

"Very good, Sir" The corporal moved on.

"It's all in the tone of voice, I guess," said Susan.

"Hi, Dad. How did it go?" asked Megan.

"I found Bruce Wallace and we did what we needed to do. Sorry I'm late. Let's cross the bridge and get on the road before it pours. We can talk on the drive home.

In sight of the bridge, Megan, who was in the lead, stopped. "What, Pete?"

"I didn't say anything."

"Someone called my name."

"I didn't hear anything," said Susan. "Let's get to the car before the downpour."

"Megan!" This time they all heard it.

Through the trees, a man ran toward them. He had run a long way and needed a moment to catch his breath. Megan hugged him. "Mark!"

"I am happy to see you, Megan. When Standing Elk told me you were here, I ran the long way around town to avoid the Redcoats." He paused again for breath. "Mister and Missus Sinclair, Peter, I am glad you came back. For five years, I have wanted to thank you again for what you did to help so many people."

"You're welcome, Mark. From what I hear, you've helped many yourself."

"I am part of a team, Mister Sinclair, people you brought together. We have done what we could over the years, but we have not been able to end the fighting."

"How have you been, Mark?"

"Things are miraculous, Megan. I kept in touch with my former master, Anderson, who relocated to Richmond when the capital moved. Through our Indian friends, we warned of the raid by Benedict Arnold. The warning allowed Governor Jefferson to escape when Richmond was sacked. Anderson hid his iron and was back in business when Arnold left."

"You did a great thing, Mark."

"I have been promised grants of land by General Washington, Governor Jefferson, the Congress, and my former master for my services. I will need many hands to work those lands but as Bartholomew and Maggie taught me, I will keep no one in bondage and will pay a fair wage. We shall rotate crops and let lands lie fallow, and renew them with leaves, ashes, bone meal, and the other things Bartholomew taught me. I will give some of the land grants to native peoples and work with Standing Elk to be the best of neighbors. Much healing will be needed among peoples when this war ends. I pray I live to see the dream come true."

John spoke again. "Mark Smith, Edmond Brown, you're a good man and I'm glad my daughter became your friend. I spoke with Bruce Wallace today and gave him reason to expect the war will not continue much longer. The British will move to Yorktown and prepare a deep-water port there. They will be in a trap and when it snaps shut, most of the fighting will be over. Are you still close to Lafayette?"

"I am."

"Good. When your business is done here, get past the British sentries alive and back to Lafayette. Tell him I am certain that Washington and Rochambeau will arrive at the end of summer and, before this year is over, the world will be turned upside down. Will you deliver that message for me?"

"When I tell the Marquis that the message comes directly from John Sinclair, the General who created the Chain of Information, he will take my report seriously."

"Good. We must cover many miles before nightfall. Mark, live a long and happy life. Megan, can you walk Mark down to the road then run back here? We should leave together."

"Thanks, General Dad."

"Don't take long, Megan. Rain is coming and there are Redcoats all over town."

Megan walked Mark around the bend in the road and took his hand. "I feel embarrassed about public displays of affection, Mark, as my father knows. He sent me back with you so I can kiss you goodbye. May I kiss you?"

"You do not need to ask," said Mark. He leaned toward her and kissed her lips.

"Goodbye, Mark. I am sad to be leaving. I'll remember you the rest of my life."

"Megan, must we say goodbye? Tell me how to find you in Northern Virginia when the war ends. I will have the means to give us a good life together."

"Mark, I wish we could. I will never forget that you wanted to be with me. Please live that good life with an amazing woman. You'll be in my heart forever."

"But, Megan..."

"It can't possibly work, Mark. I have to go very far with my family now. It's not safe for you or me to be out after dusk and with this rain starting, it's dusk now. Goodbye, dear Mark." Megan kissed him and ran back along the path. She looked back at the curve and saw him still standing there. She blew him a kiss and he returned the gesture. Then she turned and hurried ahead.

Her parents and Peter were standing by the bridge. They crossed together and reached the car just before a heavy rain began.

5-9.   Remembering the Ancestors

John drove cautiously as the wipers barely kept up with the rain. The Sinclairs rode in contemplation. After half an hour, the rain let up a bit. "What an extraordinary time," said Susan. "I didn't think I'd be able to go back in time again, but I contacted Jane and it felt good to know she is well in 1781. Did you guys find the people you knew?"

"When I ran into Bruce Wallace, I took a chance on revealing some of the future in order to motivate him to have Cornwallis move his forces to Yorktown."

"That had an impact, Dad. They ought to put your statue up there," said Megan.

"Megan, you said goodbye to Mark. How was the rest of your afternoon?"

"I was sitting quietly by myself when Standing Elk walked into our time. It was amazing. We were watching dragonflies when an Indian chief from 1781 saw an airplane overhead. How did it go for you, Pete?"

"I finally found Annie behind the Powell House. She encouraged Evie to leave for the North with her boys because Samuel Abdul Latif would help them get settled before he sailed to England and then Africa. I encouraged them to take the opportunity and go."

"What happened?"

"They got into the wagon and disappeared. Dilli gave me a painting he made after they tried to find freedom last time." Peter handed the painting to his mother.

"Look at this!"

"What, Mom?" Megan asked.

"We have a small watercolor like this at home!"

"We do?" asked Peter. "Where?"

"It's tucked between the pages of the Bible your dad's father gave him. Grandpa inherited the Bible with the painting from his grandmother after her husband Robert Sinclair died. He wanted it to stay in the Sinclair family. Grandpa told us his ancestor came to Ohio in the 1800s. His family was in Nova Scotia since the Revolution."

"Were they Loyalists?" asked Megan. "If they lived in Nova Scotia they may have been."

"We don't know who they were, Megan. I'll show you the painting. At the top it says 'Freedom Sky' and at the bottom, 'D. Sinclair. Dartmouth, Nova Scotia, September, 1782'. That was one of your ancestors and we don't know anything about him—except that he lived in Nova Scotia and gave this painting to his grandson who was leaving for Ohio, and asked him to pass it on in the family."

Peter closed his eyes and heard the sparkle of Dilli's laughter in the wagon. "I can tell you about him," he said quietly. "His name was Dilli, named after a man whose father came to Virginia from India and who died in battle. Dilli's father was Augustus, a healer who escaped to freedom and died of smallpox near Norfolk on

277

January 2, 1776. His mother was a beautiful slave named Evie, a laundress at the Powell House, who took the risk of running north two generations before the Underground Railroad because she prayed for a better life for her sons. It looks like they made it."

"That's the family you helped, Peter. A grandfather of the man who settled in Ohio and married the German widow was an escaped slave you helped get away to freedom," Megan said. "They took our family name."

"If Evie and Dilli had not gotten to freedom, Dad, Megan, and I would not have been born," said Peter. "They lived before we did so we carry their name." Everyone was quiet as that knowledge settled in. The windshield wipers counted off the seconds going by.

"We had to go back to the colonial era in order for us to be here at all," said John.

"We followed the path that was there to be walked," said Peter. "We may never understand how it happened, but I'm grateful it did."

John drove onto the ramp for I-95 North toward Washington.

Megan pulled a notebook from her backpack and began to write. After a few minutes she said, "The history we learned that got me an A on that paper is not as interesting as how we learned it. We lived it. I will write a story instead of a history paper. It doesn't matter if I get college credit or not. Is it all right with you guys if I write about what you did?"

"Good idea," said her dad. "We can tell our stories on a rainy night by the fireplace."

"That will be great. I can record you and work it into the story." The rain abated to a light mist. Megan stared out the window at the patterns in the trees they sped by. She wrote and scratched something out and wrote again. "I've got the beginning for the story that starts on our way to Williamsburg. Do you want to hear it?"

"Sure, Honey."

"All right, here it is:

To the people of the Virginia Colony in 1775, the forests and fields flanking Interstate 95 would look familiar. The smooth highway from the Potomac to the Tidewater would seem a marvel. But the cars hurtling through a misting rain early this Friday morning in May would be beyond their wildest imagining."

Selected Bibliography

Bailyn, Bernard, and Barbara DeWolfe. *Voyagers to the West: A Passage in the Peopling of America on the Eve of the Revolution*. New York: Knopf, 1986.

Boorstin, Daniel J. *The Americans: The Democratic Experience*. New York: Random House, 1973.

Butler, Jon. *Becoming America: The Revolution before 1776*: Cambridge, Mass.: Harvard University Press, 2000.

Catton, Bruce, and William Bruce Catton. *The Bold and Magnificent Dream: America's Founding Years, 1492-1815*. Garden City, N.Y.: Doubleday, 1978.

Ferris, Robert G., and Richard E. Morris. *The Signers of the Declaration of Independence*: Arlington, Va.: Interpretive Publications, 1982.

Harms, Robert W. *The Diligent: A Voyage through the Worlds of the Slave Trade*. New York: Basic Books, 2002.

Hartoonian, Michael H., Van Scotter, Richard D., White, William E., *The Idea of America: How Values Shaped Our Republic and Hold the Key to Our Future*. Williamsburg, Va.: Colonial Williamsburg Foundation, 2013

Hibbert, Christopher. *Redcoats and Rebels: The American Revolution through British Eyes*. New York: Norton, 1990.

Hibbert, Christopher. *George III: A Personal History*. New York: Basic Books, 1998.

Isaac, Rhys. *The Transformation of Virginia, 1740-1790*. Chapel Hill: Published for the Institute of Early American History and Culture, Williamsburg, VA., by University of North Carolina Press, 1982.

Jensen, Merrill. *The Founding of a Nation; a History of the American Revolution, 1763-1776.* New York: Oxford University Press, 1968.

Klein, Herbert S. *Slavery in the Americas: A Comparative Study of Virginia and Cuba.* Chicago [Illinois: University of Chicago Press, 1967.

Maier, Pauline. *From Resistance to Revolution; Colonial Radicals and the Development of American Opposition to Britain, 1765-1776.* New York: Knopf, 1972.

Olmert, Michael, and Susanne E. Coffman. *Official Guide to Colonial Williamsburg.* Williamsburg, Va.: Colonial Williamsburg Foundation, 1998.

Raphael, Ray. *A People's History of the American Revolution: How Common People Shaped the Fight for Independence.* New York: New Press, 2001.

Roberts, Allen E. *Freemasonry in American History.* Richmond, Va.: Macoy Pub. & Masonic Supply, 1985.

Schlesinger, Arthur M. *The Almanac of American History.* New York: Putnam, 1983.

Selby, John E. *A Chronology of Virginia and the War of Independence, 1763-1783.* Charlottesville: Published for the Virginia Independence Bicentennial Commission by the University Press of Virginia, 1973.

Sutton, Ann, and Myron Sutton. *Eastern Forests, National Audubon Society Guide.* New York: Knopf, 1985.

Tunis, Edwin. *Colonial Living.* Cleveland: World Pub., 1957.

Wood, Gordon S. *The Radicalism of the American Revolution.* New York: A.A. Knopf, 1992.

Excerpts from the Proclamation of 1763 of King George III

WHEREAS we have taken into Our Royal Consideration the extensive and valuable Acquisitions in America, secured to our Crown by the late Definitive Treaty of Peace, concluded at Paris the 10th Day of February last; and being desirous that all Our loving Subjects, as well of our Kingdom as of our Colonies in America, may avail themselves with all convenient Speed, of the great Benefits and Advantages which must accrue therefrom to their Commerce, Manufactures, and Navigation, We have thought fit, with the Advice of our Privy Council, to issue this our Royal Proclamation, hereby to publish and declare to all our loving Subjects, that we have, with the Advice of our Said Privy Council, granted our Letters Patent, under our Great Seal of Great Britain, to erect, within the Countries and Islands ceded and confirmed to Us by the said Treaty, Four distinct and separate Governments, styled and called by the names of Quebec, East Florida, West Florida and Grenada...

And Whereas, We are desirous, upon all occasions, to testify our Royal Sense and Approbation of the Conduct and bravery of the Officers and Soldiers of our Armies, and to reward the same, We do hereby command and impower our Governors of our said Three new Colonies, and all other our Governors of our several Provinces on the Continent of North America, to grant without Fee or Reward, to such reduced Officers as have served in North America during the late War, and to such Private Soldiers as have been or shall be disbanded in America, and are actually residing there, and shall personally apply for the same, the following Quantities of Lands, subject, at the Expiration of Ten Years, to the same Quit-Rents as other Lands are subject to in the Province within which they are granted, as also subject to the same Conditions of Cultivation and Improvement; viz.

To every Person having the Rank of a Field Officer – 5,000 Acres.

To every Captain – 3,000 Acres.

To every Subaltern or Staff Officer – 2,000 Acres.

To every Non-Commission Officer – 200 Acres.

To every Private Man – 50 Acres.

And whereas it is just and reasonable, and essential to our Interest, and the Security of our Colonies, that the several Nations or Tribes of Indians with whom We are connected, and who live under our Protection, should not be molested or disturbed in the Possession of such Parts of Our Dominions and Territories as, not having been ceded to or purchased by Us, are reserved to them, or any of them, as their Hunting Grounds – We do therefore, with the Advice of our Privy Council, declare it to be our Royal Will and Pleasure, that no Governor or Commander in Chief in any of our Colonies of Quebec, East Florida, or West Florida, do presume, upon any Pretence whatever, to grant Warrants of Survey, or pass any Patents for Lands beyond the Bounds of their respective Governments, as described in their Commissions: as also that no Governor or Commander in Chief in any of our other Colonies or Plantations in America do presume for the present, and until our further Pleasure be known, to grant Warrants of Survey, or pass Patents for any Lands beyond the Heads or Sources of any of the Rivers which fall into the Atlantic Ocean from the West and North West, or upon any Lands whatever, which, not having been ceded to or purchased by Us as aforesaid, are reserved to the said Indians, or any of them.

And We do hereby strictly forbid, on Pain of our Displeasure, all our loving Subjects from making any Purchases or Settlements whatever, or taking Possession of any of the Lands above reserved, without our especial leave and Licence for that Purpose first obtained.

And We do further strictly enjoin and require all Persons whatever who have either wilfully or inadvertently seated themselves upon any Lands within the Countries above described or upon any other Lands which, not having been ceded to or purchased by Us, are still reserved to the said Indians as aforesaid, forthwith to remove themselves from such Settlements.

And whereas great Frauds and Abuses have been committed in purchasing Lands of the Indians, to the great Prejudice of our Interests, and to the great Dissatisfaction of the said Indians: In order, therefore, to prevent such Irregularities for the future, and to the end that the Indians may be convinced of our Justice and determined Resolution to remove all reasonable Cause of Discontent, We do, with the Advice of our Privy Council strictly enjoin and require, that no private Person do presume to make any purchase from the said Indians of any Lands reserved to the said Indians, within those parts of our Colonies where We have thought proper to allow Settlement: but that, if at any Time any of the Said Indians should be inclined to dispose of the said Lands, the same shall be Purchased only for Us, in our Name, at some public Meeting or Assembly of the said Indians, to be held for that Purpose by the Governor or Commander in Chief of our Colony respectively within which they shall lie...

Given at our Court at St. James's the 7th Day of October 1763, in the Third Year of our Reign.

God Save the King

ushistory.org, Proclamation of 1763, Accessed June 30, 2015
http://www.ushistory.org/declaration/related/proc63.htm Copyright 2015

Excerpts of Letter from George Washington to Wm. Crawford

Mount Vernon, September 21, 1767.

Dear Sir: From a sudden hint of your Brother I wrote to you a few days ago in a hurry, since which having had more time for reflection, I am now set down in order to write more deliberately, and with greater precision, to you on the Subject of my last Letter; desiring that if anything in this shoud be found contradictory to that Letter you will wholely be governd by what I am now going to add.

I then desird the favour of you (as I understood Rights might now be had for the Lands, which have fallen within the Pensylvania Line) to look me out a Tract of about 1500, 2000, or more Acres somewhere in your Neighbourhood meaning only by this that it may be as contiguous to your own Settlemt. as such a body of good Land coud be found and about Jacobs Cabbins or somewhere on those Waters I am told this might be done. It will be easy for you to conceive that Ordinary, or even middling Land woud never answer my purpose or expectation so far from Navigation and under such a load of Expence as those Lands are incumbred with; No: A Tract to please me must be rich (of which no Person can be a better judge than yourself) and if possible to be good and level; Coud such a piece of Land as this be found you woud do me a singular favour in falling upon some method to secure it immediately from the attempts of any other as nothing is more certain than that the Lands cannot remain long ungranted when once it is known that Rights are to be had for them...

The other matter, just now hinted at and which I proposed in my last to join you in attempting to secure some of the most valuable Lands in the King's part which I think may be accomplished after a while notwithstanding the Proclamation that restrains it at present and prohibits the Settling of them at all for I can never look upon that Proclamation in any other light (but this I say between ourselves) than as a temporary expedient to quiet the Minds of the Indians and must fall of course in a few years especially when those Indians are consenting to our Occupying the Lands. Any person therefore who neglects the present oppertunity of hunting out good Lands and in some measure marking and distinguishing them for their own (in order to keep others from settling them) will never regain it, if therefore you will be at the trouble of seeking out the Lands I will take upon me the part of securing them so soon as there is a possibility of doing it and will moreover be at all the Cost and charges of Surveying and Patenting &c. after which you shall have such a reasonable proportion of the whole as we may fix upon at our first meeting as I shall find it absolutely necessary and convenient for the better furthering of the design to let some few of my friends be concernd in the Scheme and who must also partake of the advantages.

By this time it may be easy for you to discover, that my Plan is to secure a good deal of Land, You will consequently come in for a very handsome quantity and as you will obtain it without any Costs or expences I am in hopes you will be encouragd to begin the search in time. I woud choose if it were practicable to get pretty large Tracts together, and it might be desirable to have them as near your Settlement, or Fort Pitt, as we coud get them good; but not to neglect others at a greater distance if fine and bodies of it lye in a place. It may be a Matter worthy your enquiry to find out how the Maryland back line will run, and what is said about laying of Neale's (I think it is and Companys) Grant.[86] I will enquire particularly concerning the Ohio Companys that one may know what to apprehend from them. For my own part I shoud have no objection to a Grant of Land upon the Ohio a good way below Pittsburg but woud willingly secure some good Tracts nearer hand first.

I woud recommend it to you to keep this whole matter a profound Secret, or trust it only with those in whom you can confide and who can assist you in bringing it to bear by their discoveries of Land and this advice proceeds from several very good Reasons and in the first place because I might be censurd for the opinion I have given in respect to the King's Proclamation and then if the Scheme I am now proposing to you was known it might give the alarm to others and by putting them upon a Plan of the same nature (before we coud lay a proper foundation for success ourselves) set the different Interests a clashing and probably in the end overturn the whole all which may be avoided by a Silent management and the [operation] snugly carried on by you under the pretence of hunting other Game which you may I presume effectually do at the same time you are in pursuit of Land which when fully discovered advise me of it and if there appears but a bear possibility of succeeding any time hence I will have the Lands immediately Surveyed to keep others off and leave the rest to time and my own Assiduity to Accomplish.

If this Letter shoud reach your hands before you set out I shoud be glad to have your thoughts fully expressd on the Plan I have proposd, or as soon afterwards as conveniently may be as I am desirous of knowing in time how you approve of the Scheme. I am, &c.

G. Washington

Library of Congress, Letter from George Washington to William Crawford, Accessed June 30, 2015,

http://www.loc.gov/teachers/classroommaterials/presentationsandactivities/presentations/timeline/amrev/britref/crawford.html

The Declaration of Independence
IN CONGRESS, July 4, 1776.

The unanimous Declaration of the thirteen United States of America

hen in the Course of human events, it becomes necessary for one people to dissolve the political bands which have connected them with another, and to assume among the powers of the earth, the separate and equal station to which the Laws of Nature and of Nature's God entitle them, a decent respect to the opinions of mankind requires that they should declare the causes which impel them to the separation.

We hold these truths to be self-evident, that all men are created equal, that they are endowed by their Creator with certain unalienable Rights, that among these are Life, Liberty and the pursuit of Happiness.--That to secure these rights, Governments are instituted among Men, deriving their just powers from the consent of the governed, --That whenever any Form of Government becomes destructive of these ends, it is the Right of the People to alter or to abolish it, and to institute new Government, laying its foundation on such principles and organizing its powers in such form, as to them shall seem most likely to effect their Safety and Happiness. Prudence, indeed, will dictate that Governments long established should not be changed for light and transient causes; and accordingly all experience hath shewn, that mankind are more disposed to suffer, while evils are sufferable, than to right themselves by abolishing the forms to which they are accustomed. But when a long train of abuses and usurpations, pursuing invariably the same Object evinces a design to reduce them under absolute Despotism, it is their right, it is their duty, to throw off such Government, and to provide new Guards for their future security.--Such has been the patient sufferance of these Colonies; and such is now the necessity which constrains them to alter their former Systems of Government. The history of the present King of Great Britain is a history of repeated injuries and usurpations, all having in direct object the establishment of an absolute Tyranny over these States. To prove this, let Facts be submitted to a candid world.

He has refused his Assent to Laws, the most wholesome and necessary for the public good.

He has forbidden his Governors to pass Laws of immediate and pressing importance, unless suspended in their operation till his Assent should be obtained; and when so suspended, he has utterly neglected to attend to them.

He has refused to pass other Laws for the accommodation of large districts of people, unless those people would relinquish the right of Representation in the Legislature, a right inestimable to them and formidable to tyrants only.

He has called together legislative bodies at places unusual, uncomfortable, and distant from the depository of their public Records, for the sole purpose of fatiguing them into compliance with his measures.

He has dissolved Representative Houses repeatedly, for opposing with manly firmness his invasions on the rights of the people.

He has refused for a long time, after such dissolutions, to cause others to be elected; whereby the Legislative powers, incapable of Annihilation, have returned to the People at large for their exercise; the State remaining in the mean time exposed to all the dangers of invasion from without, and convulsions within.

He has endeavoured to prevent the population of these States; for that purpose obstructing the Laws for Naturalization of Foreigners; refusing to pass others to encourage their migrations hither, and raising the conditions of new Appropriations of Lands.

He has obstructed the Administration of Justice, by refusing his Assent to Laws for establishing Judiciary powers.

He has made Judges dependent on his Will alone, for the tenure of their offices, and the amount and payment of their salaries.

He has erected a multitude of New Offices, and sent hither swarms of Officers to harrass our people, and eat out their substance.

He has kept among us, in times of peace, Standing Armies without the Consent of our legislatures.

He has affected to render the Military independent of and superior to the Civil power.

He has combined with others to subject us to a jurisdiction foreign to our constitution, and unacknowledged by our laws; giving his Assent to their Acts of pretended Legislation:

For Quartering large bodies of armed troops among us:

For protecting them, by a mock Trial, from punishment for any Murders which they should commit on the Inhabitants of these States:

For cutting off our Trade with all parts of the world:

For imposing Taxes on us without our Consent:

For depriving us in many cases, of the benefits of Trial by Jury:

For transporting us beyond Seas to be tried for pretended offences

For abolishing the free System of English Laws in a neighbouring Province, establishing therein an Arbitrary government, and enlarging its Boundaries so as to render it at once an example and fit instrument for introducing the same absolute rule into these Colonies:

For taking away our Charters, abolishing our most valuable Laws, and altering fundamentally the Forms of our Governments:

For suspending our own Legislatures, and declaring themselves invested with power to legislate for us in all cases whatsoever.

He has abdicated Government here, by declaring us out of his Protection and waging War against us.

He has plundered our seas, ravaged our Coasts, burnt our towns, and destroyed the lives of our people.

He is at this time transporting large Armies of foreign Mercenaries to compleat the works of death, desolation and tyranny, already begun with circumstances of Cruelty & perfidy scarcely paralleled in the most barbarous ages, and totally unworthy the Head of a civilized nation.

He has constrained our fellow Citizens taken Captive on the high Seas to bear Arms against their Country, to become the executioners of their friends and Brethren, or to fall themselves by their Hands.

He has excited domestic insurrections amongst us, and has endeavoured to bring on the inhabitants of our frontiers, the merciless Indian Savages, whose known rule of warfare, is an undistinguished destruction of all ages, sexes and conditions.

In every stage of these Oppressions We have Petitioned for Redress in the most humble terms: Our repeated Petitions have been answered only by repeated injury. A Prince whose character is thus marked by every act which may define a Tyrant, is unfit to be the ruler of a free people.

Nor have We been wanting in attentions to our Brittish brethren. We have warned them from time to time of attempts by their legislature to extend an unwarrantable jurisdiction over us. We have reminded them of the circumstances of our emigration and settlement here. We have appealed to their native justice and magnanimity, and we have conjured them by the ties of our common kindred to disavow these usurpations, which would inevitably interrupt our connections and correspondence. They too have been deaf to the voice of justice and of consanguinity. We must, therefore, acquiesce in the necessity, which denounces our Separation, and hold them, as we hold the rest of mankind, Enemies in War, in Peace Friends.

We, therefore, the Representatives of the united States of America, in General Congress, Assembled, appealing to the Supreme Judge of the world for the rectitude of our intentions, do, in the Name, and by Authority of the good People of these Colonies, solemnly publish and declare, That these United Colonies are, and of Right ought to be Free and Independent States; that they are Absolved from all Allegiance to the British Crown, and that all political connection between them and the State of Great Britain, is and ought to be totally dissolved; and that as Free and Independent States, they have full Power to levy War, conclude Peace, contract Alliances, establish Commerce, and to do all other Acts and Things which Independent States may of right do. And for the support of this Declaration, with a firm reliance on the protection of divine Providence, we mutually pledge to each other our Lives, our Fortunes and our sacred Honor.

National archives, Declaration of Independence, Accessed June 30, 2015, http://www.archives.gov/exhibits/charters/declaration_transcript.html